Another creak reverberated off the walls of the gorge. "It was louder that time," Kasri said, though it wasn't aimed at anyone in particular.

"It's the mountain," came a reply. "It's moaning."

She turned to see one of Gelion's warriors leaning against the low stone wall built as a defensive structure. "Have you not heard that in Ironcliff?" he asked, turning the gear to load his arbalest.

"No, but Ironcliff is a single mountain that juts into the gap, unlike here, where the mountains surround you. How often do you hear noises like that?"

"You don't, not unless someone's digging rock and upsetting the mountain's base."

"You know this, how?"

"I spent a year as a miner before joining the warriors guild." He dug through his quiver, selected a bolt, carefully placed it on his bow, then rested his arbalest on the wall for greater comfort. "Don't worry. If anything comes out of that mist, I'll hit it."

"It would help if our view wasn't so obscured," said Kasri.

The archer suddenly sniffed the air. "Wait. That's no mist; it's smoke. There's magic afoot here."

A scramble of feet drew their attention as the rest of Gelion's command came up from behind them, crowding the wall, followed by more Dwarves, armed with axes, ready to repel any enemies who got past the arbalests.

"What have we got?" called out Gelion.

"Smoke," replied Kasri, "and plenty of it unless I miss my guess. I assumed it was mist at first, but your sentry here sniffed it out."

"Good work, Skodan. I'll remember to mention your name in my report." The Dwarf captain moved up to the wall and squinted. "I can't be certain, but I might have noticed some movement. Murdan, send a fire bolt their way, and let's see if we can't get a better look."

The Dwarf in question poked through his quiver, pulling forth a bolt with an oversized head. He held it out while one of his companions struck it with flint and blew on the end, causing it to ignite.

"Magic?" said Kasri.

"No," replied Gelion. "Simply Dwarven ingenuity."

PERIL OF THE CROWN

Heir to the Crown: Book Thirteen

PAUL J BENNETT

Dedication

To my wife, Carol.

N
EIDDENWERTH
GREAT NOR
NORLAND
IRONCLIFF
THE CLANS
WELDWYN
MERCERIA
STONECASTLE
TROLLDEN
HALVARIAN
EMPIRE
STORMTOP MOUNT
SEA OF STORMS
VARENA
CALABRIA
T
THE SOUTHERN CONT

968 MC/1110 SR
RN SEA
RUZHINA
REINWICK
ABELARD
EIDOLON
BURGEMONT
ANDOVER
WILDERNES
ARNSFELD
ERLINGEN
RUDOR
ANGVIL
THERENGIA
GOTFELD
ZOWENBRUCH
RFELD
DEISENBACH
TADT
HADENFELD
PETTY KINGDOMS
THE WILDLANDS
THE PIRATE COAST
HIMMERING SEA
THE GREAT SEA
NT

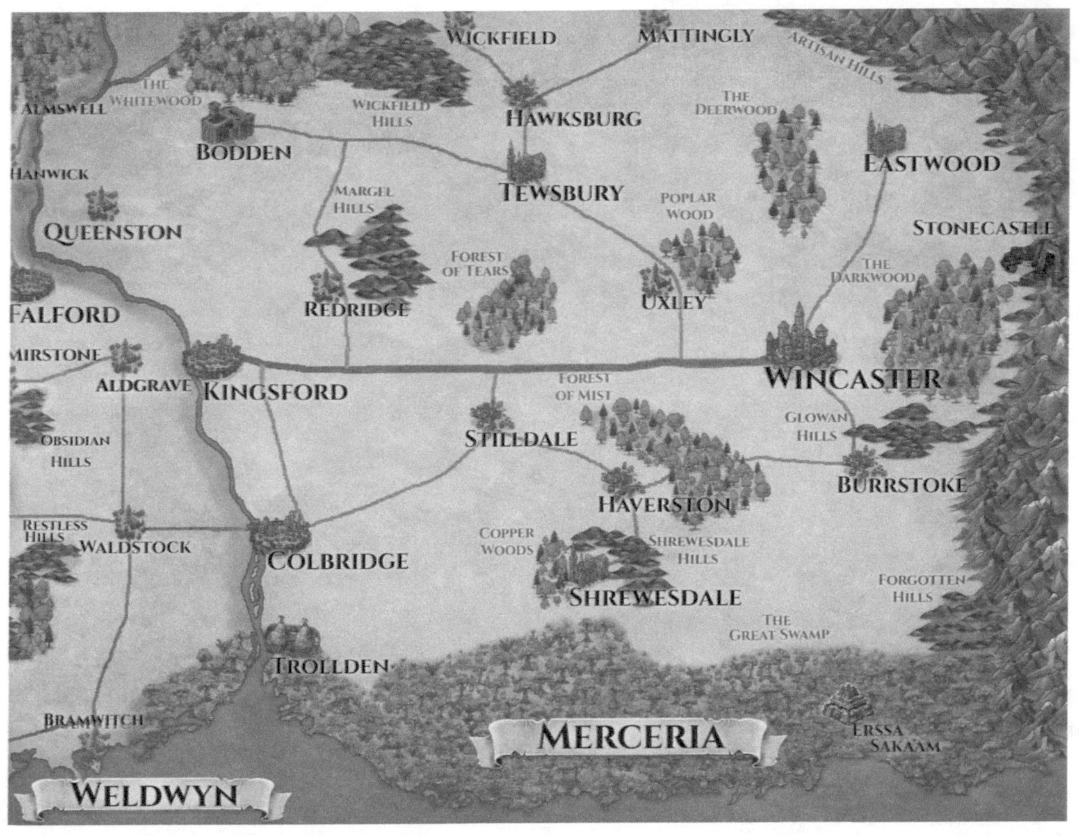

Map of Merceria

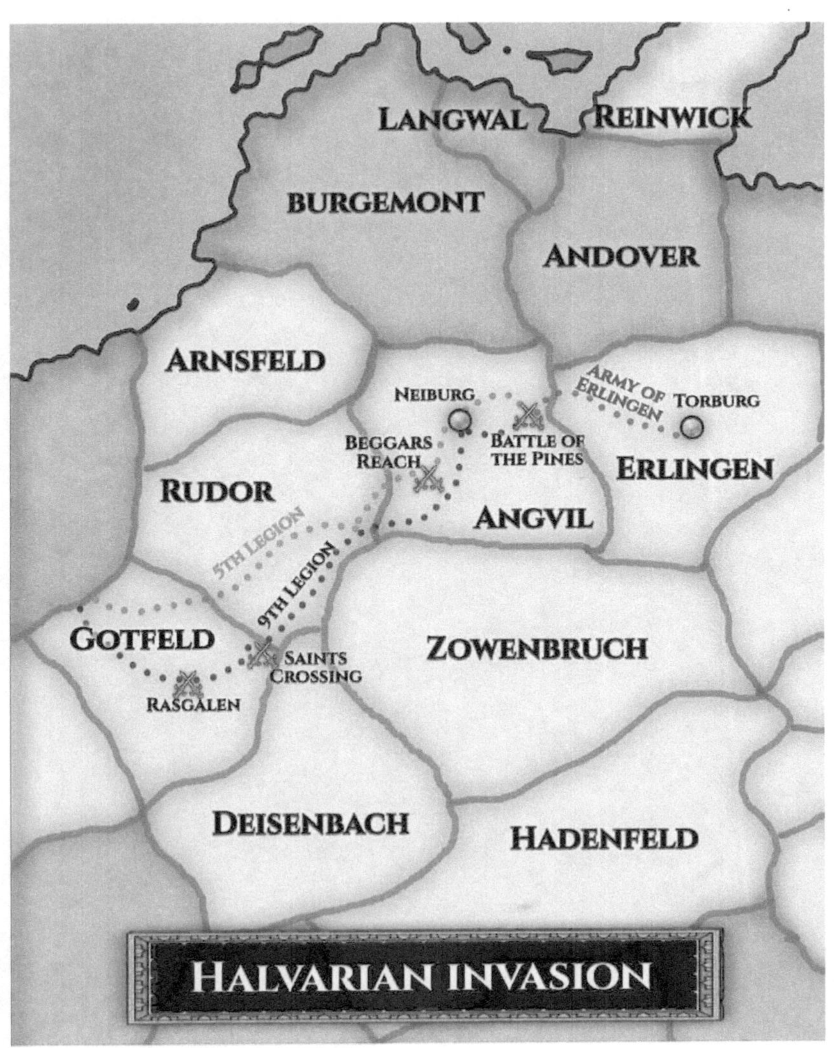

Halvarian Invasion

ONE

Kharzun's Folly

WINTER 967 MC* (MERCERIAN CALENDAR)

Kasri Ironheart stared into the early morning mist, a crispness filling the air, the near-constant winds having subsided for now. She stood before the ruins of Kharzun's Folly, a great bridge of rock that had once spanned a tremendous gorge. Herdwin had almost died destroying it last year; the memory sending a shudder through her.

"Everything all right?" asked Herdwin, standing by her side.

She smiled. "All's calm for now, but for a moment there, I thought I heard something."

"You certain it wasn't the mist playing tricks on you?"

A strange creaking noise echoed towards them.

"There it is again. What do you think it could be?"

"I've no idea, but whatever it is, it's likely not good news. I'll go fetch Gelion. He'll need to prepare his arbalesters." He disappeared into the cave, leaving Kasri with her thoughts once more. Another creak reverberated off the walls of the gorge. "It was louder that time," she said, though it wasn't aimed at anyone in particular.

"It's the mountain," came a reply. "It's moaning."

She turned to see one of Gelion's warriors leaning against the low stone wall built as a defensive structure. "Have you not heard that in Ironcliff?" he asked, turning the gear to load his arbalest.

"No, but Ironcliff is a single mountain that juts into the gap, unlike here, where the mountains surround you. How often do you hear noises like that?"

"You don't, not unless someone's digging rock and upsetting the mountain's base."

"You know this, how?"

"I spent a year as a miner before joining the warriors guild." He dug through his quiver, selected a bolt, carefully placed it on his bow, then rested his arbalest on the wall for greater comfort. "Don't worry. If anything comes out of that mist, I'll hit it."

"It would help if our view wasn't so obscured," said Kasri.

The archer suddenly sniffed the air. "Wait. That's no mist; it's smoke. There's magic afoot here."

A scramble of feet drew their attention as the rest of Gelion's command came up from behind them, crowding the wall, followed by more Dwarves, armed with axes, ready to repel any enemies who got past the arbalests.

"What have we got?" called out Gelion.

"Smoke," replied Kasri, "and plenty of it unless I miss my guess. I assumed it was mist at first, but your sentry here sniffed it out."

"Good work, Skodan. I'll remember to mention your name in my report." The Dwarf captain moved up to the wall and squinted. "I can't be certain, but I might have noticed some movement. Murdan, send a fire bolt their way, and let's see if we can't get a better look."

The Dwarf in question poked through his quiver, pulling forth a bolt with an oversized head. He held it out while one of his companions struck it with flint and blew on the end, causing it to ignite.

"Magic?" said Kasri.

"No," replied Gelion. "Simply Dwarven ingenuity. The tip of that quarrel is soaked in a flammable substance." He watched as Murdan took careful aim and then released his bolt. It flew into the smoke and bounced off something before plummeting into the gorge.

"Something's wrong, Captain," said the archer. "That bolt couldn't have been more than halfway across before it hit."

A low rumble shook the ground.

"What's happening?" said Skodan.

A spire of rock pierced the smoke, the end looking like an enormous spear. Kasri feared it would crash into them, but it stopped, its tail consumed by the smoke.

"What in the name of Gundar's forge are they doing?" shouted Gelion.

"Magic," replied Kasri. "They're growing stone spikes!"

Herdwin reappeared at her side, his sturdy axe clenched tightly in his hands. "They're getting set to cross."

Yelling erupted from the smoke, a sign the enemy was gathering the nerve to cross.

"Ready your weapons," ordered Gelion. "Loose on your own time, but make each bolt count. I don't want anyone emptying their quivers prematurely."

Skodan chuckled. "Can't say I've ever received a complaint like that."

Kasri spotted a shadow in amongst the smoke. She held out her hammer, discharging a bolt of lightning, followed by a thunderclap echoing off the walls of the gorge. Moments later, a cry echoed back towards them, and then a smudge of darkness fell into the gorge. "Got one," she yelled.

Rocks groaned as more spikes emerged, each pointed at a slightly different angle. She moved up to the edge and looked down. "They're growing spires of stone to close the gap." Beneath her, more spikes protruded forward, reaching for the Dwarven side of the gorge. She now understood the cause of the rumble they'd felt earlier. Yet, to do this, a mage must have a clear view of their target.

Herdwin joined her, peering down towards the stream that cut along the bottom. "There," he said, pointing. "Near that bend. Do you see them?"

She reached out again with her hammer, lightning flying forth, but it missed her target, only serving to warn the mages they'd been spotted. Moments later, a blast of fire flew back at her.

Herdwin grabbed Kasri, pulling her back as the flame soared past them. "Watch your noggin," he warned. "Those people mean business."

Gelion pointed at a pile of stones carefully piled behind the defensive wall. "Grab those rocks and toss them into the ravine." A trio of Dwarves moved up to carry out his command: not the most effective defence, but it would keep the enemy mages on their toes.

The smoke cleared, revealing a multitude of giant spikes emerging from the other side where the Halvarians had built that strange tower, its purpose still a mystery. Several men straddled the spikes, although nobody on this side could fathom their purpose. Gelion ordered his arbalesters to concentrate on those fellows, their bolts finding their mark more often than not.

Kasri was trying to work out what they were up to when two hidden doors at the base of the tower swung open, releasing a large roll of wooden planks tied together at each end. The enemy unfurled it, rolling it across the spikes to form a bridge.

An arrow flew from atop the tower, bouncing off Gelion's mailed shoulder. "It's about to get uncomfortable here," he said.

Herdwin watched the wooden bridge unroll and quickly realized the purpose of all those men perched on the rock spires as they moved to tie it off, preventing it from sliding from side to side. "This doesn't look good," he said. "Have we any way to stop them?"

"Aye," replied Gelion. "With our axes."

The planks kept coming until the end flopped down atop the wall in front of the Dwarves. A swarm of Halvarian warriors advanced, shields up, forming a wall of their own.

The arbalesters switched targets, sending bolts flying into this formation. Men fell and were quickly pushed aside as others stepped forward, taking their places. The column advanced towards them like some vast, unstoppable force, a wave of Humanity that appeared to stretch on forever.

Herdwin was no coward, but even he saw the futility of remaining here. They must withdraw in good order, whittling the enemy down until they lacked the numbers to continue.

Of the same mind, Gelion issued orders for his archers to fall back. Dwarves are fearless fighters, but their short stature makes it difficult to retreat once engaged. Their only chance was to keep some distance between them and the enemy, letting the arbalest bolts do what they were designed for.

Herdwin tapped Kasri on the arm. "Fall back," he said. "We can't risk being overrun."

She nodded, letting loose with a final bolt of lightning that struck a Halvarian's helmet, then arced towards another warrior. The first fellow fell prone, while the second shook his head and continued on.

The lead Halvarians were closing in on the Dwarves' defensive wall when a hail of fire came from nowhere as if the sky had opened up and poured lava upon the defenders. Despite the terrifying effect, very few of Gelion's warriors went down, retreating in good order, their armour smouldering as rivulets of flame slid off the metal.

Herdwin glimpsed Skodan wetting his fingers to extinguish a fire in his beard. Under any other circumstances, it would have elicited a laugh from him, but now it spoke to the archer's calmness in the heat of battle.

Herdwin and Kasri fell back, taking a position on the left of Gelion's line. Smoke curled up from the ground as the warriors of Halvaria left their strange bridge, charging towards their adversaries. A final volley of arbalest bolts took down a bunch, and then the forces of the empire met the Dwarves of Ironcliff in a mighty clash of wills.

Herdwin swung his axe, cleaving off an arm, blood spouting everywhere. Beside him, Kasri released a lightning bolt, a terrific roar of thunder rending the air. His ears rang, but the enemy was left worse off, as many stood there, stunned. Herdwin struck out with the edge of his shield, then poured all his strength into an axe blow, felling his opponent, but another quickly took his place.

The enemy came in ever-increasing numbers until it felt as if they were swimming in a sea of Halvarians. All around them, Dwarves went down, but it cost the empire dearly, for they lost five men for each defender slain.

Herdwin witnessed Margel's cousin Tindal fall beneath a horde of sword wielders, and then Gelion leaped into the fray, his arbalest discarded in favour of a two-handed axe. He disappeared into the group of Humans gathered around him, with only the tip of his axe appearing over their heads as he struck out again and again.

"Back! Back!" shouted Gelion as he pulled Tindal from the mass of bodies surrounding him. A lull in the fighting occurred as the Halvarians struggled to advance over their dead comrades.

Pain shot up Herdwin's leg when a spear pierced his shin, the tip somehow working its way past his mail. Stumbling as his limb went numb, Kasri grabbed his arm, doing what she could to hold him up.

Herdwin's head spun as he looked down to see blood pouring from the wound, soaking his mail and leaving a trail of crimson in its wake. Hands gripped his arms, hauling him backwards as Kasri moved to face the enemy.

The empire sent fresh warriors against them, experienced men with heavier mail. They advanced in formation rather than a rush—they clearly knew their business. Overwhelmed by their taller adversaries, the Dwarves suffered serious casualties.

"*We must abandon this fight!*" shouted Kasri, using the Dwarven tongue to confuse their enemies, but the noise of the battle was so loud she had no idea if anyone heard her.

Gelion dragged Tindal to the rear of the line. The young Dwarf had lost a lot of blood, but thanks to his fine mail and the resilience of his Dwarven body, he would survive.

"Second rank, withdraw!" Gelion cast about, seeking the other Dwarf captain, but he was no longer amongst the living. "Form a line across the pass. We'll use the Teeth of the Serpent to withdraw." He looked down at Tindal. "Can you walk?"

"Aye. I believe so."

"Then get moving. We haven't much time."

Kasri and Herdwin staggered towards him. "Move behind those arbalesters," Gelion said, pointing to his new defensive line.

He waited as they fell into position. The Teeth was a tricky manoeuvre, which called on precision and discipline. Thankfully, the companies currently under his command were up to the challenge.

The archers spread out, an arm span between them. Each odd-numbered arbalester let loose with a bolt, then withdrew three paces to reload, allowing the even-numbered ones to release their own volley. This staggered approach provided for a continuous discharge of volleys, but their quivers quickly emptied.

It was easy enough to avoid hitting the Dwarves who were still engaged in melee, for the Humans stood a head taller. However, their defence was crumbling, and when those last brave defenders fell, the enemy would sweep any who remained from the passes.

"We have but one chance," said Kasri, "but it'll mean abandoning those fighting at the gap."

"They knew this might be a one-way trip," replied a grim-faced Gelion.

"Withdraw fifty paces, and I'll take care of the rest."

"What are you going to do?"

"This pass narrows, with a steep drop on one side and a rising cliff on the other. I aim to bring down a rock slide to block their advance. It won't hold them forever but will buy us some time."

"Do it," said Gelion, then ordered his archers to withdraw. His warriors closed ranks, turned around, and marched west towards Stonecastle.

Kasri stood her ground, witness to the desperate melee unfolding before her. Her heart ached for all the Dwarves who would sacrifice their lives this day, but it couldn't be helped. Every delay imposed on the enemy allowed Stonecastle to prepare for the inevitable assault.

She waited, biding her time until she could strike. The Dwarven line collapsed, and the empire's heavily mailed warriors advanced, keeping their formation, shields interlocked to form a wall.

She turned, aimed her hammer high, and let loose with a lightning bolt that struck the cliff, sending a smattering of stones flying. Not content with such a poor showing, she repeated her actions, and this time, a sizable chunk of rock sluiced off, tumbling down to the pass, slowing the enemy's advance, but not by much.

Kasri's gaze wandered higher to where a twisted root stuck out from the cliff face. Her lightning struck again, and a great slab of stone parted from the cliff, rolling and bouncing towards the pass. Each time it hit, it loosened additional stones until a huge wall of the stuff raced towards her. She turned and ran, ignoring the enemy advancing up the pass.

The roar of stone was deafening. As she waited for the downpour of rocks to stop, a great plume of dust flew past her, and then everything went quiet. A jumble of stones lay between her and the bridge, the dust slowly dissipating as a winter breeze arose.

Kasri moved to the edge of the pass and peered down. Bodies lay strewn below, a sure sign the collapse had done its job. She was ready to congratulate herself when an arrow flew over her head. It appeared the enemy was loosing blind volleys, for the trajectory was high above. When an arrow bounced off her helmet, she wisely chose to join Gelion and the other survivors.

"What now?" she asked.

"We withdraw," he replied. "We'll leave plenty of traps behind to slow their advance. I've sent a runner back to Stonecastle, informing the vard of what's happened here, but he'll have to keep his warriors close to defend the city."

"And what of us?"

"We head to the watchtower and prepare for the next engagement."

"How's Herdwin?"

"He's lost some blood, but you know how he is; if a fall from Kharzun's Folly didn't kill him, I doubt a simple leg wound would do him in."

"Good, because we have yet to forge."

"After all that's happened, I would've thought you'd have done it long ago."

She placed her hands on her hips. "I'll have you know, it's not easy organizing a forging, particularly when your father is a vard, and we've had to deal with all these Halvarians!"

Gelion held up his hands in surrender. "My apologies, Kasri. I didn't mean to offend. I was merely suggesting you consider forgoing the usual flummery and get it done. After all, forging is meant to be a private matter, not a spectacle."

"And I would, were I not the Designated Successor to the Throne of Ironcliff. As you say, forging is a private matter, but our friends are in Merceria, Ironcliff, and Stonecastle, and we don't want anyone to feel left out. What was it like when you forged with Margel?"

"It was one of the happiest days of my life, but if you mention that to the Stonemason's Guild Master, I'll deny it."

"Why is that?"

"He thought himself a better match for her, but we all know Dwarven females—once they make up their mind, no one changes it."

TWO

Preparations

WINTER 967 MC

Idraxa Shozarin bent her neck back, staring up at the great trebuchet. "Finally. I wondered when you were going to introduce this beauty."

Commander-General Bastien Lambert, head of the Seventh Legion, smiled. "We prepared it in secret, employing magic to transport it here to Ironcliff, bit by bit. It's modelled after Colossus."

"Wasn't that the one they used against Dun-Galdrim?"

"It was indeed. A finer siege weapon you'll not find this side of the Shimmering Sea, or any sea, for that matter."

"Your hope is that this can breach the doors of Ironcliff?"

"The outer doors, yes. The inner doors, however, are an entirely different matter. This launches its payload in an arc, but the Dwarves have protected the entrance to the mountain against an attack of this nature."

Idraxa bristled. "I'm well aware of how siege weapons work, Commander. I was trained as a battle mage while you were still bouncing on your mother's knee."

"My apologies, Your Grace. I didn't mean to offend."

"Yet that's precisely what you did, despite your good intentions."

He bowed. "What can I say? I was raised in a provincial town."

She waved his comment away with her hand. "What are your intentions here regarding the Dwarves?"

"I'm not sure I understand your question?"

"How do you intend to carry out the assault?"

"The siege engines will reduce the outer city to rubble," replied Lambert. "Then, we'll send in our footmen to occupy it. Once that's done, work begins on the inner-city door, what these Dwarves call the under-mountain. The army's experience at Dun-Galdrim will serve us well in that regard."

"Interesting," said Idraxa. "What lesson did you draw from that siege?"

"The Dwarves set up numerous traps, including pits and collapsing walls and ceilings. They often lured our warriors down long corridors, then struck from adjoining hallways, cutting off any hopes of retreat. They might be physically shorter than us, but their resourcefulness more than makes up for it."

"A fair assessment. Once you've taken the outer city, how do you intend to get into that mountain?"

"In a word, rams. Two are ready to use at a moment's notice."

"Those doors are reinforced with iron, perhaps even shadowbark. Are you certain there isn't a better way?"

"I'm quite capable of doing my job. Might I remind you that I am the commander of this legion, not you!"

"And I am your superior and could have you removed from your position. Do you wish to reconsider explaining yourself, or shall I be forced to assert my authority?"

Lambert struggled with how to reply.

"Well?" she said. "What will it be?"

He finally gave her a slight nod. "My apologies, Marshal. If you'll come with me, I'll show you what I have in mind."

"Follow you where?"

"To my command tent. I have several maps there that will offer a clearer perspective."

The map was skillfully drawn with a steady hand and a flair for the artistic. However, Idraxa found its accuracy questionable as it depicted the Gap, including the relative positions of Ironcliff and Wyburn, but lacked detail farther to the west. Her messages from the High Strategos, Exalor, were most descriptive, including sketches of the area, yet this mockery of a map bore none of that information.

"As you see here"—Lambert pressed his finger down on the map—"we've sealed off the area and posted our cavalry to the south and west, ensuring no interference is possible from the troublemakers at Holdcross."

Idraxa recognized the name from her study of Exalor's maps. "Troublemakers?" she said. "Why have I not heard of this before now?"

"I only just received word of it myself, Your Grace."

"And what is it you've received word of, precisely?"

He met her gaze, struggling to find a suitable explanation.

"I haven't got all day," she pressed.

"A reinforced cohort sent to secure the Gap's western entrance was met by a small army of defenders."

"First it was troublemakers, and now it's an army. I'm curious to hear what you define as small?"

"Our estimates put their numbers at seven hundred or so."

"That's the equivalent of an entire cohort," said Idraxa. "That hardly qualifies as small. Why were they not dealt with?"

"I was busy here with the Dwarf mine."

"Ironcliff is a distraction, you fool. The objective was always to march the legion into the open countryside beyond the Gap."

"That was not my understanding," said Lambert. "I was specifically told capturing Ironcliff was paramount."

"I'm telling you right now, it's nothing more than a diversion. While taking that Dwarf mine would make things easier, we must not lose sight of our true objectives. Considering what you've told me about this small army, you need to rethink your position regarding the siege and revert to containing them. We can't afford them marching in behind us while we send the bulk of our army into Merceria."

"Then why all these questions about how I'm conducting the siege?"

"It was a test, one which you failed."

"I can't follow your strategy if I don't know all the facts."

"Then learn to ask questions."

"What exactly do you expect of me?"

"You can start by giving me the details of this small battle you spoke of. You mentioned Holdcross. Were they defending the town?"

"No, Your Grace. They were east of it, formed up with their footmen in front and their archers to the rear. I'm told both flanks were fortified by Earth Mages. If you want more than that, you'll have to speak to Lindman."

"Who is?"

"He commanded the second cohort."

"Then send for him," said Idraxa.

The commander-general dispatched a warrior. "It will take a bit to fetch him; his wounds are being tended to."

"I'm not happy about this," she continued, "so much so, I'm considering removing you from your position as commander-general. Who am I to trust if not the leader of one of our legions? You disappoint me, Lambert. I expected better." Her gaze wandered back to the map. Holdcross stood at the western end of the Gap, the name given to the flat area of land between the Thunder Mountains to the north and the Sullen Peaks to the south.

Only the Dwarven mine of Ironcliff stood in their way. Exalor's plan was to force the Dwarves beneath their mountain and keep them there.

Lambert remained sitting until the guard reappeared. "Captain-General Lindman is here, sir." He stood aside, allowing the cohort leader to enter.

Captain-General Stivern Lindman had served the empire for over thirty years, attested to by his peppered-grey hair and moustache, which had been out of fashion for decades. His breastplate bore a tremendous gash, and his left arm hung in a sling, a testament to his personal involvement in the battle. He bowed reverentially towards Idraxa. "You wanted to see me, Your Grace?"

"I understand you commanded the cohort at Holdcross. Is that correct?"

"It is, Your Grace."

"I want an account of what happened."

"I made a full report."

"I would hear it from your own lips."

"Where would you like me to start?"

"From the point of first contact. You were scouting out the western reaches of the Gap, were you not?"

"We were, Your Grace. When we sighted the town of Holdcross, the enemy was formed for battle in a line running north to south. To counter this threat, we deployed in a traditional line, archers on the flanks with our lighter footmen and cavalry to the rear, ready to exploit any breakthrough."

"And your estimates of the enemy's strength?"

"Remarkably similar to ours, although with fewer footmen and more archers. I should point out that one-third of their number consisted of Orcs, and they employed mages to create artificial hills on either end of their line to aid in their defence. Either that or they just happened to find the most convenient terrain to camp on."

"Had they any cavalry?"

"They did, Your Grace, although they appeared to be unarmoured. They were situated on either flank."

"How many horses?"

"Two companies, one of which was Orcs."

A silence filled the room. "Orcs?" repeated Idraxa. "Are you certain? We've never had reports of mounted Orcs before."

"I know what I saw."

"Who were the rest of the defenders? Mercerians?"

"If they were, we saw no signs of it. The only flags we could see were Norland ones."

"Norland?" said Idraxa. "Are you positive?"

"Exalor's briefing on this campaign was thorough. The Mercerian colours are red and green, are they not?"

"They are."

"The warriors we saw were dressed in brown tunics for the most part. Hardly the most professional looking."

"And yet they defeated you."

Lindman looked at his feet. "Yes, I'm afraid they did."

"To what do you attribute this loss?"

"The Orcs' bows, Your Grace. They proved most adept at penetrating our armour."

"The emperor's legions have fought Orcs for centuries. Are you now suggesting they somehow developed a powerful new bow?"

"I cannot answer how they came to have them, but the effects were devastating."

"You should have countered with your cavalry."

"Under normal circumstances, I would have, Your Grace, but the vast majority of my horsemen were stripped away from me to guard our main army, leaving us with only a small reserve."

"Yet you failed to utilize them."

"Imperial doctrine insists the reserve only be deployed after a break-through, and the enemy footmen proved unusually resistant to our efforts."

"I'm afraid I'll need some clarification on that matter," said Idraxa. "Are you suggesting you were unable to inflict losses?"

"Not at all, Your Grace. We inflicted substantial damage to their line, but they refused to break. Had we some Imperial troops rather than only provincials, it might have been a different matter, but they were busy preparing for the siege."

The Marshal of the North shifted her attention to the commander-general. "Would you care to explain this?"

"We were assembling the siege engines," replied Lambert, "and there was a distinct possibility the Dwarves might counterattack to destroy them. I thought it best to keep our heavily armoured men close by."

"Yet by doing so, you only worsened our situation. Our legions' reputation as unbeatable is an important part of our campaign, and you threw that away by handing our enemy a victory. It wouldn't have been so bad were they a seasoned army of Mercerians, but you allowed a group of amateurs to destroy a cohort! And to make it worse, they were Norlanders! If there is a more pathetic excuse for an army, I'm not aware of it."

Lambert waited, eager to speak yet wise enough to let her finish her rant. "Allow me to dispatch a larger contingent," he said at last. "I can have an Imperial cohort there in a matter of days."

Idraxa ignored him. "Captain-General Lindman, how many of your men survived?"

"Approximately one-third, Your Grace."

"And where are they now?"

"Posted west of here, watching for any enemy advances into the Gap."

"I trust you won't underestimate the enemy again?"

"I will not, Your Grace. I have already spread my cavalry out to screen what's left of my cohort, and I shall send word as soon as we spot any enemy movement."

"He should be removed from command," said Lambert.

"I could say the same for you," replied Idraxa. "None of this would've happened had you stuck with the High Strategos' original plan. I will only repeat this once more, gentlemen, and let there be no mistaking my intent: Ironcliff is not the primary objective here. Our task is to draw the Army of Merceria north to deplete its defences."

"I can take that Dwarf mine," insisted Lambert.

"That is not your objective. Either you follow your orders, or I will remove you from your position as Commander-General of the Seventh."

A long silence ensued, a test of wills, but Idraxa held his gaze.

Lambert sighed. "I shall do as ordered."

"Good. Now begone, the two of you. I must make my report to the High Strategos, and I don't imagine he will be happy with these developments."

Exalor Shozarin, the High Strategos of the Halvarian Empire, broke the connection. The reports from the north were distressing, to say the least.

His aide, Wingate, opened the door and peered in. "Trouble, Your Grace?"

"Certain elements of my plan have gone astray."

"I assume the Mercerians intervened?"

"No, but I failed to consider the hubris of the Seventh's commander-general."

"I'm afraid I don't understand, Your Grace."

"He wishes to make a name for himself." He noted the blank look on his aide's face. "He took it upon himself to prioritize the capture of Ironcliff, even though that was not the task."

"Perhaps he felt they represented a danger to the campaign? Wouldn't the Dwarves be able to attack our supply lines?"

"With an army besieging them? I think not! The idea was to bottle them up in their mine while the rest of the legion marched through to the other side of the Gap. The main objective was to lure the Mercerians north, and our warriors swarming across Norland would have done just that. Now they've occupied Holdcross, effectively blocking our advance."

"Do we know who commanded them?" asked Wingate.

"Unfortunately, no."

"Your Grace," said Wingate, "might I offer an observation?"

"Go on."

"Our information tells us the Norlanders are weak and poorly trained, but what if the Mercerians took it upon themselves to whip them into shape?"

"They had no advance notice of our invasion, and it would take months to do anything with that rabble." Exalor noticed the smug look on his aide's face. "What is it you're holding back?"

"As you know, Your Grace, I sift through many reports concerning Merceria."

"And?"

"If I recall, Queen Bronwyn of Norland was provided with a Mercerian advisor, a man called Heward Manton."

"What do we know about him?"

"He was a Knight of the Sword who switched sides during the Mercerian civil war. Queen Anna made him a Knight of the Hound for his service and, later, the Baron of Redridge. I propose he led that Norland expedition. After all, he's spent significant time in the Norland court and has a wealth of experience."

"He's a Knight of the Hound?"

"Indeed, Your Grace. And we know only the most trusted and capable of the queen's people are given that honour."

"That helps explain their sudden competence in battle."

"I sense something else is bothering you, Your Grace?"

"There is," said Exalor. "According to Idraxa, Orcs were present at Holdcross."

"But that was expected, surely?"

"It was, but they're equipped with a superior bow capable of penetrating our armour."

"Even our heavy cavalry?"

"Not that we know. These were provincials with simple mail, but it's troubling we didn't have advance notice of it."

"Our agents are experienced at infiltrating courts," said Wingate, "but even the best would find it difficult pretending to be an Orc."

"Yes, I suppose you're right. With the army at Holdcross blocking our way, we must alter our plans."

"Would it not be better to send the entire legion to Holdcross?"

"We can't do that without the Dwarves having access to the rear of our lines, which would prove catastrophic." He smiled, though it seldom meant something good. "It appears Commander-General Lambert may get his wish after all."

"That being?" said Wingate.

"Everlasting glory. I shall issue orders countermanding those of Idraxa. Going forward, he must make all efforts to reduce and remove the threat from Ironcliff."

"And what about the army at Holdcross, Your Grace?"

"The legion's cavalry will have nothing to do at the siege. I'll have him reassign them to watch this Heward fellow closely." He paused momentarily. "We don't have any of our agents in the area, do we?"

"I'm afraid not."

"Pity. I hoped we might eliminate this nuisance without a battle."

"Would the Mercerians not send a replacement?"

"That's just it," replied Exalor. "There are only a few Knights of the Hound, and we know the location of almost all of them."

"What about General Fitzwilliam? We still don't know her whereabouts, do we?"

"As a matter of fact, we do. A few days ago, I received word she's been found."

"I saw no such report," said Wingate.

"Kelson told me in person. It appears she's gotten herself in amongst the Petty Kingdoms, although I've no idea how."

"Could she be trying to drum up support for Merceria?"

"That would be my first guess, but I doubt she'd make much progress. No one in those parts has even heard of Merceria, let alone would be willing to go to war with us in support of them."

"Do we send agents after her?"

"We'll leave others to take care of that. We must concentrate our efforts on taking Merceria."

THREE

Beverly

Beverly awoke to find the place beside her empty. She looked around, spotting Aldwin tossing fresh wood on the fire.

"You're awake," he said. "I was beginning to think you'd sleep all day."

"Where's everyone else?"

"Fetching water."

"Even Owen?"

Aldwin chuckled. "Aubrey insisted on it, said he needed a lesson in humility."

"Really?"

"No. I believe she wanted to give us a moment alone."

Beverly rose and stood beside him, warming her hands by the fire. They'd been stranded in the Petty Kingdoms after passing through a magical portal some months ago and were still seeking a way home. The only saving grace was that her husband had accompanied her. She enjoyed his smile as their eyes met, then noticed his frosted breath. "It's chilly this morning."

"Well, it is winter, although I must admit it's not as bad as back home."

"I'll agree with that. Bodden's likely half buried in snow right about now."

"We will return. Eventually, Aubrey will be within range of her recall spell."

"I'm certain of it, but I'm thankful I get to spend more time with my husband in the meantime. That hardly ever happens."

"Doubtless, you'll eventually grow bored with me."

"Never!" said Beverly.

The snap of a branch drew their attention, and then Krazuhk came into view carrying a bundle of sticks. *"I gathered these for the fire,"* said the Orc in her native tongue. *"Heavy snow is coming."*

"How can you be so certain?"

"I am a master of air. As such, I sense the change."

"The change?" said Aldwin.

"Yes. A feeling that the weather is about to turn. My father tells me I inherited the gift from my mother."

"What's going on?" Sir Owen entered the campsite with each of their waterskins slung over his shoulders.

"We were discussing the weather," replied Beverly. "Krazuhk says snow is on the way."

"More?" said the knight. "Well, I don't suppose it'll matter much. We'll soon be across the border and into Erlingen."

"Where's Aubrey?"

He glanced over his shoulder. "She was right behind me."

"I'm here," Aubrey called out. "I snagged my dress on a branch but managed to free it." She moved closer to the fire, warming her hands. "We should pick up some warmer clothes. How many coins have we left?"

"Plenty," replied Beverly. She'd defeated a knight in a joust back in Deisenbach, his ransom giving them the funds they needed to continue their journey. They would've arrived in Reinwick by now had they not become embroiled in a plot to poison the king, an event that very nearly cost Aldwin his life. "We can make those coins go further if we avoid staying in the finest establishments."

"This one was pretty cheap," said Aldwin.

"Too cheap," replied Owen. "No disrespect intended, but if I must sleep outdoors, I'd much rather do it inside a pavilion."

"But then it wouldn't be outdoors."

"Precisely my point."

"You mentioned we'll soon be across the border," said Beverly. "What can we expect after that?"

"This road goes through the village of Adelwel, but I recommend we press on to Salzing."

"Is that the capital?" asked Aubrey.

"No, but it's a major city, which will allow us to catch up on news before we get to the capital."

"What is it you're hoping to hear? We're on our way to Reinwick, remember?"

"True, but we have to pass through the capital, Torburg, to get there. As a knight, I'm expected to pay my respects to the duke."

"Have you family in Salzing?"

"No. I was born in Chermingen but spent most of my life in Torburg."

"Why is that?"

"It was the only way I could get an apprenticeship."

"Did you always want to be a farrier?"

"No. I wanted to be a merchant, but I was low on funds by the time I reached the capital. Becoming a farrier was the only job I could find."

"And now you're a knight, and an experienced one at that," said Aubrey. "You've certainly come a long way."

"Experienced?" replied Owen. "I don't know about that."

"You're being modest. Did you not fight alongside the Orcs back in Deisenbach?"

"I did."

"And you faced Beverly in the joust; that accounts for something."

"Need I remind you I lost that particular competition."

"As did the king's champion. Even a failure can result in personal growth."

"What are you, some kind of seer?"

"I'm a Life Mage, so I suppose I am, in a way."

"Orc shamans do both," added Beverly.

Sir Owen turned to Krazuhk. "Is that true?"

The Orc stared back. "Not understand," she replied.

"He wants to know if it's true that shamans are seers?" asked Aubrey in Orcish.

"Most definitely," the master of air replied. *"As you saw for yourselves, the Sky Singers' shamans are an important part of the inner circle who advise the chieftain. Bloodrig will often offer counsel, even when not requested."*

"What did she say?" asked Owen.

"She said yes," replied Beverly. "You'd know that if you took the time to learn Orc."

"True, but Krazuhk could learn the common tongue."

"Did you not hear her first answer? She's learning, but it takes time. You, however, have yet to learn even a single word of her language."

"I fail to see why it would be necessary. Aside from our companion here, it's not as if I'll spend much time amongst her people."

"You will if you come with us to Merceria. You still want to be a Knight of the Hound, don't you?"

"I do," replied Owen.

"Then I suggest you learn the Orc tongue; in our army, it's mandatory, at least amongst senior ranks."

"Why is that?"

"All our written orders are in their language."

"I didn't know they had a written tongue."

"They don't, but our scholars worked out a way to write it."

"Why in the name of the Saints would they do that?"

"If the enemy intercepts a messenger, they'd be unable to read any letters they carried."

"That's clever," said Owen. "I promise I'll endeavour to learn the language."

"Good. Now that's settled, let's pack up, shall we? I'd like to get across the border before that snow comes."

They proceeded on their way, skipping breakfast, hoping a roadside inn might soon be found. Owen had indicated as much but refused to commit to how far away it was.

With their stomachs still empty, they encountered a trio heading towards them. A man led, holding the reins of a mule, upon which sat an older woman. Beside her walked another man who matched her in age, using a staff to keep his balance.

"Greetings," called out Beverly, slowing Lightning as she approached, the rest of her group following suit.

"We don't want no trouble," the younger man said. "We're heading to Kurslingen."

"Which is?"

The fellow stared back. "How can you not know the capital of Zowenbruch? You must've ridden right through it."

"We crossed into the kingdom by way of Santrem," offered Sir Owen, "on the Deisenbach side of the Rasfeld River, so we bypassed it completely."

"Are you a knight, sir?"

"I am. My name is Sir Owen. Yours?"

"Kinmar, and these are my parents, Eadric and Milgyrd."

"Unusual names," said Owen, moving slightly closer. "Are you Therengian, by chance?"

The man's hand went to the knife in his belt. "What if we are?"

"We mean you no harm," said Beverly. "My husband, Aldwin, has the same grey eyes as you."

Kinmar relaxed. "I know of no Therengian in these parts who'd dare ride a horse, especially one so fine as what you got there."

"We're from a distant land where they don't judge people by the colour of their eyes. My name is Beverly Fitzwilliam, and this is my husband,

Aldwin. Accompanying us are my cousin, Aubrey Brandon, and Krazuhk, a master of air."

"An Orc?" said Kinmar. "That's most unusual in these parts."

Aldwin dismounted, handed the reins to Beverly, then moved closer, holding out his hand in greeting. "I'm told I am of Therengian descent," he said, shaking Kinmar's hand, "but I'm afraid I know little of our common ancestors."

"That's to be expected," piped up Eadric. "Our people have faced persecution for centuries, ever since the Old Kingdom fell. For many generations, laws forbade all from talking about how things used to be."

"And now?"

"Erlingen has lessened its restrictions considerably since the invasion."

"Invasion?" said Aldwin.

"He talks of Andover's invasion," replied Owen, "back in ninety-five. Sorry, I forgot you use a calendar that's different from ours. I should have said fourteen years ago."

"You were there?"

"No. I was too young but learned all about it when I worked as one of the duke's farriers."

"I'm curious," said Aldwin, "when you say the restrictions were loosened, what do you mean, precisely?"

"It's no longer illegal for us to bear arms or protect ourselves, nor is there a ban on holding high office, although I daresay none of our people have had much opportunity to do so."

"Might I ask why you're headed to Zowenbruch?"

"We have family there," replied Kinmar. "My sister and her husband."

"Then I wish you much happiness and joy. May Saxnor look over you."

"And you, all of you."

Aldwin returned to the saddle, looking quite pleased with himself as the three travellers continued along the road.

"What are you smiling at?" asked Beverly.

"I no longer need to worry about facing arrest for carrying a weapon. You have no idea how liberating that is."

"Trust me, I understand completely. When they arrested you back in Deisenbach, I was ready to take on the entire Royal Guard. If it hadn't been for Aubrey, I'd have ended up in the dungeon beside you."

"You're welcome," said Aubrey. "I bet you never thought your little cousin Aubrey would be the one to keep a cool head under such unusual circumstances."

"I doubt anyone calls you little anymore. And just for the record, I've never doubted your ability to keep calm under the most trying of situations."

"That's enough of that, you two!" Aldwin looked at Owen. "They will continue to compliment each other all day long if we let them. It comes from being such a close-knit family."

"I can't help it if we get along so well," said Beverly.

"Nor can I," added Aubrey.

The Grey Goose Inn wasn't much to look at, but the food was plentiful and the ale of passing quality. Their arrival caused a bit of a stir, especially the presence of Krazuhk, but when they placed gold on the table and bought a round for everyone in the place, no one cared anymore.

They soon settled down to a hearty meal, although Beverly picked at her food. "It's peaceful here. Much more so than back home, I should think. I wonder how things are going there?"

"I talked to Kraloch two days ago," replied Aubrey. "There was nothing new then, and I doubt there'll be when I do so tomorrow."

"This is all so fascinating," said Owen, leaning forward and resting his elbows on the table. "Tell me again how you contact someone so far away?"

"It's a spell called spirit talk, which the Orcs taught me."

"Yes. You've mentioned that before. What I don't understand is how it works."

"Are you familiar with the spirit realm?"

"You mean where ghosts reside?"

"Yes."

"I've heard of it. What else is there to know?"

"It is a realm existing parallel to our own."

He stared back, at a loss as to what she meant.

"Let me put it another way," she continued. "The realm of spirits surrounds us like an invisible fog that's always there. When someone sees a ghost, they actually see a manifestation of a spirit in the physical realm."

"So, you're talking with ghosts?"

"No. Kraloch lives in Merceria."

"This I understand," said Owen. "What I don't get is how you're able to talk to him yet cannot use your magic to go home."

"The spirit realm has different laws when it comes to distance. That is to say, the spell of spirit talk is not bound by range like recall is. Rather, it's based on the familiarity with the person on the other end."

"Could you communicate with your cousin Beverly, for example, without worrying about distance?"

"I can only use the spell to communicate with someone capable of using it."

"So, another Life Mage or shaman?"

"Almost," added Beverly. "She's the only Human Life Mage to learn the spell. Kraloch is an Orc."

"I gathered so from the name. I've watched you cast the spell, but from our perspective, you're talking to thin air. How do you know you've reached the right person?"

"Because I see his spirit," replied Aubrey, "just as he sees mine, which is why the mages at either end of the connection must understand how to contact spirits."

"Nope," said Owen. "I'm still not understanding."

"Do you believe in ghosts?"

"I'd be a fool not to after what you've told me."

"Tell me this, then: what is a ghost?"

"That's an easy one; it's the spirit of someone who's died."

"Where lies this spirit when the person is alive?"

"I… I've never considered that. Inside their body, I would presume."

"That's the spirit I contact when I use the spell."

"We each have a ghost inside of us?" said Owen. "I find that most disturbing."

Aubrey laughed. "You'll get used to it."

"That being the case, couldn't you contact Kraloch whenever you like?"

"I could, but using the spell requires magical energy, and although I have plenty to spare at the moment, I can't guarantee the same is true of Kraloch."

"Why not?"

"The Mercerian mages recall people all over the place."

"But that's simply a matter of memory, isn't it?"

"No," replied Aubrey. "I mean the spell of recall we use to transport people across great distances. It's how we intend to return home."

"But doesn't that require more power than you presently have?"

"Yes, but the closer we get, the more likely I'll be able to do so."

"Is there any way for you to increase your power?"

"My, you're inquisitive today. Yes. I can increase my power through study and constant practice, but that's a little hard to do while travelling. Also, I don't want to use my magic any more than necessary in case it's needed for healing."

"Most fascinating," said Sir Owen. "Have you any idea how close you need to be for your recall spell to get you home?"

"The farthest distance I've ever travelled by recall was from Wincaster to

Summersgate, the capital of Weldwyn. That's reckoned to be just shy of five hundred miles."

"Miles. The one unit of distance that varies between different kingdoms. They say the Old Kingdom defined it as one thousand paces, measured on the off-foot, whatever that means, but some argue they stole it from the Thalamites. Very few rulers amongst the Petty Kingdoms were willing to adopt a measurement favoured by the Old Kingdom, so they changed it. They kept the name, of course. You couldn't change that after centuries of use, but the distances involved… Well, that was something else entirely."

"Out of curiosity," said Aubrey, "how would you define a mile?"

"I try to avoid any commitment in that regard. I trust in my feet, or rather, my horse. I once heard it said a good horse can take you thirty miles a day, assuming decent roads, so I use that to estimate travel times."

"Then think of my spell being the equivalent of two weeks. That shouldn't be too far off the mark."

"That's astounding," said Owen. "Why, with magic like that, we could cross the Petty Kingdoms in days rather than months."

"Not quite. A mage's magical energy recovers in time, but a trip of that distance would require adequate rest, not the sort of thing you can do in the wilderness."

"But we're not in the wilderness; we're nearly in Erlingen."

"Perhaps she's not being clear," said Aldwin. "The recall spell can only take a mage to a magic circle, one the mage is familiar with."

"Where do these magic circles come from?"

"Skilled artisans craft them, and then a mage empowers them. It's a lengthy process and expensive."

"Why's that?" asked Owen.

"The amount of gold required to hold the magic puts it well out of most people's price range."

"So you're saying only kings would have them?"

"I can't speak for the Petty Kingdoms, but back home, the Crown financed them, except for those in the Whitewood—the Meghara created those two."

Krazuhk suddenly leaned forward. *"Did you say Meghara?"* she asked, using her native tongue.

Her interest caught Aubrey off guard. *"You know that name?"*

"Indeed. She was amongst the first of our Ancestors."

FOUR

Ironcliff

WINTER 967 MC

Thalgrun Stormhammer, Vard of Ironcliff, stood on the city's outer wall, staring out over the plains at the enemy camped before his walls. They remained well out of range of his arbalesters, but he knew it wouldn't be long before the assault commenced, for their massive siege engines were poised to reduce the outer city to rubble.

He wondered if there might be some way to stop them, but it was nothing more than a dream; his warriors had no cavalry or siege engines to bombard the enemy. And why would they? Ironcliff had stood safe for centuries, but the arrival of the Halvarians changed all that.

"Quite a sight, isn't it?"

Thalgrun jumped at the sound of Agramath's voice. "When did you learn to be so quiet?"

"Quiet? I would say I was loud. Perhaps you should get your hearing checked?"

The vard turned on him, ready to explode, but the mirth on the master of rock and stone's face softened the blow. "I feel so old, as though my time amongst the living is drawing to an end."

"Don't say that. I'm even older than you, and I'd like to think I've a few more years left amongst the living."

"You may think what you like, but it doesn't change the fact we're both ancient, even by Dwarven standards."

"Ah, but not so much by the reckoning of an Elf."

"That's different—they're immortal." Thalgrun nodded towards the distant army. "What do you make of them?"

"Their numbers are impressive," replied Agramath, "but it will take more than that lot to break into the mountain. Unfortunately, the same can't be said for the outer city. It would have been much better for us had we not built outside the mountain."

"It couldn't be helped; we still need to eat, and there's only so much food you can grow underground."

"That didn't stop our ancestors from surviving."

"True," said Thalgrun, "but there's a big difference between surviving and thriving. Thanks to our farms, our population has tripled over the last century alone."

"Yet it seems these Humans will reduce us once again to our former numbers."

"Don't think of them as Humans; they are Halvarians or simply the enemy. After all, the Mercerians are Human, and they've sent help."

"A fat lot of good it did. We've lost their cavalry to Gods know where, and the footmen will likely be a mixed blessing, assuming the enemy gets through our front door. It's not as if they're skilled in fighting in Dwarven halls."

"And here I thought I was the pessimist." Thalgrun swept his gaze once more over the enemy army. "I wish Kasri were here. She'd know what to do."

"More to the point," said Agramath, "I'm eager to meet this new Mercerian commander they promised, now that Lanaka is out there, somewhere."

"Then you're in luck. She's already here."

"She is?" said the mage. "Why wasn't I informed?"

"I'm the vard, remember? Not you."

"True, but I'm the one responsible for the magic circle. Who did they send?"

Thalgrun smiled. "You'll have to be patient. She's supposed to meet me out here once she's settled in."

"Settled in? What in the name of Gundar does that mean?"

"That she's taking time to ensure those under her command know their business here." Behind him, the great doors to the under-mountain opened. "Ah, this looks like her now."

"She's vaguely familiar."

"She is Lady Hayley Chambers, the High Ranger of Merceria and Baroness of Queenston."

"No. I don't think so."

"She is, trust me. I wouldn't lie about something like that."

"No. I mean, that's not how I know her. I seem to recall her being connected to someone else."

"Revi Bloom, perhaps?"

Agramath snapped his fingers. "That's it. The last time he was here, he talked about her at great length. Speaking of which, where is Revi?"

"Back in Wincaster, the last I heard. He's one of their more powerful mages and thus in great demand for moving their warriors between all those magic circles."

"He's a gifted healer as well. We could certainly benefit from his expertise if we expect a siege."

"Then I shall send word asking for him to be sent to us."

They waited as Hayley made her way through the outer city. She disappeared into the base of the tower, soon emerging on the same wall they'd been watching her from.

"Majesty, Lord Agramath," she said. "I bring greetings from Queen Anna of Merceria."

"You're an archer," noted the master of rock and stone. "I'm not certain your bow will prove all that effective once we're inside the mountain."

"True, but my rangers can pick off enemy warriors from these very walls until then."

"Assuming they get close enough. Those siege engines have an extensive range."

"You must pardon the master of doom and gloom," said Thalgrun. "Agramath is in a dour mood this day."

"I'm dour?" replied the mage. "You're the one complaining about how old you felt!"

"See what I mean? He argues about everything!" His words were accusatory, while his mood was light. "Now, enough of this banter. Tell me about these rangers of yours."

"I could only bring one company; the rest are required in Trollden."

"Trollden? Where's that?"

"On our southern coast, Majesty. Our marshal fears another attack and believes that the most likely place for the enemy to invade."

"A seaborne invasion? Well, we don't have to worry about that here." He nodded towards the Halvarians. "Give me your opinion of that army."

"They have a preponderance of footmen, which I expected for a siege, but where are all their archers?"

"A good question," said Thalgrun. "I suspect they're waiting behind those engines of war."

"And their cavalry?"

"Thanks to Lord Lanaka, they're off hunting him down."

"They'll have a hard time," said Hayley. "He's a gifted cavalry commander."

"Do you think the Halvarians brought enough men to defeat us?"

"Without seeing what preparations you've made, it's hard to say. They certainly seem to have numbers on their side. A traditional siege calls for outnumbering the defenders by at least three to one. Might I ask how many warriors you have under arms?"

"The warriors guild has four hundred Dwarves ready to fight, a quarter of which are arbalesters. We've armed the citizenry, but they are, for the most part, ill-equipped and woefully under-trained."

"You forgot the Mercerians," said Agramath.

"Yes, my pardon. With Lanaka's cavalry no longer with us, we have one hundred of your footmen and an equal number of archers, not including your rangers."

"You mentioned the citizenry. How many can you muster?"

"A thousand, give or take. We can't arm everybody; we still need to evacuate the outer city, not to mention moving stores and looking after the wounded. You get the idea."

"It seems to me the siege engines are the biggest concern."

"You have the right of it," said Agramath. "But what can we do about them? It's not as if we Dwarves could march out and burn them to the ground—we'd be slaughtered."

"True, but my rangers might be useful with that."

"What are you proposing?"

"Come nightfall, they'll slip into the enemy camp and see what havoc they can wreak."

"But they'd recognize you, surely?"

"I shall take pains to acquire some Halvarian armour first."

Thalgrun held up his hand. "One moment. Something's happening."

Past the wall, a small group of riders headed towards the city's gates. They halted before the long stairs and then dismounted.

"It appears they wish to talk," said Hayley. "That looks like a flag of truce."

"I'm not about to surrender," replied the vard.

"Nor would I advise you to, but it would be to your advantage to meet them if only to learn what they want."

"They want us to surrender!"

"Most likely, but perhaps we can stall their attack. Would you be amenable to me accompanying you to the parley?"

"Parley?" said Agramath. "What strange customs you Humans have."

"Come on, then," said Thalgrun. "Let's go see what this enemy commander wants."

They returned to the under-mountain to gather the Hearth Guard. These elite warriors surrounded their vard, escorting him to the outer gate.

The Halvarian delegation waited patiently as the great doors swung open, and then Thalgrun and Hayley descended the steps with the Dwarven warriors formed up on either side. They halted ten paces from the enemy.

"Greetings. I am Bastien Lambert, Commander-General of the Seventh Legion. To whom do I have the honour of speaking?"

"Thalgrun Stormhammer, Vard of Ironcliff and master of this mountain. Why have you brought an army to my doorstep?"

The Halvarian bowed. "I have come at the behest of my lord and master, Nevarus, God-Emperor of the Halvarian Empire."

"Oh yes? And what does he want?"

"He invites you to lay down your arms and accept him as your lord and master."

"And why would I do that?"

Lambert swept his arm to indicate his army. "Must I spell it out for you? You are vastly outnumbered. A siege would only result in the needless death of so many of your countrymen."

"Countrymen, is it?" said Thalgrun. "My subjects are not men; they are Dwarves."

"Yet you meet me in the company of a Human." He glanced at Hayley. "I know who you are, High Ranger. You should return to your queen and tell her to surrender to the inevitable." He turned back to Thalgrun. "Tell me what the Mercerians promised you, Majesty, and I shall double it."

"What they offered, you cannot provide."

"Which was?"

"Friendship."

"Friendship? Is it friendship to ask your people to die to keep Merceria safe or simply an excuse to let you suffer while they sit at home in their capital?"

"You're not a Dwarf, so I'll excuse your ignorance. We mountain folk don't make friends easily, but once we do, we'll stick by them no matter what."

Lambert sighed. "I assume that means you wish to fight?"

"That obvious, is it?"

"I warn you, Majesty. This will end badly for you."

"For me? You have that the wrong way around, General. You are a general, aren't you?"

"Commander-General, yes."

"Good, because I wouldn't want to get your rank wrong for your epitaph."

"Have it your way," said Lambert. "I shall give you two days to change your mind. Then the bombardment will begin."

"Most generous of you," replied Thalgrun. "I would wish you a good day, but under the circumstances, I think that inappropriate, don't you?"

"Indeed." Lambert and his escort turned and walked back to their horses.

Thalgrun headed up the steps with the rest of his entourage. "What did you make of him?" he asked.

"He's confident," replied Hayley, "but I can't decide whether that's experience talking or mere bravado. He didn't appear disappointed with the result, so I assume he expected us to refuse."

"That was my conclusion as well. Strange, though, how he gave us two full days. I wonder what he's up to?"

"Likely still preparing his siege engines. I understand they can be temperamental beasts. Still, seeing him up close was worthwhile, if only to note how he and his guards were dressed. It'll make infiltrating his lines much easier for my rangers."

The vard barked out a laugh. "You remind me of Kasri."

"I take that as a compliment."

That night, twelve rangers slipped over the wall, using ropes to lower themselves to the ground. Hayley watched them disappear into the darkness before turning to see the vard approaching.

"Are they away?" he asked.

"They are. If all goes according to plan, they should be back before midnight."

"And if not?"

"Then we'll likely hear a commotion amongst the enemy."

"I'm surprised you didn't go with them."

"So far as we know, the Halvarians don't employ women as warriors. My presence would only call attention to the raiding party."

"Congratulations. You've learned an important lesson in leadership."

"I have?"

"Sometimes you must trust in others."

"Does it get any easier?"

"No," said Thalgrun. "Not unless you completely trust those you delegate in your stead."

"Like Kasri?"

He nodded. "Aye. She's a rare breed, that one. Fearless, yet not foolhardy. She'll make an outstanding vard when the time comes."

"I understand it's rare amongst your people for a child to be chosen as a successor."

"It's true; I'll not deny it. A vard typically picks someone they believe will carry on with their policies. In most cases, that means an older, trusted advisor."

"Yet you picked your daughter."

"I did, but not why you think. I wanted someone to embrace the future, not bury it behind centuries of tradition and ceremony. The fact she's also a capable army commander is the crowning stroke."

"Do the guild masters feel the same?"

"You're more familiar with our culture than I realized. The answer to that question is yes and no. Some feel as I do, particularly the warriors guild, although admittedly, it took time for them to accept Herdwin as her forge mate."

"And the rest?"

"Let's just say they'd prefer someone whose head is buried in the past."

"Traditionalists—there's plenty of them back in Merceria."

"Don't get me wrong," said Thalgrun. "Tradition has its place, but not when it comes at the expense of others. Take the guilds, for example. They're so concerned about holding on to their power that they've caused our culture to stagnate. Kasri, on the other hand, looks beyond the walls of Ironcliff, seeing us as part of a larger world."

"She takes after you," said Hayley. "You decided to support us during the war."

"I did, but it was a desperate ploy to gain an ally. We knew the empire would be coming for us, just not when."

"So you knew about Halvaria?"

"We knew the Humans to the east would eventually try to expand into our lands. We didn't know how large their empire was or what they called themselves, merely that they were warlike. At least, that was the consensus amongst the leaders of the warriors guild. The rest of the guilds expressed no interest whatsoever in the reports. It's difficult preparing a kingdom for war when others place more importance on their coffers than the well-being of their own people."

"I assume you don't like the guilds?"

Thalgrun looked around, ensuring no one else was within hearing. "This may be an unpopular opinion, but they're a plague on Ironcliff. We'd be better off without them."

"Have you given any thought to getting rid of them?"

"Plenty, but if I took action, I'd soon be minus a Crown, possibly even my head. The guilds are very protective of their influence, which is difficult to overcome. Instead, I've settled on another solution."

"Which is?"

"I'll let Kasri deal with it once she's vard."

"Wouldn't that be setting her up for failure?"

"You don't know her very well. She might not be able to get rid of them, but she'll certainly put them in their place."

"How does Herdwin fit into this?"

"Ah," said Thalgrun, a grin spreading across his features. "I'm glad you asked. He's the key to the future of us Dwarves."

"He is?"

"Never before has a vard forged with a guildless Dwarf. He's a shining example of what can be achieved when the rules of guild membership don't restrict us. Having said that, I'm sure one of those greedy masters will offer him membership if only to curry favour with Kasri, but I doubt that'll have quite the effect they think it will. My daughter's not the type to curry favour. In her words, 'A fool's a fool, regardless of the length of his beard.' That was her mother's favourite expression."

A great flame leaped skyward, illuminating one of the enemy's catapults.

"Look," said Thalgrun. "That's a sight for sore eyes. It appears your rangers hit their mark."

"Something must have gone wrong. They were supposed to strike the trebuchet first."

"Perhaps they couldn't get close enough?"

"Well, there is an entire army out there." Hayley stared into the darkness, willing her people to return. Time seemed to stretch out forever, and she found herself holding her breath several times until, finally, her rangers emerged from the shadows. She counted heads and then ordered the ropes lowered to bring them back to safety.

Bertram Ayles was the last to regain the wall, seeking out Hayley to make his report. "Two wounded," he said. "Nothing a Life Mage can't fix."

"You burned a catapult?"

"We did. We wanted to destroy the trebuchet, but it was too heavily guarded. Oh, that reminds me, we also set fire to a store of arrows while we were at it."

"I'm surprised you had enough oil."

"Turned out we didn't need it; barrels of the stuff were lying all over the place. I think they intend to use it during the siege."

"Good work. Pass on my thanks to the others. Now go and get some rest. You've earned it."

She waited as the rangers headed back towards the under-mountain.

"They did well," said Thalgrun.

"It was a small victory."

"It was, but an important one. When word of their success spreads throughout the city, it'll bolster morale."

"Let's hope that'll be enough to hold out against that army."

FIVE

Push for War

WINTER 967 MC

A bitterly cold breeze blew in from the west, but Edora Sartellian had other matters on her mind. The campaign on the western border had begun and, by all accounts, was moving along nicely. Everything looked to be going according to plan for the empire, yet she knew success there could spell doom for the current political landscape.

Exalor Shozarin was an accomplished military commander, a considerable benefit where the war was concerned. However, his unbridled quest for power was more important to her. No one denied that the man was a military genius, but that very thing made him a dangerous adversary.

She halted at the door of an ordinary-looking house and knocked three times. Agalix Sartellian opened it and peered past her, searching for anyone else in the area before ushering her inside. A servant took her cloak, and then her host led her into a large sitting room where a roaring fire warmed a trio of visitors.

"You know the others?" asked Agalix.

She recognized Freya Stormwind immediately, but it took a moment for her sight to adjust to the subdued lighting to identify the others. Enelle Sartellian, who acted as the empire's High Purifier, was not someone to be trifled with. To her left sat Kelson Shozarin, whose presence was utterly unexpected.

"I see we've surprised you," said Agalix.

"What's he doing here?" she asked.

Kelson spoke before Agalix could answer. "I'm as concerned about Exalor's plans as you are. Take a seat. We were talking about recent developments."

"Those being?"

"It seems Exalor changed his priorities concerning the northern offensive."

"In what way?" asked Edora.

"The original plan was to seal the Dwarves in their mine before marching the rest of the legion into Norland to draw out the Mercerians. Instead, he's decided to pursue more direct action against Ironcliff."

"Won't that upset his plans for conquest?"

"I'm not privy to his thoughts, but Exalor never acts without considering all the options. We are of the opinion this is part of some master plan to seize the Throne."

"An opinion I share," said Edora. "The question we must address today is what we intend to do about it."

"Yes," added Agalix. "A most perplexing problem. We know Exalor holds great influence amongst the empire's legions. We need something to keep them busy so they can't assist him in his mad grab for power."

"How do you propose we do that?"

The old mage scanned his companions before answering. "We believe the best option is war."

"With Exalor? That's a recipe for disaster."

"Actually, it was my idea to invade the Petty Kingdoms. It's not as if a legion can march on the capital when they're traipsing all over the lands to the east."

"Things like this need to be planned out well in advance."

"They do," agreed Kelson. "Thankfully, Exalor has already done the work required."

"Truly?" said Edora. "That surprises me."

"It shouldn't. Exalor has plans for scores of possible wars, all kept inside his private study."

"How do we get our hands on them?"

"That's just it—we already have. Last fall, when he presented his plans for his western campaign to the emperor, His Eminence insisted on seeing what his High Strategos had worked out for the final war against the Petty Kingdoms."

"What, might I ask, is the main strategy behind this supposed campaign? Not another attack in Arnsfeld, I trust?"

"Not at all," replied Agalix. "The plan calls for two legions to mass on the border with Ilea while the main thrust occurs in the north. Two other legions would then march across the border at Oberfeld, turn south, and push into Talstadt, threatening the central kingdoms. At the same time, another marches into Rudor, then Arnsfeld, rolling up the border." He waited for a response, but Edora remained silent. "You don't agree?"

"That strategy risks the enemy cutting off the southern advance by pushing into our rear. Better to send all three legions east, forcing an encounter with our enemies before they have a chance to properly call up their armies. If I recall, the so-called Northern Alliance is expected to field the greatest majority of men. I therefore suggest we march directly for their territory. What can you tell me concerning the strength of Hadenfeld?"

"We don't think they'll be effective," replied Freya. "Ever since their new king took over, they've been quiet."

"What of their obligations to allies?"

"Those still stand, but they wouldn't field much of an army. Two civil wars in less than five years reduced their fighting strength considerably."

"Two?"

"Yes. The last was some five years past, if I recall correctly. Hadenfeld might have been powerful a century ago, but it now pales compared to its glory days."

"Which other kingdoms can stand up to a legion?"

"Erlingen is a possibility," offered Agalix. "Although they'd be no match for two."

"You've had some time to think through this idea," said Edora, "but failed to consider one important fact."

"Which is?"

"You have no marshal to conduct the campaign. Both the Marshal of the North, or rather, the acting Marshal of the North, and the Marshal of the Empire are performing their duties in the west. Unless you're suggesting the Marshal of the South take precedence?"

"He can't," said Freya. "He's busy down south, dealing with the Orcs of the southern Continent."

"Then who is to lead this invasion?"

Agalix cleared his throat. "We hoped you'd consent to that honour."

"Me?"

"In preparation for this meeting, we contacted Korascajan. Their records on you were highly informative. You scored well in training, going on to success after success in the courts of the Petty Kingdoms. It's no small wonder the Sartellians sent you here, to the empire, to represent them."

"I agree," added Freya. "You've always kept a level head in council meetings, which will serve you well in dealing with the empire's legions."

"Providing they accept me as their marshal," replied Edora.

"Oh, they will," said Kelson. "I shall make certain of it."

"That's another thing that confuses me about this entire ordeal. Why are you, a Shozarin, plotting to act against your line-brother?"

"Exalor represents a threat to the natural order of things. I refer not only to his aims for the empire but also those concerning the Shozarin family. After careful consideration, I have determined he must be stopped, no matter the cost."

"How do we know this is not an elaborate plan to lure us into a false sense of security?"

"If that were the case, wouldn't I try to convince you he's no threat? Instead, I'm putting my head on the proverbial chopping block. He'd gut me with his sword if he learned of my presence here today."

"Fair enough," replied Edora.

"So," said Agalix. "Do you accept our offer of command?"

"I need some answers before committing to such an endeavour."

"Then ask away, and we shall do our best to answer."

"Which legions would be involved in the northern campaign?"

"The Eighth, Ninth, and Eleventh. Even as we speak, they're marching for the border. We'll arrange for them to mass on our side, close to Gotfeld, which puts them in a relatively good position, regardless of our strategy."

"I would like to read each legion's history to better judge their roles in the upcoming campaign."

"I'll see that they're sent to you. Anything else?"

"I would like a fourth legion in case something goes wrong."

"Wrong?" said Freya. "What could possibly go wrong when you have three legions at your disposal."

"Nevertheless, I must insist. This fourth legion would occupy the conquered lands, freeing up the rest of my command to bring the Petty Kingdoms to their knees."

"I like how you think," replied Agalix, "although I shall have to get back to you concerning which legion is available. I'm afraid I hadn't anticipated your request."

"Out of curiosity, how am I to be named marshal when no openings exist? Surely you're not suggesting I be appointed as the new Marshal of the North?"

"Not at all," replied Kelson. "In truth, the emperor has been enamoured of the great dream for some time. He wants to be the one who sees it through to fruition."

"A unified Continent," added Enelle. "Who would've thought it possible in our lifetime?"

"It isn't here yet," warned Edora. "We must still deal with a multitude of enemies, not to mention Exalor and his people."

"Fair enough," said Agalix. "Does this mean you're with us?"

"It does."

"Good. Now, there are other matters to attend to. As you all know, we have good reason to believe Exalor will use his legions to march on us here in Varena. To avoid that eventuality, we need to take steps to identify those loyal to him and eliminate them."

"I can help with that," offered Kelson. "I've acquired an extensive list of his allies. I suggest, however, that we do not pick them off piecemeal. That will only arouse suspicion. Instead, I propose we put people in place to exact our revenge in a coordinated effort. Call it a day of retaliation, if you like, but if we're to succeed, we must do this with the utmost secrecy. If Exalor gets one whiff of what we're planning, it'll all be for naught."

"Our one saving grace," said Freya, "is he's busy with events in the west. Is there anything we can do to ensure it remains so?"

"We can't undermine his campaign, if that's what you're asking. The consequences of such a move would be catastrophic. A loss to the Mercerians would open us up to an outright invasion."

"Is that really the case?" replied Edora. "I'll admit the Mercerians have a capable army, but they employ nowhere near the numbers we can field."

"Yet a victory at their hands would give hope to our enemies. We've already seen how our loss in Arnsfeld affected the rest of the Petty Kingdoms. Do you want that spreading throughout the known lands?"

"Can I suggest an alternative," offered Enelle. "Why not go after the dragon himself?"

Kelson shook his head. "Surely you're not suggesting we kill Exalor?"

"Why not? After all, he's the one who has designs on the Throne. Eliminate him, and the threat is gone."

"It won't work. There's already been one attempt on his life. Since then, he's increased the number of guards responsible for keeping him safe. He won't offer another opportunity."

"Then we shall attack with more warriors."

"How exactly would you mass that many in one place without attracting attention? Exalor is no fool; he knows someone is out to get him. I'm not saying the man doesn't deserve death for his plotting, merely that it's foolish to consider such an action until we've substantially weakened his power base."

"She's right," said Agalix. "Making Exalor the prime target at this point would be foolish. That's not to say we won't take the opportunity if it presents itself, but our efforts are better spent chipping away at his power base. To that end, I propose we start with Edora investigating the legions she is to command."

"To what end?" said Kelson.

"Three commander-generals will be under her command, four including the occupation force. She'll need to ensure they're all loyal to the cause; by that, I mean they don't hold any loyalty to Exalor. The last thing we need is a legion turning on us."

Enelle Sartellian cleared her throat. "As High Purifier, I keep notes on all the legion commanders. I shall be happy to share those with you, Edora."

"Thank you, although I do have a question concerning them. What happens if I deem one of them unacceptable?"

"If you report it to me, my people will deal with the problem immediately."

"And that would involve?"

"He would be arrested and removed from command. His subsequent fate remains dependent on the circumstances of his unsuitability. If, for example, he is a rabid follower of Exalor, we shall have to execute him. On the other hand, if he objects to your appointment as temporary marshal, on legal grounds, then we will reassign him to less-glamorous duties. Have you dealt with legions before?"

"I know all about them but have never been in a position where I interacted directly with them."

"Let me go over how they work. On paper, a legion consists of four cohorts, each under the command of a captain-general. These individuals, in turn, report to the commander-general, who is responsible for their overall employment. Theoretically, this makes a legion a fully integrated army capable of operating... well, almost anywhere, save for the sea. However, the bonds formed between the commander-general and his captain-generals are often overlooked. Many develop lifelong friendships. Removing one of these individuals can oftentimes unsettle the legion's effectiveness, undermining morale and leading to distrust between the various officers."

"Which means?"

"It is often better to replace the entire command structure rather than just one individual."

"All of them?"

"Well, all the generals, at least. Fortunately, there's no shortage of captains eager for promotion. The trick is finding the most competent and loyal ones. Loyalty will be particularly important going forward, as it may become necessary to meet Exalor's legions on the battlefield if things go awry."

"You're talking of civil war now?" said Edora. "I thought we were only dealing with Exalor's ego. Do we really believe he'd take it to that extreme?"

"We'd be fools not to treat it as such."

"Agreed," added Agalix. "No one ever lost a war by being too prepared."

"History has many examples of just that," said Edora, "but I understand what you're implying. This whole discussion, however, raises an important point, that of politics. You've all agreed to make me, a Sartellian, the acting marshal for this campaign, but what restrictions will I face if I appoint new commander-generals for these legions? Am I to pick from a list of acceptable candidates, or will I be free to assign whomever I choose?"

"I think we can trust you to make the right decisions without our interference, don't you?" Agalix turned to his companions.

"Most definitely," agreed Enelle. "We want victory in the east as much as you."

"Yet you are to place four legions under my direct command, and I've not gone through the usual scrutiny that would be expected of an Imperial Marshal. What if I'm tempted as Exalor is and try to take the Throne for myself?"

"You won't," said Enelle. "I've studied your background; you're a loyal subject of the empire, not a glory-seeking narcissist. If I believed otherwise, I would never have backed this enterprise in the first place."

"She speaks the truth," added Agalix. "We three families don't always get along, but this is bigger than us. It's our way of life at stake, a power structure that's kept us at the top for centuries. Even Kelson, a Shozarin, knows what will happen if we let Exalor seize the Throne. It'd be the end of everything we've worked so hard for."

Part of Edora was thrilled about leading the final campaign against the Petty Kingdoms, but was it the right move? She worried that they were manipulating her somehow, but try as she might, she couldn't figure out how. Was the objective here about conquering the Continent, or were they using her to raise an army to fight Exalor? And what did that say about their motives? Were they truly concerned about defeating the High Strategos or in a rush to claim the Throne for themselves?

She'd lived with the reality of the family's politics for her entire life, yet nothing prepared her for this. Edora found herself at a crossroads, with no clear guidance on which way led to success and which to ruin. Her thoughts rushed through her head, overwhelming her, and then she noticed everyone staring at her.

"I know this is difficult to grasp," said Agalix, "but we truly do have your best interests at heart."

"Indeed," added Freya. "And to demonstrate our faith in you, we promise you the coveted position of High Strategos once Exalor is dealt with."

There it was—the ultimate prize, but Edora wasn't certain if that was what she wanted. Like her colleagues, she was a trained battle mage. Since arriving in Halvaria, it had been drummed into her that the position of High Strategos was the greatest mark of achievement, but wouldn't that make her a target, as it had Exalor?

"You flatter me," she finally said. "When am I to begin the invasion of the Petty Kingdoms?"

"As soon as you're confident everything is in place."

She stood. "Then I must be on my way to the border to meet my new command."

SIX

Contact

WINTER 967 MC

The ghostly image of Kraloch hovered before Aubrey.

"The enemy attacked at Kharzun's Folly and forced their way across. The Dwarves are retreating to Stonecastle, but a siege is in their near future."

"And what of the north?" asked Aubrey.

"The last I heard, the enemy has taken a position in preparation for a siege there. Heward halted their advance at Holdcross, but his command is small and may be overwhelmed if attacked in force."

"Not the best of news."

"It gets worse," continued the Orc. "Tog reported ships were sighted off the southern coast. They have yet to land, but his last letter was written over a week ago. The kingdom is besieged on all sides."

"Can Weldwyn send aid?"

"They are still weak from the recent war. There is also trouble brewing farther west, which may require their assistance."

"What kind of trouble?"

"Something to do with the Clanholdings. I do not know the details. How are things with you?"

"We're about to cross the border into a place called Erlingen. Sir Owen reckons we're halfway to Reinwick, but admittedly, he's never actually been there himself."

"And now you number an Orc amongst your group."

"We do, a member of the Sky Singers. Are you familiar with that tribe?"

"I am not, but our shamans lost contact with many tribes over the years.

I look forward to meeting Krazuhk, and please pass on my best wishes to Beverly and Aldwin."

"I will." She let the image fade.

"Well?" said Beverly. "Anything to report?"

"Yes, and none of it is good. The empire has begun its campaign. As we speak, they're marching on Stonecastle and Ironcliff, and now ships have been sighted off the coast, making it even more imperative we get home as soon as possible."

"I'm open to suggestions, but until something better comes along, we'll stick to the plan. Look on the bright side of things."

"Bright?"

"Yes. We could have landed ourselves in the middle of the empire. Instead, we're in the Petty Kingdoms instead of rotting in a cell."

"I was in a cell," added Aldwin, "and I'm forced to agree with Beverly. At least we're free."

"Perhaps we should head west," said Aubrey. "That would put us closer to home, at least in theory."

"*Did you say west?*" asked Krazuhk in the Orcish tongue. "*My mastery of your tongue is still in its infancy, but I recognize the word. You cannot go west.*"

"*Why not?*"

"*A mountain range separates this land from that of the west.*"

"*How do you know this?*"

"*I am a Sky Singer,*" the Orc replied, "*and a master of air. My tribe's original lands lie to the west, at the base of the Stormtop Mountains.*"

"*Interesting,*" said Beverly. "*Could those be the same mountains that house Stonecastle?*"

"*I do not think so. To our knowledge, a great Human empire lies behind those peaks, an area where Orcs are not welcome.*"

"*That must be Halvaria; it's definitely not our home. Still, the base of those mountains might put us close enough to Merceria for Aubrey's spell of recall.*"

"*And if not, we would have wasted much time.*"

"What's everyone talking about?" asked Owen, who, despite trying, had yet to master even simple phrases in the Orc tongue.

"We're discussing changing direction and heading west," replied Beverly. "Aubrey can use her magic if we get close enough to home."

"I doubt that would be far enough. You have to understand that the Halvarian Empire is big."

"How big?"

"Some say large as all the Petty Kingdoms combined. Your cousin might be powerful, but I doubt even her magic can travel that distance."

Aubrey sighed. "No, I suppose not. We'll have to continue with our original plan and head to Reinwick. Any clue what we'll discover once we're there?"

"The region has been peaceful of late," replied Owen. "A far cry from the tumultuous events of the past."

"You mean the invasion you spoke of?"

"Yes. Erlingen's been relatively peaceful ever since, but our route will take us through Andover, and that's another story."

"Isn't that the kingdom that invaded you here in Erlingen?"

"It is. They also got involved with another war last year."

"With who?" asked Aldwin.

"Reinwick."

"That's where we're headed," said Beverly. "You didn't think you should've mentioned this sooner?"

"The war ended in a defeat for Andover."

"And that's supposed to make me feel better?"

"Word is, the Duke of Reinwick offered them the hand of friendship. The two realms are now allies, and there are rumours they're courting other Petty Kingdoms to join them."

"Some good news at last," said Aldwin.

"Perhaps not so much for you," replied Owen. "I can't speak for their current laws, but Andover used to have the death sentence for anyone found with grey eyes."

"Again," said Beverly, "that would have been nice to know in advance."

"Yes. I suppose it would."

"What's Andover's attitude towards Orcs?"

"I haven't a clue," replied the knight. "And I have no idea how they'd be treated in Erlingen, either. As far as I know, there aren't any Orc tribes in the duchy."

They arrived at an old, rickety bridge that passed over a small stream.

"There it is," said Owen, sweeping his arms wide. "Erlingen, the jewel of the Petty Kingdoms."

"It looks like Zowenbruch," replied Aldwin. "How can you tell this is the border?"

Owen pointed north, across the bridge. "That village over there happens to be Adelwel. Admittedly, it's not much to look at, but if you follow the road that cuts through it, you'll soon find yourself in Salzing. Now, that's a city worth visiting."

"Considering the makeup of our group, perhaps we should go around it?"

"Nonsense," replied Owen. "Several taverns in Salzing are known for measuring the pulse of the realm."

"I'm not entirely sure what you mean."

"He means," said Beverly, "it's a place of gossip."

"We prefer the term 'enlivened news'," replied the knight, "but you are essentially correct. As I mentioned the other day, we would be wise to learn more about recent events, particularly as we're travelling north. Why north, you ask? Because that's the source of greatest concern to the duke's court."

"How long have you been away?"

"For some time, and I'm eager to learn if relations with Andover have improved of late. You gave me grief earlier this morning for not informing you of our relations with Andover, so I'm trying to make up for that deficiency."

"You must admit," said Aubrey, "he means well. I say we follow his advice."

"I agree," said Beverly, "but I'm warning you, if anyone tries to arrest my husband again, Nature's Fury comes out."

Aldwin smiled. "It's nice to be appreciated."

Sir Owen looked at him. "Are you not insulted?"

"Why would I be?"

"She's treating you like a possession."

"No, she's not. She's looking out for me as I do for her."

"I'm confused," said Owen. "In what way do you look out for her?"

Beverly smiled. "In many ways. Can't you tell?"

The knight blushed profusely.

"I was referring to my armour," said Beverly.

"Your armour?"

"Who do you think made it?"

"I'm sorry. Are you suggesting your husband made your armour?"

"Did you not see him repairing it after the joust?"

"I did, but there's a marked difference between making armour and repairing it."

"He also made me this hammer." She tapped Nature's Fury, hanging on her belt. "I KNOW you've seen me use that."

"Yes, of course. I apologize quite profusely," said Owen. "I meant no slight."

"Yes, you did. You called into question his manhood. Let me assure you, my husband has no shortcomings in that regard."

"Oh, look," said Aubrey. "We're ready to cross the bridge. Shall we?"

"Lead on," said Owen, "before this tongue of mine gets me into even worse trouble."

Even though Salzing rivalled the major cities of Merceria, the walls encapsulating it were neglected, evidence of a lack of trouble in these parts. The guards there looked equally forgotten, contenting themselves with standing there, watching everyone passing through the gates. Krazuhk was the only one who attracted their attention, although they maintained their distance even then. The townsfolk, however, were another matter.

Upon entering the city streets, a gaggle of children followed in their wake, the green-skinned Orc and the woman dressed in ornate armour intriguing them. Eventually, Owen had enough and turned to confront them.

"Off with you," he called out, "or I'll sick the Orc on you."

They fled in fear while Beverly stopped her horse, staring at the knight. "A Knight of the Hound should be honest in all things."

"I am being honest."

"You have a lot to learn about diplomacy. Actions have consequences, Owen. You may find it entertaining to frighten children with the threat of an Orc, but parents might not be so understanding. A few more choice words like that, and we could find ourselves chased out of town."

"I suppose I never thought of it that way. You Mercerians are far more aware of treating others as equals. It surprises me, all things considered."

"What's so surprising about that?"

"Well, you're a noble, as is your cousin."

"And?"

"In the Petty Kingdoms, nobles are a privileged class; all others serve at their whim. Is it not so back in Merceria?"

"Some would agree with that," replied Beverly, "but in that regard, my father was a bit of an eccentric. To his mind, nobles exist to serve their subjects, a trait I admire."

"As do I," added Aubrey. "Have you no like-minded nobles here in Erlingen?"

"I couldn't really say," replied Owen. "I didn't spend much time at the duke's court." He slowed as they approached a two-storey building with a couple of armed men stationed outside. "Ah. Here it is, the Silver Chalice."

They drew closer, then he halted and swung down from the saddle. A guard called for help, and a collection of young men appeared to take the horses away. After them came an older gentleman with silver hair and a closely trimmed beard.

"Ah, Sir Owen," he said. "It's been a while since you last graced us with your presence." The old man's eyes flicked to Owen's companions, lingering on the Orc. "I see you've brought guests."

"I have indeed. Nobles from a foreign land."

"And an Orc. How interesting. Might I enquire whether you've eaten?"

"We have not," replied the knight.

"If you'll follow me, I'll show you inside. They've made some changes since your last visit, so I wouldn't want you to get lost."

He led them through the doorway into a long entranceway with a floor covered in a thick carpet and walls adorned with what looked like colourful paper. Numerous doors stood on either side, but their host took them straight to the end, where the hallway opened into a large room. Inside, dozens of men sat at various tables, some alone, others in small groups. This was obviously a tavern of sorts, although Beverly had never seen its like before.

"What is this place?" she asked.

"It's a gentleman's club meant for the exclusive use of the upper classes of society. Have you nothing similar back home?"

"We have the Queen's Arms," offered Aubrey. "The rich and powerful frequent it."

"Yes," said Beverly, "but not at the exclusion of others."

Owen looked aghast. "Are you suggesting your nobles socialize with the common folk?"

"I would certainly hope so, or I never would have met my husband. Nor, for that matter, would I have been trained by my mentor."

"Your mentor?"

"Yes. Gerald Matheson, the Marshal of Merceria."

"But he's a noble, isn't he?"

"He is now," replied Beverly, "but he was my father's sergeant-at-arms when I was a little girl."

They were conducted to a table.

"Today's offering is a suckling pig in an herb wine sauce," announced their host.

"That will do fine," said Owen. The fellow left them, heading into the back room.

Their arrival caused considerable interest amongst those already in attendance, particularly the presence of Krazuhk. A tall individual rose from his seat and approached them.

"I sense trouble," whispered Beverly.

"Hush now," soothed Aubrey. "Give the fellow half a chance. He might surprise you."

The man in question halted beside their table. His well-groomed facial hair spoke of nobility, while he had the musculature of a warrior, likely a knight.

"Can I help you?" said Beverly.

The fellow ignored her, concentrating on Sir Owen. "You, sir, have violated the rules of this club."

"And what rules are those?" asked Beverly.

Once more, he ignored her. "Well? What have you to say for yourself?"

"This, Sir Myles, is Lady Beverly Fitzwilliam, Baroness of Bodden, and her cousin, Lady Aubrey Brandon, Baroness of Hawksburg."

The tall man paled but recovered quickly, offering up a bow. "My apologies, ladies. I shall leave you in peace." He shuffled back to his seat.

"What was that all about?" asked Aubrey. "One moment, he's berating you for some reason; the next, he's offering an apology and retreating."

"Women are not usually allowed in this club, but nobility is the exception to the rule."

"Has it always been so?"

"Not at all. Before Erlingen was invaded, the duke permitted the barons to feud amongst themselves. This nearly led to disaster, for when the Army of Andover crossed the border, the infighting had weakened the duke's army. Following the subsequent events and the great victory, he vowed to stop such senseless petty jealousies. Proper respect must now be shown to all nobles, regardless of their station."

A server appeared, filling their glasses with wine. Sir Owen waited until he finished before taking a sip. "Ah. A Torburg Gold. How I've missed this. Now, where was I?"

"You spoke of the duke's reforms," offered Aubrey.

"That's right. Of course, those were under the old duke, Lord Deiter Heinrich. Unfortunately, he died fighting in the Crusades."

"Yes. At the Battle of the Standing Stones, if I'm not mistaken, although I believe you refer to it as the Battle of the Wilderness."

"How could you possibly know that?"

"Through my contact with Shaluhk."

"You've mentioned that name before," said Owen. "It sounds Orcish."

"That's because it is," replied Aubrey. "She's the Shaman of the Red Hand, and they live in Therengia. I suspect her version of events differs significantly from yours."

"Meaning?"

"Her people do not view your so-called crusade in the same light as you.

To them, it was an invasion of their homeland. You may have cause to celebrate the life of your old duke, but to them, his death was a cause for celebration."

"And rightly so," added Beverly. "You can't invade other people's lands and expect to be loved."

"The same could be said of the Old Kingdom," replied Owen.

"I'm not defending the Old Kingdom. I'm talking about Therengia!"

The room fell silent at the mention of the name.

"It appears we've garnered some interest," said Aldwin. He lowered his voice. "But as long as they're not interested in my eyes, I'm happy to let them stare."

"I wonder," said Beverly. "You don't suppose we could convince Therengia to join the cause, do you?"

"The cause?" replied Owen. "Surely you don't expect them to help Merceria? The two kingdoms are thousands of miles apart."

"It was just a thought."

"Then again, you may have inadvertently raised an interesting point."

"I did?" asked Beverly.

"By all accounts, Therengia has proven remarkably successful on the battlefield. When the empire finally makes its move, it would be to our advantage to have them as allies."

"And how would we do that?"

Owen shrugged. "Who knows? The current Duke of Erlingen doesn't carry the flair for diplomacy his father did. I've heard rumours that Reinwick formed some agreement with this new Therengia, but I couldn't tell you what it entailed."

"Interesting," replied Aldwin. "I note you said when the empire makes its move, not if. Are you that certain they'll invade?"

"The greatest minds of the Petty Kingdoms think so, not to mention every knight I've ever run across, aside from your good wife."

"Why is that?"

"Halvaria has a history of expansion. Added to that is every knight's secret wish to distinguish themselves in battle and win everlasting fame and glory." He held up his hands to forestall any argument. "You've convinced me killing is not glorious, but you need to understand the mindset of our knights. They're bred for war; you might even say it's their destiny to fight, regardless of the hopelessness of the situation. In some ways, it's romantic."

Aldwin stared at him incredulously. "Romantic?"

"Yes. I don't mean in terms of romance, but the idea of someone fighting a desperate battle against hopeless odds stirs the heart, don't you think?"

Beverly shook her head. "Those kinds of thoughts led to the Order of the Sword's downfall."

"Have you ever fought against the odds?"

"I have, but only when absolutely necessary. I understand sacrifice, but throwing away your life without any hope of achieving your objective is senseless. I'd much rather withdraw my army to fight another day."

Sir Owen forced a smile. "Let's hope that doesn't become necessary."

SEVEN

From the Sea

WINTER 967 MC

The mist burned off, revealing that the enemy fleet anchored off the coast had grown even larger.

"*It is as the marshal predicted,*" said Tog, speaking in his native tongue. "*I wonder why they do not land their warriors.*"

"*As do I,*" replied Gral, "*although I am more perplexed why they wait and why Trollden is the object of their interest. We are nothing more than a small village.*"

"*We guard the river, and until they remove that chain, their ships cannot move up to Colbridge.*"

"*And so we must fight? Would it not be wiser to let them pass?*"

"*If the enemy seizes Colbridge, the entire kingdom would be at their mercy. Make no mistake, my friend; we may not be great in numbers, but we hold the fate of the kingdom in our hands.*"

"*And how do we deal with an enemy that comes in such numbers?*"

"*We dispatched a messenger to Colbridge, where Lord Preston waits with our reserve.*"

"*Do you want them sent here?*"

"*No,*" replied Tog. "*Not until we know the enemy's true intentions. They may try to hold us in place while most of their ships press up the river.*"

"*To do that, they must seize the winch that controls the chain.*"

"*Precisely, which gives us the advantage of knowing their target before they strike. Of course, they are here in much greater numbers than we suspected, so they may assault the village as well.*"

"*But why would they if the chain is so important to them?*"

"*My guess is they spied on us from afar and expect us to protect our homes. Thus, an attack on the village would draw our people away from the winch. Unfor-*

tunately for them, they failed to take into account our culture. To us, buildings are replaceable."

"Do we ignore them?" asked Gral.

"Not quite. We shall set the bulk of our people to guard the river while a small number remain here to resist their efforts to take Trollden." He grinned. *"They expect us to stand and fight as the Humans do, but the swamp is our natural habitat."* He gazed out to sea. *"They are lowering boats. It appears they have finally decided to land their army."*

"Do we oppose them as they land?"

"No. Let them enter the swamp, where we have the advantage."

Captain Claudio Zalango of the Fourth Halvarian Legion watched as his company climbed out of the boats. They were at full strength, one hundred of the empire's finest warriors, ready to come to grips with the enemy. Unlike other legions, the Fourth was comprised of three Imperial cohorts and only one provincial, meaning more men armed in mail and veterans to ensure success. They employed more footmen than usual, for the High Strategos had wisely decided horses would be useless in this difficult terrain.

He formed his men into a line, ready to advance, then waited as the crossbowmen took up a position on his flank. They'd been warned about the likelihood of Trolls, vile creatures said to have skin as thick as stone. To ensure success, the legion's archers carried steel-tipped bolts specially enchanted to punch through the creatures' hides. These were only available in limited quantities, but of the three companies provided with them, one stood on his right.

The archer captain gave him the thumbs up, and Claudio ordered the advance. Initially, the shoreline was relatively firm, but after only a few steps, it was like walking on a sponge. He slowed the march to enable his men to keep their lines. Soon they were grappling with ankle-deep water, and the complaints started as boots became waterlogged.

"Quiet," he called out. "Keep your eyes to the front."

With discipline restored, he gazed upon their target, a small group of wooden buildings at a range of two hundred paces or so, raised up on posts jutting out of the swamp. Although larger than Human buildings, they were crudely constructed, with the gaps between planks visible even at this distance.

The sight made him glance right, but the crossbowmen wisely held their volleys, waiting for the enemy to appear. Closer and closer they went, the water now waist-deep.

Claudio waved a hand, slapping away an insect buzzing around his head. The air had been fresh when they'd landed, blown in from the Sea of Storms, but it grew stagnant here. He absently noted the algae spread out before them and the twisted tree trunks nearby that seemed to sprout multiple roots. His boot sank into the mud, and he struggled to free it.

All along the line, his men were experiencing similar troubles. They were in the middle of winter, and this swamp should be frozen, yet they were waist-deep in lukewarm water, struggling to make any progress.

He urged on his men, slowing the pace even more. The line became uneven, understandable considering the terrain, and Claudio fought back the impulse to force the men into a tighter formation. It was exhausting work, the captain breathing heavily, the stench of rotting vegetation invading his nostrils.

An arrow appeared out of nowhere, striking the warrior to his left. "'Ware archers!" one of his men warned just before an arrow took him in the throat.

Claudio checked around them, searching for the source. A figure shifted amongst the buildings in the distance, not Troll-sized, but more akin to a Human.

Moments later, a trio of green-skinned Humanoids revealed themselves, letting off a volley. It was only three arrows, yet every single one somehow found its mark.

"Orcs!" he shouted. The crossbowmen halted, focusing on suppressing the enemy's volleys.

Captain Zalango wanted to warn them to save the special bolts, but they'd already loaded their weapons. One hundred crossbow quarrels flew forth, sounding like hail as they struck the side of the building. Ordinarily, this would persuade an enemy to remain hidden or flee, but these Orcs stood and loosed another three arrows, each taking down an enemy in the densely packed Halvarian line.

With a start, he realized the enemy knew the empire's weakness. A volley of crossbows can be devastating, particularly at short range, but it takes considerable time to reload once discharged.

"Halt," he called out. "Raise shields and straighten the line."

He waited as the men shuffled into place, then raised his sword on high. "Advance!"

Claudio kept his gaze on the target. The enemy knew their business, for other archers soon appeared, adding to the mayhem. His men, however, retained their discipline despite the difficult terrain. Arrows stuck in shields, but few fell.

As they drew closer, he risked glancing over his shoulder. The warriors of his company were eager to come to grips with the enemy, to release their rage upon the Orcs, picking them off one by one.

Suddenly, a dark shape rose from the swamp, and a fist of stone swung out, launching his body through the air. He landed with a splash, certain his ribs were broken. As he struggled to keep his head above water, all around him was chaos. Claudio had never seen a Troll, and though his cohort commander had warned him what to expect, the reality was far more terrifying than he ever imagined.

Swords scraped across the creature's tough hide, the sound making his skin crawl. A scream of terror escaped his lips, and then someone grabbed his arm, pulling him free of the water's cloying grasp. His sergeant's grim face stared down at him as he dragged him backwards, and then a massive club swung out, taking the sergeant in the head and crushing his helmet. Blood gushed out. As the captain opened his mouth to scream, he choked on bits of flesh.

The great Troll loomed over him, then lifted its foot, bringing it crashing down on the captain's head.

"Your archers proved most effective," said Gral, using the language of Humans to converse with the Orc.

"They are not just archers," replied Gorath. "They are the Queen's Rangers."

"I was under the impression they included Humans?"

"Ordinarily they do, but all were sent north to Ironcliff, along with the High Ranger herself. She thought they could be better used to infiltrate the enemy camp rather than us Orcs."

"And if the enemy comes close enough to engage in hand-to-hand fighting?"

"Rangers are well-trained to do both."

"I wish we had more of you."

"More will come, but their other duties preclude their presence here for now."

"Other duties?"

"Yes. Keeping the roads safe. There has been trouble of late."

"What type of trouble?"

"Bandits attacking the army's supply wagons. Those behind this invasion have taken great pains to tie down our warriors wherever possible."

"And now they are here," said Gral, "in such numbers, it boggles the mind. How shall we ever defeat them?"

"Our job is not to defeat; it is to delay."

"Would it not be better for us Trolls to charge directly into them?"

"No," replied Gorath. "The marshal specifically warned us against such tactics. This enemy we face has put considerable effort into organizing their campaign." He plucked a crossbow bolt from the railing in front of him and examined its tip. "See this? It is made of hardened steel. I suspect it was specifically designed for use against you Trolls."

"Thankfully, our rising out of the swamp surprised them."

"It did, but I doubt the tactic will work a second time. The enemy is disciplined, and whoever planned their strategy will adapt quickly to changing conditions." He gazed seaward. "Look for yourself. As we speak, men in even greater numbers line up for the next attack."

They watched as the first wave of defenders, the Trolls who'd hidden in the swamp, loped back to the village. They'd destroyed two Halvarian companies, giving the enemy a reason to be wary, but was that enough?

The next attack came in the early afternoon: six full companies of heavily mailed men, led by horsemen in an extended line, who prodded the water with spears.

They advanced slowly, creeping forward only a pace or two at a time, checking the water-filled swamp for traps or hidden Trolls. Closer and closer, the enemy drew until the horsemen rode off on either side, their task now complete.

Tog watched with great interest as the footmen advanced to within spitting distance, ready to close. He lifted his arm and swept it down. A Troll to his left blew a horn, the sound being picked up and echoed elsewhere.

In preparation for the battle, Tog had ordered cut logs lined up against the sides of the buildings, with ropes holding them in place. Troll axes now slashed down and cut those restraints, releasing their burden to tumble into the swamp.

The Halvarians, already struggling through waist-deep water, now faced a new obstacle—wood that crushed some while displacing others. So busy were they that no one noticed the strange, sticky substance the logs were encased in.

"It is time for your archers to do their part," said Tog.

At Gorath's command, his rangers stood up, bows at the ready. However, rather than regular arrow tips, theirs had been dipped in tar. They waited as another ranger ran past, lighting them with a torch before loosing towards the unsuspecting enemy.

The first log failed to ignite, but the second roared to life with flames, hissing and popping as the fire spread down its length. More arrows hit their mark, and the swamp was lit up. Much to their credit, the enemy footmen didn't break, but they wavered, their advance stalling.

"Now!" shouted Tog, then jumped into the swamp, his great club gripped tightly. All along the defensive line, other Trolls followed his example, using their weapons to push the flaming logs closer to the enemy.

The tactic succeeded, for the previous clean lines of the Halvarians were in disarray. The Trolls, engrossed in the attack, overlooked the crossbowmen behind the enemy line.

One of Tog's Trolls cried in pain as a quarrel took out the poor fellow's eye. He fell with a crash, and then the Halvarians swarmed him, heedless of the danger from the flaming logs.

The battle devolved into a series of vicious melees, with the empire's finest crowding around individual Trolls while their crossbow bolts sought the large defenders' heads.

Tog swung his club, crushing someone's shoulder and sending them flying into the water. Something hit his arm, and he looked down to see an embedded crossbow quarrel. As he was about to pluck it out, another pierced the back of a Halvarian trying to slash at his leg. The fellow pitched to one side, then sank beneath the surface, a victim of his own archers.

All around Tog, the Trolls fought back. Their initial counterattack had done significant damage, but the enemy rallied, and it wouldn't be long before they flanked his defence. He struck out one more time, his club smashing into a chest, and then called for his warriors to withdraw.

Pulling back when the enemy overwhelmed some of his folk was difficult, but he consoled himself with the knowledge that such sacrifice was necessary. He ducked, passing under the support that held up the building, emerging on the other side. He spotted Gorath waiting for him and gave a wave, signalling it was time for the next phase of their defence.

The surviving Trolls fell back, abandoning the buildings of Trollden, flooding west towards the winch that controlled the river chain. Others, already stationed there, lifted massive timbers and put them into place. The logs were prepared in advance, with notches cut for the fast construction of wall segments. The Trolls' strength made short work of the task, the defensive wall materializing almost instantly.

Tog took up a position here, directing his people to prepare for the onslaught. He gazed back towards the village at the Halvarians, cheering as they entered the buildings. The wait seemed interminable, and then he spotted Gorath and his rangers running away as smoke drifted up from the thatched roofs, flames quickly consuming the tar-soaked walls. They had taken a gamble, for if the enemy had used fire arrows, it would have driven them from their own defensive line. Now, however, the empire was deprived of cover.

A few Halvarians, caught up in the rush of battle, emerged from the cluster of burning huts, running for Tog's new position. The Troll leader picked up a rock the size of his fist and hurled it towards them, striking one in the chest and knocking him from his feet. More stones rained down on them, thrown by Tog's companions.

The Orcs entered their new defensive works in single file, careful not to tread on either side lest they sink into the mud. They soon added their arrows to the rain of stones, shattering the enemy's spirit. The footmen broke and ran.

"It worked," said Gorath. "Though the price was heavy. You lost your homes."

"Houses can be rebuilt," replied Tog. "A kingdom is another matter."

"What happens now?" asked Gral.

"We sit behind our log walls and wait for the next assault."

"How can you be certain they will come?"

"They must," said Tog. "They cannot conquer Merceria without moving up the river, and their ships cannot pass while that chain blocks their path."

"They have paid a heavy price so far," said Gorath. "Your preparations proved most effective."

"We inflicted casualties, but they are slight compared to the size of their army. This will not set them back for long, and when they return, it will be in even greater numbers."

"They might try to flank us."

"That is possible, but the swamp is unforgiving, and we have taken measures to make that strategy difficult."

"What measures are those?"

Tog grinned. "There are Saurians to our east, along with some of their three-horns."

"But the three-horns are not beasts of battle; they are beasts of burden."

"True, but I doubt the enemy knows that. Their mere presence should be enough to halt any thoughts of going around us. In the meantime, we must be patient." He looked at the ranger's bow. "I suggest you unstring that. My understanding is that a wet bowstring is not as effective as a dry one, and the clouds tell me rain is coming."

"Good," said Gorath. "That will make things even more uncomfortable for the Halvarians."

EIGHT

Invasion

WINTER 967 MC

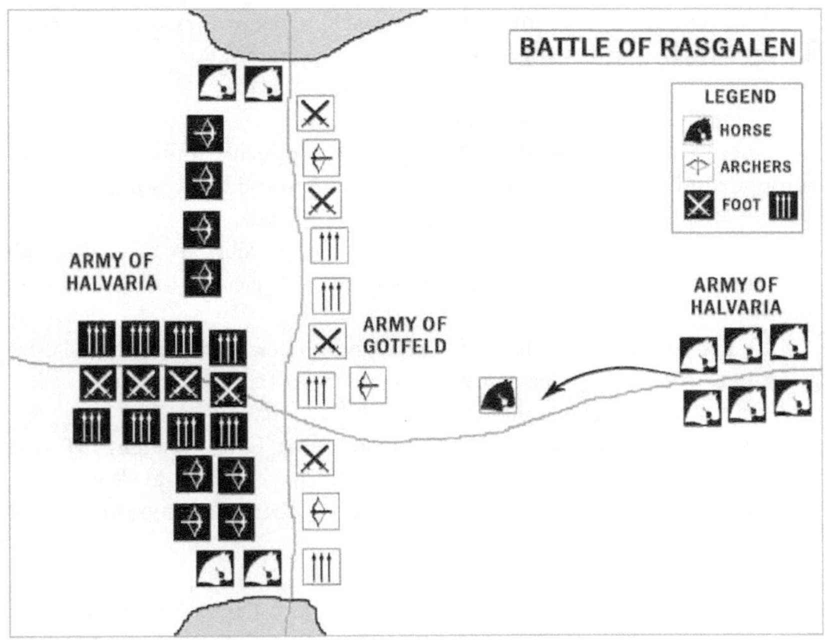

Commander-General Vorinus Moreau watched with pride as the Ninth Legion, his legion, crossed over the frozen river. This march heralded the completion of the final stage of the great dream laid down more than a thousand years ago by the founders of Halvaria. Behind him marched three more legions, the largest force the empire had ever assembled in one place. There would be no chance of a repeat of the debacle of Arnsfeld here. They would brush aside the warriors of the Petty Kingdoms as if they were flies.

His aide appeared: a humourless fellow he'd taken to calling Grim, if only for his countenance.

"Well?" Moreau snapped. "What have you to report?"

"The cavalry screen has reached the village of Volkenstag, my lord, with no sign of opposition."

"That's to be expected. A day or two will pass before word of our crossing reaches their capital, and he must still assemble his army to oppose us."

"We'll be at his doorstep by then."

"Precisely. There is, however, the chance he might withdraw eastward, allowing him time to gather allies."

"Not south, my lord?"

"South would take them into Deisenbach, a realm they are reportedly not on friendly terms with. Rudor, however, is much more likely to be of assistance."

"Could that spell trouble for us?"

"Not at all," said Moreau. "In fact, quite the opposite. It presents us with an opportunity to crush two armies at once. Remind me again how many warriors the King of Gotfeld has under his command?"

"Estimates place the number at six hundred, possibly six fifty, although that is assuming he has time to gather them. Have we information on Rudor?"

"It's presumed they will field a similar number. Arnsfeld has a larger army, but they'd have to leave some at home to protect their borders."

"Arnsfeld could spell trouble," said Grim.

"It's not so much their army as those annoying Temple Knights. During our ill-fated expedition to conquer them, they fielded at least three hundred, possibly more. I shouldn't like to see that effort repeated. Mind you, the situation here is vastly different."

"In what way, Lord?"

"We march with three times the numbers, and I shan't be tricked into fighting an enemy in a position of their choosing. This will be a campaign of mobility, Grim, where WE decide when and where to fight. Trust me; as long as we maintain the offensive, we can overcome any obstacle."

"Securing the border will be a simple matter, Lord, but once the other Petty Kingdoms hear about the invasion, they'll send help."

"I'm counting on it, as is our new marshal. In fact, this entire campaign is designed to lure them into our clutches so we can finish them off." He paused as a group of horsemen rode past. "There they go, the finest horsemen the empire has to offer. We have eight hundred, and that's only counting the Ninth. Why, if we wanted to, we could defeat these border realms with nothing but our cavalry. We certainly have enough to do so."

"We still need footmen to hold the cities, my lord."

"Naturally. I wouldn't think of doing things any other way. I merely point out how vast our invasion force is compared to that of our foe." He glanced eastward, but the legion's lead elements were already out of sight. "What was the name of that village you mentioned?"

"Volkenstag, my lord."

"Let's go look at it, shall we?" Without another word, the commander-general rode off.

Three days later, Vorinus Moreau looked down from a hilltop at an enemy army blocking the road, a thin stream their only defensive terrain.

Grim rode up to him. "It appears our estimate of their size is spot on, my lord, although they surprised us with the speed of their deployment."

Moreau looked past the enemy line. "What's the name of that village?"

"Rasgalen?"

"Then you may inform the captain-generals to commence the Battle of Rasgalen. I assume they're prepared for the advance?"

"The provincial cohorts stand ready, my lord, while the imperials remain out of sight."

"Then let them begin the attack." Grim rode off to pass on his orders.

The men of Gotfeld deployed archers on the flank with a small cadre of knights standing to the rear while the rest, footmen all, lined the stream as if it were some great defensive works. Moreau had hoped for something a little more challenging, where he could display his military prowess. To his mind, the King of Gotfeld was throwing his men away. He wondered, briefly, if it might be a trap. Were Temple Knights waiting to outflank him?

It was extremely unlikely, for he'd sent the bulk of his Imperial cavalry out wide on either side. If reinforcements were coming to aid his enemy, he would have heard by now. He considered offering the fools the chance to surrender, but he wanted to deal them a devastating blow early in the campaign. If he displayed leniency in this first encounter, the enemy might be more determined to make a stand later on. No, it was better to annihilate them, sending the survivors running home with tales of the empire's ferocity.

His two provincial cohorts deployed their light cavalry out in front, which would peel off on either side once they drew closer, threatening the ends of the enemy's line. Behind them came the bulk of his footmen, formed in one massive column, set to march straight down the road, engaging the enemy head-on while their archers peppered both flanks with their volleys. It wasn't the most elegant solution, but it didn't need to be. These cohorts outnumbered their opponents by odds of two to one, more than sufficient to win a victory, and that wasn't accounting for the rest of his legion.

The battle unfolded slowly, with the men of the Ninth taking time to close. Moreau let his attention drift to the defenders. He admired their courage for standing against such impossible odds, but at the same time, he wanted this battle over and done with so he could continue on with the campaign.

His mind rebelled at the thought. A victory here, no matter how easy, would enhance his reputation. To that end, he should, by rights, offer this battle his total concentration, yet he found it challenging to take it seriously. He yearned to make a name for himself by defeating a powerful enemy, not some ridiculously small army of a border king.

His archers peppered the enemy, pinning either end of their line in place, while in the north, the light cavalry of the Fourth cohort had already crossed the stream and was threatening the rear. In the south, the provincial horsemen took a more direct route, riding straight into the end of the enemy line.

The gamble paid off, for those facing the cavalry had little stomach for fighting and fell back, leaving the southern flank vulnerable.

The two armies clashed head-on in the centre, the line quickly devolving into a mass of warriors fighting for their lives.

"Any moment now," said Moreau. After circling beyond the sight of the enemy army, his Imperial cavalry rode out of Rasgalen, advancing into the foe's rear.

It was a masterful stroke, and he congratulated himself on pulling it off. Timing had been the most critical component of the plan, but his captains had shown outstanding professionalism, arriving precisely when necessary.

His footmen held the bulk of the enemy army in place, the king having nothing in the way of reserves. The Knights of Gotfeld turned to face the threat behind them, but the numbers were against them.

With their army caught between a large cavalry force and a mass of footmen, they could do little. They fought while their knights engaged the empire's horsemen, but soon the warriors of Gotfeld threw down their weapons and surrendered.

· · ·

Moreau sat beneath his awning, his feet resting on a stool. The enemy was beaten, their army destroyed, leaving the march into Rudor open. He had yet to write his report detailing the day's events, and he amused himself by considering how he could inflate his victory by overestimating the enemy's size while remarking on how well his warriors had fought. Perhaps a desperate melee at the bridge would liven up the retelling or an epic horse battle in the rear of the enemy. Anyone of import would easily see through the lies; however, a legion commander was expected to emphasize his own role in the conflict.

He noted a trio of warriors approaching with a prisoner amongst them.

"Ah," he said. "Captain Zoran, isn't it?"

The officer beamed, pleased to be recognized. "Yes, my lord."

"I see you come bearing a prisoner. Would you care to introduce him?"

"This is Lord Argalin Krantz, King of Gotfeld." His men forced the monarch to his knees.

Moreau stood, advancing to stand before the prisoner. "Well, well, well. What a pitiful excuse for a king."

"Please, spare me," begged the king.

"You resisted us. That can't be ignored."

"What else was I to do? Let you ransack my entire kingdom?"

"Ransack? Is that what you think we do? My dear fellow, we offered you the enlightenment of our emperor. You should have fallen to your knees and welcomed us." He regarded the king's escort. "You have his sword?"

Captain Zoran held it out, hilt first. "It is here, my lord."

Moreau drew it, holding the blade up to examine its quality. "A fine weapon you have here, Majesty. Might I ask where you acquired it?"

"It was my father's, as it was his father's before him."

"Ah. An heirloom. How quaint. It looks to be a fine blade. I wonder, though, how efficient it is at cutting flesh." He grasped the weapon in both hands, thrusting it into the king's chest without warning.

His Majesty stared down in disbelief even as the life ebbed from his eyes. The former King of Gotfeld's body slumped to the ground.

"You may dispose of the body in any manner you see fit."

"Yes, my lord."

"Oh, and one more thing, Captain."

"Yes, my lord?"

"You did well today. Congratulate your men on my behalf." Moreau held out the sword. "Here, take it. You've earned it."

Captain Zoran took the blade, bowing deeply. "You honour me, Commander."

"With that out of the way, you may return to your company. If you see my aide, tell him I require his services."

"Yes, my lord." The captain wheeled around, marching off smartly while his men dragged the corpse of King Argalin away.

Grim finally found him, although late in the day. One of his duties required the poor fellow to determine the toll the battle had taken. As he approached his commander-general, his shoulders slumped in exhaustion, yet a look of something lingered on his face.

"You bear good news, I assume," said Moreau.

"I do indeed, my lord. We suffered very few losses today while we completely routed the enemy."

"How many did we lose, exactly?"

"One hundred and twenty-five wounded, of which the vast majority should be fit to return to duty within the week."

"And dead?"

"Fifty-three, my lord. Mostly amongst the footmen who fought at the bridge."

"Ah, good," said Moreau. "That will fit in nicely with my narrative. What of the enemy?"

"We're still counting bodies, I'm afraid, but my estimate puts their losses at close to three hundred and at least a hundred wounded."

"I assume there are prisoners?"

"There are. I counted more than a hundred. That, by the way, brings me to my next question. What are we to do with them?"

"I want you to pick eight and let them go. They'll serve to spread the word of our great victory."

"And the rest?"

"Execute them. I can't spare the resources to guard them."

"It will be as you command, my lord."

"Good. Now summon my captain-generals. I wish to discuss our next move."

"Shall I send word to the marshal of our success?"

"I will do that myself," said Moreau. "Her Grace is a powerful member of the Sartellian line, and I wish to ensure she properly understands the magnitude of our victory this day. Any word on the other legions?"

"Indeed, my lord. The Eighth is camped only two miles west of us."

"And the rest?"

"Our last reports had them ten miles away, clearing the villages on either side of our advance."

"Then everything is proceeding according to plan. Send our heavy cavalry to Rasgalen to secure the town."

"Are you certain, my lord? It's almost dark now. Marching into town will take considerable time."

"I don't care if it takes all night," insisted Moreau. "By the time the sun rises, I want our men in Rasgalen. Is that clear?"

"Yes, my lord."

"Good. Now get to it before I tire of your presence."

Moreau paced, a habit he'd acquired early in his career. He'd begun as a captain, working his way up the ranks. Many doubted his ability back then, but he'd shown them he had it in him to make it to the exalted rank of commander-general.

He spotted a white horse riding towards him, its rider wearing a long, flowing cape.

"Marshal," he called out. "To what do I owe the pleasure of your company?"

Edora Sartellian regarded the commander-general before answering. "You engaged with the enemy."

"We did, Your Grace. It was a great victory."

"Don't mince words, Moreau. You and I both know they offered little more than token resistance."

"My apologies. I was under the impression the empire wished to glorify even the smallest success."

"And it does, but I'm not the empire, I'm your superior. To that end, I expect a faithful and accurate accounting of events. Do I make myself clear?"

"Absolutely, Your Grace. I shall endeavour to do so, going forward."

"Good. When will your legion be ready to continue their march?"

"It's common practice to rest a day after battle to bury the dead."

"Bury them tonight. I want you on the road first thing tomorrow morning."

"Your Grace, there are far too many enemy dead to deal with."

"Then let them rot in the open air. The key to this campaign is a rapid advance. If we are to bring the Petty Kingdoms to heel, then we must push deep into their territory, forcing a confrontation before they have time to gather their forces. Any delay, no matter how small, gives them more time to prepare."

She dismounted, handing her reins to a nearby foot soldier.

"You have done well today," she continued, "but more fighting is to come. These border kingdoms are weak and offer little in terms of opposition. Our objective is to engage the armies of Erlingen and the so-called Northern Alliance before they can gain the initiative."

"I assume we're planning to march through Rudor and Zowenbruch?"

"Angvil is a more direct route to Erlingen and the north."

"That would put us dangerously close to Arnsfeld, Your Grace."

"It would, and that, too, is important, as I'm eager to make up for the failure of our last invasion. However, that won't be your concern as my other legions will handle such things. No, the Ninth will march as quickly as possible into Rudor, then turn directly east. Ideally, I'd like you on the border of Erlingen before spring. That's when the game truly begins."

"The game?"

"Yes, the shuffling of armies as each side seeks the advantage—marches and countermarches, all aimed at giving us the perfect opportunity to crush them. Erlingen will be the first enemy we encounter with a decent-sized army. Your task is to pin them down, preventing them from joining with the Northern Alliance."

"How am I to do that without engaging them?"

"Have you learned nothing from your time as a commander-general?" She let out a sigh. "I shall spell it out for you. If they attempt to move north, you go south, threatening their cities. I have yet to hear of a king, or duke in this case, who willingly abandons his people to an invader."

"And when he responds?"

"Then you withdraw until another legion is within striking distance."

"The Ninth is more than capable of defeating them."

"I'm sure it is, but we must do more than defeat them. We must annihilate them, sending a message to all the Petty Kingdoms that opposing us is useless. Of course, if you don't think you're up to the task...?"

"My legion will do what's needed. You have my word."

"Good. You've made an excellent start to this campaign, Commander. Now show me you can keep the pressure up on our enemies."

NINE

Rumours of War

WINTER 967 MC

"There it is," said Owen, his breath frosting in the chilly winter air. "Torburg, the capital of Erlingen."

Aubrey scanned the area. "What are all these tents for?"

"That's the tournament grounds, but it should be empty this time of year."

Beverly spotted a warrior carrying a bucket of water. "Let's go and ask that fellow, shall we?" She trotted Lightning closer to the man, who halted, turning to face her.

"Something I can do for you?" he asked.

"Who are all these people?"

"Those aren't people, they're the Torburg Wolves."

"Who are?"

"Mercenaries. Don't you have them where you're from?"

"Not anymore."

He set down the bucket. "Then allow me to introduce myself. Name's Rudolf Sturgess, and I'm the captain of this company. Yourself?"

"Beverly Fitzwilliam, but I'm afraid I'm new to these parts. Might I ask what your mercenaries are doing here?"

"We've come to fight. What else would you expect?"

"Fight whom?"

"The empire, of course. Have you not heard the news?"

The rest of the party rode up beside her.

"What's going on here?" asked Aubrey.

"This fellow brought his company of mercenaries to help fight the empire."

"I didn't know Erlingen was at war," said Owen.

"Aye," replied the captain. "You haven't heard the news, then. Word is the Halvarians crossed into the Petty Kingdoms again."

"I assume the duke ordered his army to mass?"

"He has, although it'll take some time."

Beverly glanced around. "Don't take this the wrong way, Captain, but your mercenaries appear to be… How shall I put this?"

"Old?" supplied Sturgess. "That's because they are. My warriors are all experienced soldiers considered too old to be pressed into service. I'm hoping His Grace, the duke, will be willing to contract our services."

"Do you know the duke well?"

"I knew his father. I was there when he died."

"At the Battle of the Wilderness?" asked Owen.

"Yes, and let me tell you, that was a terrible day." He caught sight of Krazuhk as he was about to say more. "What's this, now? You bring an Orc here? Have you no shame? Orcs killed the duke's father during the crusade, hacking him apart with their axes."

"You're lying," said Aubrey. "Who are you, really?"

"I told you. I'm a mercenary captain."

"Who happened to arrive in Torburg as news of an invasion sweeps through town? I find that far too convenient."

"We mercenaries wander around, from city to city, seeking employment. I can't help it if we were lucky enough to arrive as the invasion started. Besides, who are you to talk? I was in the east and witnessed the duke going down with my own eyes. You're just some spoiled daughter of a noble with too much time on her hands."

"Spoiled, is it?"

Beverly held up her hand. "Let's not start saying things we might regret. For your information, Captain, my cousin is a Life Mage and far more experienced with battlefields than you."

"How would you know? One of the Sisters from Arnsfeld, are you?"

"I'm not a Temple Knight, if that's what you're implying. I've also seen my fair share of battles, but you don't seem the type to me."

"Meaning?"

"Most men who've seen battle bear a haunted look in their eyes. I won't deny you've been trained well; your stance and weapons speak to that, but I can't help but feel you're exaggerating your experiences. Tell me, Aubrey, what makes you say he's lying?"

"I know precisely how the duke died. While the Orcs were there, they didn't cause his death. Rather, a large shard of ice punctured his chest, cast by someone named Natalia Stormwind."

All colour fell from Sturgess's face. "How could you possibly know that?"

"Shaluhk, an Orc shaman present at the battle, told me."

"She's lying."

"Orcs don't lie. You'd know that if you spent any time amongst them."

"Why in the name of the Saints would I spend time in the company of greenskins?"

Aubrey turned to her cousin. "This is getting us nowhere."

"Let's put the matter aside," replied Beverly. "Tell us about Halvaria crossing the border."

"Word reached us that one of the empire's legions crossed the border."

"Which border?"

"Arnsfeld, though it turned out that was wrong. Yesterday, we received word Halvaria had slain the King of Gotfeld and destroyed his army."

"Gotfeld," said Beverly. "Where is that?"

"Northwest of Deisenbach," replied Sir Owen. "It's one of four kingdoms bordering Halvaria. If what this fellow says is true, they must have crossed the border while we travelled through Zowenbruch. Word would spread quickly; by now, couriers are likely heading to every court in the Petty Kingdoms."

"Word could reach here in so short a time?"

"The King of Gotfeld would've sent riders the moment he learned about the empire crossing the border."

"I may have exaggerated my experience," said Sturgess, "but that's not uncommon amongst mercenaries. We live or die based on our reputations; surely you understand that?"

"I'm a descendant of mercenaries," replied Beverly, "so I'll forgive you the lie, but you'd best not repeat it."

"And my men?"

"As far as I'm concerned, you're free to seek employment with the duke."

"Would you consider putting in a good word for us?"

"You appear to be under the mistaken impression we know His Grace."

"You're well-spoken," said Sturgess, "so I assumed you were nobles."

"And we are, just not from around here, except for Sir Owen; he's from these parts."

"Then perhaps you might consider offering our services to His Grace?"

"I shall mention you're available. Have you a full company?"

"Yes, fifty-two men, armed and ready to fight."

"If he's anything like his father," offered Owen, "he'll likely take you into service, especially if this news is real. Then again, he may hire you even if the rumours are false; such is the fear the empire generates."

"What of yourselves?" asked the captain. "Will you seek service with His Grace?"

"We're on our way to Reinwick," replied Beverly, "to charter a ship."

"Good luck with that. With the empire moving, the ships will all remain in port."

"Why is that?"

"Halvaria wants to dominate the Great Northern Sea, especially after losing at Lidenbach."

"Was that part of the invasion of Arnsfeld?"

"It was," said Sturgess. "The Temple Fleet destroyed all their ships, but that was some years ago. By now, they've probably replaced their losses."

"Thank you for the news," said Beverly. "Good luck with your future endeavours."

The fellow nodded respectfully, picked up his bucket, and continued on his way.

"You showed him far too much respect," said Aubrey. "The man outright lied."

"He did, but he and his company may face death in the coming months. I'll not wish ill of anyone who marches to war."

"Unless it's the enemy?"

Beverly smiled. "Precisely."

"What's our next step, Cousin?"

"That's an excellent question."

"I have an idea," suggested Owen. "How about we seek out the Temple Knights of Saint Mathew?"

"Why? Are you thinking of joining their order?"

"No, of course not, but the Mathewites offer financial services to travellers, which means they may have heard things."

"Financial services?"

"Yes. They arrange the transfer of coins from one location to another."

"They guard the wagons?"

"No. They accept coins in one city, then write a promissory note so the traveller can retrieve it at another location without having to lug around a chest full of gold."

"And they do this for free?"

"They charge a fee, usually a small percentage of the amount in question. It's how they defray the cost of maintaining their order. It also helps keep them in the good graces of the courts of the Petty Kingdoms. After all, their main customers in that regard are nobles."

"Fascinating. And we can visit them at their barracks?"

"They're called commanderies, but yes, they accept visitors, though admittedly, it's rare for women unless you're a Temple Knight of Saint Agnes."

"Will there be a fee to learn about recent events?"

"I wouldn't think so," replied Owen. "They're as concerned about protecting the Petty Kingdoms as most folk, perhaps more."

"Why's that?"

"The fighting orders are the bane of the empire's existence. If Halvaria succeeds in taking over the Continent, they won't hesitate to execute all the Temple Knights."

"Are they truly that ruthless?"

"That's what we've been told. I imagine many stories are designed to spread fear, a typical tactic in any war, but where the empire's concerned, I think there's more than a grain of truth to them."

"What kinds of stories?" asked Aubrey.

"It's said they don't take prisoners. Those who refuse to follow their ways are executed."

"How would you know if this were true?"

"That's just it," said Owen. "I wouldn't. When it comes to Halvaria, everything is hearsay, yet you can't escape that they've conquered every kingdom standing in the way of their expansion."

"How many realms have fallen to them?"

"I don't know the exact count, but in the last fifty years alone, they've swallowed up three, and their empire's been around for over a thousand years."

"Would there be an expert around here that might know more about them?"

"What would you like to know?"

"Anything we can get our hands on," said Beverly. "Particularly concerning their army."

"As I mentioned earlier," replied Owen, "they're called legions, and each one is a complete army, larger than anything any single Petty Kingdom could raise on its own."

"You say each one; have they many?"

"Most certainly, although I can't give you an exact count."

"This bodes ill," said Aldwin. "Last we heard, we were fighting in both Ironcliff and Stonecastle while Gerald fears a possible seaborne invasion to the south. That would seem to indicate Merceria is facing three legions."

"It likely is," replied Owen. "You've told me how your home is a place of near-constant warfare; the empire would take that very seriously."

"It's strange to think," said Beverly, "that had the Halvarians attacked a decade earlier, it would've been easier for them. These last ten years made the Army of Merceria what it is today."

"Why is that?"

"Seven years ago, our queen came out of hiding and helped prevent the overthrow of the king. She wasn't the queen then, merely a princess, but our history would be so much different without her."

"Say," said Aldwin. "You don't think the empire was behind that, too?"

"We had no idea about them then, but in hindsight, we'd be fools to ignore the possibility."

"It also explains other things," said Aubrey.

"Such as?" asked Beverly.

"How Sir Randolf happened to be in Bodden when your father died."

"There was no indication my father died of anything other than natural causes."

"True, but what are the odds that someone else with a rightful claim to his title happened to be there, waiting."

"You think the empire kept him close by?"

"It makes sense. The fellow would need coins to remain there unobserved, and had his claim been successful, it would've weakened the kingdom."

"I can't fault your logic," replied Beverly, "but it matters little, given our present circumstances. Surely you aren't suggesting Revi sent us here on purpose?"

"No. Most certainly not. That WAS an accident. Revi's calculations were correct. I checked them myself, but neither of us expected the ley lines to send us way out here to the Petty Kingdoms."

"This is all interesting," noted Aldwin, "but dwelling on the past won't help us. We need to concentrate on the present."

"Good point," said Beverly. "Captain Sturgess told us Halvaria would contest control of the Great Northern Sea. Do you think that's likely?"

"I would say yes," replied Owen. "Were they to control it, they could move up and down the coast at will. The only thing stopping them presently is the Temple Fleet."

"What can you tell us about that?"

"Not much, I'm afraid. I've already told you they destroyed a Halvarian fleet during the Arnsfeld invasion. They patrol the Great Northern Sea to reduce piracy, but I know nothing else."

"I assume the Church runs it?"

"No. The Temple Knights of Saint Agnes command it, which is why we call it the Temple Fleet rather than the Holy Fleet."

"Are you suggesting there's a Holy Fleet elsewhere?"

"Yes. On the Shimmering Sea, far to the south. The waters there are calmer, so they employ ships much different from those in the north."

"Different, how?"

"They're much larger," replied Owen, "and tend to be galleys of various descriptions."

"Which are?"

"Rowed vessels, though they have sails, just not as their primary means of travel."

"I'm confused," said Aldwin. "I understand the ships are different, but aren't both fleets controlled by the Church? After all, that's what Temple Knights are, aren't they? Servants of the Church?"

"Ah. I see your confusion. The difference is all about who commands them. The Primus of the Church controls the Holy Fleet, while the Temple Knights of Saint Cunar man it. The Temple Fleet, on the other hand, is under the exclusive control of the Temple Knights of Saint Agnes, reporting directly to their Grand Mistress."

"That sounds most confusing. Back in Merceria, we have only one church and no fighting orders."

"What about the Order of the Sword?"

"I meant no fighting orders of a religious nature. We prefer to keep our spiritual needs separate from our army."

"Interesting," said Owen. "Here in the east, we rely on the Temple Knights as a deterrent. Unfortunately, recent events indicate that's no longer the case."

"Yet you would have us seek out these Temple Knights to learn more about recent events."

"The Mathewites are respected across the length and breadth of the Continent. If anyone could shed light on this newest invasion, it would be them. Besides, the worst-case scenario is we visit them and learn nothing new, leaving us no worse off than we are now."

"That makes sense," said Beverly. "But before we go and speak to someone in charge, what's considered proper etiquette?"

"I'm not sure I understand the question?"

"How do we address them? Is it, sir, Lord, Your Grace? Must we wait until spoken to?"

"To get any meaningful information, we need to speak with the regional commander. As such, he would be addressed as Temple Commander or Commander, if you prefer. Think of him not as a member of the Church but as a military commander."

"Do you know this fellow?"

"I know OF him, assuming he hasn't changed in the last year or so—that does happen occasionally. His name is, or rather was, Temple Commander Roland."

"Has he no surname?"

"No," replied Owen. "At least none that I know of. It's common practice for members of an order to give up their surname when they become Temple Knights. Some even select a completely new given name. If I recall correctly, Roland came here after the failed invasion from Andover. I'd heard he opposed supporting the eastern crusade that led to the death of the previous duke."

"That still doesn't give us any idea what we can expect from the fellow," said Aubrey. "Will he help us or not?"

"It's worth a try."

"He's not going to arrest me, is he?" asked Aldwin.

"First of all, Temple Knights don't have the power to arrest. Secondly, the Mathewites deal with the poor and sick of the Continent, of which many are descendants of the Old Kingdom, making him more sympathetic to our plight."

"Even though we bring an Orc with us?"

"Ah. Well, that's an entirely different matter. Perhaps it might be better to leave Krazuhk behind while we visit?"

The Orc perked up at the sound of her name but said nothing.

"No," said Beverly. "She's one of us, and I'll not risk another encounter like the one in Deisenbach. If the Temple Commander doesn't approve, then we'll go elsewhere."

TEN

Colbridge

WINTER 967 MC

The cold breeze blowing across the river whipped the snowflakes into a frenzy as Lord Preston stood on the walls of Colbridge, staring westward towards Weldwyn.

"Do you think they will send help?"

He turned, looking upon his wife, Sophie, approaching, a thick robe wrapped around her shoulders. The sight made him smile despite his worries.

"I doubt it," he replied. "They lost too many warriors in the last war. Recovering from that takes years."

"Yet we here in Merceria did."

"True, but then we're a warrior culture, used to hardships. I've always thought of Weldwyn as a place of enlightenment."

"Enlightenment?" She laughed. "You're very poetic this morning." The smile fell from her lips as she beheld the worry etched upon his face. "I sense a great weight has been placed upon your shoulders."

He nodded. "It has. Word reached me that Trollden will soon be under attack. The war has finally come to us here on the coast."

"But the marshal predicted they'd use precisely that strategy. Surely this comes as no surprise?"

"It does not, but the timing leaves me with a decision. Do I fortify the city and wait for them to march on Colbridge, or send what warriors I have to Trollden?"

"You must march, surely? Enemy ships couldn't possibly navigate a frozen river."

"They could if they had Fire Mages."

"Does Tog report their use in Trollden?"

"No, but then again, he sent word as soon as the enemy ships appeared. If any mages were present, they wouldn't have revealed themselves yet."

"The message would have taken time to reach us. Do his Trolls still hold the village?"

"I expect him to abandon it and withdraw into the swamp. Their likely target is the chain blocking access to the mouth of the river."

"Wouldn't the ice present an obstacle?"

"No. The area near the swamp refuses to freeze. There's ice farther upstream, but getting past that chain allows them to bypass Trollden altogether."

"Then they are lost."

"Not so," said Preston. "Some weeks ago, Tog sent word of his preparations." He grinned. "Let's just say he has a flair for the unconventional. By now, he's behind a defensive wall of thick logs, with ditches hidden in front of it."

"Hidden, how?"

"They're beneath the water level. The enemy will advance to swarm his defences only to find themselves in water over their heads. Of course, it's only neck deep to the Trolls, making the occasional counterattack possible."

"How many warriors does Tog have at his disposal?"

He smiled. "You're asking a lot of questions."

"I can't help it; I'm one of the queen's closest companions, and she insists on talking freely. Would you rather I remained quiet?"

"No, of course not. I value your opinions; they remind me I don't have to do this alone."

"So then answer the question. How many warriors does Tog have to defend the mouth of the river?"

"That's difficult to say with any certainty. I know Gorath took two companies of Queen's Rangers down there, and Tog has three companies of Trolls, but then there are also an unknown number of Saurians who volunteered to help."

"Unknown?"

"Yes. They're still a secretive people. We know they have three-horns in the area. I suspect there'd be the equivalent of three or four companies of foot troops, but they're lightly armoured and more usefully employed as skirmishers rather than forming into a line of battle."

"They have one big advantage over the Halvarians," said Sophie. "They can move through the swamp with ease."

"Indeed. They also see reasonably well in darkness. I imagine Tog will use them to raid the Halvarian camps at night."

"Then it's settled. You'll march to their aid come morning."

Preston smiled. "How did you know I'd decided on that?"

"Do you really need to ask?"

"Humour me."

"Because you're an honourable man and a stalwart friend and ally. Your only remaining question is how many you'll take."

"Right again. I have four hundred, of which half are foot. I'll take those and the hundred archers under my command."

"And the rest?"

"Knights. Not the sort of troops to prove effective in a swamp."

"You have the Kurathian Mastiffs as well," Sophie reminded him.

"I do, but they're better against mounted men. Ideally, they'd best be employed once the enemy is well clear of the swamp, but if I lured them that far north, it would be hard to contain them."

"Shall I ask the queen for more men?"

"I don't think she has them to give. The last I heard, we were hard-pressed to meet our obligations to Ironcliff and Stonecastle."

"I shall send word, anyway. She'll want to be kept informed of what's happening."

He smiled at her. "I'm so lucky to have you on my staff."

"Lucky? I've spent the last few years running the queen's household. Organizing an army is much simpler. Besides, this is far more interesting than sitting around the Palace all day."

"Careful what you wish for," said Preston. "War is a bloody business."

"I didn't mean to infer otherwise. I loathe war as much as anyone else, but if someone brings it to our shores, I'll do everything in my power to punish them."

"I've made up my mind; we'll take everyone. The town watch can man the walls in our absence."

"What about the cavalry?"

"We'll bring them with us, but leave them to camp north of the swamp, where the terrain doesn't hinder them. The same goes for the mastiffs. Notify the captains to assemble here this afternoon and then pass on my decision to the marshal."

"I shall have Kurghal send word right away, Commander, or should I say, Brigade Commander?"

Preston laughed. "Tog is the brigade commander, not me."

"Still, you're an essential part of this. Now, let's get you inside, shall we? You'll catch your death of cold out here."

. . .

The captains gathered in the dining hall, a room that seemed incredibly large with such a small assembly.

Sophie sat at the table, taking notes, while Preston paced. His captains fidgeted nervously. Some, like Captain Galloway, had gained experience in the last war, but most were new to their rank, the veterans dispatched to assist their Dwarven allies. Now, it fell to him to lead them against a well-trained and disciplined enemy.

"As you know," Preston began, "we march south tomorrow. Before we set out, I thought it best to inform you what I expect. I received word only this morning that the enemy has landed, and by the sounds of it, they've come in overwhelming numbers. Our big advantage is that they've chosen to attack through the Great Swamp, and if anyone feels at home in that terrain, it's the Trolls."

Galloway raised his hand.

"Yes?"

"Might I ask, my lord, how long ago word was sent?"

"The rider took two days to deliver the news. A remarkable feat, considering the distance involved. Why do you ask?"

"Are we certain our companies still hold the town?"

"Tog briefed me on his preparations, so I can confidently say the enemy will fail to take it. Each day we delay, however, increases the risk."

"Our numbers are small," offered the archer, Captain Robbins. "Wouldn't it be better to hold here, in Colbridge?"

"Do that, and the enemy could bypass the city, allowing them free rein to flood into the heartland of Merceria."

"And if the Halvarians have already broken our southern army?"

"Then we'll run across the remains on our march down there. I know it's not ideal, but we must do something, even if it's only buying more time."

"Time for what?" asked Robbins.

"For the Crown to raise more warriors. I have it on good authority they've pressed more into service, but it takes time to prepare them for battle, and we likely won't see them till spring. In the meantime, we must do everything possible to delay the enemy's advance."

A voice boomed from the doorway. "I can help with that!"

All turned to see a well-dressed man enter and scan the room, taking in the occupants. "Which one of you is Lord Preston?"

"I am."

The fellow bowed. "Allow me to introduce myself. I am Arcanus Osbourne Megantis, the Fire Mage of Weldwyn. While my kingdom is unable to provide you with troops, I have taken it upon myself to offer you my humble services."

"Thank you," said Preston. "That's most gracious of you. I've worked with mages before, but none commanded the element of fire. Have you any inclination how you might best be put to use?"

The mage moved to stand at the table. "For the moment, I would suggest I travel with you, my lord. Once I've seen what you're dealing with, I'll be better positioned to make suggestions."

"And how do we address you?"

"Arcanus will do, although, I suppose, in a pinch, you could call me Lord Megantis. Though we Weldwyn mages have no claim to nobility, we are often treated as such."

"I've only just been informed about the trouble in Trollden. How did you come to be in Colbridge so fast?"

"I crossed the river intending to continue on to Wincaster, but when I heard the news, I thought it prudent to offer my services here."

"Could you not recall directly to Wincaster?" asked Sophie.

The mage regarded her. "And you might be?"

"Lady Sophie Wright, Baroness of Wickfield, and acting aide to my husband, Lord Preston."

His eyebrows shot up, but he quickly recovered. "My apologies, my lady, for assuming you were a common scribe. Have we met before? You look familiar?"

"You likely saw me at the Weldwyn court. I was lady-in-waiting to Queen Anna of Merceria."

"Ah, yes. I remember now."

"Tell me, Arcanus, what can you do with your magic?"

"A great many things," replied Megantis. "The more basic of my spells create flames, either as a streak or a ball, which can then be rolled towards the enemy. I can also delay the release of my magic to create a fire trap that would activate when someone walks across it. Such a spell works well if you can pick the location of a battle. Of greater use would be conjuring a phoenix, a flying creature of flame whose eyes I could see through. Effective against individuals such as other mages, but against a large army, it's better employed as a method of spying on their movements."

"That could prove useful," said Preston. "We have yet to determine the enemy's strength."

"I assume, from this gathering, you're preparing to march?"

"We are. First thing tomorrow morning."

"Then I shall accompany you, should you wish it. Once we are closer to the enemy, I will employ my magic to discover their numbers."

"Thank you. That would greatly help us. I don't suppose we can expect any other mages to join us?"

"Not as far as I know. I'm not certain if you are aware of this, but the mages of Weldwyn suffered greatly in the recent war. Aside from myself, the only two left are needed to ferry His Majesty, the king, back and forth from Summersgate to Wincaster."

"I note you did not answer my wife's enquiry. Why did you not use the same spell to travel to Wincaster yourself?"

"The trip is exhausting," replied the mage, "both to me, physically, and to my magic reserves. I also don't like spreading myself out over such a long distance."

"I'm not sure I understand?"

"For a mage to travel in such a fashion, their body is transported through an unknown realm of magic. I shudder to think what creatures lurk there, and the thought of an incorrect casting stranding me in such a place is too horrifying to contemplate."

"Our own mages frequently use the spell of recall."

"Yes, precisely. And look at what's happened." He scanned the room, finding a sea of blank looks. "Surely you've heard how your Life Mage stranded Lady Aubrey in the east?" He snapped his fingers. "There was also the other two, lady something or other and her husband, if I'm not mistaken."

"You mean Lady Beverly and Lord Aldwin," supplied Sophie.

"Yes, that's the pair of them. I'm glad they're safe, but I shudder to think what they passed through on their way east. It positively makes my skin crawl."

"I assume that means you're unable to cast the spell?"

"I've learned it, but reserve its use only for the most dire circumstances."

"You may need to cast it if we're forced to abandon the swamp in a hurry."

"Swamp?" said Osbourne. "No one said anything about a swamp."

"Is that a problem?"

"Most definitely. The vapours given off by such a place play havoc with my constitution. Given the circumstances, I think I might be better deployed elsewhere."

Preston frowned. "Have you any other limitations we should be aware of?"

"Not that I can recall."

"Then might I suggest you continue on to Wincaster? Your presence would likely make a bigger impact in Stonecastle or Ironcliff."

"Isn't Stonecastle high up in the mountains?"

"It is," said Sophie. "Let me guess, the height disturbs you?"

"You might say that," replied Osbourne. "I manipulate the element of fire, not air."

"I tell you what," said Preston. "We'll let the queen decide where best to employ your services."

"A most sensible approach." The mage bowed. "I'm sorry I couldn't be of any further help."

Queen Anna sat at her desk in Wincaster, a stack of papers haphazardly spread across it, Storm's tail thumping the floor as footsteps approached.

"Come in, Gerald," she called out.

The Marshal of Merceria entered through the door. "How did you know it was me?"

"How do you think?" She pointed the end of her quill at her mastiff. "He recognizes your footsteps, either that or the creak of your bones." She grinned. "Are you here for a social visit or something official?"

"Official, I'm afraid. Things are not going well."

"Could you be a little more specific?"

"I received word Halvaria has forced their way across Kharzun's Folly. Herdwin is conducting a fighting withdrawal, but it's looking increasingly like he'll be forced back into Stonecastle. I've sent a messenger to warn Lord Greycloak of this development, but Elves aren't suited for fighting in that terrain."

"We knew it was only a matter of time."

"Yes, but it gets worse. Ironcliff is now under siege. Hayley led an assault to destroy one of their siege engines, but it didn't slow them down much."

"And Commander Lanaka?"

"Rulahk reports he reached Heward's army up in Holdcross. They're the only thing standing between Norland and the enemy army."

"You predicted an attack at Trollden. Any word yet?"

"We received word that ships were sighted, but we have no shamans in Trollden to report on more recent developments. Preston has a reserve in Colbridge, but if the enemy comes in numbers as they did at Ironcliff, he'll be hard-pressed to contain them."

"We need more men," said Anna, "and soon."

"What we need is time. We have men in training, but it takes time to forge weapons and armour. Could Weldwyn help? I know they suffered greatly in the war, but if we can't stem this invasion, they'll be in the same situation as us."

"Alric is well aware of our situation, but barely has enough warriors to man the walls of Summersgate, let alone send an expedition to help us."

Gerald took a seat, absently scratching Storm's head. "This invasion has caught us at the worst time."

"Is there ever a good time for an invasion?"

"No, I suppose not, but we'd be in a better position had they waited until spring."

"The Dwarves will hold," said Anna. "Both Ironcliff and Stonecastle are fortresses; neither will be easily conquered."

"I doubt that's the enemy's intention. All they need do is keep them locked up in their mountains and send the rest of their armies marching past."

"That's certainly a possibility where Ironcliff is concerned, but I doubt that tactic would work with Stonecastle. According to your own reports, the mountain pass runs outside its walls."

"I must be getting old. I'd forgotten that."

She smiled. "Then it's good I'm here to remind you." She stared up at the ceiling. "If I recall, Lord Arandil fielded six hundred Elves at the Siege of Summersgate—what he was willing to commit to the campaign without stripping away the Darkwood's defences. I imagine he could increase that by as much as half again if his lands were threatened. Would you agree?"

"It seems a reasonable assumption."

"Let's say, by some miracle, the empire sieges Stonecastle, sending the rest of their army west. The only route into Merceria is through the Darkwood. I feel confident in saying Merceria is safe for the moment."

"True," replied Gerald, "but it's not Stonecastle I'm worried about as much as Trollden. It's little more than a village, and even Trolls have their limitations when it comes to fighting. We can't expect them to hold out forever, and if the enemy gets out of that swamp, there'll be no stopping them."

Anna stood. "I have an idea."

"Care to share?"

"We have plenty of men in training. What if we sent them to Summersgate to learn their business instead of keeping them here?"

"Which frees up the city guard to help us! I like where this is going. Assuming Alric agrees, what numbers could we expect?"

"No more than a few companies of foot, but that's better than nothing."

"When do we leave?"

She walked around the table and held out her hand. "How about right now? I'll send for Kraloch; he'll have us in Summersgate by dinner."

ELEVEN

Plotting

WINTER 967 MC

Encased in shadows, the room relied upon a single candle to provide what little light illuminated the six people huddled around a circular table.

The tallest, an older gentleman with a touch of grey to his beard, let his gaze wander over his fellow conspirators. They were an eclectic bunch, ranging from an ex-commander-general of an Imperial Legion to a powerful criminal mastermind. Yet they all held one thing in common: the quest for power.

"Well?" he asked. "What have you got to report?"

A high, nasal voice answered, "It is as you predicted. A rival group initiated the invasion of the Petty Kingdoms."

"Are you certain that's desirable?" came a woman's voice, harsh with age. "We have enough troubles without the empire fighting two wars."

"Desirable?" said the tall man. "Why, it does half our work for us." He leaned in closer to the flame. "We are approaching the time to make our move. The war against the Petty Kingdoms ties up four legions in the north, and the Mercerian campaign… Well, it, too, works to our advantage."

"I don't see how," replied the high voice.

"How many legions does the empire have?"

"Twelve at present, although I understand it was recently proposed to add more."

"Which will take considerable time. As such, it won't affect our plans."

"Still," said the woman, "we've only accounted for seven legions."

"Ah, but you forget. Two are massed on the border of Ilea and are thus unable to withdraw to defend the capital, leaving us three legions at our disposal. More than enough to accomplish our goals."

"Which are?"

"To march on Varena," replied the tall man. "How else did you think we'd seize control of the empire?"

"I'd assumed," said the woman, "that this is a political takeover, not a military one."

"Incredible," remarked the gruff-voiced ex-commander-general. "Did you honestly expect the emperor to willingly turn over his Crown? Without an army to back us up, we'd end up having our necks stretched."

"He's right," said the tall man. "We engineered events in our favour, but it would be suicidal to proceed without securing the loyalty of a few legions."

A middle-aged woman with auburn hair shifted uncomfortably. "While I support the idea in principle, I dislike the thought of marching on the capital. Too many things can go wrong. I've been on the receiving end of the emperor's wrath before, and I have no intention of experiencing that again."

"You speak nonsense," replied the warrior. "We've covered off every eventuality. What could possibly go wrong?"

"The empire has legions in both Merceria and the Petty Kingdoms. If any withdraw to deal with us, the entire Continent will have time to gather their forces and march into Halvaria."

The tall man hesitated. "You present a valid point, but if we seize the Throne quickly enough, we can restore order long before those remote legions are even aware of our existence."

"What of those who oppose our plans?" asked the woman with the auburn hair.

"Our rivals provided us with the means to deal with them."

"Meaning?"

"We shall execute them and blame it on the other faction. Exalor will think it's the Sartellians, while they will blame it on the High Strategos. They're about to be at each other's throats, giving us the perfect opportunity to advance our plans."

A fair-haired woman, who had thus far remained silent, sat back in her seat. "I'm well-acquainted with all the plotting at court and shall keep my ears open for anything that could upset our plans. We stand with you, Your Grace, but to pull this off, we must be aware of the timetable."

The tallest of the group smiled. "Muster your resources now, for we shall commence the march, come spring. With good fortune, we'll gain full control of the Throne before the first day of summer."

·   ·   ·

"How long will they keep us here?" grumbled Arnim. He turned to look at his wife sitting in a chair, reading a book.

"As long as they feel it necessary," she replied. "In the meantime, I suggest you find something to occupy your mind. Staring out the window won't help relax you."

"Relax me? We're prisoners, Nikki, not guests, despite their attempts to make it appear so." He paused, looking down at her book. "What's that you're reading?"

"It's about the early days of the empire. I considered it best to learn as much as possible."

"And?"

"I'm not certain what you're asking."

"I was merely enquiring what that book has told you about them."

"Quite a bit. It turns out Halvaria was originally a relatively small kingdom under constant threat of invasion from one of its neighbours, a place called Aloria."

"Never heard of it," said Arnim.

"Nor I, but we know almost nothing about our ancestors before they came to Merceria. In any case, this Aloria finally invaded, which didn't go well for the Halvarians, at least in the beginning."

"Oh?"

"When it looked like all was lost, one of their warriors, a fellow named Kaladesh, usurped the Throne. What followed was a series of harsh laws forcing everyone to support the war effort. By this means, he raised a massive army, destroyed the enemy, and marched on the Alorian capital, which he captured."

"This is how the empire was born?"

"Not quite. The story's a little more complicated. After conquering the Alorians, he absorbed them into Halvaria, doubling his land. Not content with this single victory, he expanded his borders by attacking any adjacent kingdom that might threaten his supremacy. Six years later, he'd absorbed four more realms and formed the basis of what's now called the empire."

"I assume this Kaladesh fellow became the first emperor?"

"Surprisingly, no. He was murdered by someone trying to take over. His son, Erkinwald, destroyed the usurper and then proclaimed himself emperor. The date of his coronation is considered the true birth of the empire; their calendar even uses it as a reference."

"All very interesting," replied Arnim, "but it doesn't help us."

"On the contrary, it explains much. Ever since its birth, the empire has expanded, absorbing their neighbours to pre-emptively prevent them from invading."

"That's a weak excuse to attack one's neighbours, don't you think?"

"Yet here it is, spelled out in a neat and tidy hand."

"Might I ask where you acquired this book?"

"Off the shelf to your right. Why? Interested in reading all of a sudden?"

"It couldn't hurt. I don't suppose there's a book on their military tactics here?"

"Not that I found. The vast majority seem to be concerned with manners and etiquette."

Arnim picked a tome, flipping through it. "I wonder if they employed mages back in those days."

"If they did, there's no mention of it in my current read. Do you think that's significant?"

"Likely not. Mages have existed in Merceria since its founding, but you'll seldom find them mentioned in books."

"Why is that, do you suppose?"

"It's a natural reaction to magic."

"Meaning?"

"People like to think they control their own destinies, rather than being manipulated by some invisible, mystical force."

"You and I both know that's not how magic works."

"Yes," said Arnim, "but it's still widely believed, especially amongst the common folk."

"I don't think that's necessarily true anymore," replied Nikki. "The queen has gone to great lengths to use magic for the betterment of her people."

"But old beliefs are hard to change. I'm sure, given time, the average Mercerian will accept the presence of mages. Still, I believe users of magic will always be viewed as something separate and mysterious to the average person."

A knock on the door interrupted their conversation.

"Yes?" called out Nikki.

The door opened, revealing an older gentleman dressed similarly to the other servants, although the material was of a finer quality.

"My pardon," the fellow said. "My name is Janek, servant to His Eminence, Nevarus, the God-Emperor."

"What can we do for you, Janek?"

"I was sent to prepare you for an audience."

"We're finally meeting this emperor of yours?"

"Eventually, but I fear it will take time to prepare you."

"Prepare us, how?" asked Arnim. "We've been in the company of kings before. We know how to behave."

"Ah," said Janek, "but that's just it. Don't you see? Nevarus is more than a king; he is the chosen leader of all mankind."

"He's not our leader."

"He will be soon enough. However, that's beside the point. If you wish to see the emperor in person, you must be prepared."

"How, exactly?" asked Nikki.

"A strict set of behaviours is to be observed when in the presence of a god, and they cannot be taught in a single day."

"Are we now to be tutored in the rules of his court?"

"Correct."

"Where do we start?"

Janek stared back, silent for a moment. "I'm sorry, you caught me off guard. I was expecting more resistance to the idea."

"Wouldn't your own people wish to learn Mercerian etiquette if they were at the court of our queen?"

"The empire does not negotiate with foreign courts; it only makes demands."

"Yet no such demands were made to Queen Anna."

Janek's mouth flapped open. "How could you possibly know that?"

"I didn't," she replied. "It was a guess, but you've confirmed it."

"Oh, I see. An example of trickery. I must confess I know little of such tactics. His Eminence has always insisted on the people around him being honest."

"I very much doubt that's the case," said Arnim.

"I beg your pardon?"

"Oh, I'm certain that's the intention, but an emperor ruling an empire the size of yours must have an almost infinite number of people who report to him. Are you telling me none are above bending the truth?"

"What are you insinuating?"

"Merely that everyone lies, particularly when it's in their best interest to do so."

"What my husband is trying to say," explained Nikki, "is that many of your emperor's advisors are likely not telling the truth, at least not the full truth."

"I'm afraid I wouldn't know anything about that," replied Janek. "In any case, it has no bearing on your preparations to meet His Eminence."

"I wonder," said Arnim, "is this emperor of yours a god?"

"He is."

"Wouldn't that make him immortal?"

"No, that is a misconception. He is the descendant of gods, his line being born through Human women, which would make him a demigod, but there is little difference in our eyes. His divinity is beyond question."

"I'm curious," said Nikki. "How does a god choose a wife?"

"They are chosen for him. That is how we ensure his line remains pure."

"Pure?"

"Yes, untainted by undesirables. After all, we wouldn't want the blood of an Elf corrupting his divine offspring."

"And who, might I ask, makes these choices on behalf of His Eminence?"

"The Imperial Council, but how such things are decided is far removed from one of my humble station."

"Just out of curiosity," said Arnim, "what is the current date, according to your empire?"

"It is one thousand two hundred and five years since the founding of the Halvarian Empire. We are, I believe, the oldest calendar still in use amongst civilized lands."

"Do you consider us civilized?"

"Of course. In our eyes, your kingdom is merely… misguided."

"When do we get to see this emperor of yours?"

"That depends on how your instruction goes," replied Janek. "We shall start by introducing you to the proper way to address His Eminence before moving on to how you're to respond should he deign to speak with you."

"That doesn't sound so difficult," said Nikki.

"You think that only because we have yet to begin. The manual of Imperial etiquette is thick, coming in at just over five hundred pages. Much of that deals with eating, not to mention the proper address for your social superiors."

"Have you earls and dukes in your empire?"

"No," replied Janek. "Why do you ask?"

"I am the Viscountess of Haverston; my husband, the viscount; and in our society, earls, dukes, and royalty outrank us. What is the equivalent of those titles in Halvaria?"

"I'm afraid our society is structured quite differently from yours. We have no nobility, only positions of authority filled by the most capable individuals."

"They're not hereditary?"

"No," said Janek. "The vast majority of those positions are held by mages of various types, most commonly Shozarins, Sartellians, and Stormwinds."

"I'm sorry," said Arnim. "Did you just say the positions weren't hereditary and then turn around and say they were filled by family members?"

"Technically, they aren't so much families as lines."

"The difference being?"

"Members earn their place in a line through their magical ability, not blood relations."

"But magic is passed down through the bloodline; even we Mercerians know that."

"I…" Janek's words trailed off. He appeared out of his depth in such a discussion.

"Never mind," said Nikki. "This is best left for someone else to explain. You mentioned we were to begin our training. Can you give us an idea of how much time this will involve? Are we talking days or weeks?"

"Likely a good deal longer than that. I hope to be able to introduce you to His Eminence by the spring."

"Spring? That's months away, surely?"

"Not at all. Your incarceration has, I fear, warped your sense of time. Well, and that you're in a more southerly climate than you're used to. Spring is, in fact, just around the corner."

"When do we start?"

"Tomorrow, if you feel so inclined. With your permission, I shall alert the educators their services are required."

"We look forward to it."

"Have you any questions before I leave?"

"I do," said Arnim. "Which god?"

"I beg your pardon?"

"Which god is your emperor descended from?"

"Maleus."

"Never heard of him."

"Hardly surprising, given your background. Will that be all?"

"Yes," said Nikki. "You may go."

She waited until the man left before turning to her husband. "What do you make of that?"

"I've a hard time believing their emperor is descended from a god."

"As do I, but Janek believes it, which begs the question—how many others do?"

"True," said Arnim. "I'm also curious to know more about Maleus. He's certainly not one of our Gods."

"Perhaps he was a mage? It wouldn't be hard to convince a society without magic that he was a god."

"You're suggesting all these emperors are descended from a spellcaster?"

"It bears considering, doesn't it?"

"But if that were true, wouldn't the emperor possess magic potential?"

"One would assume so."

"But they haven't mentioned he can use magic."

"Nor have they indicated he can't," replied Nikki. "It's too bad Aubrey isn't here. She could use her magic to find out."

"I doubt they'd let her cast her spell in the emperor's presence."

"No. I suppose not."

"In any case, it's mere speculation at this point. Perhaps Maleus wasn't a mage, but another race, like an Elf or something else we've yet to encounter?"

"I suppose he could be a lesser god we've forgotten about. After all, we Mercerians worship Saxnor, while Weldwyn worships Malin."

"Possibly," said Arnim, "but the Gods don't directly intervene in mortal matters."

"They don't now, but if what Janek told us is true, this happened over a thousand years ago."

"At which time our ancestors were plying their trade as mercenaries here, yet there is no mention of the name in any of our histories."

"How would we know if there were?" replied Nikki. "It's not as if either of us has combed through ancient texts looking for a reference to such a thing."

"I suppose you're right, not that it makes any difference. Knowing the truth won't change our present circumstances. We're still the empire's prisoners, even if the cage is gilded."

"Agreed. And if we somehow escaped, we'd have no idea where to go. We must be thousands of miles away from home by now, with absolutely no way of knowing how to return." She wandered over to the window, gazing out at the Palace grounds where snow blanketed the fields, giving them a pristine appearance. "We're never going to see home again, are we?"

"Hush, now," soothed Arnim. "Only a short time ago, we expected to be executed. The fact that we're still alive indicates the Gods have something bigger in mind for us."

"The Gods? You're the one who just said the Gods don't directly intervene in mortal matters."

He grinned. "I did, didn't I? Well, I suppose I can't have it both ways. Still, I can't help feeling we're not done yet, as if there's something we can contribute to the cause, as it were."

"It would be much easier if we knew what that something was."

"True, but that takes all the mystery out of it."

"Mystery? This isn't a game, Arnim. This is our lives. How can you sit back and be so nonchalant about it?" She turned to face him as he approached.

"I'm not trying to be flippant, Nikki. I'm merely thankful that if these are to be our last days, we'll spend them together."

TWELVE

Temple Knight

"So that's what they call a commandery?" Beverly observed the building at the end of the street—a two-storey affair, arranged in what appeared to be a solid block. The front door stood in the centre, with a larger set of double doors off to the right, presumably leading to stables.

"It is," replied Owen. "I'm told the design is used throughout the Petty Kingdoms. It's also rumoured to be highly defensible."

"Has one ever been attacked?"

"Not to my knowledge. Then again, who other than the empire would be foolish enough to challenge the might of a Temple Order?"

They continued down the street, blatant stares marking their progress.

"Perhaps it would have been better had I stayed at the inn," said Krazuhk.

"Nonsense," replied Beverly, easily reverting to Orcish. *"You are a valued member of our party. If these Temple Knights can't see that, then they're not worth speaking with."*

A knight stood on either side of the main door, but at the group's approach, one entered the commandery.

"That was rude," said Aldwin. "Don't they like company?"

"They're likely warning their superiors," replied Owen.

"Simply because we're riding near their commandery?"

"I think," said Beverly, "they've realized we're riding straight for them. Admittedly, we make quite the sight. I don't imagine it's every day they see two knights, an Orc, and a man with your good looks, riding past."

"Hey, now," said Aubrey. "What about me?"

"You look like a proper lady, Cousin; as such, you represent the familiar."

"She means less threatening," added Aldwin, smiling.

"What are you grinning at?" asked Aubrey.

"Beverly called me good-looking; didn't you hear?"

The Life Mage shook her head. "Don't you two ever get tired of all the compliments?"

"Not at all," they both answered simultaneously. A smile passed between husband and wife, but the remaining guard challenged them before anything further could be said.

"Halt, in the name of Saint Mathew."

Beverly raised her hand, signalling everyone to stop. "Greetings," she said. "I am Lady Beverly Fitzwilliam, Baroness of Bodden. I come seeking an audience with whoever is in charge."

The man looked her over, taking in her armour, his gaze lingering on her shield. "I do not recognize your coat of arms," he said. "Is that the mark of Saxnor?"

"It is."

"You are not an adherent of the Saints. Why do you wish to see our captain?"

"We seek only information. I was told your order gathers news from across the Petty Kingdoms."

"Aye, it does, but such knowledge is not meant for the ears of unbelievers."

"I am a knight of Erlingen," replied Owen, "and a devoted servant of the Saints. Can't you make an exception for these travellers?"

"You are in the presence of an Orc. Are you so foolish to imagine that would be well-received, or are you ignorant of their crimes?"

"Crimes?"

"They obliterated the Holy Army sent to bring the word of the Saints to the east."

Beverly opened her mouth to speak, but Aubrey quickly intervened. "My pardon," she said. "I wasn't aware any Temple Knights of your order fought at the Battle of the Wilderness."

"They weren't there," replied the guard, "but it's said the entire eastern establishment of the Cunars was wiped out. One does not forget the sacrifices of a brother order."

The second guard returned with another individual wearing a sash tied around his waist, indicating rank.

"Ah, Captain," said Owen. "At last, someone with whom we can have an intelligent conversation."

The Temple Captain clenched his jaw as he surveyed the group. They sat motionless on their mounts, waiting for a greeting, but none appeared forthcoming.

"Captain," said Owen. "Might I introduce—"

"Quiet," the fellow snapped. "You have no standing here."

"I beg your pardon. I am a knight of Erlingen. I have every right."

"This is a Temple commandery, not the duke's court. Your standing amongst the nobility of this realm means nothing here."

"My apologies," said Beverly. "We did not mean to cause offence."

"Yet you come here begging for answers. A Temple commandery is not a place of refuge for your kind, nor are they the havens of gossip as you seem to think. Be gone from our doorstep, or my Temple Knights will evict you."

"This is most unusual," said Owen. He turned to regard his companions. "Come. It appears the legendary welcoming nature of this order was greatly exaggerated. Let us find somewhere more hospitable."

They turned their horses around and rode back up the street.

"What was that all about?" asked Aldwin. "I thought you said these Mathewites were friendly?"

"Normally, they are. I don't know what's gotten into them."

"So where do we go now?"

"There's a tavern up the street if I recall. We passed it on our way here."

"Yes," said Aubrey. "The Fox and Hound."

"You have a good memory."

"And she's very observant," added Beverly. "It's what sets her apart from the other mages."

"The Fox and Hound it is, then," said Owen.

As far as taverns went, the Fox and Hound was nothing exceptional. The entrance led to a large common area with a fireplace at one end, tables scattered around the room, and a rickety set of stairs leading to the second floor. A door on the right of the entrance opened into the kitchen.

As the group entered, the half-dozen patrons there lapsed into silence. The proprietor must have noted the sudden quieting, for he wandered into the common room to investigate the cause.

"Ah." He approached them, wiping his hands on a filthy apron. "What can I get for ya?"

"Ale," replied Owen.

The fellow stared at the Orc. "For all of ya?"

"Indeed." The knight noted the man's hesitancy. "I assure you, we have ample coins, if that's your worry."

The fellow knuckled his forehead. "Of course, my lord. I'll see to it right away." He went back into the kitchen, his bulk making the floorboards creak.

"Let's get a seat, shall we?" Owen selected one close to the fire, giving those nearby a good stare. "This is none of your concern," he said. "Be about your own business."

They squeezed in around an empty table. The place smelled of sweat and stale beer, not the nicest of combinations.

"What do we do now?" said Aldwin.

"I say we continue north," replied Beverly. "It appears we'll get no answers from the Temple Knights here."

"I could always try the duke," offered Owen. "I am a knight, after all."

"A knight errant, not a member of his order of chivalry. Knights of the Sceptre, wasn't it?"

"Indeed, though I'm still puzzled why the Temple Captain treated us so callously."

"Perhaps I can answer that?" A man in a brown cassock, with an axe in his belt, stood in the doorway.

"Can I help you?" asked Owen.

"I doubt that very much, but perhaps I can be of assistance to you." He moved closer. "My pardon, I should have introduced myself. I'm Brother Cyric, a Temple Knight of Saint Mathew."

"You're not dressed like a Temple Knight."

"I'm not on duty at the moment. I assume you're the group who tried to visit the commandery?"

"We are. What of it?"

"I couldn't help but overhear your exchange with Temple Captain Alonso."

"You were there?"

"I was. I happened to be visiting on the regional commander's behalf. I act as one of his aides from time to time."

"You work for the Temple Commander?"

"I do. Father Roland. Do you know him?"

"Not personally," replied Owen, "but I believe he's been in his current position for a while."

"That he has," said Cyric.

"I'm curious why Captain Alonso was so hostile towards us. Did we upset him somehow?"

"Ah, the good captain's brother died in the east some years ago."

"At the Battle of the Wilderness?"

"Precisely. I imagine seeing your Orc friend there reminded him of that loss."

"I wasn't aware the Mathewites served in the east?"

"They didn't, at least not officially. Alonso's brother was a Cunar. Such a terrible waste of life, but the Crusade shouldn't have been called in the first place—"

"Wait a moment," interrupted Aubrey. "You said you weren't on duty, yet you claim to have been visiting with the Temple Captain when we were there."

"I suppose that requires some explanation. Part of my duties to the regional commander include investigating matters for the order. I'm not at liberty to discuss those with outsiders, but I've often found that people are more accommodating when I'm not wearing my armour. Not to sidestep your interest any further, but might I enquire what you were trying to ascertain at the commandery?"

"We were seeking news," said Owen.

"May I sit?"

"Of course."

They waited as the Temple Knight pulled up a chair. He nodded towards Owen. "You're from Erlingen, but I sense the rest of you are far from home."

"How could you possibly know that?" said Beverly.

"Your armour, while well-crafted, is of an older design. There is also the matter of your shield, which, amongst its heraldry, includes the mark of Saxnor, one of the old Gods." He held up his hands. "I say this only as an observation, not a criticism. In addition, you travel accompanied by an Orc, a most uncommon sight in this part of the Continent." He let his gaze swivel to Aldwin. "Then there's you, a man of Therengian descent who is married to you." He looked back at Beverly. "Unless it's common for two people to wear matching rings for other reasons? And if I'm not mistaken, those are made of skystone, although you might know it by another name."

"Remarkable," said Aldwin. "Is there anything else you'd care to observe?"

"There's a slight resemblance between you two ladies. Are you cousins, perhaps?"

"My name is Beverly Fitzwilliam, and this is my cousin, Lady Aubrey Brandon, and my husband, Aldwin Fitzwilliam. This other gentleman is Sir Owen."

"Your speech indicates you are a person of means," said Cyric, "yet your husband's manner of speaking is more common. I assume he was not noble born?"

"I was not," replied Aldwin. "Does that matter?"

"Not to me, I assure you. I'm afraid I'm not familiar with social norms concerning Orcs. Might I ask who your friend is?"

"Krazuhk, a master of air from the Sky Singers, a tribe found in Deisenbach."

"Deisenbach? My, you've come a long way. You didn't run across Temple Captain Giselle, did you? She and I go way back."

"We did, as a matter of fact," replied Beverly.

"This is all very impressive," said Aubrey, "but you indicated that perhaps you could help us?"

"I did, didn't I? I've travelled extensively, and part of my responsibilities includes collating information for Father Roland. Sorry, I should say, Temple Commander Roland. He gets a little fussy over titles from time to time. Is this to do with the invasion?"

"Invasion?" said Owen. "Do you mean to suggest the empire has reached the borders of Erlingen?"

"No, but I fear it's only a question of time until the duke gets dragged into the latest Halvarian war. He's obviously expecting to march soon, as he's already begun massing his army."

"Captain Sturgess seemed to think His Grace was already prepared to march."

"That would be the belief of most, but he won't move west until his barons assemble their forces." He hesitated. "Might I ask why it's of interest to your group?"

"Our home is at war with the empire," said Beverly. "We're from a land called Merceria, which lies far to the west."

"Would that be near Weldwyn, perhaps?"

"You know of it?"

"I'm friends with a ship captain who has travelled those waters, though admittedly, I've not seen him in some years."

"Merceria shares its western border with Weldwyn. Our queen is married to their king."

"How intriguing. I should very much like to visit it sometime."

"You'd have a hard time," said Aldwin. "The empire's invaded us."

"When did this come about?"

"At the onset of winter."

"A curious time to launch a campaign of conquest."

"That's what we thought," said Beverly. "We expected them to wait until spring."

"That would have been the wisest move, but the Halvarians like to keep their enemies on their toes. I'm curious, however, why they would invade the Petty Kingdoms while still fighting in the west. I assume your kingdom is resisting the invasion."

"It is. We're a warrior culture, descendants of mercenaries who fled to our land almost a thousand years ago. We won't surrender."

"The invasion of your homeland is a great tragedy. I assume you're trying to find a way home?"

"We are. How did you know?"

"Your manner. You're still adjusting to life in the Petty Kingdoms, which indicates you haven't been here long."

"What makes you say that?"

"I saw the face your husband made when he drank his ale. I'm guessing they don't put spices in your drink where you're from."

"They don't," admitted Aldwin.

"Might I make a suggestion?"

"By all means," replied Beverly, "though we're under no obligation to agree to it."

Cyric smiled. "Well said. I was going to suggest I bring you to meet with Temple Commander Roland. I think he would be most helpful to you."

"Surely you're not suggesting we take up arms under the banner of your order?"

"No, but if your home to the west is under attack, it would be in your best interest to hurt the empire here, on the Continent. If nothing else, it might draw off some of the empire's legions from your homeland."

"What makes you think we want to fight?"

"Your armour, though decorative, has obviously seen many a battle. The workmanship is exceptional, but I know my armour, and there are signs the original design was modified to allow more freedom of movement."

"How do you know so much about armour?" asked Owen. "I thought Temple Knights of Saint Mathew only wore mail?"

"We do," said Cyric, "but I wasn't always a Temple Knight. Now, what do you think of my idea? Would you be willing to sit down with my superior to discuss the possibility of aiding us in our time of need? After all, not only is Erlingen going to war, but the Temple Knights will be joining… well… two of the orders, at least."

"We'll have to discuss this amongst ourselves first."

"Fair enough. I shall arrange a meeting with Father Roland for two days hence, say, at noon? I'll understand if you decide not to accept my offer."

"Where do we find this Temple Commander of yours?"

"His offices are at the Cathedral of Saint Mathew. It's the largest building in all of Torburg. Simply head towards the centre of town; you can't miss it." With that, he rose, then stopped. "I hope this won't be the last I see you, but regardless of your decision, I wish you well."

A pair of grey-cloaked figures waited outside the Fox and Hound. "Is that him?" asked the shorter one as Cyric left the building.

"Aye. He's the troublemaker."

"He doesn't look so dangerous to me."

"Looks can be deceiving. The danger isn't in his skill at arms, it's what he might uncover. Our master has put considerable effort into convincing the good Captain Alonso to refrain from committing his company to the coming campaign. I should hate to see that undone by anyone, especially a simple Temple Knight."

"What of his superior?"

"Roland? You know as well as I that his order is only permitted here in Erlingen if he keeps them out of trouble. Besides, I doubt he'll want to commit to a war that might find them facing off against the Cunars."

The shorter fellow grinned. "So, they've committed to our cause?"

"If by 'committed', you mean they've agreed to remain neutral, then yes."

"Neutral? I thought they were going to join us?"

"And they likely will, but at present, they serve our purpose better by giving our enemies hope. Then, when the moment is ripe, they'll turn on them to the ruin of the Petty Kingdoms."

"And what about those people he met with?"

"They could prove troublesome. It might be a good idea to see them eliminated."

"I wager it'll take more than a few to bring down that knight."

"Sir Owen is not particularly known as a great swordsman," said the taller of the two.

"I was talking about the woman, Lady Beverly. If you recall, we were warned she might show up here. You don't think Brother Cyric passed something on to them, do you?"

"No. He works for the Church. If he's discovered anything noteworthy, he would head straight to his superior."

"Still, I don't like it. It can't be a coincidence that the two people we're to keep an eye out for are here in Torburg at the exact same time."

"A good point. Best we assemble the others."

"To take them out?"

"We'll watch until an opportunity presents itself."

THIRTEEN

Summersgate

WINTER 967 MC

Gerald waited as the light dissipated from the magic circle.

"We have arrived," announced Albreda. "If you'll excuse me, Your Majesty, I must rest and recover my strength."

"I understand," replied Anna. "And once again, thank you. I know this takes a toll on you."

"I'll admit it's a bit draining, but it's nice to be back in the Dome."

"The Dome," said Gerald. "I still find that name strange."

"It's better than the Grand Edifice of the Arcane Wizards Council," replied the mage. "I get a headache even thinking about it. The founding mages of Weldwyn obviously thought a lot of themselves."

When travelling to Weldwyn, the queen was usually accompanied by guards, and this trip was no exception. Evard Brenton had proven his loyalty on several occasions and even guarded the magic circle back in Wincaster, but never before had he experienced travelling by the recall spell. He craned his neck, looking up at the ceiling, stumbling as his head swam.

"Careful," said Gerald. "Your sense of balance will be off because of the spell. Don't worry. It'll wear off soon enough."

"Are you dizzy, Your Grace?" asked Brenton.

"No, but I'm used to travelling this way, and stop calling me Your Grace."

"But you're the Duke of Wincaster, Your Grace."

"True, and I'm also the Marshal of Merceria. Sir will do, or simply Marshal."

Albreda smiled. "It's good to see you still have a level head on your shoulders, Gerald. Lesser men would let such lofty titles convince them they're better than others."

"That's why I keep him around," said Anna. "Well, that and he's my oldest friend."

"Hey, now," replied Gerald. "How about you stop using the term 'oldest'?"

The door opened, and the Enchanter, Gretchen Harwell, entered, followed by a trio of guards. "Welcome, Majesty. The king sent an escort to see you safely about town." She paused briefly. "Not that he believed you needed protection; it has more to do with appearances."

Anna held out her arm. "Shall we, Gerald?"

"Brenton, you and Harper remain here. We'll call for you when we're ready to return."

"Aye, Your Gra... I mean, yes, sir."

Gerald smiled. "That wasn't so hard, was it?"

"Are you done?" said Anna. "We need to be getting on our way."

"Yes, sorry. Didn't mean to be a bother."

"You're never a bother, but the Earls Council awaits us."

They followed the trio of guards through the building and into the street. The sun hung in a cloudless sky, promising a warm day, the first in a long time.

"Spring is just around the corner," noted Anna.

"It can't come soon enough, if you ask me," replied Gerald. "I'd feel much better about it if we weren't facing an enemy on three fronts."

"Let's hope the nobles of Weldwyn are willing to help."

"I still don't understand why Alric can't order them to march. He is their king, isn't he?"

"You know full well he is, just as you know the King of Weldwyn doesn't hold the same authority as I do. He can't order the army to do anything without the earls' support."

"I'm afraid they'll refuse us. Weldwyn is in a precarious position, and it doesn't help that King Leofric led their army to ruin in a foreign land."

"And here we are, asking them to send an expedition to Merceria to face yet another enemy. Sometimes, it seems all we ever do is fight."

"We've made friends along the way, too," said Gerald. "Never forget that."

"Yes, but those same friends led us into another war. I wonder if we would've been better off staying out of other people's affairs."

"Perhaps, but that's not your way, Anna. You want a better life, not just for our people but for our neighbours as well. That's to be admired."

. . .

The palace in Summersgate had been reduced to rubble during the invasion of Weldwyn, so the Earls Council took up residence in one of the finer houses of the city. Additional guards met them at the entrance, along with a familiar face.

"Jack Marlowe," said Gerald, "as I live and breathe."

"That's Lord Jack," said Anna. "He is the Viscount of Aynsbury."

The cavalier bowed. "Good to see you again, Your Majesty, and you, Gerald."

"Is His Majesty inside?"

"No. He thought it best if you presented your case directly to the earls without him being there. He doesn't want to give the impression he's trying to force their hand."

"Why send you?"

"So you'd have a friendly face present. After all, I'm a viscount, not an earl."

"Anything I should be aware of before we enter?" asked the queen.

Jack lowered his voice. "Lord Beric is in a bit of a mood today. It seems his new wife saw fit to remain in the south without him."

"Anything else?"

"I have it on good authority Lord Dryden is favourable to helping, providing the cost isn't too high. The recent invasion left many coffers low on funds, particularly those whose holdings were captured."

"Thank you," said Anna. "I shall keep that in mind when I address them."

"Is Gerald to address them as well?"

"No," replied the marshal. "At least not directly. I'm here to offer my military expertise, should it prove necessary."

Jack nodded. "They'll want to know the details of your plan to defeat the empire before they commit any men." He hesitated. "Oh, I suppose there is one more thing I should warn you about."

"Which is?"

"Some people may be observing the proceedings."

"Are you suggesting they'll wander around or sit at the table?"

"Neither. The council meets in a great hall with a balcony that runs overhead. You might recognize a few faces up there, but I'm afraid the noble lines of Weldwyn received a shakeup in the wake of recent events."

Anna took a deep breath. "You may escort us to the earls at your leisure, Jack."

The chamber was quiet as the Queen of Merceria entered. Gerald instinctively looked up, spotting at least a score of onlookers on the balcony. Only five individuals sat around the table in the centre of the room; each one of the earls who held so much power over the realm. Anna moved to the seat at the end of the table, but not a single Weldwyn noble stood in recognition of her position.

Lord Elgin, the Earl of Riversend, began the discourse. "Your Majesty, I understand you've come here to beg for our help."

"I came," she replied, "to ask assistance from an ally whose homeland we helped liberate at considerable cost to ourselves."

"If you are attempting to shame us into helping you fight off these invaders, then you are wasting your time."

"Let us not be hasty," said Lord Dryden, the Earl of Loranguard. "She only just arrived and has yet to make her case."

"Case?" replied Elgin. "What case is there to be made? They want our warriors to give their lives, fending off an attacker—an attacker, I might add, that has come in significant numbers, if rumours are to be believed. Weldwyn has suffered enough these last few years. We cannot afford to fight another kingdom's wars."

"That is not your choice alone," replied Lord Julian. "This decision must be made by the consensus of the council."

"That is true, but even if we all agreed to send help, we lack the men to do so in any meaningful way. Need I remind you of the losses we sustained during the invasion?"

"Do not lecture me on our past. I'm well-aware of it."

"Please," said Lord Dryden. "Can we not put aside our own self-interests for the good of the realm? Her Majesty came to us because we are trusted allies. We owe her the courtesy of hearing her out."

Elgin sat back quietly in his chair, not looking pleased with the rebuke.

"Your Majesty," said Dryden. "Would you care to speak?"

"Thank you, my lord. As you surmised, I come seeking your help against our enemies. I understand the immense loss your kingdom has suffered of late, and I fully sympathize with your current plight. Rebuilding an army, particularly one devastated by war, is a long and time-consuming process. Following the civil war that put me on the Throne, Merceria was in a similar state. We had a kingdom to rule, a people to reunite, yet lacked sufficient means to ensure their safety, let alone fight off a foreign army. I say this not to boast but to illustrate that we suffered as you have."

She paused, looking at each earl in turn. Gerald had seen this before— her way of sizing people up.

"We first learned of trouble on our border some months ago, thanks to one of our Dwarven allies. Since then, we've been diligently rebuilding our strength, but, as you know, this takes people, time, and coins. People we have, along with enough coins to double our army, and if that were the only obstacle, I wouldn't be here. What we don't have is time. Even as I speak, an army threatens our southern coast, the same enemy that holds our Dwarven allies under siege."

"Your southern coast?" said Lord Oliver. "Isn't that nothing but swamp?"

"The vast majority is," replied the queen. "But the enemy has chosen those lands south of Colbridge as the target for their seaborne invasion."

"South of Colbridge?" said Elgin. "But that's right on our border!"

"Which is precisely why I'm bringing it to your attention now."

"How far inland have they pushed?"

"We held them at Trollden," said Anna, "or at least we had the last we heard. Lord Preston and his reinforcements should already have joined them to keep the enemy at bay."

"Would it not be better to withdraw them to Colbridge, a walled city?"

"No," replied the queen. "They arrived in great numbers."

"What kind of numbers?"

"Enough that they could use a small portion of their army to siege the city while still sending the rest into the heart of Merceria."

"I'm curious," said Lord Dryden. "What is your marshal's opinion on the matter?"

Anna nodded at Gerald, who stepped forward to stand at her side. "Once our Dwarven allies came under attack, I reasoned we were the true objective. Anticipating trouble along the coast, I sent the Queen's Rangers to assist the Trolls in their defence, then ordered Commander Preston to mass reinforcements at Colbridge with the intent that he would take whatever action he deemed necessary when the attack finally came."

"Shouldn't you be there yourself to oversee this?"

"Merceria is threatened by multiple sources. Am I to abandon my responsibilities to our allies to oversee only the direct threat?"

"I fully support my marshal's actions," added Anna. "He devised our defence strategy, and he makes all decisions regarding the employment of our warriors."

"Yet he failed to hold back the enemy," said Elgin. "Or at least you believe his strategy has failed. That's why you're here, isn't it? To convince us to bail you out of trouble?" He turned to the other earls. "Merceria is a sinking ship, and she wants us to go down with her."

"That's enough of that!" said Dryden. "We owe them a great debt. Without their aid, we would never have freed ourselves from occupation."

"Then what do you suggest we do? We can't send what we don't have!"

All eyes turned to Queen Anna. "Well?" said Lord Julian. "Elgin made a good point. While it behooves us to send aid, we haven't the numbers."

"Might I make a suggestion?" said Anna.

"By all means."

"We have men training in Merceria, but they lack the armour to stand in a line of battle. Would you consider allowing them to guard your city walls in exchange for your trained men?"

The earls exchanged glances, shaking their heads at each other.

"I'm afraid that's not something we're willing to consider," replied Dryden. "I suggest you ask your husband to send word west. Perhaps Princess Althea could convince the Clans to lend aid?"

That evening found Anna sitting with Alric before a roaring fire in the drawing room of the makeshift Palace.

"It's no use," she said. "They flat out refused."

"I was afraid of that," replied Alric. "They can be a stubborn bunch, particularly when they have the opportunity to hold power over someone. Much as it pains me, though, they make an excellent point. We don't have the people to send."

"So I am to return home, defeated?"

"I've written to Althea, but the Clanholdings are distant, and we have no magic to speed along a response."

"Do you think they'd help?"

"Dungannon most likely will, and from what she's told me, perhaps Drakewell, but I doubt much more than a company or two. Even then, they would take weeks to assemble before marching clear across Weldwyn. We wouldn't see any of them before summer. You might have better luck seeking help in Norland."

"I'd considered that, but the earls there are a fractious bunch."

"As they are here. Perhaps it's something to do with the title?"

A servant entered and then bowed respectfully.

"Yes?" said Alric.

"Lord Parvan is here, Majesty. He wishes an audience with Queen Anna."

"Send him in."

"Of course, Majesty." The servant left, closing the door quietly behind him.

"I wonder what this is about?" said Alric.

"We shall soon see."

A short time later, the door opened, allowing Lord Parvan Luminor, the Elven Baron of Tivilton, to enter.

"You honour us with your presence, my lord," said Anna.

"The honour is all mine," he replied. His eyes flicked to King Alric.

"You may speak freely," insisted the queen.

"I was on the balcony at the council meeting today."

"And?"

"There is a possibility I can find you some aid."

"Oh? Are you volunteering your Elves to help our cause?"

"I lack the necessary numbers, but I know someone who may be of assistance."

"Go on."

Once again, the Elf glanced at the king.

Alric stood. "Lord Parvan clearly doesn't wish to speak in my presence, so I shall leave you to discuss things privately."

"Your Majesty is too kind," replied the Elf.

They waited until the door closed and they were alone.

"Well?" said Anna. "Who is this mysterious benefactor?"

"Lord Tulfar Axehand, the Baron of Mirstone. His warriors fought beside you at the liberation of Weldwyn."

"I'm well-aware of that. The Dwarves made a significant contribution to the campaign. What makes you think he'd consider helping?"

"You helped persuade His Majesty to lend his ear to us concerning matters unique to our two peoples."

"And you couldn't say that in front of my husband?"

"I did not wish to infer he was under your influence, Majesty."

She held up a finger. "Wait there for a moment, will you?" She went to the door and peered out. "Gerald, come in here, will you? We have something to discuss."

"Be right there," came the response.

She returned to her guest. "I'll need my marshal's assessment of your proposal."

"Of course."

They waited silently for the elderly marshal to enter the room. Gerald noticed the Elf lord's presence and offered a bow. "Lord Parvan, good to see you again."

"And you."

"Might I ask what this is about?"

"He's suggesting we seek out Lord Tulfar," explained Anna.

"Indeed," said Parvan. "I believe he would prove most amenable to helping you. Mirstone is close to the border, making it possible to send aid much sooner than others."

"I fought alongside him," said Gerald. "We'd be lucky to have his warriors on our side."

"I cannot guarantee he would agree to such an arrangement, but there is a likelihood he would be willing to assist you. Unfortunately, he is not here in Summersgate, necessitating I take a trip to Mirstone on your behalf."

"Thank you, Lord Parvan," said Anna, "but I think it would be more expeditious if we undertook the trip ourselves."

"That would be even better. Lord Tulfar is much more amenable to ideas when presented in person."

"Then we have a trip to plan."

"Mirstone is, what?" said Gerald. "Just over a hundred miles?"

"Closer to one hundred twenty," replied Anna.

"We'll need a carriage and some guards to keep you safe. Should we send for Revi? I don't like you travelling without the Royal Life Mage."

"I sent him up to Ironcliff, remember? We're travelling with Albreda and she can recall us to Wincaster if need be. Will that suit you?"

"It will," said Gerald.

"Good. Now, if you'll excuse me, I must see my husband and make arrangements." She rushed from the room, the eagerness of youth lending a spring to her steps.

"She is full of energy, that one," said Parvan.

"Oh, you have no idea!" replied Gerald.

FOURTEEN

Resistance

WINTER 967 MC

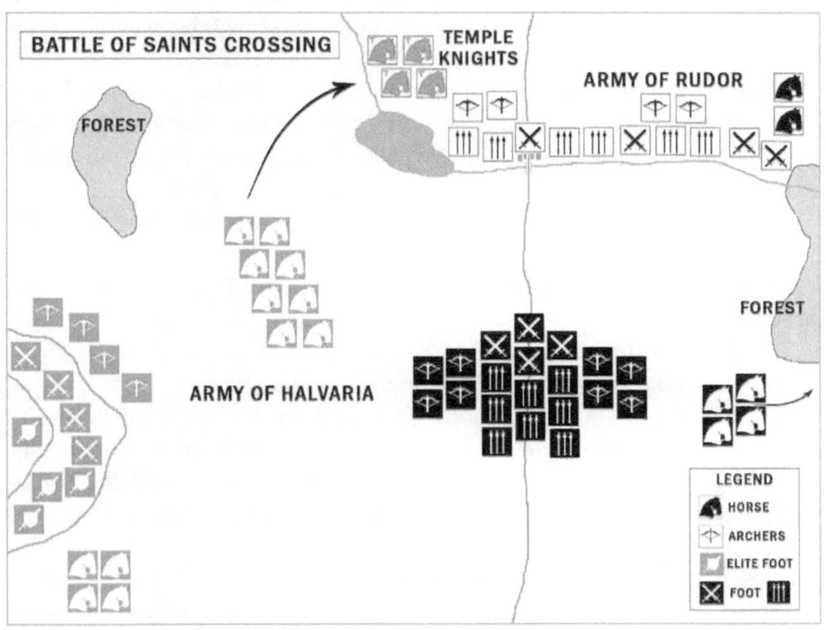

King Gwayne of Rudor sat astride his horse, staring off at the distant army. "I don't like this," he said. "Not one little bit."

Lord Wilmot, one of his barons, shook his head. "There is not much choice, Majesty. If we do not make a stand here, all of Rudor will be open to the empire's legions."

"True, but they outnumber us by a considerable margin."

"At least we have a defensible position."

The king studied his army formation. They'd taken up a position centred on the village of Saints Crossing, which guarded the bridge at the Traverne River. His warriors formed a line stretching out on either side, anchored on the western end by Silver Lake. To the east, the Nockwood guarded his flank, giving him a solid line of defence.

"Bring me the Temple Captain."

"She's a Temple Commander, Majesty."

"I don't care what she is," snapped the king. "Bring her to me this instant!"

"Yes, sire."

The baron rode off while the rest of the Royal retinue kept their distance. His Majesty was in a testy mood this day, and with good reason. He'd marched into Gotfeld to help his ally, King Argalin, only to discover the ruler had been killed in battle and his army scattered to the four winds. Now, all that stood between the enemy and his lands was his woefully small collection of warriors.

To the south, a Halvarian legion marched towards him, one solid mass of footmen moving up the road at a slow and deliberate pace, with archers on either side spread out in a thin line while their cavalry rode even farther afield.

A crimson-clad knight reined in her horse, then bowed respectfully. "You called for me, sire?"

"Yes, Commander Isabeau. You've fought these Halvarians before, haven't you?"

"Back in Arnsfeld, Your Majesty."

"Any advice on how to deal with them?"

"You've already taken up a defensive position. We can do little else to prepare, but I caution you to be mindful of the hill over yonder." She pointed to the southwest, where a prominent rise overlooked the battlefield, but more disturbing were the warriors massed there. "Those are Imperial troops, Majesty."

"Aren't they all Imperial? After all, it is called the Empire of Halvaria."

"True, but their warriors are broken into two distinct groups. The initial assault will be carried out by provincials, who are men recruited from the lands the empire has conquered. They refer to those from the heart of Halvaria as Imperial troops; they have better armour and training and are considerably more disciplined. If the enemy general commits them to the battle, it's a sure sign you're doing your job."

"And just how many men have they?"

"I cannot speak to their exact numbers," she replied, "but a full-strength legion consists of twenty-four hundred souls. This legion, which we believe is the Ninth, took losses at Rasgalen, but they've had plenty of time to replace them, so I imagine they're back to their original strength."

"But wouldn't they need to disperse men to occupy the conquered territory?"

"Ordinarily, but from what I see, that legion appears to be at full strength, which can only mean one thing—another legion is operating in the area."

"Saints alive," said the king. "And here I thought one legion was bad."

"I doubt it is within striking range, or our scouts would've reported their presence. The bad news is that even if we successfully hold off their attack, we'll have to retreat before they bring this second legion into range."

"So what you're saying is, no matter what happens here today, we must retreat?"

"Precisely, sire."

"I would think a Temple Commander would have more faith."

"Faith alone won't defeat this enemy, sire. Only the armies of the Petty Kingdoms can do that, assuming they can keep themselves from ripping out each other's throats."

"You're not exactly filling me with hope."

"We don't need to win here, Majesty, merely slow their advance."

"Perhaps I should withdraw back into Rudor?"

"I'm afraid it's too late for that. If you move to march, those Halvarian horsemen will tear your army to shreds."

"Surely your Temple Knights could protect us?"

"I possess two hundred knights, a significant number, but they can't be everywhere at once." She pointed. "More than eight hundred horsemen wait there to pursue an undisciplined army."

"Undisciplined? How dare you impugn the quality of my men!"

"Half your army is little more than country folk, pressed into service with a minimum of training. They'll hold the line so long as the river blocks the enemy's advance, but if the Halvarians cross that bridge, don't expect your men to throw their lives away."

The king went as pale as a ghost.

She considered her next words carefully. "Fortunately, you've got your best men holding that bridge, with more waiting behind to replace losses. That forces the enemy to mass at one point, where numbers won't make so much of a difference."

"And your Temple Knights?"

"I shall keep them northwest of the village, ready to react to any developments."

The king nodded. "Good. My cavalry is positioned in the east. If the enemy tries to outflank us, they'd need time to ride around the Nockwood, but the last thing I want to do is underestimate them."

"With your permission, Majesty, I should like to return to my command."

"You may go," said the king. He glanced around, spotting Wilmot and waved him over.

"The enemy draws closer, sire."

"Indeed they do, but I daresay the stalwart men of Rudor will do their duty this day."

Temple Captain Marlena watched as her commander rode back to join them. The Grand Mistress had sent Temple Commander Isabeau to assume duties as the regional commander three years ago. While a competent administrator, she lacked the personal touch her predecessor possessed.

"Have we any new orders?" asked Marlena.

"Not presently, but if all goes according to plan, we'll do little but sit back and watch."

"And if it doesn't?"

"Then we'll find ourselves in the fight of our lives." The Temple Commander turned in her saddle to regard her senior captain. "You've fought in battle before. Is there anything you'd care to pass on?"

"Keep your wits about you and trust in your training. There'll be a lot of screaming, and once we're in the thick of it, it all becomes one big, confusing mess. The key to survival is keeping formation and not straying from the other sisters."

"I shall bear that in mind." The commander turned, staring out across the lake to where the enemy waited atop the hill, a lurking menace reminding everyone of how large a single legion was.

Commander-General Moreau watched with great interest as the bulk of his provincial troops made contact with those guarding the bridge. The hilltop gave him an outstanding view of the fight, but, more importantly, a clear view of his cavalry racing forward to envelop the enemy's western flank.

Even as he watched, they galloped around the lake, eager to come to grips with their sworn enemies, the Temple Knights.

He sat back in his saddle, smiling at the thought. The sister knights were responsible for the empire's defeat at Arnsfeld. He refused to allow them to do the same here, so he'd sent every horseman under his command against them, save for the two hundred provincials headed eastward. Six hundred horsemen should be more than enough to deal with the troublesome Temple Knights.

He focused on his cavalry rather than the main thrust at the enemy's defensive line, for he knew the bridge would hold. The real test of his strategy was the horsemen who'd envelop either flank.

The provincial horsemen would be turning the flank far to the east, although the Nockwood blocked his view. The west was another matter, for the Imperial cavalry advance was visible, stretching out before him in an epic panorama. Even as he watched, the lead elements rounded the lake, crossing the river, their mounts shoulder-deep in its waters. The Temple Knights rode to counter the threat, leading to a water-soaked melee.

Moreau couldn't take his eyes off the action. The Temple Knights of Saint Cunar had always offered the greatest threat to the empire, so much so that a concentrated effort was undertaken to destroy them from within. In recent years, however, the Agnesites surprised everyone by making a stand in Arnsfeld, helping to defeat an entire Halvarian legion.

He forced himself to look back to the centre of his attack. The fight for the bridge had become a meat grinder, the two opposing armies fighting for the wooden planks stretching across the Traverne. Archers lined the banks on either side, loosing massed volleys in a vain effort to thin out the opposing side.

Had he been in charge of the defenders, he would've deployed additional footmen on either flank, ensuring an envelopment could not gain traction, but it appeared the King of Rudor was no tactician.

"Look, my lord," said Grim. "The provincial cavalry has cleared the woods."

The distinctive pale-green riders came into view, Rudor's horsemen charging straight at them. The defenders took a terrible risk, for their hundred attacked more than double their number, and that's when Moreau realized how weak the enemy line was. His attention wandered back to the fight at the bridge, and then his gaze strayed left and right, noting the other warriors lining the river.

He couldn't help but smile. "The battle is over."

"My lord?"

"Half the men lining the riverbank are a levy. They won't stand, not with cavalry threatening their flanks."

"Our men are having a hard time against the Temple Knights, my lord."

"They are proving more troublesome than I'd anticipated, but they can't keep up the pressure for long, not once the enemy begins to break."

"The bridge is still in their hands," said Grim. "How can you be so certain?"

"Watch and learn. The key is the eastern flank. The Rudor cavalry is badly outnumbered, so all we need to do is get riders past them." He held his breath. "And there it is, the moment we've been waiting for."

Resistance crumbled in the east, starting with a half company of provincials riding into the rear of the Rudor line. The first company of Rudor cavalrymen turned, allowing more of the empire's forces to push behind their defences.

The poorly trained militia broke first, leaving gaps in the line. The trained warriors of Rudor attempted to take their place but were spread too thinly. Additional provincial horsemen appeared behind them, and panic overtook even the most seasoned.

"Wait for it," said Moreau. "The Temple Knights will soon realize they're in a hopeless position. See? Their line is already thinning."

Marlena swung out, her sword discarded in favour of a mace, smashing into an enemy horseman's arm. The rider tried pulling his mount away, but she followed up with an overhead strike that landed on the man's helmet with a sickening crunch. The fellow tipped over to one side, falling from the saddle.

Her muscles ached, and her breath was laboured, yet Halvarian riders continued filling in for their fallen comrades. She pushed her horse forward, then struck at an enemy in plate armour, her mace making a dull thud, failing to do any real damage. A counterstrike came towards her face, but she brought her shield up in time to block it.

She readied herself for the next blow, and then her opponent toppled from the saddle, the victim of an attack by a fellow Temple Knight.

Sister Johanna rode up beside her. "Commander Isabeau is dead. It's your command now."

"Status?"

"We're taking heavy casualties. I don't know how much longer we can hold them back."

"And the rest of the army?"

"They've sounded the retreat. If we don't move now, we'll be cut off."

"Sound the horn, then withdraw in good order."

Johanna nodded, then pulled a horn from her belt. A trio of notes echoed forth; she paused momentarily before repeating them.

The Temple Knights were highly disciplined, a discipline put to the test as they attempted to disengage from the enemy. It was a tricky manoeuvre, but the empire's cavalry was tired after forcing their way across the river.

Marlena led them north along the road to Rudor.

"Are we to abandon King Gwayne?" asked Johanna.

"His Majesty is most likely dead, and we will be, too, if we don't leave immediately. It won't take long for their cavalry to pursue us."

"Surely it's better to die fighting than to withdraw a coward?"

Marlena moved to one side, allowing her command to continue north while she dealt with her aide. "I hold no qualms about dying in battle, but to throw one's life away without meaning is the very definition of foolishness. Yes, the empire defeated us here, but others will be willing to take up the fight."

"But the Army of Rudor is defeated. Who else can we turn to?"

"We cross the border and continue north until we turn into Angvil. That should buy us some time."

"I don't understand."

"The empire is the invader here. They can't keep marching without securing their supply lines. They'll need to subdue Rudor first, and that will take time, time which we can hopefully use to raise another army."

"We're Temple Knights, not a kingdom. We can barely afford the upkeep of the knights we have, let alone raise an army."

"Then we shall find one. Word of the invasion will already have travelled deep into the Petty Kingdoms. Our task is to discover who will resist it and then stand with them."

"You saw the size of that legion. It's hopeless!"

"Have faith, Johanna. We can survive this."

"How are you so certain?"

Marlena had patterned herself after Temple Commander Charlaine, possibly the most gifted leader the order had ever seen. Charlaine's faith remained unwavering throughout all, yet it was her openness that won people over.

"I can't," she finally said, "but I have every confidence our faith guides us in even the darkest of times. Let that belief be the glue that holds us together."

Johanna sat up straighter. "You're inspiring, Commander. I should never have doubted you."

"You spoke your mind and were honest about your fears. That is the very embodiment of what we represent."

"Shall we resume the march?"

"You ride ahead," said Marlena. "I'll wait here and bring up the rear."

The icy cold rain came in droves, signalling spring was just around the corner. The road soon turned to mud, forcing the Temple Knights to travel over the fields to save their horses from struggling.

Marlena rode past her small command, marvelling at their good order. Despite the gruelling pace and lack of rest, no one fell behind. One hundred and fifty-seven Temple Knights survived the battle out of an initial force of two hundred and twelve. The loss of so many sister knights plagued her, for she was fully aware of the treatment they could expect from the empire. Her heart went out to those they'd left on the battlefield, too injured to withdraw.

A drenched Temple Captain Enna waited at the crossroads, her cloak proving ineffective against the weather. "This is it," she called out. "The road to Angvil."

"There's been no sign of pursuit," replied Marlena, "but we shouldn't become complacent. Have your company take over as rearguard while Bernelle takes the lead." She glanced skyward, but the clouds indicated no end of the storm was in sight. "Order the horses rested and distribute what rations we have remaining. If we're to be wet and cold, we can at least have full bellies."

"Yes, Commander."

Her aide appeared, shivering as she came closer, her breath frosting despite the rain. "Is it my imagination, or is this rain letting up?"

Marlena raised her eyebrows. "Letting up? Surely you jest? It's heavier now than this morning."

Johanna smiled. "You must have faith, Commander."

"Ah. Using my own words against me is a clever tactic. What do you propose next, that we pray for this rain to cease?"

"It couldn't hurt?"

"That's true." Marlena closed her eyes. "Blessed Saint Agnes, hear this plea. Watch over us as we serve in your name and see the spirits of the slain safely to the Afterlife, that they may serve you in death as they have in life." She considered her next words carefully. "And if you can spare a thought for us, blessed Saint, could you lighten up a little on the rain?" Another pause. "Saints be with us."

"Saints be with us all," said Johanna.

Marlena glanced skyward. The rain continued to pour down, yet it now struck her not as a punishment but as a reward.

"It's still raining," said her aide.

"It is, but consider it a comfort, for the tears of Saint Agnes will wash away the roads, making it difficult for the empire to advance."

"The tears of Saint Agnes?"

"Yes," said Marlena. "An apt name for it, don't you think?"

FIFTEEN

Cathedral

WINTER 967 MC

Aldwin looked up at the tall spire of the building. "When Brother Cyric said the Cathedral was large, he wasn't exaggerating."

"Yes," replied Owen. "It's odd when you think about it."

"Odd?"

"The order takes a vow of poverty, yet that building must've cost them a fortune." The knight shook his head. "It seems even the well-meaning can't resist a display of wealth."

"Where do we find Commander Roland?" asked Beverly.

"I couldn't say, not that it matters. Anyone working in there should be able to direct us to his office."

They'd advanced down the street on foot, leaving their horses at the inn where they were staying. Those they passed looked on in wonderment at the sight of the Orc, yet none challenged her presence.

A pair of Temple Knights stood beside the entrance, their brown surcoats identifying them as Mathewites. Sir Owen approached them to enquire how they might find their regional commander. He returned shortly with good news.

"I've got directions," said the knight, "and it appears he's expecting us."

"How did he know we'd show up?" asked Aubrey.

"I imagine that is Brother Cyric's doing, and those guards knew him by name."

"Why wouldn't they? They're from the same order, aren't they?"

"They are, but it was more than simple recognition; it was akin to respect. Not something I'd expect, were they strangers."

"He did say he worked for the regional commander. I imagine that puts him in good stead."

"I suppose that must be it. In any event, if you'll follow me, I'll show you the way. Their directions were most explicit."

They entered the wooden double doors leading into the main worship hall. Owen took them through a door on the left that brought them to a narrow corridor.

"This hallway leads to the back of the building, where the offices are."

They made their way down the hallway, paralleling the nave, squeezing against the wall occasionally to allow others to pass by.

"Ah, here we are," he said at last, knocking at a door.

"One moment," came a voice, and then the door creaked open, revealing Brother Cyric. "You've decided to take me up on the offer. How marvellous. Come in and have a seat, won't you? I'll let the Temple Commander know you're here."

The small room was similar in size to Beverly's childhood bedroom back in Bodden Keep but without a window. Chairs lined the left wall, while a desk stood on the right. Directly opposite the entrance was the door Cyric went through to notify his superior of their arrival.

Aldwin was the first to sit. "This reminds me of the Cathedral back in Wincaster."

Aubrey laughed. "If I recall, you punched Lord Montrose the last time you were there."

"That was years ago, and the man was a traitor, if you recall."

"He was," added Beverly, "but we've been there plenty of times since."

Cyric reappeared at the inner door. "The Temple Commander will see you now, although I'm afraid his office isn't overly large. It might be better if only two of you came in."

"You and Aubrey go," said Aldwin. "The rest of us can wait here."

"You don't mind?" asked Beverly.

"Not at all. You're the general, and Aubrey's been at court long enough to know Queen Anna's mind."

Beverly turned to Cyric. "It appears you have your answer. Should I leave my weapons here?"

"I don't think that's necessary." He stood aside, allowing them to enter.

The office barely had enough room for the regional commander's desk and a pair of chairs arranged for his visitors. Cyric stood off to one side, his back to the corner.

"Good day," their host began. "I am Temple Commander Roland. Unless I miss my guess, you're Lady Beverly, and this is your cousin, Lady Aubrey?"

"That is correct," replied Beverly. "We come from Merceria, although I doubt you're familiar with its location."

"I am not, but from what Cyric told me, it's somewhere west of the Petty Kingdoms?"

"In point of fact, it lies beyond the Halvarian Empire."

"Remarkable. I assume you travelled to the Continent by ship?"

"Actually, no. We came through an accident of magic, but I suspect my cousin could explain that better than me."

Aubrey cleared her throat. "I am a Life Mage, as is my mentor, Revi Bloom. Some time ago, we learned how to use the magic of ley lines to transport over great distances. Are you familiar with such things?"

"Ley lines? Most assuredly, although I've never heard them referred to as magical in nature. Should I assume your trip ended up being one-way?"

"It did. Due to a miscalculation, we are stranded in the Petty Kingdoms, seeking a way to return home."

"I'm afraid I can do nothing to help you in that regard. I'm no mage."

"We weren't expecting you to," said Beverly. "Our homeland is under attack from the very same enemy threatening the security of the Petty Kingdoms."

"You mean Halvaria?"

"I do."

"I knew they were large," said Roland, "but if what you say is true, it speaks to a vaster empire than we imagined."

"We came here because we thought we might be able to help you."

"Me? I don't see how."

"Not you personally," said Aubrey, "rather, you in the context of those who fight this empire."

"And what is it you think you can offer?"

"Beverly is a general in the Mercerian Army, as well as an experienced warrior. As for myself, as I said earlier, I'm a Life Mage and could use my magic to heal the injured."

"This is a most intriguing idea," said Roland. "I could bring this to the duke's attention if you like. Or better still, I could introduce you to him directly. Might I ask, Lady Beverly, what command experience you possess? That is to say, what type of warriors have you commanded?"

"A regular assortment, including foot, horse, and bow, and more unusual companies, such as Orcs, Saurians, Elves, and Dwarves, not to mention Kurathian Mastiffs."

"What's a Saurian?"

"They are an ancient race. I suppose you would describe them as lizard-like. They are native to the swamps in the southern part of Merceria."

"As I said," added Aubrey, "my cousin has extensive experience."

"So it would seem. Have you any of your warriors with you?"

"I'm afraid not," replied Beverly. "We three were meant to be a scouting party."

"Three?" said Roland. "But I thought you numbered five?"

"Sir Owen joined us after our arrival, as did Krazuhk."

"I assume that's the Orc?"

"It is. She is a master of air, what you would refer to as an Air Mage."

"And she would be willing to use her magic in service to His Grace, the Duke?"

"I believe she'd be willing to aid him, yes. We all would. We see it as a means of striking back against the same enemy threatening our home."

"I can't make any promises, but I shall endeavour to bring your offer to the duke's attention."

"Do you think him likely to accept our help?"

"Erlingen has seen its fair share of wars over the years, but I'd hardly call their army seasoned. Their most recent conflict was nearly fifteen years ago, and even then, it consisted of a single battle. They were victorious, but that mainly came down to one of their knights capturing the enemy king. I doubt the empire would be so accommodating."

"Excuse me, sir," said Cyric, "but perhaps Lady Beverly might give us a bit of additional information about her experiences in battle?"

"Yes," said Roland. "An excellent idea. Lady Beverly?"

"I was knighted back in nine fifty-two… Pardon me; that would be sixteen years ago. Since then, our home has seen little peace. Before that, I was a member of the Bodden Horse, a group of riders responsible for patrolling the frontier and keeping raiders at bay. My true war experience began when I swore service to Princess Anna, who later became our queen. We suppressed a rebellion eight years ago, then fought a civil war that placed her on the Throne. Somewhere in there, we fought off a Clan invasion of our western neighbour, Weldwyn, and then destroyed an enemy army that marched down from the north. We then returned to Weldwyn to help stave off disaster. All told, I've seen many battles, running from small skirmishes up to thousands of warriors per side."

"She hasn't told you everything," added Aubrey. "The man who's now the Marshal of the Mercerian Army trained her, not to mention she was made Knight Commander of the Order of the Hound. Have you such ranks here on the Continent?"

"We do," replied Roland, "or at least something similar. My own order uses the term Temple Commander rather than Commander, but it amounts to the same thing."

"If you don't mind me saying so, you don't appear surprised a woman could have such a career."

"And why would I? My own order works closely with the Temple Knights of Saint Agnes, and Saints know they've had their successes in recent years." He leaned forward, suddenly taking an intense interest in Beverly. "Your actual name wouldn't happen to be Charlaine, would it?"

"No. Why do you ask?"

"Just curious. A Temple Commander of Saint Agnes and many of her sister knights disappeared some time ago."

"Disappeared?"

"There was a bit of an upheaval in the Antonine. Rumour is she marched out of the city with a substantial number of Temple Knights. No one has heard of her since."

Cyric cleared his throat. "With all due respect, sir, this is hardly the place to bring up such things."

"No, I suppose it isn't. Kindly disregard my comments, Lady Beverly. It was wishful thinking on my part."

"Would you be willing to tell us what's been happening lately?" said Beverly. "We are aware that the empire invaded, but it might prove useful to know the full story."

"Ah," replied Roland. "Now, that I can answer. The Halvarians crossed over into one of the border realms, a place called Gotfeld, destroying the king's army and killing him in the process, then marched north, towards Rudor."

"Any idea of losses?"

"According to our estimates, the Army of Gotfeld numbered some six or seven hundred souls, hardly enough to confront a legion, but King Argalin had little choice. It was either that or give the invaders free rein to plunder his kingdom."

"How many survived?"

"As far as we know, the army was annihilated at Rasgalen. He would've left a garrison to guard their palace, but we've heard nothing of their fate."

"Any idea where they'll march next?"

"Several. I suspect they'll go north, into Rudor, and then Arnsfeld to exact revenge for their failed invasion all those years ago. Cyric, however, disagrees. He thinks they'll march into Angvil and strike towards Erlingen."

Beverly turned to the Temple Knight. "Might I ask why?"

"The three strongest armies of the Petty Kingdoms are Erlingen, Hadenfeld, and the Northern Alliance. While any could be the target, hitting us early, before we fully mobilize, would prevent the other two from uniting."

"I don't agree with his reasoning," countered Roland. "It's a long march from Rudor to Erlingen, which would make their supply lines dangerously thin."

"Could they not live off the land?" asked Aubrey.

"Only if they possessed the manpower to occupy it. A legion is large but not enough to occupy as they go and fight off the duke's army at the same time."

"I think Brother Cyric has the right of it," said Beverly. "What you haven't considered, Commander, is that they likely have more than one legion at their disposal."

"What makes you say that?"

"The last we heard, they attacked our home, Merceria, with three. It's abundantly clear the Petty Kingdoms cover a vaster area, so it only makes sense Halvaria would send even more legions to conquer them."

"I must admit, I hadn't considered that possibility. Until recently, the empire was content with absorbing those realms lying on its borders. It now appears they are going for the very throat of the Petty Kingdoms. Unfortunately, that makes Erlingen a prime target. I should bring this to the duke's attention immediately." He rose, prompting the others to do likewise. "Please excuse me for calling an end to this meeting. I'm certain you understand why."

"Of course," said Beverly.

"Excellent. Now, I must leave you. Cyric will see you out." The Temple Commander moved around his desk, then squeezed past his visitors, making his way from the room.

"Thank you," said Cyric.

"For what?" replied Beverly.

"For agreeing with my assessment of the invasion. I'm afraid the Temple Commander sometimes gets mired down in administration, but now that he's come around to the idea, he'll be an invaluable resource for His Grace."

"And what will happen to us now?"

"Don't worry. I will keep you updated on the situation. Father Commander Roland will speak with His Grace, but I doubt you'll have a chance to meet the duke for a few days. Such are the demands upon him in times of war. You understand, I hope?"

"I do," said Beverly. "This isn't the first time we've been involved in news of this magnitude. Has the duke a marshal?"

"No. He commands the Army of Erlingen himself. Why do you ask?"

"I was curious about his military experience. Has he fought a battle before?"

"Regrettably, no, which makes it all the more imperative he has competent advisors. Some of his barons fought at the Battle of Chermingen, but once again, that battle was short-lived, and the number of people engaged was relatively small. Not that I'm complaining, mind you. Far better to have less death when war comes to your door, but I fear a few nobles now fancy themselves experts, based on their limited experience. I shall endeavour to suggest to His Grace that you be employed as a military advisor, Lady Beverly, if that's acceptable?"

"I would be pleased to offer whatever support I can."

"As will I," added Aubrey. "Speaking of which, how many mages does His Grace employ?"

"None, presently, I'm afraid. The previous duke had a Stormwind at court early in his reign, but they had a disagreement of some sort. Since then, not a single mage has come to take her place."

"There was a Stormwind at the court of Deisenbach, who was involved in a plot to poison the king, so you are better off not having them here in Erlingen."

Cyric raised his eyebrows. "Is that so? You must tell me more."

"Her name was Ludmilla, and from all appearances, she was a close confidante of the queen."

"Might I ask the nature of the poison she used?"

"Are you an expert in such things?" asked Aubrey.

"On occasion, I've found myself investigating deaths due to the application of poison."

"You mean murder?"

"Correct," replied Cyric.

"But I thought you only investigated matters internal to your order?"

"That is my primary responsibility, but occasionally, I'm called on to investigate other problems, usually when no other authorities are willing or able to conduct a full enquiry. As such, I've become somewhat of an expert on poisons."

"In this case, she used a glowing green liquid, an essence of the ley lines. We've run across something similar back home, though in that case, the poisoning was accidental."

"And what did this essence do?"

"My mentor, Revi Bloom, was studying the magic of the ley lines as part of his research into portals. His constant proximity resulted in an altered state, a sort of miasma of the mind. Thankfully, with a shaman's help, I countered the effects, which I also did in Deisenbach."

"Where would Ludmilla have come across this essence?"

"That remains a mystery," replied Aubrey. "Someone obviously discovered a way to extract it from the ley lines, but we shall likely never know how or where they did it."

"I assume she was not cooperative?"

"We placed her in a holding cell, but when we finally got around to interrogating her, we discovered she'd used her magic to escape. Have you encountered something like this before?"

"I've travelled much during my time with the order and came across some remarkable people, amongst them a woman named Natalia Stormwind. She was a powerful Water Mage, but if she was capable of some sort of teleportation, she never told me."

"Natalia Stormwind?"

"Yes," replied Cyric. "Why? Do you know her?"

"I've never met her, but I know of her."

"I find that remarkable. The last time I saw her, she and her husband were heading north, trying to escape the clutches of the family."

Aubrey smiled. "Then I'm pleased to inform you that they finally found a home in Therengia."

Cyric smiled. "Therengia, you say? How remarkable. I'm surprised you know that, though, seeing as you came from the west, not the east."

"I learned through a mutual acquaintance, an Orc named Shaluhk."

"You've provided me with much to think about. Perhaps one day, I shall travel east and seek them out. I assume she's still with Athgar?"

"Yes. How did you know?"

"They shared a tight bond. You might even say that though they were each powerful mages in their own right, they were even more so together."

A bell rang outside.

"My goodness," said Cyric. "Is it that late already? I'm afraid you must excuse me. I have prayers to attend to. Be assured I shall send word once His Grace, the Duke, is ready to meet you."

"Thank you," said Beverly. "You've been most helpful."

"Quite the reverse, actually. Your presence here has proved most fortuitous for the coming campaign."

SIXTEEN

The Mountain Paths

SPRING 968 MC

Herdwin stared down at the broken mountain path. Gelion's warriors had collapsed a part of the walkway, tumbling it down the mountainside, but it wouldn't take long for the empire's mages to repair the damage.

"It's not enough," he said. "This won't even slow them half a day."

"True," replied Kasri. "Those mages of theirs will restore the path before nightfall. We need to retreat before they make contact again. We can't afford another encounter like that last one." She looked at the exhausted Dwarves behind them, who'd fought a furious night action, defending the last of the Dwarven-built watchtowers that lined the pass to Stonecastle. They'd expected it to hold for a week, but the Halvarian Earth Mages made quick work of it.

"At least Gelion was able to restock his company with some bolts. Not that it'll make much difference. The path grows wider as we approach Stonecastle. The only place left for us to defend are the walls of the outer city." He turned to her. "How many of the enemy do you reckon we've killed these last few days?"

"Hundreds, yet they keep coming as if they have an inexhaustible supply." She looked skyward. "I don't suppose we could count on the weather to hinder them?"

Herdwin shook his head. "Spring is almost here, but we don't get much rain in these mountains. I'm afraid the weather is more likely to help the enemy than impede their progress."

"Gundar's axe!" The curse came from behind, causing them both to wheel around. Gelion sat on the ground, his back leaning against a large outcropping of rock while one of his arbalesters extracted an arrow from his hip. It was the third arrow wound he'd suffered in the retreat from Kharzun's Folly, yet the most painful by far.

The Dwarf captain met the gaze of his cousin. "The leg was one thing; I can hobble along, and then the arm? Well, I can fight one-handed if need be. But the hip? By the Gods, I've lost the use of the entire leg." He stared down at the blood-soaked ground. "I can't continue leading my warriors like this. I yield my command to you, Herdwin." He spared a glance at the warrior looking after his wound. "Did you hear that?"

"I did," replied Murdan. "The burden of command passes to Herdwin Steelarm."

"And you're all right with that?"

"Why wouldn't I be?"

"He's not a guild member."

"No, he's not," replied the arbalester, "but he's more than proved his worth in battle. Now, here, bite into this." Murdan offered the shaft of one of his bolts.

"No," replied Gelion. "I'll take it like a Dwarf. Now get on with it before I pass out and embarrass myself."

Murdan dug in with his knife, cutting the flesh to allow the extraction of the arrowhead. His captain looked as though he might faint, but then he grumbled and let out something unintelligible. Murdan pulled the arrow free, staunching the wound with a compress. "We'll need a litter. He won't be able to walk."

"I'll arrange one," said Kasri.

Herdwin waited as Murdan finished bandaging the wound, then pulled the fellow aside. "How bad is it?" he asked.

"He's lucky to be alive, but I doubt he'll walk again. Perhaps it might be better to spare him the agony?"

"Don't talk such rot. A Life Mage would have him back on his feet in short order."

"We have no such thing in Stonecastle."

"I'm well-aware of that, but I have friends in Wincaster. You keep him alive, and I'll see to it he regains the use of his leg. You think you can do that?"

"Aye, Captain."

"Good. How many Dwarves are standing after last night's fiasco?"

"Thirty-two arbalesters and twenty-seven axes. Not including yourself or Lady Kasri."

"And bolts?"

"Enough for another few volleys, and then they'll take the fight to the enemy."

"It's too late for that," replied Herdwin. "They'd just be throwing their lives away. It's time we were back behind the safety of the city walls."

"That's still a half-day's march," said Murdan.

"Aye, and that's what bothers me. We must buy ourselves some time." He snapped his fingers. "Wait. I just had a thought." Herdwin looked around, searching the survivors. "Tindal?"

"Right here," came the exhausted reply. The young Dwarf approached, crouching by Gelion. "Will he survive?"

"Of course I'll survive," said Gelion. "I'm not dead, you know."

"He's relinquished command," added Murdan. "Herdwin is now the acting captain."

"Wasn't he already the commander of this expedition?" asked Tindal.

"Don't argue the point," said Gelion. "Every company needs a captain, and rules are rules. By Gundar's beard, if we didn't follow proper procedure, the guild would have our mustaches, then where would we be? You don't want people seeing your upper lip, do you?"

"No," replied Tindal. "Of course not."

Kasri reappeared along with a pair of warriors. "We're going to carry you, Gelion, but before we lift your sorry arse up, I want you to chew on this." She held out her palm, revealing three small leaves.

"Numbleaf?"

She nodded. "It's all we have left, so use it sparingly. Might I suggest half a leaf rather than a full one? At least that way, it'll last."

He opened his mouth to argue, then as pain lanced up his side, he clamped his lips together in a grimace. When it finally passed, he grudgingly accepted the leaves. "I'll take your advice," he said, then bit into one. The result was remarkable, for his whole body relaxed. "Ah. The sweet taste of mint." His stomach let out a loud rumble. "I don't suppose we have any stonecakes left, do we?"

"I'm afraid not," replied Kasri. "Unfortunately, that last tower only held enough for a small garrison. By the time we finished feeding everybody, nothing was left."

Tindal looked back and forth between Gelion and Kasri. "Surely I'm not to carry him all the way to Stonecastle?"

"No," said Herdwin, "but there's an important task for you, providing you're up to it. I need you to take word to Harold Wainwright, a Mercerian captain back in the city."

"What's the message?"

"He is to bring both companies of Mercerian archers here to cover our retreat. Oh, and tell him to fetch lots of arrows. Have you the strength to do that?"

"I can muster it," replied Tindal.

"Good. Then be off with you, and let them know we're retreating in the face of overwhelming odds, so we'll likely meet them along the road."

"I shall not fail you, Commander." Without another word, Tindal turned, jogging up the path towards Stonecastle.

"He's a good lad," said Gelion.

"Aye, that he is."

"Listen, Herdwin, I'll only slow you down. Leave me here. I'll take out my fair share of the enemy before I die."

"Don't be daft, Cousin. Margel would have my beard. Besides, once I find a Life Mage, you'll be as good as new."

"You know as well as I that we'll be sealed up inside the mountain. We Dwarves of Stonecastle possess no magic circle with which to escape or bring additional help. But it's not too late for you and Kasri."

"What kind of Dwarf would I be if I let my kin face the enemy alone? I'm afraid Merceria is in this with you, whether you want them or not. Now, these two Dwarves of yours will carry you."

"They won't manage it. I'm too heavy."

"Nonsense," said Kasri. "I carried Herdwin all by myself when he was wounded last year, and you've got two of your own warriors to do the heavy lifting. Are you suggesting they're not up to the task?"

Gelion slumped. "No. I suppose not."

"Good. Let's have no more talk of leaving anyone behind." She nodded at the two warriors, who threaded poles through a couple of jackets to make a stretcher.

Herdwin watched as they carefully laid his cousin on it and hefted him up, testing the weight. They nodded at their new captain, then headed off.

"What's this about you being named captain?" she asked. "Gerald already appointed you the commander."

"Guild rules, I'm afraid. A company shall not remain without a captain. Don't you have the same back in Ironcliff?"

"Not that I'm aware of, but our warriors guild is run differently than yours. In times of emergency, the vard can put anyone in command of a company. Is the same not true here?"

"Not unless they're a member of the guild."

"But you don't belong to the guild."

"No, I don't," said Herdwin. "Which is why it was so important for Gelion to make it clear I was in charge."

She grinned.

"What are you smiling at?"

"It might be different in Stonecastle, but if this were Ironcliff, you'd be considered a guild member."

"How so?"

"As I said earlier, the vard can appoint anyone to command a company, but once done, they automatically become guild members."

"The vard didn't appoint me."

"No, he didn't, but a Dwarf captain in good stead has the right to appoint his successor, does he not?"

"He does."

"And he holds his rank under the vard's authority, does he not?"

"Aye, he does."

"Then your cousin has done us a great service."

Herdwin broke out into a grin. "I suppose he has when you put it that way. Of course, we must survive for it to mean anything."

"Oh, we'll survive. We've endured too much to lose each other now."

"That's what I like about you—always the optimist."

She cast her head down. "Not always. When I believed I'd lost you, I was despondent."

Herdwin reached out and took her hand. "I know, and for that, I'm truly sorry." He suddenly became aware that the entire area had become quiet, everyone's gaze locked on their exchange. He cleared his throat. "Let's get to work. We've still got a long march ahead of us. Murdan, select half your arbalesters and bring up the rear. If you see any signs of the Halvarians, call out, then let loose with a volley. Skodan, you take the others and lead the way. The rest will be in the middle, ready to turn around should the enemy get too close." He paused, watching everyone picking themselves up off the path. "Keep the pace even; we're not leaving anyone behind."

Kasri met his gaze. "I noticed we're still holding hands."

He cleared his throat, although he kept his grip. "That we are, and I'll not apologize for it."

"Nor should you. Let's get this army marching before the enemy decides to interfere."

The retreat to Stonecastle was long and arduous, not only in terms of terrain but stamina, for the Dwarves had fought the enemy all night. Late in the afternoon, the Wincaster bowmen arrived, the indomitable Captain Wainwright leading them. His men formed into a line at the side of the road as the Dwarves passed, and then the bowmen redeployed across the road to deny access to the Halvarians.

"Good to see you, Captain," said Herdwin, "although I must admit to some surprise over the speed of your arrival. I wouldn't have expected you until sometime tomorrow."

"As fate would have it, Kiren-Jool arrived at Stonecastle and used his magic to scry the area. It didn't take him long to discover your whereabouts, and I took it upon myself to bring a company to assist."

"You ran into Tindal?"

"We did, early this afternoon. I've sent a runner to accompany him back to the city. I also sent word for another company of archers to join us, although it will likely be after dark by the time they arrive."

"How is Stonecastle coping?"

"The city has never been under direct attack, and some fear their defences will prove inadequate."

"What's your assessment?"

"Given the enemy's strength, I have no doubt the outer city will fall, but the mountain will most assuredly endure. I wish we had a magic circle to ferry the wounded back to Wincaster."

"As do I," said Herdwin. "Any news from Ironcliff?"

"Yes, but I'm afraid it's not good. Reports indicate the siege has begun."

Kasri joined them. "Anything else you can tell us?"

"The empire gave them the chance to surrender."

She laughed. "They don't understand us mountain folk. My father would sooner die than surrender."

"Let's hope it doesn't come to that. It appears their assessment of the situation is that they have sufficient numbers to take the undermountain."

"Who commands the Mercerian contingent?"

"The High Ranger," replied the captain. "They've already had some success in harassing the enemy."

"And Lord Heward?"

"He commands a small army of Norlanders and Orcs at Holdcross, and apparently, Commander Lanaka joined them. They lack the numbers to push the enemy out of the Gap but should be able to prevent them from entering Norland."

"That should stall their advance," said Kasri, "but it still does nothing to drive them from our lands. What has the marshal been doing about all of this?"

"I couldn't say. Kiren-Jool wasn't forthcoming about such things; that's assuming he knew anything. On the other hand, I've known the marshal for several years. I imagine he's already concocting a campaign to drive them out."

"Easy for you to say," said Kasri. "These are not your lands."

"Now, now," soothed Herdwin. "Gerald values the Dwarves. He won't let us fall under the thumb of the empire if he can prevent it."

"Then where is he?"

"He sent men to Stonecastle."

"Yes, but only six companies, hardly enough to drive back the enemy." She took a deep breath, letting it out slowly. "I'm sorry. I didn't mean to get angry, but these last few days have been very trying, and my patience has hit its limit."

"Understandable, given the present circumstances," replied Wainwright, "but you must consider the pressures on Merceria. We are assailed on three sides, with barely enough people to hold on to what we've got. What we need is additional warriors."

"Could Weldwyn be of some help?"

"I doubt it. They're still recovering from the recent invasion."

"Don't tell me—the empire engineered that?"

"I don't think so," said Herdwin. "Weldwyn has always been at odds with the Clans. Then again, they timed their last invasion to perfection."

"Meaning?" said Wainwright.

"Leofric lost the Army of Weldwyn up in Norland, but someone had to have passed that information on to the Clans so they could take advantage of it. I'm not saying the empire was behind the invasion, but it certainly worked to their advantage."

"Will Ironcliff hold?"

"It should," said Kasri. "Then again, we never believed they'd be able to cross Kharzun's Folly."

"Yes," added Herdwin, "which is our biggest problem. The enemy is always one step ahead of us."

"These are dark times," said Wainwright, "but it's always darkest before the dawn. Have faith. The marshal will see us through this."

The carriage hit a rut, sending Gerald bouncing to his right, but Storm's bulk was enough to stop him from going too far. Albreda dozed across from him while Anna looked out the window, taking in the countryside, her mind elsewhere.

"It's been some time since we travelled this road," noted Gerald.

"It has."

"But..."

"Who says there's a but?"

"I know you too well, Anna. You're worried. You haven't spoken since we left Summersgate. I'd have expected you to be in full planning mode."

She met his gaze, but it wasn't the queen he saw; it was a frightened young woman. "What if we can't stop the invasion?"

"It's not like you to look at things in such a negative light."

"I can't help it. I've wracked my brain trying to find a way out of our predicament, but everywhere we turn for help, we run into a new problem."

"I'll not deny we've had our fair share of difficulties, but we've dealt with everything that's come our way in the past, and we'll do so again now."

"How can you be so certain?"

"Do you remember your history?"

"You know I have a perfect memory. What, exactly, are you getting at?"

"You're the new Evermore."

"Not quite," said Anna. "Queen Evermore was the wife of King Ansel the Second. Her actual name was Georgette; she only took the name Evermore when she accepted the Crown. I, on the other hand, was the queen's bastard child and took the Throne by force. Hardly the type of thing that will endear me to history."

"On the contrary," said Gerald. "You ushered in a golden age, as she did."

"Perhaps, but Queen Evermore only reigned for twenty years."

"True, but she was also much older when crowned."

"And many of her reforms were eliminated after her death. Is the same to happen to me?"

"I doubt that very much. You've solidified your position as queen, and the general population of Merceria loves you. What more could a monarch ask for?"

"A kingdom not constantly under threat of war?"

Albreda sat up suddenly. "War in the east," she said.

"What's that, now?" said Gerald.

"I've had one of my visions," replied the Druid. "War has come to the east."

"And?" pressed the queen.

"I'm not certain what it portends, but somehow it involves Beverly."

"A prophesy?" said Gerald. "You haven't had one in years."

"I haven't, which only makes this one more profound."

SEVENTEEN

Audience

SPRING 968 MC

"Spring is coming, don't you think?" Nevarus, the God-Emperor, turned to Janek. "Well?"

"It is most assuredly just around the corner, Eminence."

"You're only saying that so as not to upset me. I know the rules of court."

"No, it's true," replied his servant. "The days are growing warmer of late."

"I suppose that means we'll soon be inundated with rain."

"The Stormwinds predict a mild spring, Your Eminence."

"You would think an Air Mage better suited to predicting weather, but it is what it is. When am I to meet these Mercerians?"

"They are undergoing training even as we speak."

"No doubt by the time they're done, they'll be as bland as everyone else I meet. What can you tell me about them?"

"Lord Arnim Caster is the Viscount of Haverston, Your Eminence, which makes his wife the viscountess, although where that sits in their hierarchy, I couldn't say."

"A viscount is below an earl," replied Nevarus, "putting him above a baron, if I recall."

"Ah, yes. You are correct."

"Are Lord and Lady Caster barbaric?"

"No. They are most civilized, though, naturally, they are unfamiliar with our ways. I think you will find them to be intriguing."

"Then let's get them down here to meet me, shall we?"

"Eminence?"

Nevarus smiled. "I am the emperor, am I not?"

"You are, Eminence."

"See that they are brought to me here, at the Palace." He hesitated momentarily. "On second thought, have them brought to me at the Victory Fountain."

"But they are not ready!"

"I shall be the judge of that. Now go fetch them. I expect them this very day."

Janek swallowed. "Might I enquire when, precisely, you wish to see them?"

"I shall meet with them right after my midday meal." He paused. "Janek, you look like you're about to faint. Surely what I ask is a simple matter?"

"It shall be as you desire, Your Eminence. Might I ask who else would be in attendance?"

"No one of import. You'll be there, as will some of my personal guards, but I'll leave it up to you to select the most trustworthy individuals."

"I'm not sure I understand the implications, Eminence."

Nevarus let out a sigh. "I do not wish any of what transpires to be passed on to the members of my court. It's enough that I'm followed around night and day by soldiers. Can't I at least have some privacy?"

"Of course, Eminence." Janek bowed. "With your permission, I shall make all the necessary arrangements."

The emperor turned back to the window. A light dusting of snow covered the gardens, but the sun was already breaking through the clouds. Soon, the warmth of spring would return, and then he would take the steps necessary to reassert his authority.

He pondered his current circumstances. He'd inherited the position of emperor as his father had. They all bowed and scraped before him, but he wasn't so dim that he couldn't figure out what they were doing. Halvaria had once been an empire under the direct control of a true emperor. He was determined to see that status restored.

"Now?" said Arnim. "You can't be serious?"

"I'm afraid I am left with little choice," replied Janek. "He wishes to see you and Lady Nicole this very day."

"Why the sudden change of plans?"

The servant shrugged. "His Eminence can be fickle on occasion."

"Are we to be brought in chains?" asked Nikki.

"Of course not. His Eminence would never deign to be in the presence of a prisoner. You are to be considered his guests."

"Guests who are not allowed to wander around freely. To my mind, that makes us prisoners."

"Your confinement is for your own protection, my lady. Were you allowed to walk freely through the Palace, those you encounter within its halls might see you as an enemy of the empire."

"And where are we to meet His Eminence?"

"Outside, by the Victory Fountain," replied Janek. "I expect you'll wish to wear warm clothing; there is a chill in the air."

"What do you think, Arnim?"

"Let's go and meet an emperor, shall we?" He strode over to the wardrobe and pulled forth a long cloak, holding it out for his wife.

Janek watched impatiently, his foot tapping the floor in irritation. Once cloaked, Nikki turned to her husband and helped him on with one.

"Lead on, Janek," said Arnim. "Let's not keep your emperor waiting."

"By all means, my lord." The servant turned, then knocked on the door. It was opened by one of the five Imperial guards standing outside the room, all bedecked in the golden armour favoured for ceremonial occasions.

"Strange," said Nikki. "They remind me of the Hearth Guard of Ironcliff, only taller."

"And not as impressive," added her husband.

"This way," snapped Janek, then led them down the corridor.

Eventually, they exited the building and entered the vast gardens behind the Imperial Palace. Though snow remained on the ground, it was easy to imagine how they might look in full summer bloom.

Some two hundred paces from the Palace stood an immense fountain, topped by a winged Human with a wreath upon his head, holding a sword in one hand and a bolt of lightning in the other. More impressive was the individual sitting on the fountain's edge, dipping his fingers in the water.

The riot of green and gold he wore gave him an almost Elven quality. Four golden-clad warriors stood at a respectful distance, their eyes glued to the new arrivals.

At the sound of their approaching footsteps, the emperor turned. "Ah, Lord Arnim, Lady Nikki. I'm so glad you could see me."

"We could hardly refuse," replied Nikki, offering a bow.

Arnim merely nodded his head. "Eminence."

"You Mercerians are a fascinating folk. What do you know of your history?"

"We are descendants of mercenaries," replied Arnim, "but you knew that already."

"That and so much more. We are not so different, you and I. We are both from warrior cultures. Are you aware of our shared past?"

"I can't say that I am."

Nevarus smiled. "I thought as much. Your forebearers were, as you said, mercenaries. What you don't know is that Halvaria employed them."

"To what end?"

"Why, to fight. What else do mercenaries do? It was relatively early in our history and a period of great conflict. We often employed mercenaries to help subjugate our enemies."

"What happened?"

"Your ancestors turned on us, forcing us to take drastic action and hunt them down before they could do damage to the empire. A large group fled west to Zefara, the very same port you came in through. They commandeered ships and forced their crews to carry them west to the land that was then known as Terengaria. The rest, I assume, you know. I tell you this not out of any animosity but to acknowledge our shared history."

"What is it you want?" asked Nikki.

"You are very direct," replied Nevarus. "I find that refreshing." He looked skyward. "What I desire," he said at last, "is for Merceria to join us."

"Join you?"

"Why not? Are you not a warrior culture like us? Imagine what we could achieve by combining our forces?"

"Did you not think to extend this invitation before launching an all-out war on our allies?"

"I'll admit mistakes were made. It's what comes from giving my advisors too much freedom. However, I am sincere in my invitation to fight side by side with the Humans of your land."

"Humans?" said Nikki. "What about the other races within our borders: the Orcs, Elves, and Dwarves?"

Nevarus flinched. "The Orcs are a savage race, and the Elves have all but disappeared from the forests of Eiddenwerthe. As for the Dwarves, they can stay, providing they remain in their mountain homes."

"Have you ever met an Orc?"

The emperor stared back, unable to formulate an answer.

Janek stepped forward. "You must not speak thus to His Eminence."

"No," said Nevarus. "It is a fair question. I have not, in truth, met one of the green-skinned folk, but I have read accounts of their savage practices."

"Which practices would those be?"

"The execution of prisoners and the eating of Human flesh."

"They do not eat Human flesh," said Nikki. "And as for the execution of prisoners, they do that as a mercy."

"A mercy?"

"Healers are rarely part of a hunting party. They see execution as preferable to a slow and agonizing death."

"It is death, regardless."

"This only happens when their shamans cannot treat the wounded."

"I've walked amongst them," added Arnim, "and always found them an honourable people, more so than we Humans."

"That has not been our experience," replied Nevarus. "They are particularly resistant to our rule in the south, where our borders expand into the southern continent."

"Would you not resist if your empire was threatened?"

"I suppose I would." The emperor smiled. "I like you two. You challenge me."

"Let me go one step further," continued Nikki. "Have you ever tried to learn about these southern Orcs?"

"That is an excellent question. Janek, inform my advisors I wish to know everything we have concerning the greenskins." He hesitated. "Or rather, the Orcs. Elves, too, for that matter." The emperor returned his focus to Arnim. "We assumed the Elves were extinct until we discovered they still lived within your borders."

"And the Dwarves?" asked Arnim.

"We've had some run-ins with the mountain folk in past years. They are stubborn to the extreme, and we found them unpleasant to be around."

"Likely because you were trying to take away their land."

"Admittedly, we were, but they should know better than to build mines in our territory."

"Your territory?" said Nikki. "The Dwarves are one of the Elder Races, and they haven't built a new colony for centuries. Are you suggesting otherwise?"

Nevarus shrugged. "What can I say? We are destined to rule over all of Eiddenwerthe. They must be eliminated if they do not submit to our reign."

"Is that the fate awaiting Merceria?"

The emperor stared back at a loss for words. The idea that a god like him could be outwitted in such a manner was beyond his comprehension. The silence dragged on, and then Nevarus nodded. "You make me think, which is commendable, but I have had enough for today. You can take them away, Janek. We shall meet again once I've had time to consider their words."

Their escort turned around, indicating it was time to leave. Janek nodded, and then they marched off, Arnim and Nikki in the middle.

"That wasn't what I was expecting," said Arnim.

"I can't say his proposal was much of a surprise. Join us or die? What kind of an offer was that?"

"From what we've seen, I'm guessing he lives a very sheltered life."

"And?" pressed Nikki.

"He has some unusual ideas of what the outside world is like. He honestly believes he's destined to rule all of Eiddenwerthe."

"But he is," said Janek. "It was foretold long ago."

"That Nevarus would rule over all the known lands?"

"Not him personally, but the emperor, most certainly."

"How long ago?" asked Arnim.

"It has been foretold since the first days of the empire."

"And have none resisted his efforts?"

"Many tried," said Janek, "but we conquered them all in the end."

"Just not the Orcs in the south?" asked Nikki.

"I wouldn't care to comment. I have no expertise in such matters."

"What do you actually know about the lands to the south?"

"It is a great wilderness where dangers lurk that one can only imagine."

"Then why go there?"

"I beg your pardon?"

"If the land is nothing but wilderness, what is the empire's interest in it?"

"I cannot answer that," replied the servant, "but the Marshal of the South has his hands full dealing with it. Three legions are employed in that region at all times." He slowed. "You must understand that the empire is immense. You could place all the Petty Kingdoms within our borders and still have leftover space. It wasn't always that way, but a kingdom should be willing to go to war to preserve what it holds most dear. Isn't that what you Mercerians do?"

"How would you know that?" asked Arnim. "You are a servant, not a military advisor."

"True, but I am one of the few servants the emperor trusts. As such, I attend all his meetings, though I am seldom noticed."

"I wonder," said Nikki, "does he truly believe it's his destiny to rule over all of Eiddenwerthe?"

"Yes. This is the closest we've been in a thousand years to fulfilling our dream."

"And then what happens?"

"I beg your pardon?" replied Janek.

"What happens once you've conquered all the known lands?"

"We rule over them, and all shall be at peace."

"I highly doubt that," said Arnim.

"What makes you say that?"

"Your empire survives by expansion. Stop growing, and you'll soon find yourselves becoming stagnant. Were you successful in this campaign to conquer the Petty Kingdoms, you'd likely begin fighting each other. The emperor said it himself—you're a warlike culture. Without war, your legions have no purpose."

"We conquer to survive."

"You're already large enough that no one can threaten you, so why not sit back and enjoy the fruits of your labour?"

"Because the law of nature is that the strong rule the weak. If we do not constantly demonstrate our strength, another realm would soon try to replace us. Is that not true of your home?"

"I'll admit we're a warlike people," said Arnim, "but we've taken great strides towards bringing peace to our region."

"Through conquest, no doubt."

"No," said Nikki, "through diplomacy. For the most part, we've attempted to aid our traditional enemies rather than invade them. It hasn't always worked, but our successes far outweigh our failures."

"But if you revealed a weakness, how many of those old enemies would resurface?"

"Our queen counts our success by the number of our allies, not enemies."

"Yet your lands will soon be under the rule of our emperor."

"I would not be so fast to count your victory," said Arnim. "Your empire may be vast, but that merely stretches your legions over a large area. One spark of rebellion and the whole thing comes crashing down all around you."

EIGHTEEN

The Duke

SPRING 968 MC

The warm westerly breeze was a pleasant respite from the chilly winds that were the hallmark of the winter season. Beverly slowed Lightning, taking in the massive estate they headed towards.

"This place looks larger than the Palace at Wincaster."

"Perhaps in terms of ground area," said Aubrey, "but it appears to be a single floor."

"The duke's estate is legendary," offered Sir Owen. "They say it's one of the most expensive Royal residences in all the Petty Kingdoms."

"Royal?" said Aldwin. "I thought he was only a duke?"

"He might as well be a king, considering the size of his lands. Erlingen is one of the larger Petty Kingdoms."

"Then why doesn't he call himself one?"

"I have no idea."

They passed through the impressive gate, which had been thrown open to admit visitors. The guards standing nearby watched with intense interest but made no move to stop them.

"We're not the only ones here today," said Aubrey, pointing at all the carriages.

"They belong to the barons," replied Owen. "If I remember correctly, the duke celebrates the anniversary of his coronation this time every year."

"I thought we were coming here just to meet him."

The knight shrugged. "Can't he do both? He's a busy man, especially with the empire breathing down his neck."

"It'll only get worse," said Beverly. "The snow is disappearing so fast the roads will soon be clear, which can only help the empire's progress. I fear the duke needs to march if he hopes to stop them from crossing his borders."

"Ah, you came. How delightful." A mailed knight in a brown surcoat bearing a white axe, the symbol of Saint Mathew, waved from atop the steps. It took them a moment to realize it was Brother Cyric, for he'd forgone his usual brown cassock. "His Grace, the Duke, is preparing to address everyone. These fellows will take your horses, and then I'll show you the way."

They all dismounted, passed the reins to the stable hands, and then followed the Temple Knight into the building.

"This is quite the place," said Aldwin, marvelling at the extravagant décor. "The duke must be wealthy indeed."

"He is," replied Cyric, "or at least his father was. Lord Alain is said to be less extravagant than his predecessor."

"Why is that?"

"I believe it was his mother's influence. She was originally from Andover."

"Is the duchess here tonight?" asked Aubrey.

"Oh, Alain's mother died some years ago under questionable circumstances, which led to a war."

"Questionable?"

"She drowned out in the river when her boat capsized."

"She couldn't swim?"

"Not in courtly attire, I'm afraid."

"How did that lead to a war?"

"Lord Deiter took a mistress from Reinwick," explained Cyric, "the woman who now holds the title of duchess. There were accusations that he arranged the death of Alain's mother to marry his mistress. As you can imagine, that didn't sit well with the court of Andover."

"And how does the current duke feel about the entire affair?"

"In a word—bitter. He banished his father's second wife from court, with a stipend involved; he's not completely heartless to her plight, but he has no desire to be in her company."

They entered a large ballroom packed with nobles, warriors, and even members of the Church. His Grace, the Duke, was at one end, standing on a set of stairs to allow him to look out over his subjects.

"He's not as young as I imagined," said Beverly. "From your description, I expected a younger man."

"You must remember," replied Cyric, "his father ruled for many years."

"Did he have any other children from his second wife?"

"I'm afraid not," added Owen. "His Grace came up short in that regard. It's why he wanted to get rid of his first wife."

"She bore him a son."

"She did," agreed Cyric, "his only one, but a single heir can often be problematic in the Petty Kingdoms, especially with rampant disease. Most rulers prefer two or three, then marry off the spares once their eldest continues the line."

"And is Lord Alain married?"

"I don't believe so."

"Why?" asked Owen. "Interested?"

"No," replied Beverly. "I'm already married to Aldwin, as you well know."

"Marriages can be annulled," countered Owen.

"Now you're just being insulting."

"Sorry. I sometimes forget your customs are different from the Petty Kingdoms."

Aldwin shook his head. "I'll never get used to your way of looking at things."

"You have to understand most marriages amongst the nobility are arranged affairs. A man and woman often marry without ever seeing each other."

"Why?"

"Politics," replied Owen. "Surely you have that back home?"

"We did," said Beverly, "but our present queen doesn't force marriages on people."

"Althea married a Clan chief," Aubrey reminded her.

"She did, but it was her own idea, not the king's."

"But he did go along with it."

"He had little choice in the matter. You've met Althea. She can be as stubborn as… Well, as Queen Anna herself. I mean that in only the most respectful way."

Aubrey chuckled. "The word you're looking for is decisive rather than stubborn."

Beverly opened her mouth to reply, but a horn sounded, silencing all in the room.

"Lord Alain Heinrich, Duke of Erlingen," announced a voice.

The duke scanned the crowd before speaking. "Greetings, everyone. No doubt, you've all heard the news, but several false rumours are floating around, so I'll start by giving you the facts."

He took a deep breath as he gathered his thoughts. "Some weeks ago, Halvaria crossed the border into Gotfeld. Unlike the empire's previous campaigns, this one came without warning. They arrived in significant numbers, marching straight on the capital. King Argalin met the invasion outside the village of Rasgalen, where they annihilated his army."

He paused, letting the crowd discuss the news, then held up his hands. The room fell into a hush once more.

"Halvaria has since pushed into Rudor, destroying another army attempting to stand in their way. Our last report is that they turned east, marching towards Angvil, making it abundantly clear they are intent on reaching us here, in Erlingen. Make no mistake—this is a grave threat, but we cannot seek out the enemy until we muster our army. To that end, I call on the barons of Erlingen to march their warriors here, to Torburg, so we can face this threat in numbers that guarantee victory."

A cheer went up; though, to Beverly's ears, it sounded half-hearted. The duke descended the stairs, vanishing from sight as the rest of the crowd broke into groups to discuss the news.

"Come," said Cyric. "Let me introduce you to His Grace, Lord Alain."

They weaved their way through the duke's guests, conversations stopping as attendees noticed the Orc accompanying them. They encountered their host conversing with one of his younger nobles.

"Ah, Brother Cyric," said the duke. "I see you've brought me some visitors."

"Indeed, Your Grace. Allow me to introduce General Beverly Fitzwilliam of Merceria. She is accompanied by her husband, Lord Aldwin, and her cousin, Lady Aubrey Brandon, a Life Mage. They come from a land far to the west known as Merceria. You may know Sir Owen, as he was knighted by your father and has been active on the circuit for the past few months. Last, and most certainly not least, we have Krazuhk, a master of air."

The duke stared back, open-mouthed, then recovered quickly, breaking into a grin. "Welcome, all of you. Did you say general?"

"Indeed, Your Grace. I thought she might be of some assistance to you as she has extensive battle experience."

"I should very much welcome your thoughts, Lady Beverly." His gaze flicked to Aldwin momentarily, raising an eyebrow when he noticed the grey eyes, but he didn't let it dampen his spirits. "Your arrival is most fortuitous. Are you familiar with the empire where you're from?"

"When we left our home, they'd started massing on our borders. Since arriving here, we've learned their invasion of our land has commenced."

"You learned how? I thought Brother Cyric said your land was far to the west. How, then, would you receive word?"

"Through the use of magic," replied Aubrey. "I'll spare you the details, but suffice it to say, I can contact mages in my homeland whenever I wish."

"What brought you to Erlingen?"

"We were marooned here through an accident and have been attempting to travel to Reinwick to seek a ship capable of taking us home."

"I doubt any ships would be willing to take you west, not with the empire on the warpath. The Great Northern Sea will soon become a Halvarian lake."

"Do not underestimate the Temple Fleet," said Cyric. "They defeated the empire before, and I'm confident they'll do so again."

"While I admire your faith, Brother, we cannot afford to underestimate the enemy."

"If you don't mind me asking," said Beverly, "how large is your army?"

"Each baron is required to muster between two and three hundred warriors, depending on their individual holdings. In addition, there are my own household troops, which number some four hundred souls."

"And how many barons have you?"

"Twelve in total," replied the duke, "although four of them are too small to offer any significant contribution of men. Theoretically, the other eight will give me somewhere in the range of twenty-four hundred warriors to deal with this invader. That is, I believe, equal in number to an entire Halvarian legion."

"Might I enquire how they're to be commanded?"

"Each baron commands their own people, and I, in turn, command them. Why do you ask?"

"In Merceria, the army comes under the exclusive control of the marshal, a seasoned leader. Have you a similar position here?"

"A few of my nobles saw battle in the last invasion, but they're mostly inexperienced. What of yourself?"

"I've led warriors most of my adult life. Merceria has experienced little peace these last few years."

"I shan't mince words. I have no military experience, nor am I particularly skilled with weapons, but I pride myself on my ability to adapt to changing circumstances. Might I ask what you would do if you were me?"

"That," said Beverly, "depends on far too many things for a quick answer."

"Things, such as..."

"The terrain in question, the quality of troops under your command, and their breakdown, not to mention the composition of this legion you intend to face."

"These are all questions I can answer in due time, but I would need my advisors and, more importantly, maps. Can I invite you to meet me here in a few days? There will be ample time to discuss these things once the barons leave to gather their men."

"I should be delighted, Your Grace."

"Good," replied Lord Alian. "Please excuse me, for I must speak with each of my barons before any take offence at being ignored. I hope you understand?"

Beverly bowed. "I do, Your Grace."

"Then I look forward to seeing you later in the week. My people will be in touch." He turned, making his way into the thick of the crowd.

The noble with whom he'd been chatting extended his hand. "I don't believe we've met. My name's Lord Hagan Stein, Baron of Mulsingen, and this is my wife, Lady Rosalyn."

"Pleased to meet you."

"I must confess," said Lady Rosalyn. "I've never met a female general before. Is that common where you come from?"

"As far as I know, I'm the only one, but surely the Temple Knights of Saint Agnes have generals, or do they use a different title?"

"I suppose they do, although I've never heard of them naming one. However, the Cunars have plenty, though they prefer the term, Father General."

"Are there any Cunars here?"

"Unfortunately not, otherwise we'd be able to count them amongst our numbers. The Temple Knights of Saint Mathew might supply a company or two, and we'd be thankful for their support, but it's not the same. I mean, they wear such archaic armour, it is a wonder they'd be any good at all." She noted the presence of Cyric. "My apologies, Brother. I didn't mean to offer insult."

"Think nothing of it, my lady. It's not the first time I've heard such remarks. You are right not to count on the Temple Knights of Saint Cunar's support. They have seen fit to withdraw their presence from Erlingen."

"Might I ask why?" said Beverly.

"I prefer not to delve into Church politics, but our brother order has taken offence to the presence of my order here in Erlingen. Are you plagued by similar problems back in Merceria, Lady Beverly?"

"We have no religious orders, but when it comes to politics, there are those who disagree with the queen's policies, some more vocally than others."

"I fear it's much the same across the Petty Kingdoms. Ultimately, it all comes down to the nobility. Get more than a dozen together, and they'll soon be at each other's throats."

"You surprise me," said Aubrey. "If your manner of speaking is any indication, you're nobly born, yet you speak so poorly of them."

"I gave up that life when I joined the order. Regarding the nobility of the Petty Kingdoms, there are a few good souls, but most think more of themselves than others."

"There are people like that back home," replied Beverly, "but our queen surrounds herself with those who share her vision."

"That vision being?"

"A land ruled on behalf of her subjects, not despite them."

"She sounds like a remarkable woman," said Cyric. "If only the rest of the Continent did likewise. Still, our order does its best to promote common decency. Perhaps we can look forward to happier times once the empire is finally defeated."

"You mean if," said Lord Hagan. "We've yet to assemble our army, let alone beat them on the battlefield."

Rosalyn placed her hand on Hagan's shoulder. "My husband is one of the few who fought at Chermingen and still bears the scars to this day."

"True," said Hagan. "I was in the thick of it, yet don't claim to be a hero like some." He lowered his voice. "You shall hear the name Sir Galrath of Paledon bandied about when speaking about the battle, but the truth is Ludwig Altenburg captured the King of Andover."

"I know that name," said Cyric.

"I would hope so. He's the King of Hadenfeld."

"I knew him as well," added Rosalyn. "He served my father."

"And he's now King of Hadenfeld?" Beverly asked. "Is it a large kingdom?"

"One of the largest," said Hagan. "Though it has been under tremendous strain of late."

"Would they be willing to help fight off Halvaria?"

"I doubt it. They underwent a rebellion recently, the second in only a few years. Given those circumstances, the last thing he'd want to do is send his army away." He paused a moment. "I wonder, would you consider observing my warriors and giving me your opinion?"

"Had the duke not already asked me to review his strategy, I would've been pleased to."

"How about once they arrive in Torburg?"

"I would be happy to."

"Excellent. I look forward to your insights. Now, you must excuse us. We are headed back to Mulsingen to collect our men."

"How long will it take to assemble the army?"

"Weeks yet, possibly even an entire month. Why?"

"Will the enemy wait that long?"

"They shall have to if we are to succeed."

Beverly held on to Aldwin's arm as they descended the steps. Carriages lined up before the estate, waiting to ferry the visitors back to their homes. Somewhere down there were their horses, but the hour was late, and the darkness hid them from view.

"Well?" she said. "What did you think?"

"Of what?" replied her husband. "The duke, the baron, the Temple Knight, or this war we're about to be embroiled in?"

"Any or all, and who says we'll get involved?"

"I know you better than that. They're fighting the empire; they'd be fools not to ask for your help."

"I'm no one here," Beverly replied. "As far as they're concerned, I'm just a woman who wears armour."

"Hardly that. That baron, what's-his-name, seemed impressed."

"You mean Lord Hagan? Perhaps."

"His wife was nice," added Aubrey from behind them. "I get the feeling she's very involved with running the barony."

"Perhaps that's how they do things in the Petty Kingdoms?"

"No," replied Owen. "It's not. Generally, noble wives are for giving birth to heirs."

"Can they not do both?"

"I suppose they can, though admittedly, I'm no expert at such things."

Aubrey laughed.

"What's so funny?"

"Sorry, but it doesn't take a genius to understand how children are born."

Owen looked away as his cheeks reddened. "That's not what I meant."

"My apologies," said Aubrey, "but you must admit, it was an entertaining thought. Speaking of which, when can we expect to see an heir for Bodden, Cousin?"

"Oh, look," said Beverly. "There are our horses. Come along, you lot. We've got things to do."

NINETEEN

Mirstone

SPRING 968 MC

"I t's great to be back in the saddle!" Anna appeared in a good mood despite the threat to the borders of her kingdom.

Gerald sat stiffly astride his mount. "I wouldn't mind so much if I could've brought my own horse."

"It's a poor rider who blames his mount," said Albreda. "It's far more likely your advanced years are causing you discomfort."

"Thanks for reminding me. I never would have guessed."

"Well, at least you have the satisfaction of knowing you're not the oldest one here."

"Let's not bicker," said the queen.

They rounded a hill, and off in the distance sat Mirstone, with homes built into the side of a great cliff—perhaps carved was a more apt description. A low wall, roughly Gerald's height, came out from this cliff, and the only towers were the two guarding the gate.

Gerald glanced over his shoulder to where the queen's two guards stood on the back of the carriage within which Storm slept. He thought travelling with so few guards unwise, but Anna insisted, saying they came to Mirstone to ask for help, not overwhelm them with displays of pageantry.

The gates opened as they approached, allowing them entry. Much to their surprise, a winding road led through fields, though no crops grew at present. A great stone structure jutted out from the cliff, and outside it stood Lord Tulfar, the very person they came to speak with.

"Your Majesty," Tulfar called out. "I'm surprised to see you here. To what do I owe the honour of your visit?"

They halted their horses, dismounted, and passed the reins off to a pair of Dwarves who advanced to take them.

"We've come to see you, my lord," said Anna. "We seek your aid."

"Have you, now? Then we'd best head inside and discuss the matter." He moved closer, offering a bow. "Your men can go over yonder." He pointed at a building built into the cliff, this one at ground level. "It's called the Stone Tankard; it's a beer hall. Don't worry. My people will watch them to ensure they don't overindulge."

"Thank you. You know my marshal, Lord Gerald, and everyone knows Albreda."

"Of course, Majesty. Good to see you again, Your Grace." Tulfar bowed deeply to Albreda. "I must confess it's an absolute honour to have the Lady of the Whitewood amongst us."

"I like this fellow," said the Druid. "But then again, I find the majority of the mountain folk I've met most sensible." She went silent for a moment. "I wonder, Lord Tulfar, if I might beg a favour?"

"Of course, Mistress."

"I am most interested in seeing this mine of yours. Would someone be able to show me around while the rest of you discuss matters?"

A Dwarf stepped forward. "Allow me, my lord."

"Ah," said Tulfar. "I can think of no one better suited. Caldrim commands a company of arbalesters. His brother, Haldrim, does as well, although he's off keeping Princess Althea safe amongst the Clans. I trust that meets with your approval?"

"It does," replied Albreda. "Thank you."

"In that case, I shall leave you to it. Your Majesty, let me show you the hospitality of the Dwarves." Gerald and Anna followed him inside the grand fortress, where thick carpet lined the entrance hall, and carved stone statues of Dwarven warriors watched all who entered. Tulfar led them to a door on one side, opening it to reveal a much smaller room, complete with a fireplace and oversized chairs.

"Please, take a seat. My guards will find us something to drink while we talk."

"This place does you credit," said the queen. "Though I read reports from the war, I never expected the Fortress of Mirstone to be so opulent."

"Fortress? This place is merely a mine, Majesty, albeit one that's been our home for many centuries. It predates Weldwyn, you know."

"Yes," replied Anna. "I've read up on some of Weldwyn's history since the Clan invasion. I understand Mirstone stood with Weldwyn when they fought off us Mercerians?"

"We did, though admittedly, you weren't our allies then; you were foreigners, come to plunder our land. Now, you're the kingdom's greatest ally, not to mention our queen."

"You are too kind. The truth is I hold no power in Weldwyn."

"Don't be thinking that," said Tulfar. "You may have no official powers as the Queen of Weldwyn, but you wield tremendous influence and are married to our king. But enough of these pleasantries. Let's talk about the real reason you came here."

"Have you heard about the invasion?"

"From this Halvaria place? I have. I understand you've sent aid to both Ironcliff and Stonecastle, which must put a significant strain on your army."

"It did, and now the enemy has landed on the coast at Trollden, although we've prevented them from moving upriver."

"But that won't last now that the river is thawing," added Gerald.

"I'm surprised the Trolls lasted that long," said Tulfar. "Then again, the terrain there is all swamp. Not the most suitable to conduct an invasion."

"True," replied Anna, "but we think they're waiting for the spring thaw to make a major push northwards, possibly to coincide with further advances at both Dwarf mines."

"It appears they wish to force you into abandoning your allies. I imagine the results would be catastrophic."

"They would," agreed Gerald. "Not to mention success in the south would put Weldwyn at risk."

"I assume the earls offered the king no troops to aid you?"

"That is correct," said Anna, "but Lord Parvan believed you might be of some assistance."

"Your warriors were effective during the war," added Gerald, "particularly at the Siege of Summersgate. I don't suppose we could convince you to send them south to help stop this invasion before it gets inland?"

"That's a tall order," replied Tulfar. "During the war, we fielded four companies of warriors, half arbalesters, but I'm afraid a quarter of them were sent west into the Clanholdings to keep Princess Althea safe." The door opened, and two warriors entered, bearing trays of food and drink. He waited as they set them down, then dismissed them.

"Tell me more about the invasion in the south. How many men were involved?"

"We believe there is in excess of two thousand facing us."

"And your own numbers?"

"The Troll Commander, Tog, has three companies of his people and two Queen's Rangers. Assuming everything is going as planned, Lord Preston should've reinforced him with four hundred more."

"Those are pretty steep odds," said the Dwarf. "Are you certain that's enough?"

"It's all we can afford to send him, hence why we're here today."

Tulfar sat back, running his hand through his beard. "You'll need substantially more than a hundred and fifty Dwarves."

"Does that mean you won't help us?" asked Anna.

"No. I'll help, but it's pointless to send so few warriors. If I commit Dwarves to the fight, I'd like to ensure they have a better than average chance of survival."

"What are you saying, precisely?"

"When we marched to help liberate Summersgate, we only sent our most experienced warriors because we needed to keep some in Mirstone in case the enemy attacked. The garrison then consisted of axe wielders and archers, not the arbalesters we're so well-known for. I propose sending all the warriors we can spare, including these less-experienced Dwarves. They wouldn't be as effective as our veterans, but I reckon they could still hold their own in a fight."

"How many are we talking about?"

"With a few days' preparation, we could manage an expedition of four hundred, of which half would be these less-experienced individuals."

"Who would command them?" asked Gerald.

"I would, at least for the march, though I hoped you might see to their disposition once we face the enemy."

"I would be honoured."

"Good," said Tulfar. "Then it's settled. I shall give the order for the ovens to commence baking."

"The ovens?"

"You can't expect a Dwarf army to march without stonecakes to fill their bellies."

Anna stood. "Thank you, Lord Tulfar. Merceria is greatly indebted to you."

"On the contrary, it is you that I have to thank."

"For what, might I ask?"

"Your influence led the king to hear our pleas for representation."

"Yet you're still not ranked as an earl."

Tulfar shrugged. "Progress is slow, but we Dwarves are patient. The important thing is that the first step was taken, and though the road may be long, the journey has begun."

"You're becoming quite the philosopher," said Gerald.

"I can't help it. It's what comes from reaching a certain age." He lifted the end of his beard. "Look at all the grey hair!"

"I think I have you beat on that score."

"Aye. At least it puts me in good company. Now, you must excuse me. Preparations have to be made if we intend to be on the road in short order. As for you two, stay and enjoy the food and drink. When you're done, someone will show you to guest quarters." With that, he left, quietly closing the door behind him.

"That was not what I expected," remarked Anna.

"Four hundred," said Gerald. "Even if they aren't all veterans, that's still a significant contribution."

"How would you like to proceed?"

"The best strategy is to march east to Aldgrave, then head south, crossing at Colbridge. If the enemy has advanced north, they'll still have to siege the city, and we can reinforce from the Weldwyn side of the river if need be."

"It will take time to ferry everyone across."

"We really should see about building a bridge down there."

"That's a bit complicated," replied Anna. "It would have to be a drawbridge to allow ships upriver. Perhaps we should talk to Tulfar about it? Dwarves are said to be the best engineers."

"True, but I doubt they have much experience with bridges. Most live in the mountains or hills, like in Mirstone. Not exactly the terrain that requires bridges."

"I think they could rise to the challenge. In any case, it's a long-term goal, not something in our immediate future. How we go about fighting these Halvarians is of more concern."

"I've been pondering that for some time," said Gerald. "Based on what I've learned since the attack on Ironcliff, these Halvarian legions employ remarkably more cavalry than us. If we're going to fight them, we need a way to neutralize that particular threat."

"Preston has the Kurathian Mastiffs."

"He does, but we'll have to use them sparingly. Once the Halvarians face them in battle, they'll adjust their tactics, and we'll lose our advantage."

"Their cavalry will be next to useless in the swamp."

"Agreed," said Gerald, "but they might dismount them and use them as extra footmen, but I didn't intend to face them in the swamp. I can hardly expect the Dwarves to fight in such terrain. Instead, I shall lure them north onto ground of our choosing."

"But the road to Colbridge is flat." She saw him smile. "You're going ask Albreda to use her magic."

"I am. You saw the reports from Heward. With a couple of mounds, it would be the perfect place to mount a defence."

"And if they come upriver?"

"I have a solution, but I'm afraid it'll be expensive."

"Expensive, how?"

"Let's just say that some merchants will have to be recompensed for losses."

"You never cease to amaze me, Gerald. You can take the worst circumstances and turn it into a victory."

"Victory? We shouldn't count our eggs before they hatch. There's a lot of work to do to put this plan of mine into action. Let's start by seeing if our host has any maps of the region."

Albreda looked deep into the pit, where steps had been carved around its interior, allowing the option of descending on foot. However, the mass of gears connected to a large winch was far more impressive. "How far down does this go?" she asked.

"All the way to the bottom," replied Caldrim, laughing. "Sorry. I couldn't resist. The main shaft leads to the deeper levels of the mine, and the lift can carry ten workers down a distance of five hundred feet. The shaft goes farther, but the engineers say the strain on the cable becomes too great at that point, so they have to proceed on foot."

"What, precisely, do you mine down there?"

"Many things. That's what makes us unique. We have iron ore, but the real profit is silver and precious gems."

"Any gold?"

"Some, though not in any great quantities. It's mainly used for coins or jewellery, but I notice you don't wear any."

"Correct," replied Albreda, "but gold is employed in the creation of magic circles."

"How much gold?"

"I couldn't tell you the exact amount, but I once heard our smith say we needed buckets of the stuff. It's inlaid in the circle to hold the magic during casting."

"I've seen the circle in Summersgate," said Caldrim. "We'd have no problem supplying enough for all your needs."

"But I thought you just said you didn't produce it in great quantities?"

"We don't, but we've accumulated a lot over the last hundred years."

"Do you not turn it into coins?"

"We supply the gold used in Weldwyn's coins, but that has to be carefully controlled, or we risk upsetting everyone's finances."

"Wouldn't the same be true if you sold the gold to us?"

"Ah, but you'd be paying in Mercerian coins that we can then turn around and use to purchase goods from you."

"What goods are you looking for?"

"A variety of things, but mostly food. We Dwarves have an insatiable appetite, and while we can survive on what we grow, it doesn't give us the greatest variety to choose from."

"I'm certain the queen would be most amenable to such an exchange."

"Shall we go deeper?"

"Most certainly," replied Albreda.

"I must admit to some surprise. I was under the impression you'd spent most of your life in the wilderness, and surely being surrounded by stone would be uncomfortable for you?"

"Nonsense. Although some call me a Druid, I still use Earth Magic, and the last time I checked, it included manipulating stone. Not that I do so very often, you understand, but your work here has inspired me."

"Is it true you're a wild mage?"

"I am, but bear in mind that only means I am not bound by a restrictive mindset."

"I'm not sure I understand?"

"Most mages are taught a rigorous set of rules concerning the use of magic, whereas I am freed from those preconceived ideas, allowing me to push beyond the boundary of a closed mind."

"I've heard you are the most powerful mage in all of Eiddenwerthe."

"I don't know if I would go that far," said Albreda, "although it might be true for Merceria. I'm capable of even greater power when within the Whitewood."

"Why is that?"

"I'm not entirely certain. I suppose I have an affinity for it as if it's in my bones."

"You mean your blood, don't you? Doesn't magic pass down through the generations?"

"So all the great scholars claim, yet to my knowledge, there were no mages amongst my family. Some believe magic is released through great tragedy, and Saxnor knows I've had more than my fair share of that! However, I don't put much credence in the words of scholars when it comes to magic. After all, how can one who doesn't wield it themselves possibly understand it? Has Mirstone ever had mages?"

"So I've been told, though long before I was born. You can see the evidence of their magic here, particularly the large surface vents. They worked closely with our engineers to bring air to the deeper levels through a series of bellows. Their operation has been explained to me numerous times, but it's as if they speak an entirely different language, one full of numbers and weight distributions. Still, you have to admit, they do fine work."

"They do indeed. You know a good deal about this mine, especially considering you're a warrior."

"My mother was an engineer, but she died when a tunnel flooded. Despite all their knowledge, there's still no reliable way of discovering the presence of underground waterways."

"I'm sorry for your loss."

"It was many years ago."

"And is your father still alive?"

"He is. He's a member of the miners guild, which is how he met my mother." Caldrim peered down into the pit. "He's likely down there somewhere, overseeing the work. Would you like to meet him?"

"Most definitely."

TWENTY

Battle

SPRING 968 MC

"Why are we not yet in Erlingen?" asked Edora.

Four legion commanders stared back, but only Moreau dared to answer. "Can you not see the rain outside? The rivers are flooding, the roads have turned to mud, and we possess no accurate maps of the area."

"The strategy is simple. You march east. You can see the sun, can't you?"

"I can distinguish east from west, but there are rivers aplenty in the Petty Kingdoms, and you can't cross them wherever you please. Furthermore, the enemy has employed a new tactic."

"Which is?"

"The common folk are removing all road signs and markers. It's made it difficult to determine our actual progress."

"Then interrogate the locals and force them to provide the necessary information."

"We tried, Your Grace, but the farther we go into the Petty Kingdoms, the more stubborn the people become. Even so, our estimates indicate we are making reasonable progress."

"We are still not where we should be!" Edora looked at the other commander-generals, but they avoided her gaze. "What do you need to rectify this deficiency?"

"We have defeated all who stood in our way," replied Moreau, "but as we push into the heart of enemy territory, there is progressively more terrain to watch. The Ninth needs closer support from the Eleventh Legion."

"That won't happen," replied Commander-General Korvin Bandros. "We are far too busy pacifying Rudor. It's easy enough for your legion to push into Angvil, but we're left to clean up after you. And don't bother accusing the Eighth; they're hunting down rebels in Gotfeld. Men who, had you not rushed the job, wouldn't be alive to cause us so much grief."

"There is still the Fifth," suggested Hamath Nordin. "My men are well-rested and capable of marching, should Your Grace permit it."

"You are tasked with occupying the conquered territory," replied Edora, "not marching into Erlingen."

"Can we not do both? The Eleventh is stalled in Rudor, while the Eighth is currently engaged in this horseplay. Does Rakert need an entire legion to chase down a few rebels? Let their cavalry deal with the troublemakers and assign the footmen to garrisoning the cities and towns of Gotfeld, freeing up my legion to assist the Ninth."

"Your proposal has merit. What do you think, Moreau?"

"It's an excellent idea, Your Grace, though I wonder how the roads will fare. Thanks to the boots and hooves of our legion, they're in terrible shape. I shudder to think what two legions would do to them."

"Then the Fifth shall take a parallel course, assuming there is one," said Edora. "In that way, their presence may escape the attention of our enemies. Then, when the trap is set, the two legions converge and eradicate all resistance."

"An excellent plan. Have we any new information concerning the so-called Northern Alliance?"

"Our agents in Andover report they have yet to issue orders to muster their forces. That was two weeks ago, so there's always the possibility they've heard of our progress. We estimate it would take them at least a month to gather their armies, then add to that the complication of two armies marching under one banner. Not long ago, these kingdoms were at war with each other, a situation our agents will seek to exploit, leaving us ample time to deal with Erlingen before we worry about the alliance."

"I'm not convinced," said Nordin. "You speak of Erlingen and this alliance as if they're the only threats. What about the other Petty Kingdoms?"

"Arnsfeld won't march," replied Edora, "not after the pasting we gave Rudor and Gotfeld. Oh, they might contribute some troops to their allies, but even during the debacle of the previous invasion, they didn't field significant numbers."

"Then how did they defeat us?"

"Because of the Marshal of the North's shortsightedness. It would've been an entirely different outcome if he attacked with a second legion. We have four legions for this campaign, giving us close to ten thousand warriors. Even if all the Petty Kingdoms combined forces, they couldn't hope to reach those numbers."

"What is Burgemont's army like?" asked Moreau. "And can we expect them to come to the aid of Erlingen?"

"Their army numbers less than one thousand, most of which consists of poorly equipped footmen, the vast majority being little more than a local militia. There is a small cadre of knights, less than fifty. I expect they will remain within Burgemont, providing we don't cross their border."

"If we are to conquer the Continent, we must still deal with their army, however small."

"Eventually," replied Edora, "but we can eliminate them later once we've destroyed the principal threats." She glanced around the room, stopping at Commander Rakert. "You've been very quiet. Anything you'd care to add?"

The commander-general regarded his peers. "The Eighth stands ready to take whatever action you deem necessary, Your Grace."

"That's it? No concerns regarding the upcoming campaign?"

"You have obviously spent a lot of time devising this plan. It is not my place to criticize it. After all, you're the battle mage here; the rest of us are mere servants of the empire."

"How long will it take to pacify the rebels in Gotfeld?"

"I have every confidence the recent arrival of purifiers will soon see an end to our problems in that regard."

"Your tone suggests you hold some reservations."

"An army of occupation is still required, Your Grace, though I daresay it wouldn't need to be so concentrated. I propose that by next month, we can take over subjugation duties in Rudor, thus freeing up the Eighth for employment elsewhere. That would, I believe, give you three legions with which to crush our enemies."

"Finally, good news, at last! I shall hold you to that timetable, Rakert. Now, we must consider how to deal with Erlingen. Theoretically, they can field numbers equivalent to an entire legion, but I doubt the duke would be willing to leave his own lands undefended, which means, if we lure him out into Angvil, we can reduce his numbers. Ultimately, the plan is to bring the Ninth and Fifth together at the last moment and overwhelm him."

"That won't be easy," said Moreau. "They have friendly eyes in that part of the country; keeping our location a secret will prove difficult."

"Nonsense," said Rakert. "Use your cavalry to cut off all the roads."

"They could still travel cross country," insisted Moreau.

"At a greatly reduced speed, making any information they carry out of date by the time it reaches our enemies."

"I don't think you appreciate the difficulty involved in carrying out this idea of yours."

"Then ignore it," replied Rakert. "It's not as if I'm your superior."

"I'll have no more arguing," said Edora. "We're on the same side here. We should be working together to develop the best overall strategy."

"Ah, there you have it," said Bandros. "Strategy is the marshal's domain, not us lowly commander-generals."

"A good battle mage seeks suggestions from those under her command."

"But you've already settled on a strategy, which begs the question: why are we even here?"

Edora closed her eyes and took a deep breath. The legion commanders stood at the pinnacle of their careers, yet all they did was argue with each other. She opened her eyes to see them all watching her closely.

"My strategy hasn't changed," she said at last, "but I have amended it to include a second prong to increase our chances of success."

"Chances?" replied Moreau. "Are you suggesting the Ninth cannot deal with Erlingen alone?"

"Have you not heard this entire discussion?" said Rakert.

Edora felt stretched to the breaking point. "Enough! The both of you. I shall remove you from command if you start bickering again." Rakert backed down, but Moreau still wore a look of contempt; she'd have to tread lightly or risk losing his loyalty. "Commander-General Moreau, should you see the opportunity to attack the duke's army on favourable ground, then by all means, take it, but do not force the encounter if the enemy has picked the terrain."

"I might remind you I did just that in Gotfeld, twice!"

"And the empire is pleased by your success, but the armies of Gotfeld and Rudor were at a significant numerical disadvantage. That will most certainly not be the case with Erlingen."

"If I'm not mistaken, the current duke there is inexperienced in battle."

"That is true," replied Edora, "but other, more recent developments could negate that lack."

"Those being?"

"We've received word of a Mercerian general in Erlingen."

"What of it?"

"She has a record of fighting against the odds and coming out victorious."

"Even if that were true," said Moreau, "I doubt the duke would hire a foreigner to lead his army."

"Evidence suggests a Temple Knight may be orchestrating precisely that."

"The Church? I thought we'd dealt with the Temple Knights?"

"Did you not fight them at Saints Crossing?"

"Only those from Saint Agnes, and in limited quantities."

"I hadn't heard that," said Rakert. "Weren't the Cunars supposed to prevent them from interfering?"

"According to prisoners, they came from Arnsfeld. The Cunars have no presence there."

"Ah, yes. The Temple Knights of Saint Agnes. Wasn't the order broken up by the Church?"

"It was," said Edora, "but several realms choose to ignore that edict. There is also the matter of the lost companies."

"What do you mean, lost?" asked Rakert.

"They cannot be accounted for."

"Surely that supports the argument that they've been disbanded?"

"They rode out of the Antonine as one," replied Edora. "There was an attempt to stop them, but ultimately, they were outmanoeuvred."

"When was this?"

"Some time ago, if I recall."

"Perhaps they've gone east," suggested Bandros. "We possess little information concerning Therengia."

"We initially believed that, but someone would have noticed that many sisters moving across the Continent."

"Not if they were moved using magic."

"Don't be ridiculous," said Moreau. "Magic is only useful for moving small numbers."

As the only mage in the room, all eyes turned on Edora. "A spell of teleportation can transport up to ten riders if the caster is powerful enough but requires knowledge of the magic circle at the destination, and we control all of those."

"Wait a moment," said Rakert. "Wasn't there a renegade Stormwind in Therengia?"

"Yes," replied Edora, "and a powerful one, at that."

"Could she have constructed her own circle?"

"Crafting a magic circle is not a simple task, and from all accounts, no one ever taught her how to empower one. There's also the matter of the expense—Therengia is not a wealthy realm."

"But it is not beyond the realm of possibility?" asked Rakert.

"I suppose it's possible, but it only makes our task that much easier. After all, better they remain in the east than nearby, where they can be used against us."

"This Therengia," said Bandros, "are they a threat we should consider?"

"It lies far to the east," replied Edora, "remote enough not to affect our current campaign. There's also history to consider; there has never been a great friendship between the Petty Kingdoms and Therengians, quite the reverse. They would never come to the aid of the very realms that once oppressed them."

"Still, we'll have to deal with them, eventually."

"Only after we've dealt with the Petty Kingdoms. Now, shall we move on to other matters?"

Edora slumped into her chair. Today's meeting had been exhausting, made so by the fractious nature of the legion commanders, but it wasn't over yet. She still had to contact Agalix to update him on recent developments. She leaned forward and stared into the fireplace, her mind a whirl.

Replacing the commander-generals when she'd first taken command might have been better, but it would have delayed the start of the offensive. The campaign had seen its share of problems, but their past experiences had served them well. Would their luck continue?

She called forth her magic, and the fire rose significantly, green flames tinging the red and yellow. "Are you there, Agalix?"

The silence dragged out, and then an aged face appeared. "I am. I trust all is proceeding as planned?"

"My legions are heading for Erlingen even as we speak, but the spring thaw is not helping."

"Take comfort in knowing that it will be just as detrimental to our enemies."

"I'm confident we can find a way to keep on schedule. How are things there?"

It took a bit for him to answer. "Progress is slow but deliberate, much as it is there."

"That's a guarded reply."

"Allow me to provide further details," replied Agalix. "We identified several of Exalor's allies and are keeping them under a watchful gaze."

"But?"

"What makes you think there's a but?"

"Your hesitancy, for a start."

"We are not as far along as we would have hoped."

"Meaning?" pressed Edora.

"We know Exalor has additional allies, yet it's proving difficult to identify them without tipping our hand."

"And the war in the west?"

"Ironcliff is reportedly under siege, with Stonecastle soon to follow. The fleet should have arrived off the coast of Merceria, but we have not heard of their progress or lack thereof."

"Are there not mages there to keep us up to date?"

"There are, but they seem reluctant to discuss details of the campaign, which means they've run into some difficulties, although I can't imagine what form that might take."

"Could the Mercerians have sent reinforcements to Trollden?"

"They most assuredly did, but they only have so many warriors and should have exhausted their reserves by now."

"Does that endanger our own plans?"

"No," said Agalix. "If anything, it helps us. With Exalor's great campaign bogged down, it keeps his focus on military matters. Who knows, perhaps he'll travel there in person and die in battle, thus solving our problem."

"I wouldn't count on that quite yet," replied Edora. "He is a most resilient man."

"An admirer, are you?"

"I'd be a fool if I said I didn't respect his abilities, but I have no desire to see him seize the Throne."

The elder mage nodded. "Good. He's a dangerous fellow, and we shouldn't underestimate him."

"Will his invasion of Merceria succeed?"

"It's still too early to tell. So far, he's reached his initial objectives, if a little later than expected, but whether that continues to be the case remains to be seen."

"Anything else I should know about?"

"I told you General Fitzwilliam met with a Temple Knight of Saint Mathew named Cyric?"

"You did," said Edora. "Why?"

"Our agents there report he then arranged for her to speak with the regional commander of the Temple Knights."

"But hasn't Captain Alonso already agreed to keep his Temple Knights out of the war?"

"Yes, but it seems this Cyric fellow has influence far above his rank. I was considering what to do about him when you contacted me."

"What have you decided?"

"You tell me—you're the strategist."

"He needs to be eliminated."

Agalix smiled. "Precisely my conclusion. I shall get word to our agents at once."

"Won't that be dangerous?"

"You don't think our people capable of killing a lone knight?"

"There is always the possibility they might be uncovered."

"If they are, it's no great loss. I've always believed such people live to serve the empire. What better way to do so than dying in its service?"

"And General Fitzwilliam?"

"She is a minor inconvenience at present, but if she proves troublesome, we shall deal with her in a similar fashion."

"What of Kelson?" asked Edora.

"He's one of us, as you well know."

"I don't trust him. He could be working in Exalor's best interest."

"How did you arrive at that conclusion?"

"He's a known confidante of the High Strategos and even healed him when someone attacked him. Why would he do that if he supports us?"

"It was too soon for him to die," said Agalix, "and Kelson knew we had not yet gathered our strength. Besides, the attack was not of our doing."

"Then who was behind it?"

"An excellent question. Perhaps a new faction has arisen?"

TWENTY-ONE

Temple Commander

SPRING 968 MC

Temple Commander Marlena reined in her horse. The flooded road forced her command to circle wide across a barren field. It was unlikely that enemy warriors had made it this far from the invasion, but she wasn't about to take chances.

"Enna, take half your company and sweep right. Ensure you spread out and be on the lookout for trouble."

"You expect Halvarians this far east?"

"We know from experience they often send people ahead of an invasion to cause problems. Let's be cautious."

"Yes, Commander."

Johanna rode up beside her. "Another week, and we'll be in Erlingen, Commander, providing the horses can make it. They're looking ragged."

"It can't be helped. Either we keep up this pace or risk being overrun by the Halvarians."

"What happens once we reach the border? Not everyone supports our order now."

"True, but I doubt the duke would refuse our help. How often do you think he has the chance to double his cavalry contingent?"

"Double?"

"Well, double his knights. I've heard he only has a hundred or so."

"Wouldn't his barons have more?"

"I would certainly hope so, but it's common practice for nobles to lead their own contingents in battle."

Johanna shook her head. "It seems a most inefficient way to do things."

"It is," replied Marlena, "but most armies of the Petty Kingdoms are ill-disciplined, making it difficult for one individual to command more than a few hundred men. The Battle of the Brinwald was the same, but fortunately, we had everyone under a strong leader."

"You're referring to Temple Commander Charlaine."

"I am. I wish she were here with us today. We'd stand a much better chance of defeating this invasion."

"Whatever happened to her?"

"She was recalled to the Antonine." Marlena wanted to say more, but knew that would be breaking a confidence. She changed the subject instead. "What did you make of the Halvarians?"

"They appear substantially more competent than they did at the Brinwald. I surmise whoever's leading this legion is far more capable."

"Agreed, and those heavy cavalrymen were the equal of knights in terms of their ferocity."

"I didn't know they had knights."

"They don't," replied Marlena. "But that doesn't mean they can't train and equip men in heavy armour. It's a smart move when you think about it."

"Smart?"

"Yes. Knights are very effective at fighting, but they're not well-disciplined. There are exceptions, but I've heard they are generally only good for one charge."

"I've never understood why."

"Usually, they're nobles. As such, they're used to preferential treatment, not to mention they see it beneath them to listen to the commands of others."

"Aren't they the decisive factor in a battle?"

"Only after the common footmen soften up the enemy. Breaking an army requires significant effort, and the horsemen are saved for the last stages of the fight."

Johanna stared silently off to her right, where the lead riders picked their way through the field while Marlena was busy with her own thoughts. Command carried a terrible burden, even more so when her promotion was unexpected. Ordinarily, a Temple Captain received training at the Antonine before assuming her new position or would at least be sent a series of books to study, but her own promotion had been sudden and unexpected, forcing her to consider if she was up to the task. She dismissed the negative thoughts and returned to Johanna, who remained staring into the distance.

"See something interesting?" Marlena asked.

The words pulled Johanna back to the present. "No. Sorry, Commander. My mind was elsewhere."

"Something troubling you?"

"It's nothing important."

"I'll be the judge of that. I made you my aide because I valued your opinion. Don't hold back on me now."

"I was imagining how all this might turn out."

"And what did you come up with?"

Johanna grimaced. "Nothing good, I'm afraid."

"You'll have to do better than that. I want details."

"We are badly outnumbered and about to enter a kingdom where our order isn't even recognized. It's hard to think of an outcome that works well for us. I know I should have faith, but these are trying times."

"I won't debate that times are difficult," replied Marlena, "but the fact still remains that the Duke of Erlingen has to face the empire on the field of battle. He won't refuse our help."

"That I understand."

"You don't think we can defeat this invasion."

"You saw the size of that army we faced at Saints Crossing. They broke Gotfeld, then marched towards Rudor and destroyed their army. There's no indication Erlingen will fare any better."

"We did our part," replied Marlena, "and lived to tell the tale."

"Agreed, but too few of us are left to make any meaningful difference. It would be different if we faced another Petty Kingdom, but this is Halvaria we're talking about. They're not about to repeat the mistakes of their past. The next time we meet, we'll have nowhere to retreat."

"I appreciate your fear, but you must understand campaigns of this magnitude are seldom settled by a single battle. The farther east we withdraw, the farther stretched out the enemy army becomes, and with each mile, their supply lines grow longer still."

"Couldn't they live off the land?"

"They could have, had they invaded in late summer, but they chose to march in winter. They're advancing across the Continent before the planting season even begins. Do you understand what that means?"

"Not entirely," replied Johanna.

"To feed their legions, they'll have to bring food all the way from Halvaria, meaning lots of wagons and horses, which, in turn, cost them even more supplies. At some point, their advance will become untenable."

"And when does that happen?"

"When the number of horses required to supply them outnumbers the actual legions."

"Yet we march without supplies."

"We do, but look at us, we're starving. Our horses haven't eaten a decent meal in days, and we're no better. If it weren't for the meagre offerings of the country folk around here, we'd all starve to death. I understand how difficult this is, and there's no guarantee the duke will take care of us, but what other choice do we have? We can't return to Arnsfeld, not with the enemy behind us. Our only option is to keep on the move."

"We could find refuge in a kingdom that would welcome us."

"I'd love to. Have you a list?"

Johanna cast her gaze downward. "No."

"Then we'll keep riding east until another opportunity presents itself."

The Fox and Hound was quiet this afternoon, unusually so, considering the rumours swirling around about a possible war. Aubrey set down her cup. "I hate to say it, but I think I'm growing used to this wine."

Beverly laughed. "It's just as well. It will likely be some time before we return home."

"I'd have to agree. This invasion makes things significantly more diffi- cult for us."

"Oh, I don't know," said Aldwin. "In some ways, it makes it easier. You can find employment healing the wounded, and Beverly can help the duke with his strategy."

"Providing he's willing to listen," said Beverly.

"When are you meeting with him?"

"This afternoon."

"What will be your recommendation?"

"That largely depends on the quality of his troops. Erlingen has enough men to take on a legion, but from most accounts, they have little experi- ence, while the empire has a history of successful campaigns."

"Except in Arnsfeld," added Owen. "Could you recreate the conditions that led to their defeat at the Brinwald?"

"What is the Brinwald?" interrupted Aldwin.

"It's a forest. The Army of Arnsfeld used it to anchor their line."

"You seem to have a great interest in this battle," said Beverly. "Tell us what you know."

"Let's see now," said the knight. "Where do I start? The battle fell under the command of a Temple Commander of Saint Agnes."

"That's a bit unusual, isn't it?"

"Very much so, for it marks the first time a religious fighting order took to the field of battle on behalf of a Petty Kingdom. There are rumours of some skirmishes up north in Reinwick, but we've received no confirmation of that."

"Go on," urged Beverly.

"The Temple Commander set up a defensive line anchored by woods on both flanks, one of which was the Brinwald. By some accounts, they prepared earthworks, although I'm at a loss to explain how, given the empire's rapid advance."

"How large was the Army of Arnsfeld?"

"I can't imagine them fielding more than a thousand, excluding the Temple Knights."

"But they faced an entire legion. They would've been outnumbered by at least two to one."

"Ah, but part of the enemy's army was tied up besieging a keep at the border, thus reducing their numbers."

"A master stroke," said Beverly, "but I doubt they'd fall victim to the same strategy twice. Could magic have created their defences? It seems to me an Earth Mage would have done wonders for them."

"I couldn't say. The accounts we have stress the Temple Knights' role in the battle. After all, they are the decisive part of any army."

Aubrey shook her head. "Footmen and archers are just as decisive as the horsemen, as I'm sure Beverly will attest."

"Agreed," added Beverly. "The key to success on the battlefield is using your army's strengths effectively. Footmen need archers to soften the enemy advance, while the cavalry takes advantage of any weakness, but they're all part of the same weapon."

"Weapon?" said Owen. "You make them sound like a sword."

"In a sense, they are, and the same as a weapon, you must care for an army's well-being."

The knight stared back. "I'm not sure I follow."

"A great man taught me to treat those under my command with respect. Like all of us, they want their lives to have meaning. Our marshal would never throw away the lives of those under his command, and in return, they offer a fierce loyalty."

"I doubt you'd find the same thing here," said Owen. "There's a hierarchy amongst the Petty Kingdoms."

"Go on. I'm curious to see where this is headed."

"The most important men on the battlefield are the king's knights, followed by any other cavalry available, then the foot, and finally, the archers."

"Do I detect a certain disdain for bowmen?"

"You do. They are largely seen as cowardly folk, lacking the bravery to go head-to-head against their opponents."

"What is the object of battle, Owen?"

"I beg your pardon?"

"Indulge me. What is the object of battle?"

"To defeat the enemy army?"

"How does one accomplish that?"

"By killing more people than they do."

"Not quite," replied Beverly. "The objective is to break the enemy's will to fight, and killing is certainly a part of that. The most important thing, however, is when you said, 'More people than they do.' That being the case, wouldn't it seem prudent to use ranged weapons whenever possible? Or is this hatred merely because a decent bowman can take out a knight before he's within melee range?"

Owen reddened. "I suppose that's part of it, yes. But it's still cowardly."

"You say that because you've been trained as a knight and wear expensive armour. Most soldiers aren't that privileged. They're expected to bear the brunt of the fighting with inferior armour while your lot sits back and waits for the final charge."

"But you yourself are a knight."

"I am now, yes, but I grew up riding with the Bodden Horse, a collection of common soldiers who patrolled the northwest border of Merceria. They so inspired me that under our current queen, I raised the Guard Cavalry."

"Which is?"

"Common cavalrymen armed and equipped as knights."

"I've seen them," added Aubrey. "I'd say they're as effective as the Temple Knights you have here."

"But you still have regular knights, don't you?"

"Oh, we do," replied Beverly, "but the Knights of the Hound aren't employed in the traditional sense. We leave that for the Knights of the Sword. Currently, they're undergoing a reorganization under King Alric. The queen thought it better to keep them under direct Royal control."

"Why is that?"

"When she came to power, most had sworn their lives to the previous king, whom she'd just overthrown."

"Why are you telling me all this?"

"To make certain you understand. We Mercerians adapt as we go, changing our tactics and strategy to defeat our enemies, but your Petty Kingdoms seem stuck in the past. Do you know if anyone ever studied Halvaria's tactics?"

"Not that I'm aware," replied Owen. "Then again, there'd have to be survivors to do that."

"You just told us they were defeated in Arnsfeld a few years ago. Had that occurred in Merceria, the queen and the marshal would've interviewed the survivors."

"I'm afraid our politics work against us."

"Whatever do you mean?" asked Aubrey.

"No one in the Petty Kingdoms wants to give another kingdom knowledge of their tactics in case they go to war with each other."

"Even if the entire Continent is at stake?"

"Well, they say the only enemy worse than the empire is each other."

"If that's true," asked Beverly, "why have all these alliances?"

"It's mostly posturing. To my mind, they're all empty promises. By the time an ally musters an army, any potential war would already be over. Take Erlingen, for example. We're one of the most powerful kingdoms, yet you won't see anyone coming to our aid, and do you know why?" He didn't wait for an answer. "Our so-called allies would rather sit back and watch us wear ourselves down so they become more powerful than us."

"That is a cynical way of looking at it."

"Yet," said Aubrey, "it's not too different from our own history. Weldwyn and Norland were both our enemies, and in times past, we Mercerians would've gladly sat back and watched them suffer. How many times has Merceria invaded Weldwyn?"

"Too many to count," replied Beverly, "but that's all changed under the queen. Like I said, we've learned to adapt to ever-changing circumstances."

"But think how different things would be had she never come to power. We'd be trapped in an endless cycle of war with our neighbours."

"I hadn't thought about that, but it's true. Still, you can't argue that we don't adapt; the Army of Merceria is nothing like it was during King Andred's reign."

"Agreed," replied Aubrey, "but that's more to do with the marshal's reforms than anything else."

"You're both correct," stated Aldwin, "but the reforms would never have been allowed without the right person on the Throne."

A scream from outside caught everyone's attention. Beverly leaped to her feet, rushing for the door, Krazuhk right behind her.

Outside the Fox and Hound, the Temple Knight Cyric lay in an expanding pool of blood. Nearby, a young woman stood screaming at the sight, while another, more composed individual, pointed down the street to a man running away.

Krazuhk, calling on her magic, sent a bolt of lightning after him, striking his back and causing him to stumble, but he rounded a corner before she could ready another spell.

Aubrey appeared at the door, along with Owen and Aldwin. Upon seeing the injured knight, she began her own spell. Her hands glowed brightly, and then she placed them on Cyric, watching as the light faded into him.

He blinked his eyes open. "What happened?"

"You tell me," replied Aubrey. "We heard a scream and came running out here to find you lying on the ground. Did you see your assailant?"

"I'm afraid not. One moment, I was reaching for the door, the next, I felt a searing pain in my back. I'm not certain if it was a sword or a dagger." He tried to sit up, but his head swam.

"Lie down. Your body needs to adjust. You've lost quite a bit of blood, but given time, you'll make a full recovery."

"I'm afraid time is a luxury I don't have. The army is assembling, and Father Roland needs my assistance."

"Could this attack be related to that?" asked Beverly.

"Quite possibly. Adding a company of Temple Knights would significantly help His Grace, and the Temple Commander was beginning to waver in his resolve."

"Are you suggesting that agents of the empire were behind this attack?"

"I'm afraid it's far worse than that."

"Meaning?"

"I fear the Church itself orchestrated this or at least elements within it."

TWENTY-TWO

Trollden

SPRING 968 MC

Lord Preston watched as the Halvarians commenced their latest advance.

"Will they never learn?" said Tog. "They throw their men against our defences over and over again, achieving nothing."

"I wouldn't say that," replied Sophie. "They've succeeded in tying down our warriors."

"Perhaps that is their plan."

"I'm surprised they haven't tried flanking you," said Preston.

"They did early on, but the Saurians and their three-horns anchor our eastern flank. The warriors who entered that part of the swamp fled in terror."

"Could we not use them to attack the empire's camp?"

"No," replied the massive Troll. "They are light troops, best employed as skirmishers. We do not want to risk their three-horns in a direct attack."

"Still, I can't help but feel we're being led astray here. Could they be trying to outflank us to the west?"

"We've had no reports of landings in Weldwyn."

"I think it's politics," suggested Sophie.

"I am afraid you have to explain that to me," said Tog.

"There may be factors at work here that we're unaware of. Perhaps there is some animosity between the leaders of the empire. Is it possible the commander here might be holding back so the attacks on Ironcliff and Stonecastle suffer?"

"Anything's possible," replied Preston, "but I think this has more to do with keeping us busy. Their presence on the coast forces us to keep a large reserve here, preventing us from reinforcing elsewhere."

"Then why keep attacking?" asked the Troll.

"Were they to let up, we might consider the extra warriors unnecessary and redeploy them. We are, in a sense, stuck. We lack sufficient numbers to attack our enemy, but at the same time, we can't afford to send any elsewhere."

"This is so frustrating," said Sophie. "Is there nothing we can do?"

"Not at the moment," replied Tog. "And our numbers are slowly decreasing, thanks to illness. Unfortunately, Humans are not well-suited to this terrain."

A voice called out from behind them: "My lord?"

They all turned to see a courier coming towards them.

Sophie smiled. "Edgar Greenfield, isn't it?"

"Aye, it is," the old man replied. "I bring a message from Colbridge." He withdrew a sealed letter from his sling bag and passed it to Lord Preston.

"I am not the commander here; Tog is."

"Aye, an' don't I know it, but 'er Majesty knows he don't read so well."

"Go ahead," said Tog. "Open it."

Preston broke the seal, then unfolded it. "It's written in the marshal's hand."

"Aye," replied Edgar, "'e gave it to me 'imself."

As was the custom for Mercerian military orders, it was written in Orcish, so Preston perused it before translating it for the others. "The marshal wants us to withdraw northward, up the road to Colbridge."

"Are you certain?" said Gorath. "That would mean giving up the advantage of terrain."

"He must have something in mind but doesn't indicate what. However, he mentions that we are to slow the enemy's advance as much as possible to give him time to prepare."

"Then why not delay our withdrawal?"

"I imagine he's concerned our present position might be overwhelmed."

"We shall do as he has asked," replied Tog, "but before we withdraw, there are a few things to deal with."

"Which are?"

"The mechanism that controls the chain must be broken to prevent them from lowering it, then we must destroy our fortifications to ensure we do not have to recapture them once we retake the coast."

"You think that likely?" asked Gorath. "From what we have seen, the enemy has a massive army. I do not see us liberating it anytime soon."

"If we are to eventually live in peace, we must defeat the invaders. I promise you, we will return and rebuild Trollden as a fortress, preventing this from ever happening again."

"I shall have the rangers form a rearguard," said Gorath. "Lord Preston, I suggest your command begin heading north at first light. Does that letter indicate how far we should go?"

"Just past the edge of the swamp. I imagine whatever the marshal has planned will occur there."

"Look at the bright side," said Sophie. "Once we leave the swamp, you can use the cavalry."

"True, but so can the enemy, and unless I miss my guess, they have considerably more."

"We could slow their advance with a little preparation," said Tog. "I shall have my Trolls dig up parts of the road as we withdraw. Their footmen will have difficulty making progress in chest-high water."

"Do your Trolls never tire?" asked Preston.

"We do, but only after several days of toiling. Once we do sleep, however, very little will awaken us."

"The question," said Sophie, "is how far do we march each day? The marshal wants us to slow the enemy, but we don't want them to overwhelm us with a sudden advance."

"I suggest no farther than five miles," replied Preston, "giving us the time to set up a fortified camp each day."

"That would also work for my Trolls," said Tog. "Even for us, it is time-consuming to dig so much."

"Then it's settled."

Gerald slowed his horse, moving off to the side of the road as the Dwarves passed by. The warriors of Mirstone were a tireless group, marching from sunup to sundown with little rest. It made an exhausting trip for the Humans amongst them, but it meant they covered many more miles in a day than was customary for Human troops.

He spotted Albreda looking skyward and rode over to her. "See anything interesting?"

"Some birds, but none with enough stamina to reach the coast."

"It's too bad Revi's up at Ironcliff. That familiar of his would've been useful right about now."

"I am more than capable of spying out the enemy once we're closer." She turned to face him. "Are you certain this plan of yours will work?"

"Nothing in war is guaranteed, but with your help, we have an opportunity to nip this thing in the bud."

"Nip in the bud?" said Albreda. "I'm afraid this particular weed has already taken root."

"Then we shall dig it out. Once we rendezvous with Tog's command, we'll have close to twelve hundred souls. The enemy still outnumbers us, but we've fought against worse odds."

"It's not the odds I'm worried about; it's the quality of their soldiers. From what we learned, they appear highly trained and well-motivated. I'm not saying I don't have faith in your capabilities, Gerald, but we've never faced an enemy like this before."

"True, but we have every advantage going into this. We're fighting on home soil. After coming out of the swamp, the enemy will be tired, which is hardly the best condition to fight under. My bigger concern is that you might not have the strength to carry out your part."

"I may be old," said Albreda, "but I assure you, I'm still more than capable of doing what's needed."

"You're not much older than I am," said Gerald.

"What's your point?"

He grinned. "Merely that it looks like it's up to us old folks to save the realm once again."

"You've been doing this all your life."

"Well, all my adult life, I suppose."

"Did you always want to be a soldier?"

"No. That came after Fitz took me in."

"He saw your potential," said Albreda.

"He did. I'll always be grateful for that."

"He's the key to everything."

"I'm not sure I understand?"

"He believed nobles should serve the common people. That, in turn, was passed on to you and Beverly, then to the queen, and that belief brought about a tremendous change in the kingdom, one I never believed possible."

"That could all be for naught if the Halvarians have their way."

"Then we shall do everything we can possibly do to ensure this invasion of theirs fails."

The withdrawal north continued, with the men of Colbridge leading the way. They marched quickly, covering the five miles well before noon, spending the bulk of each afternoon building makeshift defences. It was tiring work, with the constant dampness of the swamp making it even more uncomfortable.

Behind them came the Trolls, digging pits in the road and letting the water flood the area. For the first few days, the enemy remained at a respectful distance. However, the Halvarians began making a nuisance of themselves on the morning of the fourth day.

It started with a horde of archers, some armed with crossbows, harassing the Trolls as they tried to make the roads impassable.

Later that day, they followed up with a more determined push, supporting the volleys with an advance by axe-wielding footmen, forcing the Trolls to retreat north and abandon their work.

Gorath's rangers kept up a steady stream of arrows but were in danger of being overwhelmed. Preston called his footmen to back them up, and a deadly exchange developed. Little more than a skirmish, in the grand scheme of things, yet both sides suffered substantial losses.

By late afternoon, the Halvarians saw fit to retire, leaving a battleground littered with the dead and dying, presenting a new problem—what to do with the prisoners.

The Mercerian command met that evening to discuss the matter. Without tents to gather in, they stood around a fire, a light rain flickering the flames.

"We have little choice," began Gorath. "We must execute the prisoners."

"We can't," said Preston. "That goes against everything the queen believes in."

"We haven't the warriors to spare. Are we to weaken ourselves even further by providing guards?"

"There is another solution," offered Sophie. "What if we send them back to the enemy? They then become their problem."

"I would not recommend that," replied Gorath. "They will rearm them so they can fight us again."

"Actually," said Preston, "she has the right idea. We'll take their weapons and armour and send them back. They came here in ships. I doubt they have unlimited reserves with which to equip them."

"Who will carry the goods we take from them?"

"We split up the weapons amongst our own men."

"Their armour would weigh us down."

"We're marching beside a river; throwing it in the water is easy enough."

"We have close to one hundred prisoners," said Sophie. "That's quite a bit of armour. Could we not send it back to Colbridge?"

"We'd need wagons for that," said Gorath.

"We have those aplenty; it's how we brought our food stores. I propose we split the contents of one wagon amongst the others, then use it to carry the captured weapons and armour. We could then use them to raise and equip a militia in Colbridge."

"How long would such arrangements take?" asked Tog.

"We can have one ready to move by first light," replied Sophie.

"Then let it be so. Now, we must deal with the increased aggression on the part of the invaders. Lord Preston, what have we learned from the prisoners?"

"They are provincial troops forming a cohort under the Fourth Legion."

"Cohort?"

"Yes, a mass of men akin to one of our armies. They claim four such cohorts make up their invasion force, three of which are Imperial, whatever that means."

"It means," said Sophie, "that those we captured are likely recruited from the empire's captured territories. I suspect the Imperial warriors are more seasoned men. Their name certainly suggests as much."

"There were heavily armed men in Trollden," said Gorath, "but they kept to the back of each assault. I suspect they are saving them for a major push."

"Footmen do not concern me," replied Tog. "Their crossbows, however, have proven effective in large groups."

"What I want to know," said Preston, "is where are they hiding their cavalry."

"By now, they've likely figured out how to remove the chain barring their way, so they will be shipping them upriver in boats."

"That makes us vulnerable. The road parallels the river; they could easily bypass us, cutting us off from the rear."

"How deep is the river here?" asked Sophie.

"I do not know," replied Tog. "Why? What are you thinking?"

"You used a chain to block the river near Trollden. Could we use logs to do so here?"

"We lack the time to cut down trees. The enemy would soon overwhelm us."

"What if we placed a few in the river and buried the ends in the bottom so their tips would puncture hulls?"

Tog nodded. "A good tactic. Encountering one or two would alert them to the danger, slowing them down considerably."

"We would need to reorganize our withdrawal," said Gorath.

"We'd have to do that regardless," said Preston. "Our delaying tactics are no longer effective."

"What would you suggest?"

"We'll buy time with the cavalry."

"We are still in the swamp, hardly the terrain favourable for such warriors."

"Our big advantage is that very same terrain. The enemy must advance up the road. The swamp will slow their progress if we keep them off the road."

"How would that work?"

"We charge down, driving men off it, then withdraw, repeating the process each time they try to regain the road."

"And if they counter the tactic?"

"The advantage of the road is it's relatively narrow, making it possible for a few defenders to hold off a much larger force."

"They will just push up the road in greater numbers."

"True, but that takes time to organize, time that works to our advantage."

"Is our cavalry disciplined enough to carry out such a tactic?"

"The Guard Cavalry is."

Tog considered the idea. "What do you think, Gorath?"

"I have seen the Guard Cavalry in battle," the Orc replied. "If anyone can do this, it is them."

"Then that is how we shall proceed. Come morning, the Trolls will head upriver, looking for a narrow stretch where we can place as many stakes as possible. I want the rangers standing by to support the Guard Cavalry's withdrawal after contact. Lord Preston, I would like your archers to monitor the river closely. If their ships show up before we are ready, we must change our plans and withdraw eastward, away from the water."

Preston awoke, only to notice the space beside him empty. He looked around, spotting Sophie huddled in front of the fire. He moved closer, and she turned, revealing tracks of tears on her cheeks. "What's the matter?" he asked.

"I'm not suited for this," she replied. "I always thought I was strong, but the fear of you dying in battle overwhelms me this night."

"I've seen plenty of battles. This is no different."

"But it is, don't you see? This isn't some Norland rabble of inexperienced raiders; it's a professional, disciplined army, possibly even more accomplished than our own."

He sat down beside her, taking her hand in his. "If Merceria wishes for a future free from such conquerors, we must do what we can to make that happen."

"But why does it have to be you?"

"I'm the most experienced cavalry commander here and a Knight of the Hound. It's my duty."

"That's of small comfort should you die."

"I'm sorry for putting you through this, Soph. I truly am, but I have a duty to the queen."

"That duty does not call on you to sacrifice yourself."

"No, it doesn't, but we must buy the marshal time to prepare. I say this with all humility, but their best chance of survival is if I'm there to lead them."

She gazed into the fire. "Each time you ride into battle, a little part of me dies. I fear that in short order, there shall be nothing left of me."

TWENTY-THREE

Angvil

SPRING 968 MC

Sister Johanna galloped towards Marlena, calling out as she rode. "Commander, we've spotted an army."

"Ours or theirs?"

"It's not Halvarian. I suspect it's the Army of Angvil, heading east."

"Probably heading to Erlingen to combine with the duke's forces."

The Temple Knight slowed, coming up beside her senior officer. She was out of breath, a sure sign something else worried her. "There's more," she finally said.

"Go on."

"We spotted some cavalry on their flank, Halvarian Imperials, by the look of them."

"How many?"

"Two hundred or so, heavily armoured, like our knights. I think they're trying to outflank the Army of Angvil."

"How do you know they are Halvarians?"

"They're all dressed the same; if they were knights of the Petty Kingdoms, I'd expect each to display their coat of arms."

"Are you certain they're not Temple Knights?"

"I know the symbols of all the other Holy orders, and they wore none."

"I thought we'd left the legion far behind us, but it appears they made better time than us. This bodes ill for the Duke of Angvil."

"Actually," replied Johanna. "Lady Burghild, the duke's widow, rules there now."

"I wasn't aware the duke was dead."

"We received word of it right before we set out for Rudor."

"Why wasn't I informed?"

"Commander Isabeau knew, but I assumed she would have briefed you."

"She likely would've had she known she was going to die." Marlena took time to gather her thoughts. "I'd say his death was no mere coincidence."

"He reportedly died from a hunting accident."

"I imagine he did, only he was the one being hunted."

"You suspect the empire killed him?"

"It stands to reason. It left his army without a leader on the eve of this invasion."

"You don't suppose the duchess is commanding, herself?"

"No," said Marlena. "From what I recall of Burghild, she was a child of court."

"Meaning?"

"She spent her childhood growing up in a proper, ladylike fashion. In other words, she knows nothing about fighting."

"How do you know all this?"

"Before I was a Temple Captain, I was an aide to Temple Commander Charlaine. She always insisted on knowing as much as possible about those realms bordering Arnsfeld."

"So we have an inexperienced leader leading an army that is about to be cut off by cavalry?"

"That's the substance of it, yes. I suppose that means we'll have to intervene. Give the order for the sisters to form up. We ride to battle."

The Halvarian cavalry rode in a column, keeping a slow pace to preserve their mounts' strength for battle. They were two hundred in strength, two full companies of the empire's most heavily armoured horsemen.

Against them, Marlena brought one hundred fifty-seven knights who were tired, hungry, and mentally exhausted, yet not a single sister refused the call to battle.

The enemy saw their approach and countered by forming into a line. Marlena organized her knights in a wedge formation, then flipped down her visor and ordered the charge.

The Halvarian commander ordered his men forward, but the two forces clashed before his horsemen finished manoeuvring into a counter-charge. The Temple Knights drove into the enemy line, splitting it down the centre, and then the fight devolved into a series of individual melees.

Marlena, beset on both sides, struck out with her mace, smashing it into one opponent's visor. It failed to penetrate the armour but bent the helm, obstructing her foe's field of vision. She quickly followed up with an overhand blow, landing her weapon firmly on the top of the fellow's helm and denting it. The rider fell back, though whether he was dead or simply knocked unconscious was unknown.

A blow landed against her shield, and she twisted in the saddle, smashing her mace against her attacker's wrist. A loud clang announced the hit, and then the Halvarian's hand went limp, his weapon falling from his grasp. She attacked again, but he countered with his shield, knocking the head of her weapon aside as he pushed out, hoping to unseat her. She hooked the top of his shield with the bottom of hers, forcing it down and opening him up for another strike.

This time, she jabbed with the top of her mace, striking his pauldron. The hit unbalanced him, so she pulled her shield back, dislodging him from the saddle, and he was soon lost amongst the horses following her.

She urged her mount forward, then realized they'd pushed through the Halvarian line, cutting the enemy commander off from half his command.

Marlena wheeled to her left, ready to deal a blow against the rear of the enemy formation. A man bedecked in a gold helmet rushed at her, and she shifted her horse, presenting her shield. His sword struck, sending a shock up her arm, but her manoeuvre successfully stopped the blow.

He attacked again, this time making contact with her vambrace, but it bounced off the metal. She smashed her mace against the side of his helmet, staggering him, and then her horse pressed up against his until they were knee to knee. She swung on high, crashing it down on the top of his helmet, and his head bent awkwardly, his neck broken. His arms hung loose as his mount raced off, carrying him away from his command.

All around her, the Halvarian cavalry broke, the horsemen fleeing in small groups. The Temple Knights refrained from chasing them, instead forming into their ranks.

Temple Captain Bernelle appeared at her side. "The enemy flees west, presumably back to the rest of their army. Victory is ours, Commander."

"Dismount half your knights and take care of the wounded. We'll need the others to be on the lookout lest they return in strength. And let's see about gathering those horses, shall we? They're too valuable a resource to leave in the enemy's hands."

"Surely you don't want them killed?"

"Of course not. We'll take them with us. I'm certain the Duchess of Angvil can put them to good use."

"And if she doesn't want them?"

"Then we'll take them into Erlingen, where we can trade them for supplies." She removed her helmet and looked around, seeking her aide. "Johanna?"

"Here, Commander."

Marlena noted the blood running down her aide's thigh. "You're wounded."

"It's nothing serious."

"Clean the wound and have someone bind it. A minor cut can turn necrotic under the right circumstances, and Saints know we're not in the best of shape right now."

"Yes, Commander. Before I go, what do you want us to do with the prisoners?"

"How many have we?"

"Two dozen or so, most wounded."

"Strip them of their armour and weapons before sending them on their way." It suddenly occurred to her that they might prove to be a valuable source of information. "On second thought, let's not release them quite yet. I'd like to have a chat with them."

"To what end?"

"These are Imperial troops. They may know more than the provincials we've previously run into."

Jansen Borke was a bitter man. He'd served in the Halvarian Army for a lifetime yet never rose beyond the rank of captain. To add insult to injury, he was stripped of his armour and made a prisoner of the wretched Temple Knights.

His head ached, and he had difficulty holding it upright. He knew his time was at an end, for he'd felt something in his neck give way. Even now, he struggled to take a deep breath, and maintaining his balance was proving so challenging he was forced to sit.

A figure loomed before him, and he looked up at a blood-splattered knight wearing a sash. "I assume you command these Temple Knights?"

"Yes, I have that honour. My name is Temple Commander Marlena."

"My compliments to you, Commander. It takes great courage and discipline to break Halvarian heavy cavalry."

"Where is your legion?"

He tried to laugh as an act of defiance, but a spasm of pain shot up his neck, leading him to grimace instead. "I would go to the Underworld before I revealed the location of the Fifth."

"Thank you," she replied. "You've told me all I needed to know with that."

He tried to reason out her words, but found concentrating difficult. "Might I ask a favour?"

"You're in no shape to request anything."

"I wish only for a quick death. I am broken and shall not see another dawn. Surely you would not have me suffer in my final moments?"

She knelt to look into his eyes. "I can grant you what you wish, but to do so, you must provide me more."

"More? What else is there to know? I already told you I will not reveal the Fifth's location."

"This legion of yours is new to the area, isn't it?"

"It is."

"Who commands it?"

"Hamath Nordin. He gained much experience in the south."

"The south?"

"Yes. In the occupied lands adjoining the southern continent. Edora Stormwind herself approved his command of the Fifth."

"Stormwind, you say?"

He smiled, despite the pain, pleased he'd surprised her. "They are common back in the empire."

The woman clenched her jaw. "That is news indeed. Is she the one who orchestrated this campaign?"

"She is. After all, she's a trained battle mage."

"And the Ninth?"

"They'll be along in good time." He coughed violently, spitting out blood. "It appears my time is ending sooner than expected."

She stood, then pulled a dagger from her belt. "I cannot take the life of a wounded man, but I can give you the opportunity to do so yourself." She handed him the blade, hilt first.

Borke took the weapon. "Thank you."

"Any last words?"

"I always believed that in my final moments, I would say something memorable, but I've not been as successful as I would have hoped."

"You met your end doing your duty. Can a soldier ask for anything more?"

"My duty?" He coughed up more blood as pain lanced into his head. "Were I to live my life again, I'd curse the very name of the emperor. He has brought me nothing but misery and now death." He held out the dagger with shaking hands, the blade hovering over his heart. "I now leave this world. I wish you well, Commander, despite you being my enemy." With that, he plunged the knife in. His body jerked, and then his arms fell to the sides as his head slumped forward.

. . .

The Temple Knights of Saint Agnes formed into a column, ready to resume their march. The Halvarian survivors sat beneath a nearby tree, their hands and feet bound, their weapons broken, and their armour cast aside.

Johanna surveyed the muddied ground. "We lost another eleven knights. Was it worth it?"

"We saved the Army of Angvil," replied Marlena. "At least for now, but we've learned something far more important."

"We did?"

"Those men were members of the Fifth Legion, but we fought the Ninth at Saints Crossing. We are now facing not one legion but two. It is imperative we take this information to the duchess."

Marlena entered the Angvil camp, her battle-weary knights still riding in precise ranks despite their exhaustion. It had been a most trying day, and all she wanted to do was sleep, yet more work needed to be done.

"See to the knights, Johanna," she said. "I need to find whoever's in charge."

The Temple Commander rode through the camp, spotting a well-guarded tent near its centre. She dismounted, then passed the reins to a waiting guardsman. "Who commands here?"

"General Bertran. And you are?"

"Temple Commander Marlena of the Order of Saint Agnes."

He noted her blood-splattered armour. "You're the one responsible for saving us today."

"You should thank my Temple Knights, not me."

"Still, I imagine His Lordship will be most pleased to share his appreciation in person." He nodded to another guard standing by the entrance to the tent. "You may proceed, Commander."

"Thank you." She moved up to the warrior guarding the door. "Shall I divest myself of weapons?"

"That's not necessary," came a voice from within. "Enter, Commander, or should I say Temple Commander? I'm never sure how to properly address you religious types."

She stepped inside. A group of mud-stained men stood around a table, upon which lay a map with small stones holding down the corners. Marlena wondered how accurate their information was.

"My name is General Engle Bertran, and I have the honour of commanding the Army of Angvil. These other individuals are the barons of Angvil. Shall I introduce them?"

"I'm afraid I have little time for pleasantries," she replied. "My name is

Temple Commander Marlena. I must inform you that your army is in grave danger."

"No longer, thanks to you. We will occupy a position on ground of our choosing come morning. When the empire arrives, we shall be ready."

"You are making a huge mistake, my lord. The might of an entire legion approaches, against which you have no hope of success."

"And that is precisely what I want our enemy to believe. We lured the empire away from our capital, Neiburg, and found the perfect ground to face them. Added to that are the stragglers we picked up along the way."

"Stragglers?" said Marlena.

"Yes. Warriors of Rudor who survived the Battle of Saints Crossing."

"Cavalry, I assume?"

"No, footmen. Why?"

"With all due respect, my lord, we rode directly east after the battle. I find it highly unlikely footmen could have travelled this far in so short a time."

"Yet here they are, ready to lay down their lives. Am I to send them away? Of course not!"

"What do you know about the enemy army?"

"They are a legion," replied the general. "What else is there?"

"Which legion?"

"What does it matter?"

"The legion we fought at Saints Crossing was the Ninth," said Marlena, "whereas the horsemen this afternoon were from the Fifth. Do you understand what that means?"

The general waved it away. "Ninth or Fifth, who cares? The important thing is that we finally have a chance to crush a legion. After their losses in Gotfeld, they'll be lucky if they have half their strength."

"Their losses, my lord?"

"Yes. The survivors tell us the battle was a bloody affair."

"More so for the Army of Rudor. I was there, and from my point of view, the Halvarians suffered little."

"Your impression of the battle differs greatly from the other survivors."

Marlena shook her head. Was this man a fool? "I do not doubt your resolve, my lord, but two legions are out there. Even if you defeat one, you will take losses, and then the second will march in and annihilate you. Marching to Erlingen and combining with the forces of that kingdom would be a better choice."

"I refuse to abandon this realm! Even if what you claim is true, Erlingen needs time to raise their army, which making a stand here will buy them." He stabbed his finger down onto the map. "There is a hill there called

Beggar's Reach. Funny name that, but it shall soon become known as the place where the Army of Her Grace, Duchess Burghild of Angvil, defeated the empire."

"I admire your optimism," said Marlena, "but it will mean the decimation of your army."

"We are not afraid of death!"

"Even a meaningless one?"

The general ignored her warning. "Will your sister knights fight alongside us, or do you continue your flight eastward? I imagine you have no stomach left for fighting."

"I am not a coward. My experience in battle proves that, but I see no wisdom in throwing away what little advantage we have out of pure stubbornness."

"And what advantage is that?"

"You know the territory better than the enemy. Use it to your advantage."

"That's precisely what we're doing!"

"You should be dispersing your men and using them in hit-and-run raids against their supply lines, not making a stand on a hill."

"I shall not debate the matter any further. I have made the decision to stand firm, and by the Saints, that's exactly what I aim to do. The only question awaiting an answer is whether your Temple Knights will stand with us."

"They will," said Marlena, "though it may well cost us our lives." She cast her gaze around the room. "Mark my words carefully, my lords, for the day may come when you realize their import, assuming any of us live to reminisce about such things."

TWENTY-FOUR

Torburg

SPRING 968 MC

"Your army does you credit," said Beverly, "but you'll need to leave some here to protect Erlingen."

Alain Heinrich, the Duke of Erlingen, stared down at the map. "Despite that, we should still possess the numbers to take on an Imperial legion."

"Numbers alone won't defeat them."

"Don't you think I know that?" he snapped.

"My apologies, Your Grace. I meant no offence."

"No. I should be the one apologizing. This entire invasion has me on edge. Now, where was I?"

"You were about to explain your strategy for the coming campaign."

"Yes. Let me see..." The duke dug through a stack of papers, withdrawing a small map. "Ah, here it is. This map purports to show the region bordering us to the west, the area in which we'll be marching."

"Purporting?"

"Unfortunately, we cannot judge its accuracy until we arrive, so we shall have to be careful."

"You're basing your entire campaign on potentially false maps?"

"What choice have I?" asked Lord Alain. "Better to march into unfamiliar territory than let the Halvarians cross our border. Are you suggesting you Mercerians would sacrifice your own lands if threatened?"

"We've done precisely that, but I concede you're better off advancing into Angvil in this case."

"Thank you, that's most reassuring. You seem impressed with our numbers, but what do you think of our composition? Do you believe we have enough cavalry?"

"You have four hundred knights, a significant number, but I worry they may lack the discipline required for battle."

"My knights are the finest warriors on the Continent."

"Yet of little use if they can't follow orders. We experienced similar problems with our knights back home."

"How did you deal with them?"

"We raised professional mounted troops instead. The knights still exist but are rarely employed."

"Ah," said the duke. "I'm afraid they're a much-needed component of our army—the killing blow, so to speak."

"I assume you mean to move into Angvil on a single road?"

"We have little choice. There's only one available to us. Our route takes us from Torburg to Anshlag, up through Zurkirk, and then across the border. Once we cross, we run into trouble, for the enemy may be near."

"Had you additional light cavalry, I'd suggest sending them out as a screen."

"A what?"

"A screen—a line of horsemen who ride ahead, flanking the column to give warning should they sight the enemy. Is that not the practice here in the Petty Kingdoms?"

"Our army is not suited to such things unless my archers would prove useful?"

"No," replied Beverly. "While they might be good at skirmishing, they lack the speed to warn you of the enemy's presence."

"We have some mounted men-at-arms; they're not as heavily armoured as the knights. Would they do?"

"I would have to see them, but it's possible."

"Then I shall speak with their respective barons once the army is assembled." Lord Alain pursed his lips. "Diplomacy is necessary in these situations. The barons can be... Well, I suppose the word moody would fit."

"Surely they all serve the Crown?"

"They do, but barons are loath to release command of their own men. To them, it's a mark of their power and influence. Have you something similar where you're from?"

"We used to, but the more recent kings of Merceria put the power and influence in the Crown's hands, making for a much more effective army."

"Effective in which way?"

"It allowed us to appoint the most qualified people to command the troops rather than relying on inexperienced amateurs."

"Amateurs? Is that what you think we are?"

"No, Your Grace," replied Beverly. "I speak about the nobility of

Merceria, who, with very few exceptions, lacked any tactical or strategic sense. Our reforms resulted in a professional and extremely effective army."

"In the absence of proof, I shall take your word for it. In the Petty Kingdoms, a king's power, or a duke, like myself, lies in the ability of his lesser nobles to command large numbers of men."

"Are there any rules concerning what type of warriors these barons must raise?"

"There are not," replied the duke. "All possess footmen and archers, while few have cavalry due to the expense. Still, that gives us close to twenty-four hundred warriors. How does that compare to the Mercerian Army?"

"Our largest army to date was raised to retake Summersgate. At that siege, we had almost three thousand souls, which included many warriors from our allies."

"Allies?"

"Yes. Orcs, Elves, and Dwarves. Close to half our numbers."

"Would that we had such help today."

"Have you no allies of your own?" asked Beverly.

"Many, and we sent word to all, but such messages take weeks to reach their destination, and then they have to muster their own armies, not to mention march to our aid. I'm afraid we'll all be dead and buried long before any of our friends reach us."

"Then we need to ensure that doesn't happen."

"Any other suggestions you might have?" asked the duke.

"Quite possibly. I assume each brigade will march together?"

"Brigade? I'm afraid that's a term I am unfamiliar with."

"Sorry. It's a term my father used to describe a group of warriors under a single commander. You have, no doubt, heard the terms vanguard or rearguard. They would be along similar lines."

"Is this a Therengian term?"

"I have no idea. Why do you ask?"

"The Petty Kingdoms generally avoid terms attributed to the Old Kingdom, with the possible exception of general, although many prefer the term marshal. Have you those back home?"

"Yes. Both, actually. The Marshal of Merceria oversees the entire army, while the generals, of which I am the only one at the moment, are directly beneath him in the chain of command."

"Chain?" asked Duke Heinrich.

"Yes. How else are we to maintain control of our warriors in the event of a death?"

"Our barons lead their companies. If one dies, then his household troops are no longer to be relied upon."

"Our practice is different. Beneath our generals are commanders, then captains, then sergeants, each able to step up to fill a superior's role should it prove necessary. It's what makes our warriors so effective."

"Do you think the Halvarians have a similar organization?"

"I couldn't say," replied Beverly. "We had minimal experience with the empire before coming here. Have you any experts in the matter?"

"I believe Temple Commander Roland would know more. His people are always out and about, collecting information. Having said that, I shall send word asking him for anything he may deem useful. I realize we're a little late to make any changes to the army's organization, but are there any other insights you might offer regarding strategy or tactics?"

"We place our archers directly behind our footmen, the idea being to use a volley of arrows right before the enemy contacts your footmen, assuming you're defending."

"And the cavalry?"

"Were I in command, I'd mass them into one or two groups. They'll do you little good in dribs and drabs, especially against an enemy with so much cavalry themselves. Have we any word on the empire's numbers regarding horsemen?"

"Nothing absolute," replied Duke Heinrich, "although it's rumoured they have lots."

"How many is lots?"

"Difficult to say. I imagine the Temple Knights would know more. Their people were at the Battle of the Brinwald."

"I can think of nothing else in the way of suggestions at this time," said Beverly, "but I assure you, I shall give this situation considerable attention. With Your Grace's permission, I'll leave you to your planning."

"Of course, Lady Beverly. Thank you once again for your expertise; it is most appreciated."

Beverly was escorted from the Palace only to find her cousin waiting for her.

"Anything new to report?" Aubrey asked.

"While the men of Erlingen are brave, I am concerned about their leaders' capabilities."

"How so?"

"Their army lacks experience, particularly at the higher levels of command."

"But didn't they fight off an invasion from Andover some years ago?"

"They did, but most barons did little more than watch from a distance. Hardly the sort of thing that makes them suitable for command."

"It seems to have worked for them in the past."

Beverly nodded. "It has, but I'm not so sure it'll be effective against a well-trained Halvarian legion."

"You've advised the duke, but ultimately, it's up to him how he wants to proceed."

"It is, yet I can't shake the feeling he's heading for disaster. It wouldn't be so bad if we knew more about the enemy legion we're facing."

"Do you think it's similar to those that attacked Merceria?"

"Likely. Why?"

"I'm guessing Gerald will have gathered whatever information he could about them by now. Let's get back to the inn, and I'll contact Kraloch to see what they've learned."

Lord Hagan Stein and Beverly watched as the baron's men formed up on the tournament grounds. They'd marched from Mulsingen under the direction of one of his captains, a dour fellow who'd served his family for over twenty years.

"Well?" asked the baron. "What do you think?"

Five companies stood waiting, the bulk of which were foot. Used to the professionalism of Mercerian troops, the sad turnout disappointed Beverly. Most wore gambesons, which wasn't necessarily bad where armour was concerned, but they'd been on garrison duty so long their stomachs struggled to fit within the padded coats, and the exertion of forming up left them red-faced and sweaty. These men would perform poorly on a march, and she wondered how they'd made the trip from Mulsingen in one piece.

"That bad?" said Lord Hagan.

"I'm sorry," replied Beverly. "I was contemplating how they might be deployed. I note you only have one company of archers."

"Not just archers, crossbowmen. A far superior weapon, don't you think? Do you use them back in Merceria?"

"We have no experience with them, although they are similar in nature to the Dwarves' arbalests, which proved most effective against the Clans, but I cannot speak to the merit of your crossbows. Perhaps you might demonstrate their effectiveness once we're done here?"

"I'd be delighted. You'll note we also have a company of mounted men-at-arms, a fairly recent addition."

"Yes. I understand that's rare in Erlingen."

"Only one other baron has such troops. I considered raising a company of knights, but it takes years, not to mention far too many coins."

"You are better served by the horsemen you have. I believe you'll find they're entirely more versatile. They, at least, appear to be in good physical shape. Unfortunately, the bulk of your footmen appear overfed and under-trained, but that will sort itself out in time, providing we have it. There's nothing like a march to battle to harden warriors to the rigours of war. Do any have battle experience?"

The baron reddened slightly. "Yes. Some years ago, my father took them to lay siege to Regnitz."

"I'm afraid I'm not familiar with the name. Is it a town?"

"No, a baron's keep, although there is a village there. Some footmen saw fighting, far more so than at the Battle of Chermingen."

"How many, precisely?"

"A company's worth. More than one was present, but most have retired or moved on. My wife felt it best we group all our veterans together."

"A sensible approach," replied Beverly. "I don't suppose the other barons did likewise?"

"If they have, they haven't seen fit to inform me."

"I'm curious about your opinion on the quality of their forces?"

"I cannot claim to be an expert in such matters, but they seem impressive to me, particularly the knights."

"I'm more interested in the foot; they're the ones who'll bear the brunt of the fighting."

"I suppose they will do."

"Are any of their men veterans like yours?"

"Not that I know of. My father's feud with the Baron of Regnitz is the only baron's war in recent years. Once Lord Alain became duke, he banned such open conflicts."

"Does this mean there's bad blood between Mulsingen and Regnitz?"

"None at all," replied Lord Hagan. "In fact, my wife is the daughter of Lord Haas, the current Baron of Regnitz."

"That must make for awkward visits."

"You'd think so, but it doesn't. My father was responsible for the animosity between our two baronies, and any bitterness died with him."

"You must admit, your present circumstances are unique."

"In what way?"

"Here you are," said Beverly, "a man claiming to be lacking in battle experience, yet you have a core of men who are possibly the only ones in all of Erlingen with any knowledge of fighting."

"When you say it that way, it sounds quite ironic. Aside from that, however, what can you do to prepare us for battle?"

"How long until the duke marches for Angvil?"

"Not long now, I assure you. He waits only for the Barons of Galmund and Rosenbruck, who have the farthest to march."

"Given the time constraints, there's little I can do to make a meaningful difference."

"But you can do something?"

"I suppose," said Beverly. "What is it you propose?"

"You take command of some of my men."

"Which ones?"

"Whichever ones you think would benefit the most from your experience."

"In that case, I'll take the footmen."

"Really? I find that most surprising. I thought you'd pick the cavalry."

"While I have much experience leading horsemen, yours are in good shape. The foot, however, could benefit from a firm hand."

"Then I shall name you as the commander of my foot companies. When would you like to begin?"

"How about right now?"

"Now?"

"Certainly," said Beverly. "They're all here, armed and assembled. Not putting that to use seems like a waste."

"That makes perfectly good sense, but I thought you wanted a demonstration of our crossbows?"

"That can wait until later this afternoon."

"How would you like to start?"

"With a march around the tournament grounds."

"That shouldn't take too long."

"Then we shall do it two or three times."

The baron gasped. "Don't you think that a tad extreme?"

"Extreme? Back in Merceria, we expect our footmen to march fifteen miles a day and still fight at the end of it. I'm not saying your men could do the same after only a few days of preparation, but it's worth working towards."

Lord Hagan turned to address his warriors. "Men of Mulsingen, today we are joined by General Beverly Fitzwilliam of the distant kingdom of Merceria. She has graciously agreed to take command of the footmen to help prepare you for the coming campaign. The rest of you are dismissed, at least for now. You will, however, be required to remain in camp for the immediate future." This remark brought grumbles from everyone.

Beverly waited until the cavalry and archers dispersed before approaching the three companies of footmen.

"You don't know me," she began, "nor do I expect you to have heard of my home, Merceria, so let me begin by telling you a little about myself and my experiences."

She paused, watching their faces. Many appeared skeptical, and why wouldn't they? There was no history here of women warriors save for the Temple Knights of Saint Agnes.

"Merceria is a kingdom of warriors, descendants of mercenaries who fled the Continent centuries ago. I was raised a warrior, leading cavalry patrols against our northern neighbour. Eventually, I was knighted for my service to the Crown, then later received the honour of becoming the Knight Commander of the Order of the Hound. Many of you may wonder how that qualifies me to lead footmen."

She let the question hang a moment, keeping their interest. "The Order of the Hound is much more than a collection of knights. We are Queen Anna's chosen military commanders, not only of horse but of foot and bow. Our kingdom has been in an almost constant state of war, and I've spent my entire adult life honing my craft. I shall now pass that wisdom on to you, the footmen of Mulsingen."

She waited but sensed little enthusiasm, so she tried a different tact. "Are there any questions?"

Again, silence. "Speak freely. I shall not hold it against you."

A fellow in the back raised his hand.

"Go ahead," said Beverly. "Speak your mind."

"With all due respect, my lady, your armour is of an ancient design, and you're a woman. Hardly things that speak to your expertise."

"I tell you what," said Beverly. "Pick three of your best warriors, and I shall duel them."

Finally, a buzz of excitement. They talked amongst themselves, and then three men were pushed forward.

"Who will you fight first?" the largest fellow asked.

She grinned. "Just come at me, all at once."

TWENTY-FIVE

The Clans

SPRING 968 MC

Brogar's eyes darted about, green faces staring at him from all directions. "I don't like this. We should have brought some Dwarves to work this mine." They stood outside the doors of Tor-Maldrin, though it was now referred to as the Stonewall Enclave, thanks to the efforts of the Goblin Glisnak.

"Nonsense," replied Althea. "They've done remarkable work here, and Drakewell has done well by them."

"Sorry. I have difficulty trusting Goblins, particularly when they stare at me like I'm a side of meat."

"They're merely curious. Most have never seen a Dwarf before."

"And likely won't again." He lowered his voice slightly. "How is it their leader can speak our language?"

"He took a ring off a dead wizard, which is enchanted with a spell of tongues."

"A wizard?"

"Yes, a man going by the name of Ryfar Shozarin. From the sound of it, he was an enchanter. Glisnak said he incited the Goblins to go to war with the Clans."

As the double doors to the mine opened, the Goblins backed away, and a familiar face walked out, flanked by two wolf riders, their mounts massive in comparison.

Brogar took a step back. "I've never seen a wolf so large."

"They're mountain wolves," called out Glisnak. He nodded at his body-guards to halt, then closed the distance. "It's good to see you again, Al-tea."

"And you, Glisnak," replied the princess. "Though it's only been two days since you last visited us in Drakewell."

"Have you come to take me up on the offer of a tour?"

"Perhaps later. Other matters require my attention at present."

"Those being?"

"This is something best discussed inside."

"I might remind you that my Goblins do not speak the common tongue."

"The common tongue is not the problem; it's that I need to rest for a bit."

"Are you ill?"

"No, but I'm expecting a child."

The Goblin stared back. "Are you wishing to use our runt pit for it?"

"Runt pit?"

"Yes. Where all pitlings are placed until they crawl out."

"That is not our way," said Althea, "although I thank you for the offer."

Glisnak shrugged. "Come inside. I've had a room made up for visitors." He turned, leading them past the two wolf riders.

Brogar kept his eyes on the beasts lest they attempt to take a bite of him. Once through the door, they were led to the right.

"That's an armoury," said the Dwarf.

"It was," replied Glisnak. "I had some of our diggers bring a table and chairs up here. I believe that's how you Humans prefer to meet?"

"It is," replied Althea.

"You want something to eat?"

"No!" Brogar's abrupt reply surprised the princess. She was a little more diplomatic. "We ate right before we came here, although some water would be nice."

"I shall have the runts fetch you some."

They entered the armoury and took seats, then waited as a young Goblin entered carrying a tray of drinks on his head. Glisnak smiled as they were passed around, revealing his pointed teeth.

Althea took a sip from her cup. "That's quite nice." She looked at her Dwarf bodyguard. "It's cold, likely from an underground spring."

"We should get to the heart of the matter," suggested Brogar.

"Yes. As I told you when you visited Drakewell, we're preparing to march east. Our ally, Merceria, has been invaded and needs all the help they can get."

"And we can still help you."

"I'm not sure how," replied the Dwarf. "You lack the numbers to offer any meaningful contribution."

"Even a few Goblins could be put to use."

"How?"

"Our wolf riders could carry messages and scout the path you wish to take."

"That's an excellent point," said Althea. "And the truth is we lack cavalry at present. More importantly, it would demonstrate to others our commitment to furthering our relationship with the Goblins."

"Relationship?" said Brogar. "There's barely enough of them to fill a small village."

"That may be true now, but in time, things will change."

"I think you're overestimating their capabilities."

"I might remind you that your home of Mirstone is only a single mine, yet it's of great importance to Weldwyn. Every civilization has to start somewhere."

"Are you now a philosopher?"

"On occasion."

Brogar turned to their host. "Glisnak, do you intend to unite the Goblins of the Sunset Peaks?"

"No. Our people argue too much for that to work."

"Doesn't the same hold true of those in Stonewall?"

"No. Those who come here do so knowing we offer a new way to live. We already resumed the Dwarves' work by digging out the iron."

"Yes," added Althea. "It's having a noticeable effect on Drakewell. They now have so much iron, they're shipping it downriver. You might not see it, but their presence here will have a dramatic effect on the entire region."

"I'm not convinced," said Brogar.

"Thankfully, you don't have to be for this to work. You'll come around eventually, but your own folk have spent generations thinking Goblins pests rather than people who can contribute to the betterment of all."

"Aye. I suppose you make a good point. I shall try to be more open-minded."

"I have a question," said Glisnak.

"Go on, then. Let's hear it."

The Goblin turned, then picked up a metal helmet with teeth marks gouged across the top. "Can your people show us how to make more of these?"

"You mean a metal helmet?"

"Yes."

"I'm a bodyguard. I don't make armour."

"I know, but your fellow Dwarves have a tinker amongst them, if I'm not mistaken."

"A tinker? Oh, you're talking about a smith."

"Yes."

"I'll have a word with Haldrim. I'm sure he can arrange it. That doesn't necessarily mean your tinker has the wherewithal to work metal of that quality."

"Flint is a good tinker. He only needs to be shown once."

"I shall speak with our good captain as soon as we return to Drakewell."

"When do you march?" asked Glisnak.

"Three days from now," replied Althea. "We can delay a further day or two if you need to."

"Three days will work; that's half a six-day. By then, our riders will have returned."

"Returned from where?"

"They ride up and down the foothills of the Sunset Peaks, seeking more to join our enclave."

"How many of your people would accompany us?"

"Six wolf riders, maybe twelve if the others return in time. We'll also take some lobbers and grunts."

"Lobbers are archers," explained Althea, "while the grunts are armed with spears."

"I will also bring Virdu."

"What's a Virdu?" asked Brogar.

"My pit-sister, she's a bender."

The Dwarf stared back in confusion.

"She bends bones into shape?"

"You mean a healer?"

"Yes, but with magic."

"Ah, a Life Mage, then. That would prove most useful in the coming campaign." He looked at Althea. "I'm starting to come round to this idea of them accompanying us."

Althea watched as the Dragon Company marched out of Drakewell. The fifty Dwarven arbalesters, wearing the Dwarf mail so common to their race, were followed by a company of archers from Drakewell. The plan was simple: march downriver to Galchrest, east to Klinridge, and on to Loranguard. There, they would rendezvous with her husband, Lochlan, who would be bringing volunteers from Dungannon, Banburn, and Halsworth. There was no guarantee that any other Clan would send men to help, but it was worth the risk. To her mind, the Clans were a hotheaded group and focusing their ire on repelling the invaders of Merceria was a far better choice than letting their resentment build into open hostilities again with her homeland.

A dozen wolf riders passed by, their long hair, held in place by a topknot, flying out behind them.

"They look good," said Glisnak. "I wish I had more."

"I'll admit they're impressive," replied Althea, "but I hope you haven't sent them all eastward. I'd hate to think we've stripped your defences."

"Not at all. Tarzil will stay behind to keep an eye on things, and I have assurances from the Chief of Drakewell that they would come to our aid if Stonewall were threatened."

Another group of Goblins marched by, though perhaps marched wasn't the correct term for it. They were a motley group, with lobbers leading the way, and the grunts following. Goblins were physically weak, but their quick reflexes more than made up for the deficiency. A single Goblin wandered over to the small group.

"Ah," said Glisnak. "This is my pit-sister, Virdu. I believe I mentioned her before?"

The bender bowed.

"She doesn't speak the common tongue but is quick to learn."

"What's a pit-sister?" asked Brogar.

"Goblins are born with teeth, so we're placed in a large pit in the ground and kept fed. When we grow enough to climb out, we become runts and are accepted into the enclave. If two should climb out simultaneously, they are known as pit-siblings."

"It's their version of brothers and sisters," added Althea.

"Have you a pit-brother or sister, Master Brogar?"

"No," replied the Dwarf, "but Haldrim does, a brother named Caldrim. He commands another company of arbalesters back in Mirstone. I suppose you might say it's the family business."

"Business?" replied Glisnak. "I don't know that word."

"Doesn't that ring of yours allow you to understand our language?"

"It does, but our language, Garspeak, has no direct translation."

"A business can be thought of as a trade. Look at it this way: you're a lobber, and Virdu a bender. Think of those names as defining your trade."

"This makes sense. Those other Dwarves are lobbers, like me, but I've yet to work out what you are, Brogar."

"In your terms, I suppose I'd be a grunt. My job is to keep Princess Althea safe. Have you something similar in your culture?"

"Most chieftains have grunts who keep them safe."

"Do you?"

"I don't need them. I have the loyalty of the wolf riders. Few would argue with a mountain wolf."

"I see why," replied the Dwarf. "They're impressive."

"Yes," added Althea, "and faster than I would've thought, maybe even faster than Weldwyn's light cavalry."

"Aye. I would agree, although they wear next to no armour."

"That will change in time," replied Glisnak. "So far, Flint has had little time to work on armour."

"That reminds me," said Brogar. "How did he make out with our smith?"

"I'm not an expert at such things, but he assures me the advice was most helpful."

"So he can fashion helmets now?"

"I won't know until I return, but he sounds confident."

"Strange how things work out."

"Strange?"

"Yes. Here we are, Dwarves, Humans, and Goblins, all working together for probably the first time in history."

"It gets even better," said Althea. "Only a short while ago, Clansmen working side by side with Weldwyn would have been unimaginable."

"It's thanks to you," said Brogar. "If you hadn't befriended Glisnak's people all those months ago, we would've perished at the hands of that dragon."

"Dragons don't have hands," said Glisnak.

Brogar chuckled. "No, I don't suppose they do, now that you mention it. Might I ask, Highness, how you intend to employ these… What did you call them?"

"Lobbers and grunts," supplied Glisnak.

"Yes, that's it. I think them a fine addition, but they're not so numerous that we could use them on the battlefield."

"I've been thinking on just that matter," replied Althea. "I intend for them to safeguard the camp's perimeter at night."

"Good idea. We can position them in groups of three."

"Six would be better," Glisnak advised them. "It's our sacred number. I don't believe in such nonsense, but I can't say the same about the grunts. They're a superstitious bunch."

"Then six it shall be," replied Althea. "Did your people bring any of those mushrooms with you? The ones that let you see in the dark?"

"We did, but they need to be used sparingly. We're unlikely to find more once we leave the foothills." Glisnak stared off to the east. "Do you think we'll see any Orcs or Elves?"

"Orcs, most certainly—they form a major part of the Mercerian Army. However, the Elves will be employed farther east."

"Too bad. I've often wondered what they would be like."

"You'll have a chance to meet some Trolls, if that's any consolation."

"Trolls? I've never even heard of those. What are they?"

"Large creatures, taller than a Human and with skin akin to stone. They have two arms and legs like us but are immensely strong."

"It's hard to imagine anyone that size, let alone someone with stone skin."

"It's not stone, just very tough skin."

"Anything else to look forward to?"

"I suppose mounted warriors should be added to the list," said Althea. "Speaking of which, we'll have to show your people how to fight if confronted by them."

"My grunts already know how to fight."

"Not against horses, they don't," said Brogar. "Warhorses are massive beasts, capable of crushing us under their hooves. Think of your mountain wolves, then give them longer legs."

"A frightening thought. Do they bite?"

"Not generally. They rely more on their weight than anything else. And they won't be alone, for they'll have armoured warriors atop them. The combination can be deadly."

"I look forward to seeing them, but perhaps only from a distance. Do they use bows?"

"Of course not, they're animals."

"I meant their riders."

"I don't know," said Brogar. "None of Weldwyn's cavalry used bows, but I understand the Norlanders did when they invaded Merceria."

Glisnak thought this over. "That makes sense. Our own wolf riders don't use bows because it's too hard to cling to their wolf's hair while using one."

"They don't have saddles?"

"What's a saddle?"

"I'll explain it later," said Althea. "We need to get moving, or we'll lose sight of our troops."

At Galchrest, they picked up a company of foot before beginning the long trek cross-country to Klinridge. It was a laborious march across a dry and oftentimes harsh region, but it was worth it, for the chieftain there lent them two companies of footmen to add to the cause.

Just as welcome were the boats waiting to take the expedition downriver to Loranguard. They now numbered close to two hundred fifty warriors, not including the Goblins, a sizable contribution likely to grow once it reached the border of Weldwyn.

Althea took great pains to ensure they would not be seen as hostile, sending word in advance of their arrival. Even so, she was nervous, for the mere sight of so many Clansmen marching towards the city would cause a stir.

She needn't have worried, for her brother, King Alric, waited at the border with her husband, along with the men he'd managed to assemble.

Althea moved closer to embrace Lochlan, then turned to her brother. "Your Majesty," she said. "It feels like forever since I've seen your face."

"And I yours," he replied. He nodded at her troops, now moving into the makeshift camp. "You've been busy." He squinted. "Are those Goblins?"

"They are—from the Stonewall Enclave. I wrote to you some time ago about how they helped slay the dragon."

"You did, but I don't remember you mentioning a place called Stonewall."

"That's their name for the old Dwarven mine of Tor-Maldrin."

"You've outdone me," admitted Lochlan. "I thought I did well raising two hundred men, yet you've managed to bring more."

"Nonsense. We're on even terms once you take my Dwarven guard out of it." She waved forward the Goblin leader, though he hesitated to approach the king's horse. "This is Glisnak, Chief of the Stonewall Enclave."

Alric bowed his head slightly.

"He speaks our language," explained Althea, "thanks to a ring of tongues."

"In that case," said the king, "let me thank you for your contribution to our efforts, Chieftain Glisnak."

"You are welcome." The Goblin turned to Althea. "Is that the correct response?"

"It is. Tell me, Brother, what route have you chosen for us to travel to Merceria?"

"Rather an interesting one, if you don't mind me saying. We shall be going by ship. I have several standing by in Loranguard."

"How exciting. More time on the water. Will any Royal troops be joining us?"

"Thanks to the earl, I was able to commandeer a couple of companies from the local garrison, though it'll mean weakening the city's defences."

"Your garrison is safe," said Lochlan. "And if you should find it otherwise, you only need send word to Klinridge or Halsworth, and they will come to your aid."

"You surprise me," replied Alric. "It wasn't so long ago that the Clans invaded Weldwyn, yet now they're willing to come to our aid?"

Lochlan grinned. "What can I say? We've spent a good portion of last winter travelling from town to town, building goodwill. It was Althea's idea."

"I should say that comes as a surprise, but it doesn't. She was always the sort to take matters into her own hands, but I am curious how she convinced them we're no longer their enemy."

"In a word—flax," replied Althea. "The Clans have plenty of it, and I convinced the boat holders to ship it to Riversend and Loranguard at a considerable profit." She grinned. "It's amazing what an influx of coins does to settle differences."

TWENTY-SIX

Neiburg

SPRING 968 MC

Townsfolk fled their homes, eager to escape the capital, Neiburg, before the Halvarians arrived. They flooded the streets, hurrying east, loaded down with what goods they could carry, hoping it wasn't too late.

Rilan Paldrin raced through the Palace. News had arrived that the Army of Angvil had been defeated, and he must find Her Grace, the Duchess, to ensure her safety. He came across a maid dusting the frame of an immense painting.

"Corella," he said. "What in the name of the Saints are you doing?"

"Performing my duties," she replied.

"The empire approaches. You must get away from here as fast as possible!"

"What have I to fear from the Halvarians?"

He was dumbstruck. "I beg your pardon?"

"It's not as if I'm anyone important."

"My dear, you are a servant of the duchess, which puts you in grave danger."

"I'm a simple maid."

"You serve the ruling house of Angvil. That alone warrants your death. The empire wipes away everyone connected with the previous rulers when it conquers a realm. Have you learned nothing? Now go while you still have the chance."

She hesitated, struggling to figure out what to do with her rag.

"Give it to me," said Rilan. He waited while she turned it over to him, and then she ran off, her footsteps receding down the hallway. He stared at the rag, his mind lost in thought. They would flee this Palace, of that he had no doubt: what matter a rag?

Her Grace frequently took her morning meal in the parlour, a room gifted with large windows that let in the morning sun. He hurried on towards it, tossing the rag aside.

The empty halls gave the place an eerie feeling, but he pushed on, undeterred. He slowed to catch his breath as he arrived at the parlour. He was about to address the Duchess of Angvil; it would not do to appear rushed.

He opened the door to see the duchess staring out the window.

"Your Grace," he said, a note of relief in his voice. "We must prepare you to evacuate the city."

She remained silent, staring out the window.

"Your Grace?" He moved closer.

"All is lost," she finally said. "The army is destroyed, the enemy at our very doorstep."

"We must abandon the Palace, Your Grace."

"It will do little good. The Empire of Halvaria will conquer all the known lands."

"The Petty Kingdoms will never allow it."

She turned. There were no tears or anger, only a look of utter defeat. The light had left her eyes, and horror threatened to overwhelm Rilan for the first time in his life.

"All is not lost, Your Grace. Surely Erlingen will come to our rescue?"

"Erlingen?" she sneered. "Do you honestly believe they have a chance against the might of the empire?"

"This is not like you, Your Grace. What happened to the fire in your heart?"

"It was extinguished the moment I learned of our defeat." She turned once more to the windows. "Look at them run for their lives. Have they no dignity?"

Rilan came to stand beside her. "Dignity is a trait reserved for the wealthy."

"Perhaps."

She retreated from the window, but the scene below captivated him. A cart had overturned, spilling someone's belongings. The owners abandoned their meagre possessions, fleeing up the street while others trampled their clothes into the muck and mire of the roadway. Rilan couldn't help but be overcome. Here was the duchess, lamenting the army's loss, but the common folk always suffered the most. His heart went out to the unknown family forced to abandon their belongings. Would they survive to tell how they fled the capital, or would they die on the road, victims of war?

War. The very word brought a lump to his throat. People died on the battlefield, but far more perished, thanks to war's brothers: pestilence, plague, and starvation. Was this the fate that awaited him?

At the sound of a cup dropping, he turned to see the duchess slump to the floor. Her cup rolled across the floor, spilling its cloudy contents. He rushed to her side, picking up one of her hands and feeling the coldness.

Her eyes fluttered open. "Forgive me," she muttered. "I go now to a better place." Her eyes rolled up into her head, and then she went limp.

Tears welled in Rilan's eyes as he turned away, unable to bear the loss. Duchess Burghild had been a most gracious lady, but she'd been wrong about one thing. Defeat was not inevitable; the empire was not destined to rule over the Petty Kingdoms. Hope sprang eternal in the hearts of the Saints, and at that moment, he found it rising in his own. He would avenge the death of this woman and see the empire brought to its knees.

He rose to his feet, briefly glancing around the room. He'd led a privileged life serving the elite of the elite, yet it now crumbled before him.

Rilan looked one final time at the duchess, a wave of anger building up within him. "To the Underworld with the empire!" he shouted. "I refuse to give up so easily." He stormed from the room.

"There it is, Neiburg, the gateway to the heart of the Petty Kingdoms." Hamath Nordin was filled with good humour, and why wouldn't he be? His legion had crushed the Army of Angvil and was now heading to clear Erlingen.

His deputy commander was less enthusiastic. "The men are exhausted."

"Understandable, given the speed of our advance, but sacrifices must be made. I look forward to spending the night in the Royal Palace in Neiburg."

"The ruler of Angvil is a duchess, my lord, not a queen."

"What's your point?"

"It's not, by definition, a Royal Palace, merely a ducal one."

Nordin waved away the criticism. "It matters little. We shall still spend the night in comfort. Send my respects to Captain Borke and have his cavalry encircle the city."

"Captain Borke is dead, my lord. If you recall, we lost him before the battle."

"Oh yes. I'd forgotten. Remind me again who his replacement is?"

"Captain Desjardin."

"He's a provincial, isn't he?"

"He is, Lord, but he has faithfully served the empire for his entire adult life."

"And before that?"

"He was a child in the conquered territory of Auverney, my lord."

Nordin shook his head. "I have a hard time keeping track of all our provinces."

"It fell to the empire about a century ago," replied his aide. "You may recall the last stand was at Guilford."

"Is that a town?"

"No, a keep. It took two legions to dig them out of it."

"Has the province been loyal ever since?"

"Their men would hardly be in service to the empire if it weren't."

Nordin smiled. "That's what I like about you; you're always blunt and to the point. You'll make a fine commander-general one day, providing you play the game as well as you advise."

"The game, my lord?"

"Yes. The game of politics. The empire thrives on it. Chart your course correctly, and you'll go far. However, make one mistake, and you will soon be commanding a penal colony in the southern jungles."

"I shall be careful to avoid offending anyone."

"That would be the wisest route. Any word on the enemy survivors?"

"They are withdrawing east, towards the border of Erlingen, with our cavalry harassing them, adding to their constant state of panic."

Nordin chuckled. "This is all working out magnificently. Word of our success will soon reach the ears of Lady Edora, and then our star will rise."

"Our star, my lord?"

"Yes. Until now, we've been supporting the Ninth. This shows her that we're just as good as them."

"But they have two victories, while we have but one."

"True, but Angvil was the first opposition of any consequence. Remind me what that place was called?"

"Which place, my lord?"

A flicker of annoyance crossed the face of the commander-general of the Fifth. "That hill where we destroyed Angvil's army."

"Beggar's Reach, my lord."

"How disappointing. I was hoping for something a little more…"

"Interesting?"

"Yes, that's the word. The Battle of Beggar's Reach sounds so mundane."

"Could we call it the Battle of Neiburg?"

"I admit that is considerably more impressive," said Nordin, "but it contradicts Imperial policy. Our custom has always been to name it after the closest landmark or village, and the battle was nowhere near Neiburg. I'm afraid it's Beggar's Reach."

"Might I ask a question, my lord?"

"Most definitely."

"By all accounts, the armies facing us are growing stronger. How long do you think before we're outnumbered?"

"You worry too much. We always knew the border realms were weak. It makes perfect sense that opposition increases as we march deeper into the Petty Kingdoms. That's why we're marching parallel to the Ninth Legion: to pin the enemy in place, then overwhelm them with the might of two legions."

"I understand the strategy, but which legion will do the pinning and which the overwhelming?"

"Doubtless, the Duke of Erlingen has assembled his army and is on the march. We must see how he reacts to our advance before we make that decision. Fear not, though. We shall defeat him."

"Of that, I have no doubt."

Nordin smiled. "Ah, I see now. You're not concerned over victory so much as who receives the glory."

"The thought had crossed my mind."

"Don't worry. There'll be plenty of it to go around once the real campaign kicks off."

"Are we not already deep into it?"

"This was nothing but a warm-up, a tactical manoeuvre designed to draw out our real enemy."

"The Army of Erlingen?"

"Precisely. The plan is to defeat them and then march on the so-called Northern Alliance."

"And then?"

"Then nothing. With those two armies defeated, none will be left to oppose us."

"What of Hadenfeld?"

"I'm impressed," said Nordin. "You know your history, but you're a little behind on recent events. Hadenfeld endured not one but two civil wars of late, leaving their army much weaker than before."

"They could still pose a threat."

"I think you overestimate their strength. Let me assure you, the empire's greatest minds have determined they are no threat to us. Here's a little nugget of wisdom: when offered information that benefits your cause, do not question it."

"Understood, my lord."

"Good. Let's get the legion moving, shall we? I want to sample the delights of Neiburg."

. . .

In the wake of the army's defeat, the population of Neiburg fled east, seeking refuge from the Halvarian invaders. They took everything they could carry, but after a few miles, the burden of their possessions weighed them down. The constant fear of enemy warriors appearing convinced them to abandon all but the most essential belongings. Refuse littered the road, the sum of people's lifetimes trampled in the mad haste to escape.

It was a depressing sight, but Rilan Paldrin pushed on, determined to locate whatever remained of the warriors of Angvil. A woman resting on the side of the road beckoned to him. He moved closer, eager to offer assistance as she lay against a tree trunk.

"Water," she croaked out, her voice hoarse and dry.

He pulled forth his waterskin and dribbled some into her mouth. Only after she was done did he notice her leg had been crushed, likely by the wheel of a wagon. He could do nothing to ease the woman's pain. Panic rose within his chest, and he fought to control it. This shouldn't be happening. The Army of Angvil should have vanquished the invaders and sent them running back to the border. Their loss was a disaster of epic proportions.

A fire built within him, fuelled by anger and resentment. The duchess had chosen the coward's way out. Now, he and the other commoners were left to bear the full force of the empire's wrath! No longer content to serve a noble, he would seek retribution by fighting against the world's injustices. He saw himself as a great hero, standing atop a hill while an adoring crowd watched.

He was brought crashing back to his senses by the injured woman's sigh as her head tilted to one side. Tears filled Rilan's eyes as he realized she had passed on to the Afterlife.

Marlena watched as the remnants of the Army of Angvil stumbled past. Over a thousand men had stood at Beggar's Reach, but fewer than three hundred survived. Added to that were her own Temple Knights, who could barely field a single company.

"What do we do now?" asked Sister Johanna.

"We do what we should have done in the first place. We retreat into Erlingen and hope the duke has the men to oppose the empire."

"And if he doesn't?"

The Temple Commander turned to regard her aide. "I don't know what to say. Our only hope is that Erlingen received word of the invasion. Should that prove not the case, there's little more we can contribute."

"Are you suggesting our company will disband?"

"What choice have we? Our supplies are gone, our horses weak, and we have no funds to reorganize. Added to that are our losses. Each battle reduces our numbers: one more, and we shall be unable to field even half a company. At what point do we become useless?"

"This is not like you, Commander. You, amongst all of us, are guided by your faith."

"A faith shaken by death. How many more sisters must perish? And to what end? Will we be slowly whittled down until the last of us departs this mortal realm alone?"

"We will defeat Halvaria!"

"How?"

"I beg your pardon?"

"It's a simple question," replied Marlena. "Tell me how you see this war playing out?"

"The Army of Erlingen will defeat the legions."

"Both of them? I think you overestimate their chances."

"But they must!" insisted Johanna.

"Must? You speak as though everything is foreordained."

"Isn't it? Do we not worship the Saints for exactly that reason? Aren't their very words meant to lead us on a path towards redemption?"

"Redemption? For what? My father used to torment me. Are you now suggesting I must find redemption for his sins against me?"

Johanna averted her gaze. "Sorry. I spoke out of turn."

Marlena closed her eyes, her thoughts drifting back to her time before joining the order. She was the daughter of a duke, a luck of birth that should've had her living in splendour. Instead, her father had treated her abysmally. Only after his death did she finally find solace in the Temple Knights of Saint Agnes.

"Have you any family left, Commander?"

The question snapped Marlena out of her musings. "I do, although I haven't seen them in years. My oldest brother, Ernst, is a duke back in Abelard: at least, he was the last I heard. As for my other brother, I have no knowledge of his whereabouts. We were never the coziest of families."

"My life was one of neglect," offered Johanna. "I was the fifth child of an already impoverished merchant."

"Is that why you joined the order?"

"Not at first. I was married off to a cobbler. He was a decent enough fellow, but things took a turn for the worse when his business failed."

"You don't have to tell me this if it's too painful."

"No. It helps to talk about it. He eventually took ill, making things even worse. Unable to pay the rent, we were tossed into the streets. He died a few weeks later. I sought refuge at a Mathewite mission, later joining the Church. I was only a lay sister initially, but I've always been a hard worker, and my superior suggested I might be better employed as a Temple Knight. It wasn't so much a calling as it was a convenient way to be rid of the city that had caused me such grief."

"Thank you," said Marlena.

"For what?"

"For reminding me that our past is a part of us but doesn't define who we are. Here I am feeling sorry for myself, yet others have suffered as much, if not more." She straightened in the saddle.

"You're different all of a sudden, as if a light has been lit inside you."

"Your words have restored my faith. The situation we find ourselves in at present is neither new nor as hopeless as it appears. Like our patron Saint, we face great odds, but we will follow her example and overcome them, as she did when she stood up to the High Lord of Herani."

"Inspiring words."

"Indeed, but there is another expression I favour, said to be those of our order's very first Grand Mistress."

"Which is?"

"Have faith, but keep your sword at the ready."

TWENTY-SEVEN

Tournament Grounds

SPRING 968 MC

The Army of Erlingen stood on the tournament grounds, their numbers swelled by a second army of wagons and camp followers. They'd assembled to fight the Halvarians and awaited only the duke's orders to march towards the enemy they all feared.

Beverly looked over her small command. Lord Hagan Stein had given her three companies of footmen to whip into shape, and now, only a few days later, she was beginning to see some remarkable progress.

She'd started by marching them around the tournament grounds each morning in full armour, then followed up with weapon practice and close-order drill designed to teach them to operate as a proper Mercerian company would. The men of Mulsingen grumbled at first, then began taking pride in their progress. Standing beside the other barons' companies, their discipline became more evident with their perfectly formed ranks.

Duke Heinrich trotted out in front of his army, his barons following, which Beverly found strange. If you were organizing an army around nobles, wouldn't you think they'd stand with their men—at least, that was the Mercerian way.

She watched as His Grace came to a halt, his back to the assembled men. His barons then trotted closer, each halting in front of their own contingent of troops.

"Ah. I see now," said Beverly.

"See what?" asked Emerson, her most senior captain.

"I was curious why the barons weren't here with their men."

He chuckled. "They don't like waiting. It's an age-old story. We're to be here at noon, making us wait half the afternoon before they show up."

"Half the afternoon? The sun's hardly moved from its peak."

"Well, it feels like half the afternoon." He fell silent as Lord Hagan drew closer and took up his position at the head of his men.

The duke yelled out a command and then rode south towards the road. His own personal warriors followed, then the men commanded by the barons, in order of seniority: at least that's what Beverly assumed. If she were in charge, she'd send the cavalry out ahead even though this was considered friendly territory, but the army wasn't hers to command. Instead, she must do her duty and follow Lord Hagan's orders.

She waited an eternity for the army to move out, and then, finally, the men of Mulsingen joined the march. Her companies advanced quickly, bringing them too close to those in front, forcing them to slow. This, in turn, led to problems with those following, causing a ripple effect. It was frustrating in the extreme, but the army settled into a steady rhythm shortly after they left the tournament grounds.

The situation made her appreciate Gerald's reforms to the Army of Merceria. At the time, it had seemed like a small thing, but insisting on a standard pace made a significant difference on the campaign trail, allowing troops to carry out complex manoeuvres in the midst of battles. It had been a revolution in the conduct of war. The thought gave her pause. Was Halvaria as disciplined?

Aldwin and Aubrey, who'd been waiting alongside the road, rode over, falling into place on either side of her. Sir Owen had been asked to accompany His Grace, the Duke, along with Krazuhk, whose ability to use the common tongue improved daily.

"Well?" said Aubrey. "What do you think, Cousin?"

"We certainly have the numbers," replied Beverly. "I only hope we can get this army ready for battle."

"Ready?" said Aldwin. He twisted in the saddle to view the men marching behind. "They appear ready enough to me."

"It's not these men I'm worried about; it's the rest of the army."

"You don't believe they're up to the task?"

"Not at the moment, and therein lies the problem."

"I've seen you go into battle with less."

"True, but they were Mercerians; I had no need to worry about their resolve. The men of Erlingen are well-equipped, but at the end of the day, it's discipline that'll make the difference, and I'm afraid they'll be outmatched in that regard."

They passed a horseman wearing a brown surcoat, who then spurred on his mount to ride closer. "Lady Beverly?" he called out.

"Brother Cyric? I see you're doing much better."

"I am, thanks to Lady Aubrey." He nodded in greeting, then glanced at the men following her. "I sense you've had a hand in preparing Lord Hagan's footmen for the coming campaign."

"I did what I could in the time I had. Were you looking for me in particular or just passing by?"

"I was seeking you. We've received news from the west that I thought you might be interested in, though I fear it's not good."

"Go on."

"The Halvarians are rolling through Angvil. From what we've heard, Duchess Burghild was determined to make a stand, which would likely have already happened."

"Has your regional commander decided to join the cause?"

"He has, though only in a limited capacity. One company of our Temple Knights is to accompany the army."

"Do the duke's knights wear red?" said Aubrey. "I saw knights in that colour back on the tournament grounds."

"Those are Temple Knights of Saint Agnes, a company's worth. Not a large number, but our order works closely with them."

"And how does that work?" asked Beverly. "Do they follow the duke's orders or act independently?"

"I'm afraid that's a difficult thing to answer. The Temple Knights only follow the Church's orders, but lately, there have been some... developments."

"Those being?"

"I'm forbidden to go into detail, but suffice it to say the senior chain of command has seen great upheaval in recent years. As such, each Temple Captain will make their own decisions on the battlefield. They will consult with His Grace, the Duke, but I'm afraid he has no battle experience."

"Not the most encouraging news. I assume someone brought the situation in Angvil to the duke's attention?"

"Yes, but he has not altered his strategy one whit. He still intends to march straight to the border to confront our enemy head-on."

"I doubt he has much choice," said Beverly. "If he delays, it would see his own lands at the mercy of the enemy."

"Mercy is not a characteristic commonly associated with the empire. They are ruthless, not that the Petty Kingdoms are any better. Everywhere an army marches, there are tales of plundering, murder, even rape, and that's on both sides. Sometimes, I wonder why we bother fighting. Is it the same in Merceria?"

"War brings out the worst in people, but our army punishes that behaviour. I've witnessed several Mercerian troops hanged for such offences, though not without a tribunal."

"Fascinating."

"Do Temple Knights have such problems?"

"Not the Mathewites, I assure you, or the Agnesites. We are highly disciplined and dedicated to our respective vows."

"I noted you failed to mention the other religious fighting orders."

"I suppose I did, didn't I? Well, as our blessed Saint likes to remind us, if you can't say something nice about someone, you should refrain from mentioning them. That's not a direct quote, merely my interpretation of it." He paused, looking skyward.

Beverly let him have his moment of peace. She glanced over at Aldwin, who returned her look with a wicked grin, and blushed. After all they'd gone through, her heart still fluttered at the thought of having him near her.

"I wonder," said Cyric at last. "What do you think our chances are of defeating this invasion?"

"I'm no expert on Halvaria."

"But thanks to your cousin Aubrey, you've been updated on events back in Merceria, yes?"

"I have, but it's not exactly good news."

"Go on."

"So far, we've learned they're highly motivated and well-trained. One-on-one, they're likely superior to the men of Erlingen."

"Do I detect a 'but' in there somewhere?"

"The history of Merceria tells me it's possible to win against a superior enemy, providing you have the will to do so. The key to this battle is forcing them to meet us at a place of our choosing."

"You speak as though you've read the writings of General Axalon. The title of general is a recent affectation, but you get my meaning."

"Who was General Axalon?"

"A great Thalamite leader who lived before the rise of Therengia, responsible for the first Empire of Eiddenwerthe, or at least the first Human one. I cannot speak to the history of the Elder Races. His teachings are required reading for those wishing to achieve the rank of Temple Captain."

"Might I ask how long you've been a Temple Knight?"

"More years than I care to admit."

"Yet you haven't risen in rank. I find that surprising, considering your grasp of military matters."

"I am content to serve as a simple knight as it frees me up to indulge in my pastime."

"Which is?"

"Investigating the unusual, everything from supernatural occurrences to outright murder."

"Supernatural?" said Aubrey. "You mean magical, don't you?"

"Not everything can be ascribed to magic," replied Cyric. "My experience reveals there are things that defy both the laws of nature and magic."

"Are you a mage, perhaps?"

"No, though I have a greater understanding of such things than most common folk."

"Common folk," said Aldwin. "Your manner of speech would suggest you're high born."

"I was," replied Cyric, "but I gave that up when I joined the order."

"Let me guess, you're the younger brother?"

"No, the heir, but that is a discussion best left firmly in the past."

"Sorry. I didn't mean to offend."

"And you didn't, I assure you. On an entirely different matter, I wonder if you and Lady Beverly might be interested in meeting with the Temple Captains?"

"To what end?" asked Beverly.

"From what you've told me, your Mercerian training is very similar to that used by our respective orders. I thought it might be interesting to compare notes."

"What do you think, Aldwin?"

"Fine by me. It'll allow me the opportunity to see their armour up close."

"When would you like to meet?" Beverly asked.

"This evening," replied Cyric, "before the rigours of the march take their toll. Should they be interested, you're welcome to bring the rest of your group."

"I think I'll pass," said Aubrey. "I want to see how Krazuhk is doing, not to mention Owen."

"Would you be able to meet at dinner time?"

"I shouldn't like to impose," replied Beverly.

"It will be no trouble at all, I assure you. Now, if you'll excuse me, I have other business to attend to."

The Temple Knights' camp was separated from the rest of the army by about two hundred paces. The two orders were separated by a gap, with their tents arranged in strict lines.

A brother of the order met Beverly and Aldwin at the perimeter. He led them to a small pavilion, outside of which stood two Temple Knights: one of Saint Mathew, bedecked in the customary mail of that order, and one of Saint Agnes, wearing the plate armour more common amongst the knights of the Petty Kingdoms. They entered to find Brother Cyric in the company of two others.

"Ah, Lady Beverly, Lord Aldwin. I'm so glad you made it. Shall I make introductions?"

"If you would be so kind," replied Beverly.

"This is Temple Captain Vitaly, who commands the Mathewite company. He fought in Arnsfeld seven years ago, so he has some experience with Halvarian tactics. Temple Captain Petra commands the Agnesites and fought against the empire at Temple Bay, back in ninety-eight."

"Ninety-eight?" said Aldwin.

"Twelve years ago," explained Petra. "I've heard you Mercerians use a different calendar."

"Two experienced captains," said Beverly. "That's good to hear."

"Not as good as you think," said Vitaly. "Our combined experience tells us the empire is not to be trifled with."

"What can we expect, going forward?"

The Temple Captains looked at each other.

"You go first," said Petra.

"Where shall I begin?" replied Vitaly.

"The beginning would be best, I think," replied Beverly.

"The empire had been massing on Arnsfeld's borders for some time, so the invasion was not unexpected. It also came to the regional Temple Commander's attention that the Halvarians were trying to cause instability in the region."

"That would be Temple Commander Charlaine," added Petra.

"Wait a moment," said Beverly. "Wasn't she the one who disappeared a while back?"

"Yes," replied Petra. "Along with several companies of our Temple Knights. It appears you know our history."

"Only small bits of it. Please continue, Captain Vitaly."

Vitaly cleared his throat. "She accurately predicted the attack route and prepared a defensive position with the aid of an Earth Mage. She also lured part of the attacking legion away by convincing the local baron to hole up in his keep."

"And the actual battle?"

"It was a near-run thing, I can tell you. There was a tremendous loss of life on both sides, but the Temple Knights of Saint Agnes's charge changed the tide of battle. They cut through the enemy line and charged into their rear, creating havoc."

"Might I ask what tactic the empire used to attack?"

"They began with their usual, assaulting with their provincial troops all along the defensive line, backed up by their Imperial cavalry, and would have succeeded had it not been for the presence of the Elves."

"Elves?" said Aldwin. "We have them as allies back in Merceria."

"I'm not sure where Temple Commander Charlaine found them," replied Vitaly, "but thank the Saints she did, else the battle would have ended quite differently."

"Let's get back to the empire," said Beverly. "How would you break down their organization?"

"I estimate about a quarter of their forces were mounted, with another quarter bowmen of various descriptions. The rest were footmen, though they varied considerably in terms of equipment. They employed their foot in the usual way, marching straight into our defences in one large mass while the cavalry tried to outflank us, which is where the Elves came in. The Halvarian cavalry tends to be broken down into the heavily armoured elite horsemen, akin to our knights, and the lighter horse used more as skirmishers or scouts. My own experience in the battle involved my company charging in to save one of our flanks from collapsing. It cost us dearly, losing half our strength, but we held them."

"And you commanded?"

"Oh no. I was only a Temple Knight then. After the battle, however, I was sent to the Antonine, where I trained to become a Temple Captain. Torburg is my first assignment at my current rank."

"I see," replied Beverly. "Anything else you'd care to impart?"

"They're capable warriors, Lady Beverly, but they make mistakes, or at least they did at the Battle of the Brinwald. The trick is being prepared to exploit any opportunity that presents itself."

"I shall certainly bring that nugget of information to the attention of His Grace, providing I have the opportunity. I can't, however, guarantee he'll heed the advice."

"I thought you might say as much. His Grace is proud, and it could prove difficult to sway him."

"What of you, Captain Petra? Anything to add?"

"The Battle of Temple Bay consisted of a fleet engagement followed by an assault on their stronghold. The land engagement was more like a large skirmish."

"And your assessment of the empire's abilities?"

"One-on-one, they were no match for us. Our attacking force consisted of only Temple Knights, though all three orders were represented."

"Yes," said Cyric. "I should point out this was before the Temple Knights of Saint Cunar became more isolationist."

"One thing of note," said Petra, "is that they employed mages."

"What types of mages?" asked Beverly.

"At least one Fire Mage I'm aware of, along with someone able to summon a green mist that burned the lungs."

"I shall have to consult my cousin on that one."

"Don't bother," offered Aldwin. "What you're describing was likely a Necromancer."

"I'm surprised you know that," said Beverly.

"It comes from spending so much time with Albreda. She hates Necromancers."

"Albreda?" said Cyric.

"She's a Druid," explained Aldwin. "What you'd call an Earth Mage, and the most powerful caster in Merceria, if not all of Eiddenwerthe."

"A bold claim. Might I ask who mentored her?"

"No one. She was self-taught."

"A wild mage?" said Petra. "The presence of such would not be tolerated in the Petty Kingdoms."

"Why is that?"

"Many believe uncontrolled knowledge of magic is dangerous to the caster and those around her."

"And by many, you mean…"

"Those who run the arcane colleges across the Continent."

"Then they don't know what they're missing," said Aldwin. "While she wasn't trained in the traditional sense, her freedom to explore has made her the power she is today."

"Yes," added Beverly, "and she passed on many of her techniques to my cousin Aubrey. Albreda is highly regarded by all, including our queen."

"I see I've hit a tender spot," said Petra, "and for that, I apologize. I myself have no magic, so I can only rely on what I've been told."

"Trust me," replied Aldwin, "if Albreda were with us in Erlingen, we'd have a much better chance of defeating these Halvarians."

TWENTY-EIGHT

The Earls of Norland

SPRING 968 MC

Lord Asher, the Earl of Beaconsgate, shifted in his seat, his gaze sweeping across the rest of the Nobles Council of Norland. "I fail to understand the need for the presence of the Orc."

"She came all the way from Holdcross to attend this meeting," replied Bronwyn. "You shall address her as Ghodrug, as befitting a chieftain, particularly one who rules over such a large portion of land."

"Ravensguard is no longer an earldom of Norland."

"It is not, but if we wish for an everlasting peace between our peoples, it serves our interests to hear her opinion. Must I remind you that everyone here agreed to accept her presence when I was made queen?"

Asher sat back, steepling his fingers, a habit his queen found most annoying.

Lord Creighton, the Earl of Riverhurst, used the lull in the conversation to interject his thoughts. "We've all travelled a significant distance to be here, Your Majesty. Can we get to the heart of the matter?"

"I called you all together," explained Bronwyn, "because we face a grave threat to the realm."

"Another one?" said Rutherford. "It feels like we only recently faced an army of undead spirits."

"An army which, I might remind you, was only defeated with the Mercerians' assistance."

"Ah. I see where this is going. You feel obligated to help them with this northern war of theirs."

"This is not a trivial matter," replied the queen. "An army stands poised to march onto our lands. Are we to sit back and let them destroy us?"

"I think you overestimate the threat," said Lord Marley. "Isn't there a Mercerian army at Holdcross?"

"You know full well there is, but they cannot hold the enemy back forever."

Asher smiled, then leaned forward, resting his arms on the table. "While you may perceive this as a threat, Majesty, some here view it as an opportunity."

Bronwyn's jaw clenched. She knew she ruled only because these earls permitted it. How could she convince them to intervene? She decided this situation required diplomacy rather than a firm hand. "Go on," she urged.

"We've been under the heel of the Mercerians since the last war. We have an opportunity here to re-establish ourselves as the dominant force in the region."

"How?"

"We let the Mercerians fail. The more losses they take, the stronger we become. We might even run across the opportunity to exert our will over them for a change."

"Are you seriously suggesting we allow their northern army to be wiped out? That would leave Norland at the mercy of the invaders!"

"Could we not approach Halvaria directly?" suggested Asher. "They're after Merceria, not us. If we allied with them, it would open a clear path into the heartland of our southern neighbour."

"Only by marching through our lands," cautioned Lord Waverly. "At least the Mercerians are a known quantity; we have no idea what this so-called empire would do if they took over."

"What do you propose instead? That we all send troops to stop these invaders? I don't see your men lining up to march to Holdcross."

"Please," replied Bronwyn. "This bickering is hardly productive."

"I agree," said Ghodrug. "The Black Ravens already sent a substantial number of hunters to aid in this realm's defence despite your past treatment of us. Will you not show the same courtesy to your allies?"

"It seems to me," said Asher, "that it wasn't so long ago we fought a civil war. Are we not better served to leave the Mercerians to fend for themselves?"

"That's easy for you to propose," replied Waverly. "Your land lies in the south. Mine, however, is north. The Halvarians must march through it to continue on to Merceria."

"Regrettably," said Creighton, "none of us is in any position to do anything, even if we wished to. Our coffers are bare, thanks to the recent war, and raising troops is an expensive proposition."

"Lord Hollis did so," countered Waverly.

"He did, but he only committed them to ingratiate himself into the queen's good graces." He turned to Bronwyn. "Out of curiosity, how many did he send north?"

"Two hundred," she replied. "Just shy of my own contribution. Those men now help hold Holdcross, staving off the invader, but they cannot last. Would you throw away their lives alongside those of the Mercerians?"

"I commend the efforts of Lord Calder," said Asher, "as I do your own, Majesty, but Creighton has the right of it. We have few men at our disposal; sending them north strips our lands of their only defence."

"Will none of you offer any help to our beleaguered warriors?"

"There are only six of us," replied Creighton. "Five, if you consider Calder already made his contribution. Are you now suggesting that five companies could change the tide of battle?"

"Surely you can spare more?" said Waverly. "After all, the realm is in danger!"

"This isn't the first time we've discussed this," replied Asher, "nor do I believe it will be the last. You must face facts, my friend; we have neither the capacity nor the desire to intervene in this affair."

"Affair?" said Bronwyn. "You make this sound like an inconvenient dispute with a neighbour rather than an actual invasion."

"I've said my peice, Majesty. I do not feel any further discussion would prove beneficial to your cause. As for Lord Calder, I understand why he supplied men, considering Holdcross is part of his domain, but that does not mean we will blindly follow his example."

"In that case," said Marley, "I think we should adjourn this meeting, don't you?"

"Not yet," replied Bronwyn. "I would hear Lord Rutherford's thoughts."

"You've all made excellent points," replied the elderly earl, "and while I appreciate the difficult position we are putting the defenders of Holdcross in, I cannot commit to sending my warriors without the unanimous support of this council. Doing so would be tantamount to throwing their lives away." He stood. "I second the motion to end this session of the Nobles Council. Are there any objections?" He paused. "I thought not. Good day, my lords, Your Majesty."

Bronwyn paced while her servants looked on, afraid lest any movement on their part sour her mood even more. "This is most frustrating! We stand on the brink of invasion, yet all they do is complain they lack the necessary men to aid us! They certainly seem to have enough when it suits them."

A knock at the door interrupted her rant. "Who is it?" she snapped.

A servant poked his head into the room. "A visitor seeking an audience, Your Majesty. He claims to have travelled a great distance to see you."

"I'm busy. Tell him to come back later."

"He claims he can be of assistance, Majesty."

Bronwyn took a deep breath. Could this mysterious stranger carry the answer to her problems? She somehow doubted it, but things could hardly get worse. "Send him in."

The door opened, admitting a feeble old man who walked with the aid of a cane, his back stooped from years of labour.

"Well?" she demanded.

The visitor bowed, though his legs shook when he did so. "My apologies, Majesty. I am not the man I once was."

"Yet you come here claiming to be able to help me. I trust you're not here to fight as my champion?"

"Alas, no. Those days are now in my past."

"I am rather busy of late. It would best serve both our interests if you got to the point."

He looked around the room, his gaze lingering on the fine furniture. "It has been some years since I set foot in the king's chambers… My pardon, I should have said queen's chambers."

"You served my grandfather?"

"Not directly, no. I served Lord Hollis, the Earl of Beaconsgate at that time."

"Something about your eyes is familiar," noted Bronwyn, "but I recall no one of your advanced years while I was held prisoner at his estate."

"I was much different in those days, but I get ahead of myself. My name is Marik. I was once Lord Hollis's champion."

"Impossible. The earl's champion was in the prime of his life."

"That I was. Unfortunately, my youth was drained from me by a Necromancer named Jendrick, though that was not his real name."

"I recognize that name. I believe he died in the war."

"His false identity certainly did. What became of the Elf who wore that façade remains unknown."

"Is that why you're here? To warn me of a Necromancer's presence?"

"No, Majesty. That threat was resolved long ago. I come, instead, to offer my services."

"To do what? You certainly aren't up to the challenge of being my champion."

"That I freely admit, but while I served Lord Hollis, I was privy to many of his secrets, which I believe could now serve you."

"You have my attention," said Bronwyn. "Let's see if you can maintain it."

"As you are likely aware, Hollis was a cunning individual who craved power at the highest level. Some years before the war, he began collecting information on his rivals, from their familial connections to their preferences regarding... well, pretty much everything. This information could prove most persuasive in the right hands."

"And you have this information?"

"Not on me, but I know where to find it."

"How do I know this isn't some ruse meant to ingratiate yourself into my circle of advisors?"

"I have nothing to gain by seeking your favour."

"On the contrary," said Bronwyn. "You have a great deal to gain. You have no lord since Hollis died, and if your clothes are any indication, there is little in your coffers. My patronage would elevate your standing considerably."

"I'll not deny it would," replied Marik, "but I assure you, everything I've said is true. To prove it, I shall retrieve the documents in question and present them to you without any expectation of reward."

"Why would you do that?"

"For too long, I served a man unworthy of my loyalty. I wish to rectify that by doing what I feel will set things right."

"Well said," replied the queen. "If these documents help me, I shall reward you, but not as an advisor. Instead, I will present you with a modest stipend and a place to live out your remaining years. Does that sound acceptable to you?"

"It does, Your Majesty. Thank you."

"One more thing, if you will."

"Most certainly. What is it you wish?"

"Merely some information. You claim a Necromancer used magic to enfeeble you. Have you any way to prove this?"

"The worst of my affliction was cured by none other than Lady Aubrey Brandon, the Mercerian Life Mage."

"I recognize that name," said Bronwyn. "Wouldn't that make you loyal to Merceria?"

"Norland is my home," replied Marik, "not Merceria. While I'm grateful they helped me, I took no oath to serve them."

"When the time comes, will you swear to serve me?"

"Without hesitation, Majesty."

Bronwyn stared into his eyes, trying to read his soul. He appeared earnest in his desire to serve Norland, but that could be an act. Still, she risked nothing having him retrieve these documents he spoke of.

.   .   .

Gerald oversaw the preparations for the coming battle in the south, in person. Lord Tulfar's Dwarves had crossed the river at Colbridge and were now within sight of the Great Swamp. They'd arrived as Tog's army came into view.

"It's late already," said Anna. "Are you sure we have the necessary time to prepare?"

"Sure? No, but this is our only chance." He glanced over his shoulder at Albreda, who was deep in conversation with the Dwarven captains. "I hope she's up to this. She's powerful, I grant you, but I'm asking a lot of her."

"I'm sure she wouldn't agree if she didn't believe it was possible." Anna took a deep breath. "Now, what can I do to help?"

"You know the plan as well as I do. I need you to meet our southern forces and direct them to their places."

"As you wish, Marshal. I'll get right to it." She rode off at a gallop.

Evard Brenton moved closer. "Sir?"

"Yes?" replied Gerald.

"Mistress Albreda wanted me to inform you she is about to commence casting."

"Good. Let's hope the enemy gives us time to prepare."

"Sir?"

"There's still lots to accomplish before the night is out. I hope I haven't bitten off more than I can chew."

"We hold the advantage of terrain, sir."

"That we do, but this is a professional army we're facing, not a rabble of Norland raiders. By my reckoning, we've scraped together over one thousand warriors. What do you make it?"

"Eleven hundred, by my count, though I'm unsure how to include the Trolls."

Gerald couldn't help but chuckle. "Yes. I've often had that difficulty myself. Then there's the matter of the Kurathian Mastiffs. Do we count them as warriors as well?"

"It was a lot simpler in the past."

"True, but I much prefer these men to those who served under King Andred."

"I used to serve the king," replied Evard.

"As did I, but when the time came, we both had the good sense to join the queen, so I think all is forgiven, don't you?"

"Of course, sir."

Gerald noticed a pair of riders breaking off from Tog's forces and heading right for him. It wasn't long before he recognized them both. "Lord Preston, Lady Sophie, so good of you to accept my invitation."

"Tog sends his regards," replied the baron. "He thought it best to oversee the deployment of his troops first-hand. Her Majesty informs me you want the cavalry to the rear?"

"I do. I have a little surprise in store for the enemy, and I can't risk them getting tangled up in it."

"Isn't that precisely their job?"

"Not right away. Fear not, though; they shall have their moment to shine, but they must be fully rested first."

"Of course, Marshal. Might I ask the strategy you intend to use?"

"It's a combination of things, but let me start by asking you a simple question. What is the greatest threat to us?"

"Their cavalry outflanking us."

"Would you agree we must do something to neutralize that threat?"

"Of course. Why? What is it you're proposing?"

"By morning, a series of hills over there will give us a defensive position.

"But couldn't the Halvarians outflank us?"

"No," replied Gerald. "We have the natural anchor of the river to the west, while that set of trees over there covers us on the east."

"Those I see," said Preston, "but couldn't they range farther out and avoid them altogether?"

"Do you remember the Siege of Wincaster?"

"Unfortunately, yes. I was with the Knights of the Sword inside the city. Why? What are you getting at?"

"During that battle, Albreda and Aldus Hearn animated two giant trees."

"Yes. I recall hearing about it. They used them to get atop the city walls. Are you suggesting she'll do the same thing here?"

"That's just one of the possibilities," replied Gerald.

"One? You have more?"

"Several, in fact, but they depend on the strength of her magic. She might be the most powerful mage in all of Merceria, but her magical energy still limits her. Once that's gone, we'll rely on good old-fashioned weapons."

"What can I do to help?" asked Preston.

"How do you feel about defending a hill?"

"I'm not sure I follow?"

"We can only defeat this enemy by using the element of surprise." Gerald glanced over his shoulder. "Albreda will use one of the spells she learned from Aegryth Malthunen, the Weldwyn Earth Mage. I believe she called it a defensive mound. Heward's master of earth used something similar to defeat the Halvarians up in the north."

"Is that where we'll make our stand?"

"Yes, but it's imperative you hold on as long as possible."

"Well, the Dwarves' assistance will certainly help."

"I'm afraid they won't be with you. I have something different in mind for them."

"Then who will I have?"

"The army you brought north from Trollden."

"But that's Tog's command, surely?"

"Ordinarily, I'd agree," said Gerald, "but I need the Trolls to play their own part over by the river."

"You are a most mysterious fellow, Marshal."

"Thank you. I'll take that as a compliment. Oh, and not to put more pressure on you, but the queen will be with us."

"The Queen? Surely not?"

"Yes. The Royal Standard will be flying proudly in the middle of our line. If this is to work, the enemy's attention must remain on that hill."

"I shall not fail you, Your Grace."

"This is a military matter, Preston. I prefer you call me sir."

"Yes, of course. I shall endeavour to keep that in mind, going forward."

"Good. Follow me. There is much to do before this night is over."

TWENTY-NINE

His Imperial Eminence

SPRING 968 MC

Nevarus, Emperor of Halvaria, set down the scroll describing the fourth campaign to subdue the southern lands, a campaign that had become bogged down in the lush jungles of the region. He cast his gaze around the room, settling on Janek. "Fetch Exalor, will you? Tell him I require his opinion on something."

"I'm afraid he's not in the capital, Your Eminence."

"Then where is he?"

"He travelled north to oversee the siege of Ironcliff."

"That is most inconvenient."

"Is there someone else I can summon in his stead?"

"Are any of the marshals in Varena?"

"I heard a rumour that the Marshal of the South arrived on personal business two days ago."

"Personal, you say? I would think he would have the common courtesy to pay his respects. Remind me again who this upstart is?"

"Castimar Stormwind, Your Eminence."

"Let's get him over here today, shall we? I want an accounting."

"Accounting?" said Janek.

"Yes. Of events in the south. I'm beginning to believe that the entire campaign is nothing more than a way to bleed the Imperial treasury dry, and I would hear his excuses."

"Of course, Eminence."

"While you're at it, have a servant bring me more wine."

"Red or white, Eminence?"

"I leave that choice in your capable hands, Janek. You haven't failed me yet." He waited as the servant left, then turned to the mound of papers littering the table. They consisted of hastily scribbled notes thrown together haphazardly, indicating either a careless attitude or a deliberate attempt to hide something.

Nevarus prided himself on his education, which was the one thing he controlled. However, sifting through these notes, he soon realized how little he understood regarding the role his legions played in the south. Were the Orcs there as dangerous as they'd led him to believe, or was someone using the pretense to ask for further resources? Despite sending more coins and additional troops to quell the local population, there wasn't an increase in truthseekers or purifiers. What were they hiding?

Castimar Stormwind looked up, irritated at the interruption. "He wants what?"

"He's ordered you to the Imperial Palace, Your Grace."

"When?"

"At once, according to the summons."

"This couldn't have come at a worse time. I'm supposed to go and meet with our co-conspirators today: a little difficult to do if I'm meeting with the very person we're plotting against. Did he say why?"

"No."

"Then you should have asked more questions. Honestly, Beaufort, you should know by now how much I detest vagueness."

"I did ask, Your Grace, but the messenger knew nothing about the letter's contents."

"Any indication of the emperor's mood?"

"Unfortunately, not. Do you suppose he suspects something?"

"He would have sent warriors if he did. Still, we must tread carefully these next few days, for the emperor's attention has somehow been piqued."

"And the council?"

"I'm confident the Inner Council is still unaware of our plans, but it wouldn't hurt to offer a distraction. Do we have anyone available?"

"We have someone watching Exalor," replied Beaufort, "or did you have a different distraction in mind?"

"I was thinking something a little closer to home might be preferable. Perhaps another member of the council?"

"It would require summoning someone, which may take several days. Whom did you wish to target?"

"The individual matters little," said Castimar, "but it should be someone of note. We must ensure it looks like one of Exalor's people is responsible."

"I shall see to it at once, Your Grace."

"Good. Have the carriage brought round. It appears I have an audience with His Imperial Majesty."

Outside the carriage, the streets of Varena rolled past, but Castimar remained oblivious to them. His thoughts were elsewhere, trying to come to grips with the emperor's sudden interest. It was annoying, to say the least, especially when his plans were so close to fruition. With only a little more time, he would be rid of the nuisance of the Imperial court.

The clip-clop of horse hooves finally ceased, and a servant opened the door. "We are here, Your Grace."

He stepped down onto the cobblestones. The Imperial Palace loomed before him, the largest building in the entire capital. A fitting tribute to the present God-Emperor, and it would make a fine home for his successor. Castimar smiled at the thought. This would all be his soon, but he must be careful not to tip his hand.

Royal guards stood ready to escort him into the building, which wasn't unusual for a marshal, but a part of him wondered if he might face arrest. He nodded at them, following as they led him into the massive structure.

They kept a brisk pace, but Castimar was used to it. Even as a young man, he'd eagerly completed tasks, and his training at the Volstrum tempered that with meticulous planning and deliberation, allowing him to progress to the exalted rank of marshal, but he wasn't done yet.

They finally halted at a great set of double doors, the emperor's personal quarters. A guard knocked before opening one to reveal Janek, His Eminence's favoured servant.

"Your Grace," the fellow said in greeting. "His Imperial Eminence is expecting you."

Castimar strode in confidently and bowed. Only after completing this did he notice the table strewn with papers.

"Ah, Marshal," said Nevarus. "So glad you've agreed to meet with me."

"I could hardly refuse an Imperial summons, Your Eminence."

"Quite."

"Might I enquire the reason for calling me here?"

"This." The emperor stood aside, sweeping his arm to indicate the table.

"My apologies, Eminence, but I have no idea what I'm looking at."

"These reports detail your exploits in the south. After reading them, I feel your prolonged campaign against the Orcs warrants an explanation."

"I assure you progress is happening, but the land thereabouts is extremely inhospitable. It is mostly jungle, making it nearly impossible to navigate, let alone travel through. We're constructing roads, but they take time."

"I note you have spent a considerable amount of coins on this campaign, a cost that might need re-evaluating in light of your slow progress."

"We are doing all we can to work towards a speedy conclusion, Your Eminence, but cutting back our funds now would have devastating consequences."

"Tell me what you know about the Orcs."

The sudden change of topic caught Castimar off guard. "Orcs, Your Eminence?"

"Yes. I wish to learn more about them."

"There is little to tell. They are a savage, bloodthirsty race that often attacks in overwhelming numbers, swarming their victims in a mob of violence. I can tell you, it's quite unnerving."

"And what have you learned about their civilization?"

"Civilization? They can barely use spears, let alone form an actual society."

"Yet, by your own admittance, they present an obstacle to your advances in the south."

"With all due respect, Eminence, I said the slow advance was due to the terrain, not the Orcs."

"If that's the case, why are you still fighting them?"

"I'll admit they are a difficult foe to track down in the jungle, but we have devised a tactic to deal with them."

"That being?"

"As the road advances farther south, we build strongholds along with it."

"Your solution is to build a row of forts?"

"It has proved most effective."

"I see," said the emperor. "How far south have you advanced since the current campaign began?"

"After taking over from the previous Marshal of the South, we have pushed more than one hundred miles farther south."

"And where, might I ask, does it end?"

"I beg your pardon, Your Eminence?"

"Surely there is an end in sight to this military campaign? How do we determine when it is finished, or are you suggesting there is no way to win?"

"I assure you, nothing could be further from the truth."

"Have the Orcs a capital?"

"Not that we know of."

"How big of an area do they occupy?"

"I cannot answer that, Eminence."

"Then how do you expect to win?"

"We will win," replied Castimar, "when the Orcs can no longer carry out this war. If it requires exterminating every last one of them, then so be it."

"I think it's time for you to re-evaluate your strategy."

"What would you have me do? Surrender?"

"Careful," said the emperor. "You are close to being impertinent. One more remark like that, and I shall see you removed from office."

"My apologies, Your Eminence. I meant no disrespect. Might I ask what prompted this sudden interest in the south?"

"I am always interested in how my empire is doing, particularly regarding military matters, and"—he glanced at the table—"it was suggested to me that the Orcs are not the savage brutes they are reputed to be." Nevarus wandered over to the papers, pulling forth a scroll. "Here, in your own words, is an account of the ruins of one of their towns. A remarkable thing, considering we found no such towns when we conquered the Orcs to the north. Only in the south do they appear to have built such settlements. Why do you think that is?"

"I really couldn't say."

"But you do acknowledge you found them?"

"Your Eminence, I would never invent falsehoods to fill a report."

"Yet you saw fit only to plunder them."

"That is what we do to our enemies," replied Castimar. "We do so every time our borders expand. Only then can our sentinels and purifiers cleanse the area of all opposition. It has remained unchanged for over a thousand years."

"Yet no Orc towns are under our rule. Why is that?"

"You cannot negotiate with a savage, Eminence. There is no reason to capture a town if its people cannot be brought into the fold."

"So, instead, you choose to burn it to the ground, making us as savage as the Orcs!"

"We did not begin this cycle of violence; that was all their doing."

"Would you not do the same were our empire threatened?"

Castimar was confused. The emperor was pushing for something, but what? Even more important was understanding who'd put him up to this. "Might I ask why the Orcs have become of interest to you?"

"I am the emperor! Everything that transpires within my empire is of interest."

The marshal bit back a retort. Antagonizing His Eminence served no purpose and would only make squeezing the truth out of him more challenging. He must, therefore, adopt a different strategy. "Might I ask your thoughts on the matter, Eminence?"

"My thoughts?"

"Yes. You appear to have given this careful consideration. Might I ask how you would deal with the situation?"

"I would have you send delegates to the Orcs and settle our differences."

"To accomplish that, we must be willing to give back their land. Do so, and the rest of our enemies will see us as backing down."

"When has their opinion ever swayed us? As far as I'm concerned, they can all go to the Underworld."

"Just to be clear," said Castimar, "you are suggesting we invite the Orcs to become full-fledged members of the empire?"

"With the war against the Petty Kingdoms in full swing, we can ill-afford the added expense of fighting an unnecessary campaign in a harsh and remote continent."

"I beg you to reconsider, Eminence. The southern campaign may be on another continent, but it is closer to this capital in distance than our northern prefecture."

"Are you implying it represents a threat to the security of the empire?"

"Not while we maintain three legions in the south. Change that, however, and I cannot guarantee we could contain them."

"You are a man of contradictions," said the emperor. "First, you claim you are pacifying the Orcs, then, in the next breath, that they threaten our very way of life. Which is it to be? Do they constitute a threat or not?"

"That depends. Do you intend on withdrawing the legions?"

"Not at this time, but I seek an end to this campaign. I, therefore, instruct you to negotiate peace with the Orcs."

"The empire has never negotiated peace, only dictated it."

"Then it is time we learned a different way of doing things."

"Eminence?"

"The campaign in the west ties up three of our legions, and the advance on the Petty Kingdoms another four. Add to that the two standing by on the border of Ilea, and you see the problem. If we continue in the south, we have no reserves should disaster strike."

"Our legions are the finest warriors in all of Eiddenwerthe, Eminence; they have never been defeated."

"You and I both know that's not true. Your own reports say otherwise."

"What about the many warriors we've sacrificed for the gains thus far achieved? Are their lives to account for nothing?"

"I'm not suggesting we abandon all the progress you've made in the south, only that we give up pushing farther into enemy territory. I want you to concentrate on occupying the area you currently hold, which includes sending emissaries to the Orcs."

"And what are we to offer them, Eminence?"

"An opportunity to live in peace within the borders of Halvaria. Who knows, we may even employ them as mercenaries in our legions. That's what the Mercerians did."

"The Mercerians?"

"Yes," said Nevarus. "Have you not been updated on Exalor's progress?"

"Regrettably, I have not, though I am familiar with his original plan."

"This western realm employs all manner of creatures, including Dwarves, Trolls and, dare I say it, even Elves?"

"Surely these are exaggerations? The Elves disappeared from Eidden-werthe centuries ago."

"Yet, by some accounts, they were present in Arnsfeld."

"That, Eminence, is more likely an excuse to explain away the legion commander's failure."

"There are also reports of Elves in both Merceria and Weldwyn."

"Weldwyn?" replied the marshal. "I'm afraid I'm not familiar with that name."

"The kingdom west of Merceria."

"Just how many kingdoms lie to the west?"

"Four we are aware of, although one is a loose coalition of tribes referred to as the Clanholdings."

"Did Exalor have knowledge of this when he began his campaign?"

"I am assured he did."

Castimar realized this opened an opportunity to discredit the High Strategos. "Have we heard any recent news on how his campaign is progressing, Eminence?"

"I have a report indicating he began the siege of Ironcliff and another telling about the Third Legion's advances through the mountains, but neither provides many details. Could you shed some light on why that is?"

"If what you say is true, then I imagine Exalor has his hands full. No one has ever attempted an operation of that magnitude, and it must require his undivided attention."

"Are you suggesting these reports are inaccurate?"

"It would not be out of character for the High Strategos to exaggerate his successes to maintain your interest, Eminence."

"By lying?"

"It wouldn't be the first time someone in his position has done so."

Nevarus smiled. "You're talking about the conquest of Calabria."

"I am," replied Castimar. "It is a well-known fact our legions encountered stiff resistance during the liberation, nearly leading to disaster. Had the emperor not personally intervened, it could have led to our defeat."

"Are you suggesting the same action is warranted in Merceria?"

Castimar smiled, for the emperor had taken the bait, but how could he divert Nevarus's attention from his own efforts in the south? "It is not my place to second-guess the High Strategos," he said. "I merely strive to remind you that only one of your vast intellect can understand the western campaign's complexities."

"Your words give me much to think about."

"It was my honour, Eminence. Regarding the other matter we discussed, I shall carry out your will as soon as I return to the south."

"You impress me," said Nevarus. "Keep this up, and you may soon find yourself the new High Strategos."

THIRTY

Contact

SPRING 968 MC

Sir Owen topped a rise overlooking the border village of Zurkirk. The Army of Erlingen marched below, their footsteps bringing them towards the bridge over the Rasfeld River that marked the border. Seven days had passed since they'd left Torburg, a week full of confusion as the barons argued over almost every aspect of the campaign. First, it was the order of march, then the positioning of their tents when camp was set-up for the night. And each evening, they insisted on meeting with His Grace, the Duke, if only to pay their respects.

Lord Alain soon grew tired of it but couldn't afford to offend anyone. Instead, he hosted a nightly gathering of his nobles, discussing matters concerning the army's disposition.

Owen, who had endeared himself to His Grace, was tasked with organizing things for these get-togethers, of which the barons contributed little. They meant well, but their lack of experience proved more of a headache to the duke than a blessing, a headache that quickly became the bane of the knight's existence.

At the approach of a horse, Owen turned to see Lady Beverly. "Impressive view you have from up here," she said, bringing her massive warhorse to a halt beside him. "I assume that's Zurkirk?"

"It is. A small village, in the grand scheme of things, but important nonetheless."

"Has it a baron?"

Owen nodded. "Unfortunately, his lands are too small to contribute anything to the army."

"And is he here?"

"No. He and his family moved to the safety of Torburg."

"And his people?"

"His servants likely went with him."

"I'm not referring to his servants," said Beverly. "I meant the villagers."

Owen shrugged. "I imagine they'll flee as well."

"They don't have that luxury."

"They have legs. Surely it's better to flee than be killed by the enemy?"

"You've grown used to a life of privilege, Owen. The common folk have little choice in the matter. Everything they own is tied up in the land. Abandoning their homes would result in the loss of their livelihood."

"That is their lot in life."

"If that's still your opinion on the matter, then we have more work to do before considering you as a Knight of the Hound."

"What's that supposed to mean?"

"Queen Anna is concerned with the welfare of all her subjects, not just the wealthy and entitled ones."

"You yourself are titled."

"I am, but as I've said before, in Merceria, the obligation of the nobility is to serve their subjects, not the other way around."

"The more I learn about your home, the stranger it gets."

"You believe caring for those under your protection is strange?"

"We are the ruling class, are we not?"

"Let me ask you this, then. What makes it so?"

"Why, birth, of course. Everyone knows the blood of nobility is different from commoners."

"I assure you it's not," replied Beverly. "You were born a commoner yourself: by your own definition, that makes you ineligible to become a knight."

"Ah, but knights are different. For one thing, their titles aren't hereditary."

"Haven't any knights of the Petty Kingdoms been rewarded with a title?"

"They have. I suppose I must concede the argument on that basis."

"This is not an argument," said Beverly. "It's an education."

"But aren't your knights all born to the upper classes?"

"Not at all. In truth, I'm the exception rather than the rule, at least when it comes to the Knights of the Hound. Most of the order were common born."

"I noticed you were very specific there."

"I was. Our other order, the Knights of the Sword, consists almost exclusively of the sons of nobles."

"Is this a recent development?" asked Owen.

"Throughout our history, monarchs have knighted individuals for their service to the Crown; we are a warrior culture."

"How interesting."

"It becomes even more so when you consider our nobles."

"What does that mean?"

"Many of our newer nobles were also common born, including the Duke of Wincaster."

"A duke? Surely you jest?"

"I assure you I don't, and no one has deserved a title more."

"You hold this fellow in high regard."

"I do. He trained me to become a knight and is now the Marshal of Merceria." She paused momentarily. "I'll tell you something else; if he were here, he'd whip this army into shape and not let the barons argue over trivialities."

Owen sighed. "Ah. You've heard about the duke's problems."

"An army can't function if it's constantly at odds with itself."

"I couldn't agree more, yet I see no solution to our present dilemma."

"The duke needs to take a firm hand."

"He is, I fear, a victim of our current circumstances. He requires the barons' support to defeat the empire, and the barons are well aware of it. He fears if he presses them on anything, they will abandon the cause, leaving the realm virtually defenceless."

"Even to the extent that it endangers their own lands?"

"Admittedly so. The barons are a stubborn lot, and I've only been doing this for a short while. I can't imagine what the duke has dealt with since he was crowned."

He waited, expecting a reply, but when Beverly wasn't forthcoming, he looked at her, noting her attention focused on a distant object. "What is it?" he asked.

"Unless I miss my guess—people."

"Where?"

"Over there, across the river, heading towards the bridge."

"The empire?"

"I don't believe so," replied Beverly. "Halvarians would approach, ready for battle; those look more like stragglers. I would assume it's what's left of the Army of Angvil."

"We should alert the duke."

"You do that, and I'll ride over and see who's in charge."

.   .   .

Beverly sat astride Lightning on the Erlingen side of the bridge. A woman approached from the other side, her armour caked in mud.

"I am Temple Commander Marlena," she called out. "Of the Temple Knights of Saint Agnes."

"Greetings. I am Beverly Fitzwilliam, Knight Commander of the Hound. At present, I'm marching with the Army of Erlingen."

The knight visibly relaxed. "I'm happy to see you. We feared the duke wouldn't march to our aid."

"Is this your command?"

"Only the sister knights. The others are remnants of the Army of Angvil. Will the duke give us leave to cross?"

"I can't see why not." Beverly trotted over to meet the woman in the middle of the bridge. "Bring them across, and they can take refuge in Zurkirk for now." She waited as Marlena waved the others forward. "How many have you?"

"Sixty-two of my order, along with three hundred and fifty or so warriors of Angvil. Are the duke's forces close by?"

"On the other side of the village. Why?"

"I fear the enemy is approaching. One of their legions defeated us some days ago, and they've been on our heels ever since. Does the duke intend to make a stand?"

"Definitely, but where depends largely on how close the enemy is. You say they've been following you. Is that their entire legion or just their advanced scouts?"

"Only their light cavalry. No match for my Temple Knights, but we can't be everywhere at once."

"Is there terrain across the river that might serve us?"

"Not that I saw," replied Marlena. "The area is flat, and fighting with your back to the river wouldn't be advisable."

"Would you be willing to place your men under the duke's command?"

"As I said, they're not under my command, but I assume most would agree. As for my sisters, we intend to seek out others of our order."

"Then you're in luck," replied Beverly. "A Temple Captain of your order is with the duke, although I suppose you outrank her."

"My promotion is only one of circumstance. I was a Temple Captain when the campaign began."

"We are often forced into roles we did not seek, but you appear to have risen to the challenge."

"What makes you say that?"

"The fact that you brought these people to safety. Not to rush you, but these matters would be best discussed with His Grace."

"Yes, by all means," said Marlena. "Allow me to speak to my aide before you bring me to the duke."

"I'll meet you over there when you are finished," She pointed down the road, where it exited the village. With that, Beverly wheeled Lightning around and rode off.

The first of the duke's forces entered the village as Beverly arrived, Sir Owen and Brother Cyric amongst them, keeping an eye on their advance.

"Ah, there you are," called out Owen. "What did you discover? Are they friend or foe?"

"They're the remains of the Army of Angvil," she replied. "Led by a Temple Commander of Saint Agnes."

"Her name's not Charlaine, by any chance, is it?" asked Cyric.

"No, it's Marlena."

"Marlena?" said Cyric. "Not Marlena Falkenberg, surely?"

"She never gave her last name. Do you know her?"

"If it's who I think, then yes. I convinced her to join the order."

"Not to appear rude," said Beverly, "but why are you here? I thought you were advising Lord Alain?"

"I was, but when Sir Owen arrived with a warning of a possible threat, the duke suggested I might be of some assistance in identifying them. However, that appears to have proven unnecessary."

"The Temple Commander will be here shortly. She's just seeing to the disposition of the survivors. I hope His Grace doesn't mind, but I told them they would be safe in Zurkirk."

"So long as they keep the road clear for his army."

Beverly moved aside, clearing the way for the survivors who had crossed the bridge in one large mob, with the Temple Knights accompanying them.

Marlena spotted Beverly at once and rode over.

Cyric grinned. "Has it been so long you no longer recognize me?"

Her face betrayed her surprise. "Brother Cyric? What in the name of the Saints are you doing here?"

"I came from Torburg, along with the duke's army. You've done well for yourself."

"I serve where I am needed."

"The same can be said of us all. How long has it been?"

"Fifteen years since I joined the order, give or take a few weeks."

"And now you're a Temple Commander."

"Only through happenstance. My superior died at Saints Crossing."

"We heard about that battle," said Beverly. "I understand the losses were great."

"We never should have made a stand, not when they outnumbered us by more than two to one. The same could be said of Angvil. Their general threw away their army when he insisted on staying put once they faced a fresh legion."

"Fresh?" said Cyric. "Are you suggesting two are in the area?"

"I'm not suggesting; I'm telling you. At Saints Crossing, we faced the Ninth Legion, while our last encounter was against the Fifth."

"These are bad tidings, indeed. We must inform His Grace at once."

"Come," said Owen. "I'll bring you to him."

Finding the duke didn't take long, for he'd chosen the local inn as his quarters while his army set up their camp. Sir Owen led them in, making the necessary introductions to His Grace, who sat at a table, papers strewn about it.

Lord Alain looked up from his notes in irritation. "I'm pleased to meet you, Commander, but unless you carry valuable information, I insist you leave. I have an army to prepare."

"Temple Commander Marlena bears important news," insisted Sir Owen.

"That she brought the remnants of the Army of Angvil? I am already aware of that."

"With all due respect, Your Grace," said Beverly, "I think you should hear her out."

The duke sat back, tossing his quill aside. "What is it?"

"Two legions are operating in the area," said Marlena. "The Ninth and the Fifth."

"And?"

"That's almost five thousand men, Your Grace."

"The Rasfeld will protect us, a river so deep it makes fording impossible. All we must do is hold our end of the bridge."

"That strategy failed at Saints Crossing, Your Grace. While the bulk of the Army of Rudor was busy holding the bridge, the Halvarian cavalry outflanked them."

"That may be the case there, but as I said, the river here has no fords."

"Neither did the river on the border of Arnsfeld, yet four years ago, they crossed, thanks to Water Mages."

"I hardly think that applicable here," replied the duke.

"Your Grace," said Beverly. "Surely there is a better option than holding one end of the bridge?"

"What else would you have me do?"

"Allow me to take a detachment of cavalry across."

"To do what?"

"To assess the enemy's intent, or at the very least, push back against their scouts."

"And throw away my only advantage? I think not."

"You cannot afford to be defensive, Your Grace. Doing so puts your entire realm in danger. Our only option to defeat this invasion is to go on the offensive."

"Easy for you to say," said Lord Alain. "It's not your kingdom that's under attack."

"On the contrary. While you're here playing games with your army, my countrymen are dying in the west. You must take decisive action to defeat the Halvarian Empire."

"How? By marching against two full legions? That would be suicide."

"Then face them one at a time."

"How do you propose we do that?"

"You know this side of the river better than they do. Lure them into a trap of your choosing."

"By letting them ransack part of my duchy?"

"Then march into Angvil and seek out the enemy before they combine."

"How do you propose we do that when we don't even know where they are?"

Beverly held her tongue, trying to calm herself. Getting upset served no purpose here, but she must convince the duke to see reason. "Temple Commander Marlena, do any of your survivors know this part of Angvil?"

"Most certainly."

"Do you think they'd be interested in providing His Grace with information about the area?"

"I'd be surprised if any refused."

Lord Alain leaned back in his chair. "Fetch them, and we'll see if they can help update our maps of the area." He glared at Beverly. "Anything else you'd care to discuss?"

She ignored his tone of voice and seized the moment to offer a suggestion. "We need as much cavalry as you can spare to form a screening force. To succeed in this, we must seek out the enemy while preventing them from doing the same to us."

"And if the two legions merge?"

"Then we withdraw back to friendly soil."

The duke crossed his arms. "Do we even stand a chance of defeating this invasion?"

"We'll never know unless we take the opportunity to seize the initiative. Might we have the use of the Temple Knights?"

"I see no objections," replied Cyric, "although I only speak on behalf of my own order."

"The sister knights will do whatever is required," added Marlena. "You have my word on that."

"What do you say, Brother Cyric?" asked the duke. "Shall I entrust my army to this woman?"

"This woman is a general, Your Grace, one with far more experience than anyone else here, save for perhaps the Temple Commander."

"So she claims, but how do we know she tells the truth? There is no way to corroborate her stories or vouch for her character, save for her companions, and we have no reason to trust them any more than her."

"With all due respect, Your Grace, I detect no deceit on the part of Lady Beverly or her companions. And she demonstrated her martial prowess most eloquently by defeating three of Mulsingen's finest warriors."

"Yes," added Sir Owen, "and all at the same time. I saw her in action in Deisenbach, Your Grace, and I can attest to her skill at arms."

"That's a far cry from leading an army," replied Lord Alain.

"She IS a general."

"And I'm a duke, but I'd be the first to admit that hardly makes me a tactical genius."

"In the short time I've known her," offered Cyric, "she has demonstrated a superior knowledge of tactics. I would even go so far as to vouch for her credibility, Your Grace, so strong is my belief in her abilities."

"I shall consider your advice, but I need to see a plan before I hand over control of my army. I'll not march us into oblivion."

"Thank you, Your Grace," said Beverly. "I shall do my utmost to ensure you don't regret your decision. Now, I need every piece of information you have, including maps of the area and accounts of the survivors from Angvil. I wish to begin by discussing your experiences, Temple Commander, provided you have no objection."

"Not at all. I look forward to speaking with someone who will listen to me for a change."

THIRTY-ONE

Riverside

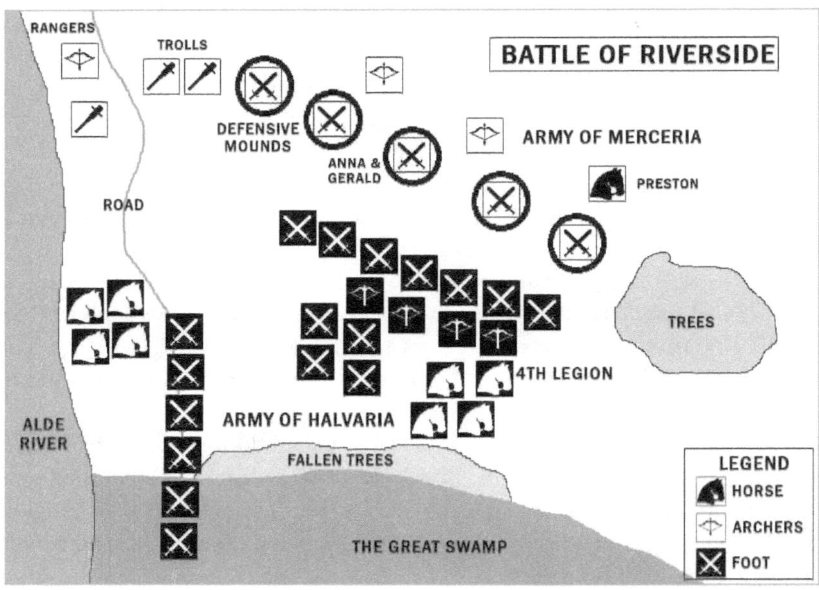

The Halvarian Legion marched north, finally exiting the Great Swamp that had plagued them for so many miles.

"It's working," said Anna. "They're doing precisely as you predicted."

"They have little choice," replied Gerald. "They must clear the swamp to have any chance of fighting. It'll be interesting to see how long it takes them."

"Interesting?"

"An enemy's manoeuvres can tell you a great deal about their discipline. If they deploy quickly, as I suspect, things should go smoothly for us."

"You mean other than having to hold the line against an overwhelming force?"

"We've faced worse odds."

"Not against a disciplined enemy, we haven't."

"Have I ever let you down before?" asked Gerald.

"No. Never. But witnessing them marching in such precise ranks is a little disheartening."

"It is, but they lack the one thing that makes us who we are."

"And that is?"

"Grit and determination."

"Why, Marshal, you're becoming quite the philosopher, and by the way, that's two things. I hope Jane appreciates your qualities. How are you two getting along? Any signs of a marriage in your future?"

"Not with this war raging. I felt it best if she remained in Wincaster, where it's safe." He stopped speaking to stare at her. "That's where I wish you could be, Anna, safe in the Palace, not in the middle of nowhere, facing the enemy in battle."

"I am the queen," she replied. "I owe it to my people to stand at their side."

"I knew you'd say that."

"I wish I had the foresight to bring my armour. I feel so vulnerable standing here beneath the Royal Standard; I'd prefer to be less exposed."

"Ah, but then our strategy wouldn't work. We need your presence to draw them in. Remember, if things go awry, you're to flee north to Colbridge."

"I won't abandon you."

"If it goes that badly, I'll already be dead."

"Don't say that." She reached out, touching his arm. "Braedon needs his grandfather, as do I."

Gerald saw tears forming in the corners of her eye. He cleared his throat. "We should concentrate on the task at hand."

"I still don't understand how Albreda made so many mounds. It must have taken a considerable portion of her magic."

"I was happy with three, but she insisted on five. I can see why. It gives us much better coverage."

"Even though the eastern woods are empty?"

"We know that, but the enemy doesn't. Whoever's in charge over there will assume we've placed men in there to anchor our flank."

"We'll soon know if your hunch is correct," said Anna. The first few Halvarian companies of footmen filed east to begin forming a line. "Are you certain we wouldn't be better off attacking them before they form up for battle?"

"We need to neutralize their cavalry, and we can't do that if they haven't cleared the swamp. You must be patient."

"I'm afraid that's not a quality I'm known for."

As more companies cleared the swamp, they filled in the line from east to west.

"There's their cavalry," said Gerald, "forming up directly behind their foot."

"I expected more," said Anna.

"And likely there will be. I suspect they mingled their horsemen in to support their foot's advance."

"They obviously weren't expecting us to make a stand so close to the edge of the swamp. You chose wisely, Marshal."

"Let's not let it go to our heads. They still have plenty of warriors advancing up that road." He lapsed into silence as a smile played over his lips.

"What are you grinning at?" asked Anna.

"The enemy has committed a blunder, though not a serious one."

"Do tell."

"He's mixed his heavier footmen in with the rest, slowing their deployment."

"Does that help us?"

"Not really, no, though it does illustrate they're capable of making mistakes, however minor."

"Let's hope they make more serious ones."

"What would you put their numbers at?"

Albreda's voice rang out, "I can answer that!"

"I thought you were resting?" said Anna.

"And so I was, but that doesn't mean I was asleep." She pointed skyward, where a hawk circled. "I blinded the enemy."

"Meaning?"

"They had a familiar at their beck and call. Swiftfeather found it to be most delicious."

"You said you knew their numbers?" prompted Gerald.

"Yes. Their army is broken down into four brigades, to use the Mercerian expression. Each is similarly equipped, with approximately three hundred foot, one hundred bow, and two hundred horse per brigade, although the last one in line appears to be at half strength. The results of their troubles in Trollden, no doubt."

"Any sign they've spotted our preparations?"

"None whatsoever, but they are in unfamiliar territory, and fallen trees are likely of little interest to them." She watched the enemy line forming up opposite the Mercerians. "How will you decide when Lord Tulfar should do his part?"

"We must wait until they've committed to the assault if this is to work. Are you certain he'll hear the signal?"

Albreda chuckled. "Don't you think you left it a little late to ask? Fear not. When the time comes, everything will go according to plan." She glanced left and right. "This is most invigorating, almost as exciting as the Siege of Wincaster."

"Let's not get carried away," said Anna. "You broke your back there, and we don't have a healer with us today."

"I suppose I did, didn't I? It's strange to think that was only six years ago."

"Not quite," said Gerald. "If you recall, we took Wincaster in the summer, although I suppose that's close enough for all intents and purposes."

"Something's happening," said Anna.

They all looked south, where a solid line of Halvarian footmen stood, with archers behind. Some heavier foot remained farther back, ready to reinforce the line wherever needed. The cavalry had split into two groups, one on the west of the road, paralleling the river, the other on the east, likely to try exploiting the Mercerian flank.

"This is the most dangerous part," said Gerald. "If this group doesn't take the bait, we're doomed. The others on the road behind them will swarm us."

He needn't have worried, for the entire Halvarian line moved north directly for the Mercerians.

"They haven't gone after the Trolls," noted Anna.

"No, they haven't," replied Gerald. "They likely had enough of them in the swamp. Ready?"

"Always."

"You may give the signal, Albreda."

The Druid closed her eyes, the air buzzing around them, and then she looked skyward, releasing a howl that seemed to shake the very ground.

The fallen trees, so carefully placed at the edge of the swamp, came to life, lifting their branches from the ground and revealing a long trench packed with Dwarves. A horn sounded, Tulfar's call to battle, and then the warriors of Mirstone emerged, their axes ready to bring death to the enemy.

Arbalests sang out, piercing the armour of the Halvarian cavalry massed on the eastern flank. Then howls erupted as the Kurathian Mastiffs burst from the trench, racing across the open ground to join in on the attack.

Unaware of this development, the empire's line continued their assault on the Mercerian defences, leaving their reserves at the mercy of the mountain folk.

Tulfar led his Dwarves forward, targeting the empire's reserve of heavily armoured warriors. His arbalesters loosed several volleys into them, and then his axes struck, creating even more confusion.

Gerald glanced east, where Preston led the Mercerian cavalry south to assist the Mastiffs. They soon struck, scattering what remained of the empire's horsemen on that flank.

Two of Tulfar's companies moved past the attack on the heavy footmen and struck the enemy forces coming up the road, making it difficult for the rest of the legion to march to their comrades aid. It was a brilliant tactic, but the Dwarven assault soon waned against the overwhelming numbers. This was the moment of reckoning, where the empire would regain the initiative or face defeat.

Tog rushed his Trolls forward, securing the western flank and driving deep into the enemy line. Halvaria's footmen had no chance of penetrating the Trolls' thick hides. Instead, they fell back, forcing their way into the rear ranks to avoid the slaughter, leading to further confusion. With both flanks in danger, the centre of the line crumbled, the footmen dropping their weapons and throwing their hands up in surrender.

"It worked," shouted Anna.

"Did you ever have any doubt?" replied Gerald.

"Of course not. You?"

He lifted his trembling hand. "Does that answer your question?"

"You did the impossible."

"Let's not get ahead of ourselves. We've hurt them badly, but that's not the same as driving them from our shores."

"You're being modest," said Albreda. "Live in the moment, Gerald. You've destroyed almost half their army, not to mention a good portion of their cavalry. Quite the accomplishment, if you ask me." She closed her eyes. "Swiftfeather has a clear view of them," she said. "Tulfar has pulled his Dwarves back, and the Halvarians are withdrawing down the road to the south. Do we pursue?"

"No," replied Gerald. "We'll advance, but only to the edge of the swamp. Unless I miss my guess, they'll head to their ships and sail away."

"What makes you so certain?"

"We've shown we can stand toe to toe with them and emerge victorious. They won't be eager to repeat the process. Their entire strategy relied on them breaking through and getting into the heartland of Merceria, and that's no longer an option."

"True," said Anna, "but they could still hold Trollden, forcing us to maintain an army in the region."

"I doubt they'd last long. The Trolls are immune to the dampness of the swamp, but once summer's here, the Halvarians will find it uncomfortable, quickly succumbing to disease and illness."

"Nature has a way of keeping the balance," added Albreda. "They're getting precisely what they deserve."

That evening, everyone gathered around a fire. Although Albreda was exhausted from all the magical energy she'd expended, the rest were in fine spirits.

"Congratulations," Gerald began. "Thanks to Albreda, you provided Merceria with a great victory. I must thank Lord Preston, whose cavalry did a magnificent job routing the eastern flank. Tog, you, too, played a crucial part, for without your advance, the rest of the Halvarian cavalry could have done some serious damage. Last, but most certainly not least, I must thank Lord Tulfar. None of this would have been possible without the Dwarves of Mirstone."

"What happens next?" asked Sophie.

"We bury the dead and see to the wounded. Gorath, I'd like your rangers to watch the road. We don't want to be surprised should the enemy try another assault."

"You think that likely?" said the Orc.

"No, but let's not take any chances."

"What of my warriors?" asked Tulfar. "They're eager to continue the fight."

"And they will, but after a night of digging trenches and an entire battle, they need to regain their strength. Preston, have your cavalry oversee the collection of weapons and armour from the prisoners."

"What do we do with the prisoners?" asked Sophie.

"We'll march them to Colbridge, but our army needs to rest first."

"And Her Majesty?"

"I shall be returning to Wincaster as soon as Albreda recovers her strength," replied the queen, "as will Gerald. In his absence, Tog has command."

The great Troll nodded his head. "What are my instructions, Marshal?"

"Hold here for the time being. We'll let the swamp take its toll on the enemy while we contemplate our next move."

"Which will be?"

"It depends on what's happening in Ironcliff and Stonecastle. We may have blunted this invasion, but that's a far cry from halting their campaign of conquest. I must now consider how we carry this fight to the enemy."

Agostino Feranti stared down at the body of his commander-general. The man lay in a pool of his own blood, the victim of a ritual suicide for failing in his duty. It now fell to Feranti to assume command and wrestle a shred of dignity from his predecessor's inability to secure a victory.

A captain appeared at his elbow, standing to rigid attention.

"What is it?" snapped Feranti. "Can't you see I'm busy?"

"Sorry, Captain-General. I thought you'd like to see the list of casualties."

Agostino turned on his aide, ready to vent his spleen, but the look of failure on the fellow's face made him change his mind. These valiant warriors needed reassurance, not blame.

"How many have we lost?" Feranti said at last.

"Almost two cohorts, sir."

"I expected no less. The enemy proved a cunning adversary."

"Do we regroup and launch a fresh attack, sir?"

"With what? Any numerical advantage we had has vanished. All we can do now is return to our ships with our heads hung low."

"The High Strategos will not be pleased."

"Nor will the emperor, but at least we'll be alive to hear of their displeasure. Would you prefer to die here in this fiendish swamp?"

"I serve where the empire sends me."

"Spoken like a true devotee, but dying here will accomplish nothing for our precious empire save our own destruction. We shall return to Halvaria to rebuild our strength."

"Surely that is the admiral's decision?"

"It is," said Feranti, "but I can't see him remaining here, can you? Not after all that's happened."

"Will we return here, sir?"

Feranti looked around, noting the downtrodden expressions. "Let us hope not."

. . .

The cylinder of light descended in the casting circle in Wincaster.

"I don't understand how you do it," said Anna. "Where do you find the strength for so much magic?"

"I'll let you in on a little secret," said Albreda. "I call it from deep beneath the surface."

"You mean the ley lines?"

"That's certainly one word for them. I've always thought of them as the lifeblood of the forest, although from a technical standpoint, they exist outside the Whitewood as well."

"Revi should've consulted with you before sending Beverly through that Saurian portal."

"Why? It would've made no difference. Just because I draw on their power doesn't mean I fully understand how they work."

"Could you teach this skill to others?" Anna asked.

"I wish it were that simple. I can only do so because of my close affinity with the Spirit of the Whitewood."

"The spirit?" said Gerald. "You make it sound like there's a living god out there."

"The spirit is not an individual; it's the sense that all things are connected. Think of it as a great tapestry, with each thread connected to another, revealing a presence much grander in scope."

"Is that what gives you your visions?"

"I assume so, though I know no way of confirming it. They could just as easily be caused by eating the wrong kind of mushrooms. I joke, but it does reveal how little we mages understand when it comes to magic."

"Well," said Gerald, "if the preparations for that battle are any indication, I'd say you're the equal of three full mages, perhaps even four."

"More like five," said Albreda with a smile, "but who's counting?"

"What does it feel like when all that magic courses through you?" asked Anna.

"I only notice it when I'm casting. Imagine standing still in a strong stream and feeling the water rushing against your legs. The feeling is similar when casting, but rather than in your legs, it permeates every fibre of your being."

"And is this true of all magic?"

"I can't say with any authority. Before now, I only felt this within the confines of the Whitewood, but there must be a node somewhere north of Trollden, for I felt its presence there. It was difficult to control at first, but as I grew used to the power, it became easier to direct it."

"Well, thank the Gods you did," said Anna. "As Gerald is wont to say, it saved our bacon."

Gerald laughed. "I don't say that, do I?"

The queen's crooked smile answered his question.

"Much as I'm enjoying the chat," said Albreda, "I have things to see to, amongst them, how the brave Dwarves of Stonecastle fare. I intend to ride up there. What do you think, Gerald? Care to join me?"

"I really would like to, but I must plan out the next phase of this war."

"The next phase? You've still got two full armies to deal with."

"I'm well aware of that. We can't go on the offensive right away, but sooner or later, we'll be in a position to turn the tables on our enemy, and when that time comes, I need to know what my options are."

"Oops," said Anna.

"I beg your pardon?"

"It just occurred to me we left my guards behind."

"Tog will see to them," said Gerald, "or Preston."

"Still, it shows how distracted I am of late."

"I doubt anyone's going to criticize you, Anna. There is a war on, you know."

"That's no excuse. I can't very well claim to care for my subjects, then turn around and abandon them, can I?"

"I'll include word for them to return the next time I send dispatches. Will that suffice?"

"Yes," said Anna. "Now, what's our next step?"

Gerald moved towards the door. "First, we head to the map room."

"And then?"

"Then we get something to eat. I don't know about you, but I'm starving."

THIRTY-TWO

Summons

Nikki placed her book in her lap. "I think they've forgotten we're here."

"Nonsense," replied Arnim. "They feed us, don't they?"

"They do, but those are palace servants. Apart from that, they've left us alone."

"How can you say that? We met the emperor!"

"That was weeks ago. All we do now is stare at the walls or read."

"But that's allowed us to learn much more about their empire. Did you know that mages were not involved in the rule of the original empire? As far as I can determine, mages only arrived in Halvaria well into their fifth century."

"And now they appear to hold the true reins of power. How interesting. It illustrates how nefarious magic can be in the wrong hands."

Arnim laughed. "It's not magic that's nefarious; it's the people wielding it. Magic simply exists, much like a sword."

"A sword most cannot see, let alone wield. Have you found anything else that might be of interest?"

"Quite a lot." He held up his latest read. "Janek provided me with this; it covers the last few centuries of their history."

"And?"

"It explores the power dynamics of the three most influential lines."

"Lines? Don't you mean families?"

"Family is generally a term used to refer to those related by blood, while mastery of magic connects the great lines of the empire."

"Go on."

"Each of the three lines has its own gifts. The Stormwinds, masters of

Water Magic, come from the east and are trained in an academy known as the Volstrum. Does that name mean anything to you?"

"No," replied Nikki, "but Kraloch might know more. He often talked at length with a fellow shaman from the east. What about the other lines?"

"There's the Sartellians, who are also from the east, though they have their own school, a place called Korascajan."

"And what type of magic do they practice?"

"Fire."

"They say fire is the most destructive element."

"I read that," said Arnim, "and that Fire Mages are sometimes consumed by their fascination, whatever that means."

"It means," replied Nikki, "they can get carried away funnelling all that power and ignite themselves."

"Truly?"

"Oh yes. I remember Aldus Hearn discussing that very subject at one of the queen's dinners."

"Let me guess, he was arguing with Albreda?"

"That he was. He was adamant it was a frequent occurrence, but Albreda called it a load of hogwash. She was of the opinion that a mage can easily tell when they reach the limits of their magic."

"She's the most powerful mage we know," said Arnim. "I wonder how she'd fare against a Sartellian?"

"Let's hope we never have to find out. You mentioned there was a third line?"

"Yes, the Shozarins. They're Enchanters, but unlike their counterparts, they're trained here in Halvaria."

"With all this attention to magic, I'm surprised they don't have a line of Air Mages, or Earth for that matter."

"I've found evidence they employ them, but the most influential positions appear to be the exclusive purview of only these three."

"Where does the emperor fit into all of this?" asked Nikki.

"I'm beginning to think he's just a figurehead. I'm sure the first emperor was the true power at the birth of the empire, but it sounds like these mages eroded his influence over the centuries."

"Does he know that?"

Arnim grinned. "That's an excellent question. What's your take on it?"

"I suspect he doesn't, and why would he? He lives a sheltered life, with only sycophants telling him what goes on outside the Palace walls. Controlling the narrative wouldn't be too difficult if these families were the true power. That does raise an interesting point, though."

"Which is?"

"Why would Janek give you that book if it reveals the emperor is a puppet?"

"Perhaps that was his intent?" Arnim snapped his fingers. "That's it. Don't you see? He wants the emperor to regain his former influence."

"We're prisoners here. How could he possibly hope we could help the emperor?"

"By planting the seeds of doubt in his mind?"

"That's a bit of a stretch," said Nikki.

"Bear with me a moment. By our reckoning, the emperor lives a life of solitude, spoon-fed information by these powerful mages. However, we hold no loyalty to any of these families."

"Lines," she corrected.

"The book uses the terms interchangeably, but I concede the point. In any case, we bring into question the very news His Eminence receives."

"So let me get this straight. We're not presenting anything new, just letting him know that he can't trust his sources?"

"Does that make sense, or am I climbing up the wrong tree?"

"But why couldn't Janek inform the emperor of his circumstances?"

"He could, but remember, although trusted, he's still a servant, whereas the emperor is a descendant of Gods, according to their beliefs."

"Does that help our current circumstances or make it worse?"

"I don't follow," said Arnim.

"The question remains: what we do with this information? We could play along with the emperor's belief and treat him as an all-knowing god, in which case we continue to live a life of relative comfort, even though we're still prisoners."

"And the alternative?"

"We reveal that these mages are manipulating him—the more dangerous approach—for he might fly into a rage and order our execution."

"Perhaps there's another option," said Arnim.

"I'm open to suggestions."

"We let him discover this for himself."

"He and his ancestors have sat on the Throne for centuries without knowing. What makes you think he'd notice it now?"

"I propose we guide him on a voyage of self-discovery."

"I'm listening."

"Here's how we start…"

"The emperor will see you now," announced Janek. "I have been instructed to escort you to the map room."

"The map room?" said Nikki. "Why there?"

"He did not see fit to inform me of his intentions."

"Will we be surrounded by dusty old parchments?"

"Not in the least. It is a large audience chamber with a mosaic inlaid on the floor depicting all the known lands."

"Will we finally learn where we are in relation to Merceria?"

"So it would seem. If you follow me, the emperor is not the most patient of individuals."

"I'm surprised you would say that," said Arnim. "Is a god not infallible?"

"I am not here to play word games," replied Janek. "I am to conduct you to His Eminence. Shall we?" He swept his hand to indicate the door.

"By all means."

Outside stood familiar guards, the same who'd been present during their initial meeting with the emperor.

Janek led them deeper into the Palace, along corridors where massive gold-inlaid columns supported the high ceilings, a sign of the empire's wealth. They eventually arrived at a set of double doors, where another two soldiers wearing the livery of the emperor's personal guard stood. At their approach, they moved aside, allowing them entry.

Nevarus was in the middle of the chamber, staring at the floor, holding what appeared to be a walking stick. As they entered the room, his gaze drifted over to them.

"Ah. There you are. I was beginning to think you'd refused my invitation."

"It was a summons," corrected Arnim. "Not an invitation."

The emperor was in a fine mood and refused to let Arnim's comment dampen his spirits. "My servants can sometimes be a little over-exuberant. Come. Look at my map, and tell me what you think."

The mosaic was a great work of art. Crafted over centuries, it depicted all the known lands of the Continent, including a remarkably accurate representation of Merceria.

"We are here," said Nevarus, pointing with his stick. "Varena, capital of the Empire of Halvaria. Our borders reach from the Great Northern Sea to the continent to our south. We are the largest empire to ever grace Eiddenwerthe."

"That you know of," added Arnim.

The words caught Nevarus off guard. "Why would you say that?"

"There is limited information about the time before the coming of Humans."

The emperor smiled, though it looked forced. "Are you a scholar, perhaps?"

"My husband prides himself on keeping well informed," said Nikki. "It comes from the belief that we can avoid making mistakes in the future by learning from the past."

"A scholar and a philosopher. How intriguing."

Arnim's attention was drawn to the floor. "What are all those coloured blocks scattered around?"

"The red ones are my legions. The other colours represent a myriad of nations. We've placed green blocks to represent Merceria and her allies."

It was a disheartening sight, for the empire appeared ten times the size of their homeland, possibly even larger. "Is this map accurate?" asked Arnim.

"As accurate as it can be. Our scholars are constantly making changes, but you know how it is in times of war, things get missed." He wandered over to the section representing the northeast portion of the empire. "You see here how we've marched into the Petty Kingdoms. The Great Dream is about to become a reality."

"Great Dream?" said Nikki. "What's that?"

"Our destiny. Ever since the founding of Halvaria, we have dreamed of one land united under the common rule of the emperor. What you see here is the culmination of that, or rather, a representation of it."

He paused, deep in thought. "But I digress. I brought you here not to boast of our victory in the east but to discuss matters in the south." He moved until he stood on the portion of the map representing the southern regions.

"This," he said, pointing with his cane, "is where our legions pushed back the Orcs into the dark recesses of the southern continent."

Arnim and Nikki both moved closer, their eyes glued to the floor.

"This region is unknown to us," said Arnim.

"As I thought it might be," replied Nevarus, "but it plays an important part in today's narrative."

"I'm not certain I understand?"

"I took your advice and read everything we have concerning the Orcs. The reports were scarce, yet at the same time, they tell an interesting tale. I believe they once had a great civilization rivalling the Human kingdoms of old." He let his gaze wander to his guests. "You're not surprised?"

"Not at all," said Arnim. "We've known about this for a while."

"Can you explain to me why their civilization crumbled?"

"Why does it matter?"

"I am building a legacy," replied Nevarus. "A united land to last through the ages. For that to be possible, we need to understand why the empire of the Orcs failed."

"There was a great war," said Nikki. "One that reportedly lasted for centuries, fought between the Elves and the Orcs."

"And the result of this war?"

"The Elves destroyed the great cities of the Orcs, scattering their people to the most remote regions of Eiddenwerthe."

"And what of the Elves?"

"Their losses were so substantial that when Humans appeared, the Elves lacked the numbers to oppose them."

"Yet the Orcs still exist; some might even say they thrive."

"They are a most resilient people," said Nikki. "Though it's taken them almost two thousand years to climb back to where they are now."

"How does a race that savage come to be embraced by your queen?"

"They are no more savage than us Humans. You'd understand why our queen accepted them if you spent the time to learn more about her."

"Then educate me."

Nikki took a breath. Had she talked herself into a corner? Was it right to discuss her queen with an enemy? She decided to take the plunge. "Queen Anna listens as much as she speaks."

"Are you suggesting that others control her?"

"No, but she surrounds herself with those she trusts." She spotted an opportunity to dig in deeper. "Is Your Eminence blessed in this regard?"

She caught him off guard, for he stared back a moment before replying. "I have many advisors."

"As I assumed," said Nikki, "but the question remains: do you trust them?"

"Why wouldn't I? Would you ask the same of your queen?"

"She is particular about who she invites into her circle of confidence."

"As am I."

"So you chose your own advisors?"

Again, the pause. She was making progress.

"My advisors are the finest minds in all of Halvaria."

"That doesn't answer my question."

Nevarus looked back at the map. "It's refreshing to hear someone speak without fear of repercussions. Are you this open with your own queen?"

"Queen Anna values honest opinions."

"As do I, else I would have you executed for your audacity."

Nikki pressed her point. "Do others not disagree with you?"

"Who would dare? I am the God-Emperor. My opinions are infallible."

"Your opinions," said Arnim, "are shaped by others."

"Explain yourself!"

"You live a life of relative solitude, Eminence. Everything you know about the outside world is presented to you on a silver platter, the Orcs being only one example of that. Your own people concealed what your scholars long suspected, that they once had a great kingdom. You saw through this when you learned more, but had you not, you would remain unaware of their history."

"What would you have me do? I cannot dismiss all my advisors. Even if I did, how would I know these new advisors were any more honest than the last? Your observation has me trapped with no way out."

"Go amongst your people," suggested Nikki. "See for yourself the hardships your subjects endure and learn the truth first-hand."

"My subjects worship me."

"Do they? Or do they offer lip service to avoid being punished?"

"I have been amongst them many times," said Nevarus.

"I have no doubt you've left the Palace on occasion, but I'm willing to bet you were accompanied by many guards. Hardly the opportunity to ensure an honest evaluation from your subjects."

"But if that's the case, wouldn't my mere presence sway their opinions?"

"Not if they don't know you're their emperor."

"A disguise? What an interesting thought. Could such a thing be arranged, Janek?"

The question caught his servant unawares as he jumped at the mention of his name. "Your pardon, Eminence. My mind was elsewhere."

"Lady Nikki thinks I should go amongst my people dressed as a commoner to discover what they truly think of my rule? Is this something that could be arranged?"

"It would take a lot of work, Eminence, and I doubt the council would approve."

"The council has no say on the matter. I am the emperor, am I not?"

"Most definitely, but you would need guards at the very least."

"Are you suggesting my life would be in danger while amongst my own subjects?"

"It is not your subjects I fear, Eminence."

Silence filled the room as beads of sweat trickled down Janek's cheeks. The emperor turned on his servant, the veins in his neck throbbing, but he stopped short of exploding in rage. Stepping back, he let out a deep breath to calm himself.

"Explain yourself," demanded Nevarus. "If it is not my subjects who cause you so much consternation, then who does?"

"The members of the council, Eminence."

"And why would they wish me harm?"

"With all due respect, Eminence, far-reaching forces are at work here."

"Go on."

Janek's eyes flicked to Arnim and Nikki. "I fear this subject is better discussed in private."

"We shall speak of this matter now, or you'll find yourself without a head!"

Janek swallowed, trying to calm himself, but his voice came out much higher than he'd intended. "There are various factions amongst the council who seek more power, Eminence."

"Name them."

"I dare not, for fear they would kill me."

"And I shall kill you if you don't. Which is it to be?"

Janek closed his eyes, his voice barely a whisper. "The High Strategos, Exalor. He plots to seize the Throne for himself."

"What?"

"It is true. I swear, and he's not the only one. Even as we speak, others plan precisely the same thing."

"How could you possibly know?"

"No one notices the servants, Eminence, and when they talk amongst themselves, you can learn all sorts of things."

"If that's true, why have you not brought it to me sooner?"

He glanced nervously towards the guards. "Nowhere is safe, for the council's ears are everywhere. I may have signed my death warrant by mentioning it even now."

"If I may, Eminence?" said Nikki.

The emperor nodded, allowing her to approach Janek. "Why collect this information if not to inform your master of the danger?"

"Initially, it was simply a way of staying on top of the other servants, but it eventually became much more. They say there's a danger in collecting secrets, but what they don't tell you is that the deeper you dig, the more dangerous it becomes until you reach a point where you are too terrified to dig your way out."

The emperor moved closer, placing his hand on the man's shoulder. "You have done right in telling me this, Janek. I shall protect you."

"With all due respect, Eminence, you lack the influence to do that."

THIRTY-THREE

Counter March

SPRING 968 MC

The horseman galloped into camp, his mount lathered in sweat. Exhausted, the rider dismounted, racing towards the duke's tent, where Lord Alain Heinrich stood at a table, poring over a map of the region.

"Your Grace," said the rider. "I bring urgent news. The Halvarians have withdrawn."

"Withdrawn, you say?"

"Aye, back towards Neiburg. We have them on the run!"

"It's a trap," said Beverly, who perused the map beside the duke. "They mean to draw us in, then hit us with both legions."

"But we've only sighted one," said Duke Heinrich.

"Because that's all they want us to see. I will expand our cavalry patrols."

"We're already stretched paper thin."

"Agreed," said Beverly, "but if we play this right, we can use their own manoeuvring against them."

"How so?"

"If I were the enemy, I'd have one legion draw us farther into Angvil while the other cuts us off from the rear. I propose we turn around and attack the legion that's supposed to surprise us."

"To do that, we'd need to know where they are."

"Oh, that won't be a problem."

"It won't?" asked the duke.

"No. We have a secret weapon."

"We do?"

"Krazuhk."

"The Orc? I don't see how she can help."

"That's because you only see her as an Orc, whereas I know her to be a master of air. Are you familiar with Air Magic, Your Grace?"

"I'm afraid I'm not. We have no mages at court, save for your cousin, and even if we did, they'd be much more likely to be those who practice the magic of fire or water. What can Krazuhk do for us?"

"She can summon a creature of the air to scout the area."

"But surely a bird is incapable of recognizing an army?"

"It only has to find a large collection of people. We already know a legion is out there; we just need to know its location."

"You suggest we trust a bird to tell us what the enemy is? I think you overestimate their capabilities."

"And I think you underestimate them. It won't be what the bird sees that counts; it's how Krazuhk interprets it."

"I would feel much better about this if it didn't rely on magic."

"Why?" asked Beverly. "Because you don't understand it? Your Grace, do you understand how a trebuchet works?"

"Only in the broadest sense of the term."

"Yet you wouldn't hesitate to use one in a siege, would you?"

"No, but that still doesn't mean I have to trust magic."

"Then trust me. You gave me command of this army, and I've spent years coordinating with mages of varying descriptions. If I can trust Albreda's wolves, I can trust a bird Krazuhk summons."

"Wolves?" said the duke. "Now you're playing me for a fool."

"I assure you, I'm not. If you don't believe me, ask Aubrey, or my husband, for that matter; he's spent more time amongst them."

"Your husband spent time amongst wolves?"

"Yes. Back when Albreda empowered Nature's Fury."

"Which is?"

She drew her hammer from where it hung on her belt, holding it out for his inspection.

"A fine weapon," said Duke Heinrich.

"It holds the power of the earth."

"Is that godstone?"

"We call it sky metal," replied Beverly, "but it's the same thing."

"That weapon is worth a king's ransom, even without its magic."

"It's not for sale."

"Very well. I shall continue to entrust my army into your care despite your reliance on magic that I can't comprehend."

"Thank you."

"So what's our next step?"

"We march west, following their retreat."

"I thought we wanted to catch that second legion?"

"We do, but we must make them believe we're falling for their trap."

"This is a dangerous game you're playing," said the duke.

"Victory favours the bold."

"I recognize that expression. It's attributed to Axalon, I believe?"

"No. Richard Fitzwilliam, my father."

"Did you take over as general upon his death?"

"I was awarded my rank due to my abilities, not my relationship to my father."

"Was he a general as well?"

"He was the first. Before that, Merceria only had one senior rank, that of marshal-general. When my mentor, Gerald Matheson, was awarded command of the army, he broke the rank into two, with marshal at the top and general just beneath. I'm only the second person to ever be awarded the rank of general."

"You've clearly experienced much."

"I've learned from the best. Now, with your permission, I need to speak with Krazuhk. Her participation will be vital over the next few days."

"You're the general," said the duke. "Can't you summon her?"

"I'm not here to feed my ego, Your Grace. I've often found a casual conversation to be much more effective than an official request."

"Then do what you think is best."

She walked through the camp until she spotted the green flag Aubrey had cobbled together that served as a marker, letting the rest of the army know anyone injured would find healing beneath it. It also acted as their group's rallying point.

"How's it going?" called out Aldwin.

A smile crept over Beverly's face. Despite the burden of command, his presence always quickened her pulse. "An opportunity has arisen," she replied, "but convincing His Grace it would work was difficult."

"Let me guess? It involves magic?"

"How did you know?"

"While you've been busy planning this campaign, I've been repairing weapons and armour. It's amazing what people tell me when they're waiting around."

"What you're saying is they don't trust magic?"

"That about sums it up, although I believe it's because they've never seen it. Those Aubrey heals are more accepting."

"We have injured already? We haven't even found the enemy!"

"Nothing major, simply cuts and scrapes. We did have one whose foot was crushed by a wagon, but her magic soon fixed it."

"Good to hear. Where's Krazuhk?"

"Inside the tent, helping Aubrey."

"Doing what?"

"Restraining patients. Apparently, we have our first case of fever amongst the army."

Beverly drew in a quick breath. Fever was the bane of any army and could easily strip them of their warriors.

"Aubrey has it well in hand," said Aldwin. "You needn't worry."

"I'm more concerned with how it started."

"Sorry. I don't know the details. You'll have to get those from your cousin. Shall I come with you?"

"That would be nice."

They headed inside the tent the duke had provided for treating the injured, but aside from its current two occupants, it had seen little use.

Aubrey had just finished laying her hands on a patient, her magic still lingering as it faded into the fellow's skin. Krazuhk stood to one side, pinning the man's arms in place.

"Trouble?" said Beverly.

"Nothing I can't handle," replied Aubrey. "This man was suffering from a throat inflammation, making it difficult to swallow. He should be fine now that I've cast my spell."

"Do we know where he caught it?"

"Back home, apparently. His wife said he wasn't feeling well when we left Torburg. I've treated her, too, just to be safe."

"*I cannot understand this,*" Krazuhk spoke in the language of her people. "*If an Orc felt ill, they would immediately seek out the tribe's shaman. There is no shame in admitting when one needs help.*"

"*True,*" replied Beverly, switching to Orc. "*But these people have little experience with magic, particularly the healing kind.*"

"*So they would rather suffer?*"

"*Superstition runs deep, especially amongst the poorer folk.*"

Krazuhk nodded. "*I am starting to understand how Human society is layered, with nobles at the top and the poor at the bottom. Orcs would never accept this.*" She shook her head. "*Sorry. I sense you did not come here to discuss the habits of Humans.*"

"*True, I did not,*" replied Beverly. "*I came because I need your help.*"

"*I am happy to be of service however I may.*"

"*I hoped you'd say that. Can you see through the eyes of a bird?*"

"I can summon a creature of the air, if that is what you mean, but I cannot see through its eyes without making it a familiar, which carries its own risks. Why?"

"I wanted you to use it to spy out the enemy. We have a Life Mage back home named Revi Bloom who does precisely that with his familiar."

Krazuhk smiled. *"I possess a much more useful spell called bird's-eye view amongst my people. It allows me to scout the area as if I were in the air. Very similar to what you described, though it has its limitations."*

"Those being?"

"Trees still block my view, much as they do at ground level, and I cannot see through the walls or roofs of buildings."

"How high up in the air is your viewpoint?"

"Several hundred paces. The only restriction is the viewpoint must be visible to me, so I cannot remain hidden while using the spell."

"Could you use it to spot an enemy army?"

"Most definitely, although it would help to know where to look. Even with a height advantage, there is still much to see. When would you like me to cast it?"

"As soon as possible. Do you need to prepare anything?"

"Only a suitable guard. While viewing things from above, my mind will be elsewhere."

"I can arrange for guards to keep you safe."

"Then fetch them, and I will try to discover the whereabouts of this enemy army."

"Perhaps we should wait until tomorrow," said Aldwin. He looked around, noting the growing shadows. "It will be dark soon."

"All the easier for me to spot the enemy camp," said Krazuhk, this time in the common tongue. "Their fires will light up the night like a beacon." She closed her eyes, waving her arms while muttering words of power. The air buzzed as if a swarm of bees filled the area, and then the Orc ceased her movements, her arms falling to her sides. She remained thus for some time, oblivious to those around her.

"What's happening?" asked the smith.

"The spell's working," replied Aubrey. "I assume it's similar to entering the spirit realm, although I'm surprised her mortal body still stands. I lie down for such a spell."

"I thought she'd be bobbing her head around like Master Bloom."

"She's extending her sight, not seeing through another entity."

"What's the difference?" asked Aldwin. "She's still elsewhere, isn't she?"

"Only her eyes. If we touched her on the shoulder, she would still be aware of us."

"Do you think she'll be able to spot the enemy?"

"We'll know soon enough."

As Krazuhk searched for signs of the Halvarians, the setting sun disappeared, bringing forth the darkness that would aid in her discovery of them. They'd picked a spot well away from the Army of Erlingen lest their own campfires play havoc with the Orc's night vision.

Aldwin counted to one hundred, then yawned. It had been a busy day, and tomorrow would likely be as hectic. Once word got around that he was a smith of some skill, everyone came to him. It wouldn't be so bad if he had a grinding wheel, but it was a tiresome chore with only a whetstone at hand.

"I found them," said Krazuhk, her sudden words making him jump. "They are north and slightly west." She paused a moment. "There is more. A distant city to the northwest is ablaze."

"That must be Neiburg," said Aldwin. "The soldiers talk of little else these days. Any idea of numbers?"

"That is difficult to determine," replied the Orc, "but judging from the number of fires, their army is similar in size to ours."

"Any sign of the other legion?"

"One moment as I shift my gaze."

Again, the waiting. To occupy his mind, Aldwin returned to the distraction of counting.

"The second legion is west of us," said Krazuhk at last, "though the distance is great."

"How great?" asked Aubrey. "Could they march to attack us tomorrow?"

"Doubtful. The region is heavily forested." She opened her eyes. "We must bring the news to Beverly."

Duke Heinrich stared at the map. "Are you absolutely certain of this?"

"Yes," replied Krazuhk. "Their campfires lit up the forest in that area."

"That's good," said Beverly. "It means we have the advantage."

"Perhaps," replied the duke, "but how do we maintain it?"

Beverly stabbed down a finger. "If this map is any indication, they'll advance here where the two roads converge, hoping to cut off our retreat."

"Assuming this map is accurate."

"It must be if the enemy hopes to get behind us."

"Then we need to arrive at the crossroads first."

"No," replied Beverly. "We march west."

"Are you insane? That puts us between two legions!"

"They're trying to execute a complicated manoeuvre, which indicates they have a means of spying on us."

"We have seen no evidence of their scouts." The duke paused, remembering their conversation earlier. "You refer to magical means."

"I do. If they see us moving in that direction, they'll assume we're going after the westernmost legion, and that's where the tricky part comes in. We'll march back eastward tomorrow night under cover of darkness, ready to confront them come morning."

"But they'll be blocking the road to Erlingen by then, won't they?"

"Quite possibly, but we could leave a rearguard there, if you prefer."

"What of our supplies?"

"We have everything we need for the next few days. After that, we'll either be victorious or wiped out, and supply lines no longer matter."

Temple Commander Marlena looked down at the map. "I suggest this legion moving to cut off our retreat is the Fifth, the same we fought at Beggar's Reach."

"And the other?" said Beverly.

"Likely the Ninth. They were responsible for destroying the Army of Rudor. Have you a plan for the battle itself?"

"I shall choose the terrain first thing in the morning. Having said that, I'd like your Temple Knights to remain at the rear of the army. That way, you'll be in the lead when we turn around to march eastward."

"Yes, General."

"When you fought at Beggar's Reach, did you inflict many casualties?"

"Enough to ensure they're not at full strength."

"Could they have pulled men from another legion?"

"Unlikely," said Marlena. "Any other legions the empire might have sent will be far too busy occupying the conquered territories."

"But not impossible?"

"Anything is possible in times of war."

"I'll have Krazuhk repeat her spell tomorrow morning. It might give us a better idea of the numbers we're dealing with."

"If they somehow replenished their losses," said the duke, "do we still fight?"

"Yes," replied Beverly. "We won't get another opportunity like this."

"What makes you say that?"

"The Army of Halvaria is, by all accounts, disciplined and experienced. We can safely assume they'll adapt quickly to changing circumstances."

"Do you believe we have a chance of winning?" Duke Heinrich asked.

"I wouldn't lead us into a battle if I didn't think that was possible."

"They still have more cavalry than we do."

"Yes, but the terrain around here is heavily wooded, which means their horsemen will be forced to stay on the road."

"Couldn't the same be said of our own?"

Marlena grinned. "I suspect that's exactly what the general wants."

"It is," agreed Beverly. "Your Temple Knights will have a much easier time holding back the empire's cavalry if you can restrict them to a narrow section of road. Don't worry. I intend to provide archers and footmen to guard your flanks."

"What about the rest of their legion?" asked the duke.

"It depends on what I find tomorrow morning. Speaking of which, Marlena, I'd like you to talk with the survivors again to see what they know about the area. Local knowledge will prove far more valuable than these maps."

Aubrey entered the tent, a smile playing across her lips. "I have news," she announced. "Gerald defeated a legion near Colbridge."

"Gerald?" said the duke.

"Our marshal," explained Beverly. "This is great news, indeed. It means their efforts to invade Merceria have failed."

"There are still legions at Stonecastle and Ironcliff," warned Aubrey, "but Gerald can now turn his attention to helping our Dwarven allies."

"Do you often refer to your marshal using his given name?" asked Duke Heinrich. "Wouldn't his title be more appropriate?"

Beverly snorted. "You've never met the man. To be more precise, he insists on a certain level of informality. It's part of what makes him so endearing."

"You harbour a fondness for him."

"I do. He taught me everything I know about battle. He's like an uncle to me."

"Let us hope his experience in the west is a sign of things to come for his protégé."

THIRTY-FOUR

Bombardment

SPRING 968 MC

Margel ducked as stones went flying overhead. The bombardment of Stonecastle had begun with flaming spheres and huge rocks raining down on the outer city. She saw an arm protruding from a pile of debris and rushed over, eager to free them. As she pulled on the hand, it came loose, bile rising in her throat.

Flames shot overhead, and then a great ball of fire struck a nearby building, flames splashing everywhere. The smoke stung her eyes, and then dust flew up, threatening to choke her. A guardsman ran past her, heading for the safety of a building, his weapon discarded in his haste. As soon as he ducked into the doorway, a massive groan erupted, and the roof collapsed, burying him under hundreds of pounds of rock.

The vard had called for the evacuation of the outer city, but Margel stubbornly refused. Out there, somewhere, was her Gelion, and she wasn't about to seek safety while he was outside the mountain.

Another explosion of rock sent shards flying in all directions, one such shard nicking her arm as it whizzed past, drawing blood. She cursed at her misfortune, then noticed a small group of people emerging from the dust. There was no mistaking the golden armour of Kasri or her forge mate's cousin Herdwin. Between them, they carried Gelion upon a litter, and for a moment, Margel feared the worst.

"This way," she yelled, waving at them. They drew closer, joined by six Dwarf warriors, survivors of the fierce withdrawal from Kharzun's Folly.

"Gundar's beard," she said, grabbing her forge mate's hand. "What have they done to you?"

"An arrow to the hip," replied Gelion. "I can't walk."

"Bring him this way," said Margel. "We'll take refuge in the lower levels of our house."

They entered to find a surprising visitor, an old man wearing dirty brown robes.

"Aldus Hearn," said Herdwin. "As I live and breathe, you're the last person I expected to see here."

The Druid smiled. "Albreda suggested I might be of some assistance here. Thankfully, I arrived right before the siege began, else I'd be stuck out there."

"But you've never visited here, have you?" asked Gelion.

"I have not."

"Then how did you come to find yourself in my home?"

"You should ask your forge mate the same question. She recognized me when I entered the city; it must be because of my hat." He doffed his headgear and bowed. "Greetings, Gelion, Captain of Stonecastle."

Margel stood with hands on hips. "Herdwin's described him enough times, and honestly, how many elderly Humans can be found in Stonecastle?"

"Admittedly, few," said Herdwin, "but still, the chances of running across him are slim, at best."

"Not so," noted Kasri. "Their house lies astride the main road into the mountain. Everyone entering the city walks right past this place."

A loud crack from outside shook the walls.

"Best get yourselves downstairs, all of you," said Margel, "before we take a direct hit."

"Wouldn't something of that nature bury us?" asked Kasri.

"You needn't fear that," said Hearn. "I'm more than capable of moving a few rocks if needed."

Herdwin and Kasri carried Gelion down the stairs between them, placing him on a bed against the wall.

Margel fussed over her forge mate. "How badly is he injured?"

"You can ask me," said Gelion. "I'm right here."

"I can, but I know you. You're too stubborn to admit when you're badly hurt." She turned to Herdwin. "You tell me, and let's have the truth."

"I'll not lie; his wounds are grievous, but with the aid of a Life Mage, he'll make a full recovery."

"There are none in Stonecastle."

"True, but I have connections in Wincaster." Herdwin moved closer, taking her hand in his. "I promise you, Margel. I shall do all I can to ensure he gets the care he needs."

"I believe you, but no one's going anywhere, not with this siege in full swing."

A horn sounded in the distance.

"What's that?" asked Hearn.

"They're abandoning the walls," replied Gelion. "That can mean only one thing: the Halvarians have broken through the gates. The streets will soon be filled with the enemy."

"I can save us from discovery," offered the elderly mage, "but it involves collapsing the upper floors."

"Do it," Margel and Gelion responded in unison.

Hearn closed his eyes and began muttering strange words. The air buzzed as sweat broke out on his face, and then he moved his arms in an intricate pattern. Above them came a rumble, and then a cascade of dust flew down the stairway, threatening to choke them all.

"Sorry," said Hearn with a cough. "I forgot about the stairwell. Is everyone all right?"

"As well as can be," replied Gelion. "Though this means I'll have to build another house once this is all over."

"You didn't build this one," said Margel. "If you recall, I inherited it from my uncle."

"Hush now," said Kasri. "We must wait and listen. Even though Aldus collapsed the building above us, the enemy may still search the rubble."

They sat in silence. Margel looked at her companions. Six warriors had joined the group when they fled to the safety of the lower floor. She recognized three as members of Gelion's company but had never met the others before. She'd decided to make introductions when Kasri spoke. "How long before the enemy reaches the gates to the under-mountain?"

"That depends on how eager they are," replied Gelion. "Not that it matters; once the great doors are shut, nothing's getting in there. Why? What are you suggesting?"

"It would be helpful if we could climb into the rubble and keep an eye on things."

"To what end? It's not as if we could take on the entire Halvarian Army?"

"Ah, but as I indicated earlier, the main road passes this place, so any attack on the under-mountain goes by us first." She shifted back to Master Hearn. "Can you create a crawl space through that debris up there?"

"Most assuredly. How large?"

"Enough for a single Dwarf to watch the road. We'll take turns and keep notes, everyone except Gelion."

"I shall see to it at once." Aldus moved to the stairwell to begin using his magic.

"Let's take stock of our supplies," suggested Kasri.

"We have our weapons," replied Herdwin, "but food might prove a problem if we're down here too long."

"Don't you worry about that," said Margel. "There's a cold cellar beneath us. I reckon what's down there will last a couple of weeks at least."

~

Captain Galman Boldhammer watched the last of the garrison enter through the gates of the under-mountain. A tremendous crash came from the direction of the outer city doors, a sure indication they had finally succumbed to the bombardment. He imagined the enemy pouring in through the gate, their weapons ready to slay all who opposed them.

Beside him, a guard shifted uncomfortably. "Sir," the fellow said, "we must close the gates before the enemy draws too near."

"Not yet," replied Boldhammer. "We've yet to see Captain Gelion and his men."

"With all due respect, sir, if they're not here now, they never will be."

Galman kept staring, willing his fellow guild member to appear. Then the bombardment halted, and the sound of large numbers of men marching through his beloved city's streets echoed off the stone walls.

Still, he hoped, delaying until a group of Humans came close enough to offer a threat.

"Close it," he shouted, "and may Gundar watch over us all."

Dwarves feverishly worked the winch, moving the gears to swing the great doors shut. Once closed, massive beams fell into place, sealing them in for good.

Esteve Solinak, Commander-General of the Third Halvarian Legion, paused at the crossroads, surveying the damage. The outer city of Stonecastle lay in ruins, its army having taken refuge beneath the mountain. The Dwarves were now sealed in stone and no longer a threat, making it possible for him to order the cavalry to continue into Merceria. This was the pinnacle of his career, at least thus far. He would gain even more fame with the invasion of Merceria, but for now, he was content to bask in the glory of his own success.

Against all expectations, he'd taken the outer city in one great push, and now, two days later, it was deemed safe enough for him to venture in and view the carnage for himself. What would history say of him? Would he be remembered as one of the greatest commander-generals of all time, or disappear into the annals like so many other forgotten legion commanders?

He found his mood souring and turned to his aide. "Where is this great door of theirs? I fancy seeing it in person."

His aide shook his head, knowing full well the commander was aware of the door's location as it lay up the street, a road so straight it could be seen from their present position. Rather than point out the obvious, he bowed, then waved his hand, indicating the direction. "It is this way, my lord."

They proceeded directly towards the great mountain, halting every two dozen paces so Solinak could examine the damage to the city. It made for a tedious trip, but no one dared argue with the commander-general.

Herdwin descended the stairs, returning early from watching over the street. "Something's happening," he announced.

Gelion's mood had soured after their entombment, not that it had been terrific in the first place. "And by something, you mean what, exactly?"

"Someone important is headed up the road."

"How do you know he's important?"

"He's dressed in much finer clothes and is accompanied by guards."

"Could he be a mage?" asked Margel.

"Anything's possible, but he's wearing a sash, which usually means an officer."

"I hope someone staves his head in."

Kasri, who'd been resting in a chair, sat up. "That's an excellent idea."

"What are you suggesting?" Herdwin asked.

"That Master Hearn clear the rubble as quickly as possible."

"What hope have we against an army?" said Gelion.

"We might not be able to take on an army, but we can cut off its head."

"I like how you think, but I'll give you one better. I'm a captain of Stonecastle."

"Meaning?" asked his forge mate.

"Like others of my rank, I carry a horn. Allow me to sound it as you attack. It's not as if I'll be any good in a fight."

"And what will that do?"

"Announce to those within the mountain a counterattack is underway, and hopefully, they'll strike while the enemy is leaderless."

"I'm in," stated Herdwin. He looked at the other Dwarf warriors, who nodded enthusiastically.

"That settles it," said Kasri. "Master Hearn, can you do what's needed?" They all looked at the Druid.

"I see no reason why not."

"How long will it take to dislodge the rubble?"

"It's only one spell," replied Hearn. "Merely a variation on creating a defensive mound. I'll push the debris outward, creating a circular wall. You must wait until I'm done casting to move since the ground will shake violently." He smiled apologetically. "I'm afraid it's not meant to be used while the ground in question is occupied."

"This is it," said Herdwin. "Our chance to finally strike back."

Commander Solinak halted yet again, this time to examine a collapsed building. An arm lay nearby, presumably severed by falling rock, though no other body parts were near it.

"I must commend those working the siege engines," he said to no one in particular. "They've done an exceptional job reducing this city to rubble."

As the ground began shaking, he wondered if the very siege engines he'd just complimented were once again at work. Looking skyward, he searched for anything flying through the air, but something about the rumble felt like it was coming from somewhere closer. Suddenly, rocks exploded from the nearby ruins, releasing a ring of dust and debris.

He moved to shield his eyes, and a horn sounded. One of his guards screamed in pain, and he turned to see a group of Dwarves emerging from the rubble. His Earth Mage, Alitor Verathras, immediately threw up his hands to ready a spell, but before he finished it, an old man came from the dust, pointing at Verathras. A tiny spark flew forth, landing at Alitor's feet, and then green tendrils reached out of the ground. The Halvarian mage, his spell interrupted, looked on in surprise as the tendrils wrapped around his legs, crushing them. With only his upper torso remaining intact, he silently slumped over, the entire event surreal to Solinak.

Two of his guards went down immediately, the victims of crossbow bolts, and then a golden-armoured Dwarf charged into the rest, a hammer taking one down with a single swing.

The commander-general drew his sword, ready to fight back. He slashed at a Dwarf about to swing an axe, then attacked another, but this one seemed more skilled and dodged his blow. Solinak hadn't fought like this in years, yet the old lessons returned quickly. He took out the second

Dwarf, then readied for the next, using the brief interlude to ascertain his position. Half his guards were down, but the sound of fighting would undoubtedly bring reinforcements. He need only hang on and defend himself until they arrived.

He parried another blow, and then the gold-plated Dwarf smashed the head in of the guard next to him, momentarily blinding him with a spray of blood. Before he had a chance to clear his eyes, something solid hit him in the back of the head, and he fell, never to rise again.

Margel glanced at the dead commander-general, then at her hand holding the frying pan. "Serves you right," she said. "No one hurts my Gelion! And what kind of fool removes his helmet during a siege?"

The horn sounded again, and then a reply came from the great horn of Stonecastle, signalling the doors would be opened. Every Dwarf who could carry a weapon would soon descend on the enemy to exact their vengeance!

Herdwin pushed past her. "Pardon me," he said, then struck with his axe, taking down the last remaining guard.

All went quiet as they waited. The great horn sounded again, and they turned to the mountain to watch the first few Dwarves emerge. As the opening widened, more followed, including the Mercerians who'd come to assist.

The Halvarians within the outer city were more concerned with looting than preparing a defence. At the sight of the counterattack, some fled, rushing up the street straight at Herdwin's small command.

"Form a line," he shouted, then ushered the others in place beside him. The Halvarians, noting their unexpected presence, turned to cut down a side road rather than face this new threat. The few who spotted their dead commander-general on their way yelled out in fear.

The great host of Stonecastle pushed up the road, their vard leading them, grinning from ear to ear.

"Well, I'll be a dull axe," he called out. "You're the last person I expected to see, Herdwin!" He slowed, allowing his warriors to push farther into the city without him.

Khazad stared down at the bodies. "Who's this, then?"

"We're not certain," replied Herdwin, "but we believe he might be the enemy commander."

"That one," said Kasri, pointing, "was a mage of some sort, although he never got a chance to cast his spell."

"And who do I have to thank for taking out their leader?"

Herdwin pointed at Margel, who still held her frying pan.

Khazad laughed, a deep-throated sound that made his stomach wobble. "For your actions this day, I award you the title Master of the Pan. We are forever in your debt, Margel."

He surveyed the rest of the group. "Lady Kasri, I'm happy to see you in good health." His gaze flicked to the Druid. "You, I don't know, although I'm sure that's easily fixed."

"Allow me to introduce Master Aldus Hearn," said Herdwin. "An Earth Mage of Merceria."

"Yes," added the Druid. "I arrived just before the siege but was waylaid before I could make it inside the mountain."

"Waylaid?"

"He means," offered Margel, "I invited him into my home as a guest."

"Your house is a popular place for Mercerians of import," noted the vard.

"Aye, it is, and I'll not have anyone claim otherwise."

"I meant no disrespect. Rather, it was a compliment."

"Then I am pleased to accept it as such."

"What happens now?" asked Kasri.

"My warriors will clear the walls," replied Khazad, "but with the enemy commander dead, I think it unlikely they can organize much of a defence. Now, you must excuse me. I have a scouring to see to."

THIRTY-FIVE

The City Burns

SPRING 968 MC

Vorinus Moreau watched as the city was engulfed in flames. The Fifth Legion had captured Neiburg and then marched northeast, ready to play their part in the coming days. Considered the key to the entire strategy, the Ninth remained in the capital, giving their allies time to get into position.

Captain Zoran stood silently beside him. Ever since he'd captured the King of Gotfeld, he had been in the commander-general's favour. With a bit of luck, he might see a promotion to captain-general.

"Glorious, isn't it," said Moreau. "The wrath of the empire is boundless and unstoppable. It won't be long now before the entire Continent bows before us."

"Indeed, my lord, though I wonder at the wisdom of burning Neiburg."

"We must set an example of how we treat those who dare to oppose us. It was their own fault; had they surrendered to the Fifth, they would have been spared all this."

Zoran nodded in agreement. Moreau was in a good mood today, and he didn't want to dampen his superior's enthusiasm.

The commander-general turned to him. "You don't agree?"

"I know it is Imperial policy, my lord, but we might have put the city to better use as a stronghold. It's difficult to defend when it's burned to the ground."

"It is, but the campaign will soon be over."

"We have news?"

"We do, indeed. The Army of Erlingen approaches as we assumed it would. We will meet them south of Neiburg, and then the Fifth will attack from their rear." Moreau grinned. "The fools fell for our little ruse. In a way, it's almost disappointing. I hoped for a bit more of a challenge."

Zoran knew coordinating two full legions was difficult at the best of times, but their marshal had done a brilliant job of it. Now, the might of two legions would crush the duke's army in one fell swoop. He imagined the carnage and saw a battle that would live on as one of their greatest triumphs.

Moreau continued. "It's interesting to look back on things. Before this invasion, I would have sworn the Great Dream was centuries away, yet here we are, deep in the Petty Kingdoms, about to rout one of its largest armies. I almost feel sorry for them."

"My lord?"

"Not that I wish them well, you understand, but I have no doubt they shall suffer tremendous losses. Lives that could otherwise have been spared."

"They would never submit to the will of the emperor."

"You're right. A pity, really. We would all be better off if they'd accepted our rule from the beginning." He paused a moment. "Have you considered what you will do once this war ends?"

"My lord?"

"Wars don't last forever, Captain. There will be little need for warriors once the Continent is ours."

"The conquered territories must still be subdued, my lord."

"Yes, I suppose that's true, and that alone could take decades. It appears your military training will still be in demand."

"What of yourself, Lord?"

"Me?" said Moreau. "I'll retire to my estate and live a life of ease in splendour and glory, my name forever on the lips of the empire's powerful elite."

Zoran bit back a response. His superior held a high opinion of himself, but who was he, a mere captain, to tell him otherwise? Instead, his nodded agreement was enough to spur Moreau on further in his musings.

"This campaign demonstrates once and for all that the aborted invasion of Arnsfeld was an aberration. Our legions crushed the armies of three kingdoms, and now we prepare to add a fourth."

"A lot can happen in war, my lord."

"Have faith, Captain. We've eliminated everyone who's stood in our way."

"The Army of Erlingen is reportedly larger than those we previously fought."

"True. Our estimate places them at similar numbers to our own legion, but that doesn't include the efforts of the Fifth. Combined, we'll outnumber them two to one. I don't know about you, but I like those odds."

"And once they're defeated?"

"We turn our attention to subduing Erlingen and then march north to take on this so-called Northern Alliance."

"Even so, things can go awry. Perhaps we should send word for the Eleventh to join us?"

"No!" insisted Moreau. "We don't need them, and even if we did, they're too far away to arrive in time. We must take a defensive position and let the enemy come to us. I'll admit it's not as exciting at taking the initiative, but when push comes to shove, it's all about destroying the enemy, and this is a solid tactic."

"Was this your idea, Lord?"

"I wish it were, but Edora Sartellian came up with it. If I were you, I would keep my eye on her; that woman is going places."

"What do you mean?"

"I wouldn't be shocked if she eventually became the High Strategos. Play it smart, and you could follow along in her wake."

"I serve you, my lord."

"Well put," said Moreau, "but I have risen as high as possible in the emperor's army."

"Did you always aspire to be a commander-general?"

"I thought of nothing else when I was a child. You might say it was a calling. As it turns out, I'm right where I'm meant to be, leading this legion when I'm most needed."

"With the enemy army being handed to you on a platter?"

Moreau laughed. "Yes, precisely! Rest assured, the crows will feast on their dead after this coming battle."

"A masterful plan," said Zoran.

"I like you, Captain. When you brought me the King of Gotfeld, I knew you were someone who got things done. Mark my words, great things are in your future."

To the east, Hamath Nordin marched the Fifth Legion south. The road from Neiburg to the Erlingen border was narrow, and the surrounding terrain heavily forested, making progress slow. The Fourth Cohort, made up entirely of provincials, led the way, their cavalry ranging ahead of their footmen. For Edora Sartellian's plan to work, the Fifth had to move quickly. Even now, the enemy advanced towards the Ninth. If his men arrived too late, the result could be the loss of an entire legion. Arrive too early, and they'd only meet the rear elements of the Army of Erlingen. To this end, Nordin stressed the need for a rapid march.

The heavy cavalry brought up the rear of the legion due to the terrain. They would have their chance once they got past this constricting roadway, but for now, it was more important for his footmen to keep their pace.

The first signs of trouble arrived before noon, when a rider pushed through the advancing columns and halted before him.

"My lord, we sighted the enemy."

Nordin sighed. The man must be exaggerating; the Army of Erlingen was miles to the west. "And when you say the enemy, what precisely do you refer to?"

"Our cavalry screen came across a group of warriors at the crossroads, my lord."

"How many warriors?"

"A hundred, perhaps a little more."

"Likely a rearguard set to keep their supply lines safe."

"Your orders, Lord?"

"Inform the captain-general of the Fourth he is to push forward in full strength. I want the crossroads cleared as soon as possible."

"Yes, Lord." The rider turned and made his way to the head of the column, a difficult endeavour considering the number of men on the road.

Having heard the exchange, Nordin's aide rode up beside his superior. "Trouble, my lord?"

"Merely a rearguard, nothing that need concern us at present. Where's our mage?"

"Resting. He spent a considerable amount of his power scrying out the enemy last evening. Shall I wake him?"

"He found the Army of Erlingen, didn't he?"

"He did, Lord. They were heading west, as we suspected."

"Good, then all is as I thought. The provincials will clear the road, and then we'll turn westward, following their trail."

"Shall I ride ahead and supervise?" asked the aide.

"No. We'll let the captain-general of the Fourth Cohort have his moment of glory. It's not often the provincials get a chance to distinguish themselves."

"Should we halt the advance until the road is cleared?"

"I think you overestimate the capabilities of those guarding the cross-roads. They won't stand. They never do in the face of a legion of the empire's finest."

Captain Nedermeyer led his cavalry towards the crossroads. The men of Erlingen stood waiting, their spears set against a possible cavalry charge. It was a pitiful number of men, especially considering how easy it would be to turn their flank. He raised his sword up high, then swept it down, the signal to begin the charge.

The one hundred provincial horsemen increased their speed until their hoofbeats echoed off the trees like thunder. Closer and closer, they drew, and then at the last moment, Nedermeyer realized his mistake.

Hagan Stein, the Baron of Mulsingen, waited behind his footmen, his horse nervously stomping the ground while the lead elements of the Halvarian legion thundered towards his position. He gave the command, and the men hiding in the forest advanced, presenting a solid line against the threat. Behind them came archers, loosing arrows at the enemy charge. The light provincial cavalry, their horses unarmoured, took tremendous casualties, and then those who remained struck his line.

His footmen should've used their spears to keep the horses at bay, but they'd never been exposed to a cavalry charge before. The sight of so many riders bearing down on them caused more than a few to waver. Then, an enemy horse riddled with arrows went down, sliding into the front rank and opening a gap in the line. The Halvarians quickly capitalized on this opportunity, and before he knew it, Hagan was fighting for his life.

Marlena picked her way through the forest. Their guide, a young local named Kip, insisted the trail led back to the main road after meandering to the east. It was a gamble, but the Temple Knights appearing in the enemy's rear would create panic amongst the Halvarian leadership. Temple Captain Vitaly's knights followed the sister knights in single file, a formation necessitated by the dense underbrush.

She'd recognized the wisdom in the tactic but knew timing was everything in battle. She only prayed they would arrive in time. Ahead of her, Brother Cyric was in fine form. Despite being an aide to the regional commander of the Mathewites, he'd insisted on accompanying them as they rode to battle.

She remembered the first time they'd met. She'd been a suspect in the death of her father. Under normal circumstances, she would have been found guilty of the crime, but Cyric had gotten to the truth. After everything was settled, he offered her a way out of her predicament by introducing her to the Temple Knights of Saint Agnes. She joined them, embarking on a journey taking her halfway across the Petty Kingdoms on a quest to halt the Halvarian Empire's aggression.

Her crowning glory came at the Battle of the Brinwald, where she led the charge that broke the enemy's back and halted the invasion. That battle, or rather the circumstances leading up to it, triggered her promotion to Temple Captain. At that time, she had an exemplary mentor to guide her. However, her more recent battlefield promotion left her struggling to find her place.

Behind her, Sister Johanna must have sensed her thoughts, for she chose that exact moment to speak up.

"Are we doing the right thing here, Captain?"

"We must have faith in the general's plan."

"I'm not suggesting she's not skilled, but can we take the word of a foreigner?"

"Foreigner? Are we not all foreigners deep down?"

"I'm not sure what you mean?"

"Are you from Erlingen or Angvil?"

"No."

"Then you are as much a stranger here as Lady Beverly."

"But she's not even from the Petty Kingdoms?"

"True, but perhaps she's here to fulfill a higher purpose?"

"Are you suggesting she's a pawn of the Saints?"

"I've said this before, and I'll say it again: the Saints do not control people; they offer guidelines for how we might live our lives."

"Yet, by your own reasoning, she is here, at this moment in time, precisely where she is needed most."

Marlena smiled, for it was the exact turn of phrase favoured by her mentor, Temple Commander Charlaine.

Krazuhk opened her eyes. *"Everything is proceeding as you suspected. They push up the road to attack the men at the crossroads."*

"Good," replied Beverly. *"We need to make our way along this trail till we outflank them from the west."* She switched to the common tongue. "Are you certain we're not lost?"

The old man leading them smiled, showing his blackened teeth. "I knows the way. Just down 'ere the path turns left, then we cross a stream."

"And this leads us behind the enemy?"

"Should do, right by Ogre's Hill. It were named after an old legend."

"Which old legend is this?"

"There was this Ogre, see? And he wanted to waylay those travelling the old road. All well and good till a knight comes along and slays him." The old man smiled at her but said no more.

"That's it?" said Beverly. "No moral to the story?"

"Nope. But the hill does overlook the road." He cocked his head to the side. "Ah, hear that? It's the stream. I told you we was close."

They continued, picking their way along a twisted route that seemed to double back on itself more than once. Beverly had visited the Whitewood on several occasions, not to mention many other forests of Merceria, but this one felt much different, like some giant maze with twists and turns appearing every hundred paces or so.

This entire tactic was an enormous risk, particularly considering the Erlingen warriors' relative inexperience. She wished she had a few Mercerian companies to bolster her forces, for going into battle with such an unknown quality of men worried her more than she cared to admit. On the other hand, if it worked, her tactic would allow them to destroy an entire legion.

She was suddenly struck by the loneliness of command. She had Aldwin and Aubrey with her, but they weren't army commanders. What she needed was someone who understood military matters, a fellow leader like Heward, Preston, or better yet, Gerald.

"*You are worried,*" said Krazuhk. "*I sense it.*"

"*I'm beginning to doubt myself, not the best characteristic in a general.*"

"*I disagree. It shows you are not infallible, an important trait in one who leads others into battle.*"

"*That doesn't exactly help.*"

"*Then let me ask you this: has your mentor ever doubted his abilities?*"

"*Yes, of course.*"

"*And did he succeed in the end?*"

"*Always.*"

"*Then you are in good company.*"

Beverly's mind settled. "*Thank you. I needed to hear that.*"

"*I did nothing but remind you of who you are. It has become apparent to me you were born to lead.*"

"*I would hardly say that.*"

"*Yet it is true. May I demonstrate?*"

"*How?*"

"*By asking you a few questions.*"

"*Go ahead.*"

"How old were you when you first rode as a warrior?"

"Fifteen," replied Beverly. *"I accompanied one of Gerald's patrols out of Bodden."*

"Had you been an Orc, you would have started sooner, but I understand that fifteen is young for a Human, particularly a female. Were any other members of the patrol your age?"

"No, but I was a follower, not a leader."

"You must let me finish," said Krazuhk. *"You are a knight and, as such, hold much regard in Human civilization. At what age did you achieve that honour?"*

"Seventeen, though I was later stripped of that title."

"Ah, but by then, you had become a Knight of the Hound, had you not?"

"I had, but I was already twenty-five."

"True, but unless I misinterpreted your words, you were the first of that order, a singular accomplishment, but it was a stepping stone to even greater things. You are now a Knight Commander and a General of Merceria. Are you suggesting this marshal of yours appointed you to such a position without having faith in your abilities?"

Beverly opened her mouth to object, but Krazuhk made a good point. Who was she to question the wisdom of the Marshal of Merceria? If Gerald had faith in her, then she had better find it in herself.

"Now," continued the Orc, *"you must honour his trust by doing what you do best."*

THIRTY-SIX

The Battle of the Pines

SPRING 968 MC

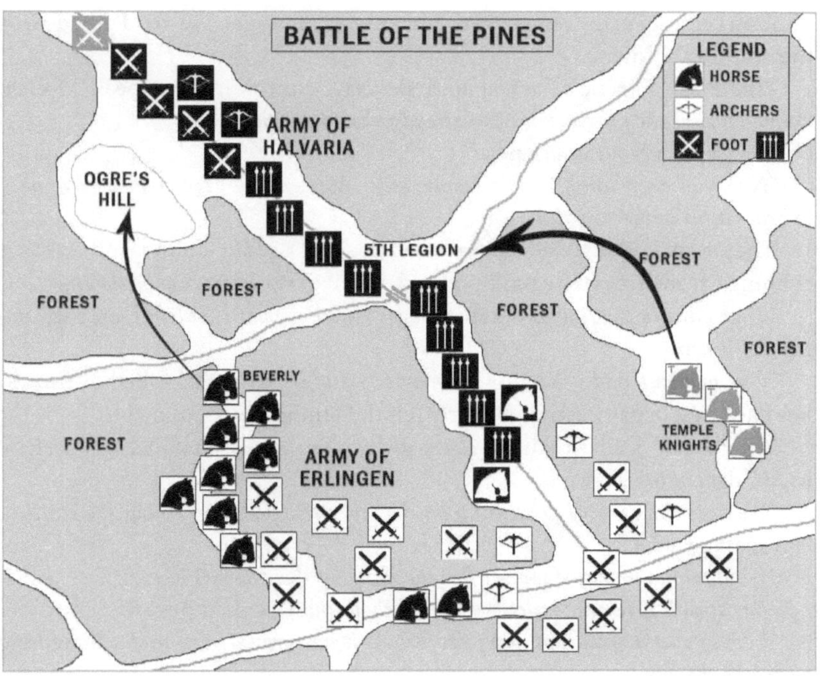

Beverly ducked, avoiding the branch. Lightning, as if sensing her predicament, let out a snort. "Not funny," she said. "I doubt you'd like it much if the leaves kept slapping your face."

"There it is," called out their guide. "Ogre's Hill."

The ground rose before them, revealing a mostly bare hilltop, save for a cluster of trees at its southern end.

"The road is just east of it," the fellow added.

Beverly halted her column. "Wait here," she ordered. "Krazuhk and I will examine the hill and determine how best to use it. I don't want the enemy getting wind of what we're up to till it's too late for them to do anything about it."

She dismounted. "You stay here, Lightning. We need to be quiet."

"*I shall lead,*" said the Orc in her native tongue. "*I am a skilled hunter and more likely to remain silent.*"

"*By all means.*"

They proceeded up the hill, the climb proving not too taxing. They heard the enemy on the march before they were halfway up. The Halvarians' habit of marching in step at all times made for a distinctive sound.

Krazuhk lay down just before she reached the top, the better to remain unobserved. Beverly soon joined her, staring down at the road filled with the empire's soldiers.

"*Those are Imperials,*" whispered Beverly, continuing to speak Orcish. "*Which means the provincials have already passed this point.*"

"*Do we launch our attack now?*"

"*No. We'll wait until Temple Commander Marlena makes her move. We need to draw them in the rest of the way.*"

They watched in silence for a while, the distant sounds of fighting echoing off the trees. Krazuhk pointed. "*Their army appears to be slowing.*"

"*That's due to fighting at the crossroads. Where is their cavalry? I don't see any signs of it here.*"

"*One moment, and I shall use my magic to find it.*" Krazuhk rolled over onto her back and began casting. Beverly felt the familiar buzz of magic.

"*I see them,*" said Krazuhk. "*They are farther up the road and will soon be within sight of this very hill.*"

"*We need the cavalry to form up on the reverse slope. I don't want the Halvarians spotting them.*"

"*Would it not be best if we muffled the sound of their horse's hooves?*"

"*I'm afraid there's not much we can do about that,*" replied Beverly.

"*I could cast a spell that dampens sound. It has proved very useful to hunting parties in the past.*"

"*Do what you can, then, but be careful not to expend too much of your strength; we may need your magic later in the battle.*"

"*Understood, General.*" The Orc left the hilltop, leaving Beverly to watch the enemy's advance.

Marlena peered through the trees from her position east of the road. Beyond lay the narrow stream that flowed across the road, not much of an obstruction but a welcome sight for the Temple Knights, as it marked the location of the attack. She determined the provincial warriors had passed through the stream heading south, leaving the Imperial crossbowmen to play catch up. Behind them came the empire's heavy horsemen, their mail gleaming in the early afternoon sun.

The Temple Commander formed her knights into a line and advanced at a trot to the edge of the woods. Their target was the point at which the stream crossed the road—seize it, and they'd divide the legion in two. More importantly, it would cut off the bulk of the enemy warriors from their commander-general.

She waited, the trees making it far more difficult to maintain their line, then yelled out the command. The Saint Agnesites exited the woods, heading straight for their targets, the Mathewites following, anchoring their northernmost flank.

Success came early, allowing them to seize the road, but then the enemy cavalry arrived from the north, determined to wipe them out by sheer numbers.

Although the Halvarians had the numerical advantage, the close confines of the road prevented them from charging. The Temple Knights, in turn, became brutal killing machines, hitting out with calm, measured strokes while remaining in a tight, efficient formation.

Beverly raised Nature's Fury to the sky, letting the light reflect off the skymetal. "Charge!" she screamed, urging Lightning down towards the enemy.

A Halvarian officer, more alert than his fellow countrymen, turned to engage her, but a bolt of lightning struck him before he'd advanced more than three horse lengths. He stood rigid in his stirrups before falling from the saddle.

On either side of Beverly rode the cavalry of Erlingen, releasing a fury that had been building inside them. For weeks, all they'd heard about was the defeat of one Petty Kingdom after another. Now, they had a chance to finally strike back at the enemy. Behind them, footmen poured out from the woods into the flanks of the Halvarian horsemen.

Beverly soon lost sight of the battle, for her own position at the head of her troops left her fighting for her life. Nature's Fury swung out, striking a foe's chest. The breastplate fractured under the force of her blow, and then she swung overhead, crashing down onto the fellow's helmet. A loud crack echoed off the trees, and the rider slumped, his part in the fight done.

Years of training had honed her skills, and her muscles took over, swinging out with her hammer even as her shield blocked attacks. Lightning, fierce as ever, stomped and bit all who came near, driving deep into the enemy horsemen.

She let the magic of nature grow within her, the animal fury building until the hammer struck out with incredible speed and precision. The weapon felt like an extension of herself, as if she had grown claws to strike down all who opposed her.

The enemy riders drew back from her blows, the horses panicking. Then a large group broke off, fleeing north, clogging the road even more.

The rest, now caught between Beverly's command in the north and the Temple Knights to the south, collapsed. Many threw down their weapons and begged for mercy, while others, hoping to escape, fled east, abandoning their mounts to make their way through the thick forest.

~

Krazuhk watched from the safety of Ogre's Hill. She'd used a bolt of lightning to help Beverly break the enemy line, but now concentrated on more important matters. If there was a mage amongst the Halvarian warriors, she must locate them before they turned the tide of battle.

The most logical place to find such a person was near their general. From what she'd learned of Human armies thus far, they tended to use a lot of flags to identify those in charge.

She closed her eyes, reaching her arms into the air, calling on her magic to summon help. The air teemed with life, so much so that she had to narrow her focus; then she saw it, a creature so small as to almost be missed —the perfect familiar. She held her hand out, and the hoverbird flitted over and landed on her finger.

"*Excellent,*" said Krazuhk. "*You can remain motionless in the air, the perfect vessel to find my target.*" She leaned in close, letting their foreheads touch, and immediately experienced a rush of senses as their minds merged, forging a bond like no other. The creature then flew off her hand, hovering momentarily before rising into the sky.

The Orc closed her eyes once more, establishing a link. She felt the connection snap into place, and then she was gazing down at the trees. It was a remarkable sight, for the bird saw colours far beyond her limited ability and a vaster field of vision. While it took a moment for her mind to adjust, she could now search a much larger area in a shorter period than otherwise would have been possible.

Below her, the warriors of Erlingen and Halvaria fought, oblivious to the tiny bird that flitted overhead. She urged the creature north, following the road packed with the empire's cavalry.

A man sat atop a white charger, his gold armour marking him as the one in charge. He conversed with a finely dressed, unarmoured fellow, clutching a staff, the mark of a magic wielder if ever she'd saw one.

Taking note of their position, she broke the connection and stealthfully made her way north, keeping to the trees to avoid detection by the warriors on the road.

~

Marlena reformed her knights. They'd cleared the road, save for the wounded and dead, and she looked south to where the bulk of the Halvarian provincials fought near the crossroads.

Brother Cyric appeared at her side. "You succeeded, Temple Commander. My congratulations on a great triumph."

"The battle is not over," she replied. "We cut the enemy in half, but we must still deal with those to the south." She glanced around at her knights, covered in blood, their armour dented and scratched, yet they were ready to fight on.

"We ride south," she called out, "straight into the rear of those provincials." With that, she lowered her visor, then raised her blood-spattered mace high to grab everyone's attention before sweeping it down.

As one, the Temple Knights advanced. There was no bravado here or shouts of triumph, merely trained warriors advancing; the only noise, the sound of their horses' hooves and the jangle of their gear.

The enemy, their focus on the fighting to the south, never saw them coming.

~

Beverly pressed on to the north, the Erlingen footmen following in her wake. The melee had thinned her cavalry, but those who remained had a fire in their blood. They rode at her side, their weapons eager to deal yet more death to the enemy.

The fighting had slackened, but then suddenly, footmen opposed them rather than just the empire's cavalry. Unlike those waging battle in the south, these men wore plate armour, marking them as the Fifth Legion's elite companies.

Undeterred, Beverly pushed straight into them, relying on Lightning's bulk to penetrate their ranks. The sudden appearance of her horsemen in amongst the retreating enemy cavalry took them entirely by surprise.

Without realizing it, she broke through their makeshift line and attacked yet another heavily armoured company following in the wake of the first. However, the cluster of horsemen farther north was of even more interest, for their Imperial standard marked them as the legion's leadership.

Beverly risked a quick glance backwards, where the horsemen of Erlingen were doing surprisingly well. The Halvarians should have formed an effective defence, but they were disorganized, with no one stepping up to take charge.

It struck her then that perhaps she'd discovered the enemy's weakness. Cut off from their commanding officer, the isolated members of the legion had fallen apart. This would never happen in Merceria, for every officer and sergeant knew their duty. This was apparently not the case in the empire.

The men before her yielded, many running for the safety of the woods. She let her cavalry catch up to her, then briefly halted their advance to issue orders.

"Over there," she said, pointing north, "is the person leading this legion. Remove him from the battle, and we shall have total victory!"

They cheered, and then she ordered them forward. They rode slowly at first, building up speed as they approached the enemy. Fifty paces away, they urged their horses into a full gallop. It was awe-inspiring, particularly considering the road's narrow confines. The sight of a solid wall of horsemen charging towards the beleaguered footmen was too much to bear. A few brave souls attempted to make a stand, but the bulk fled, leaving the small knot of horsemen behind them dangerously exposed.

Beverly charged straight at the one wearing gold armour.

~

Krazuhk witnessed the charge and the enemy mage gesticulating. She quickly countered with a spell of her own, and moments later, the Halvarian looked around in confusion, his voice muffled by a sphere of silence. Unable to cast his spell, he was quickly cut down by an Erlingen horseman.

. . .

Bodies littered the road after the destruction of the legion. Beverly led Lightning through the carnage, giving him a rest from his exertions. She ignored those who picked through the corpses, searching for anything of value—it was an age-old practice. Men fought and died in this battle. What matter then that they should seek some reward for their efforts?

She spotted Aldwin heading towards her, and relief washed over her. They embraced without words, holding each other for what felt like an eternity, yet, at the same time, wasn't nearly long enough.

They finally parted, and he looked her over with a keen eye. "Your armour looks a little worse for wear. Are you injured?"

"Not in the slightest. This armour may be archaic by Petty Kingdoms' standards, but it kept me safe. What more could a girl ask for?"

He grinned. "Come. Aubrey will be worried about you."

"Where is she?"

"Dealing with the wounded. That reminds me, you haven't seen Krazuhk, have you?"

"I have. She helped kill an enemy mage."

"Fire?"

"We're not sure, although she suspects he was more likely an Enchanter."

"What makes her think so?"

"Her knowledge of magic," replied Beverly. "We suspected the Halvarians were using magic to watch our movements, but we would've easily spotted a Fire Mage's spell."

"I suppose that's the disadvantage of using flames for everything."

"Precisely." She halted suddenly. "Actually, before we check on Aubrey, I'll need to see the duke."

"Is this about the enemy general?"

"No, he's dead, struck down by Nature's Fury. Where is His Grace?"

"Still at the crossroads," said Aldwin. "Come. I'll bring you to him."

"Let me ensure I understand you," said Lord Alain. "We just won a monumental victory, and now you say we must retreat?"

"Yes," replied Beverly. "While it's true we destroyed a legion, we still took losses, which makes it unwise to face off against another."

"So we retreat back to Erlingen with our tails between our legs?"

"We bought time, Your Grace. In the wake of their defeat, the empire will hesitate to advance until they can amass enough warriors to give them a numerical advantage."

"How much time do we have?"

"Some weeks yet, perhaps even a month. Their rapid advance left them with long supply lines within hostile terrain, which they must subdue to concentrate on invading Erlingen."

"And in the meantime?" asked the duke.

"Have you no allies you can call on for help?"

"The Northern Alliance is our only hope for reinforcements, but we have no representation there."

"Then send your finest diplomats. I'm sure they'll see reason when they discover what's at stake."

"My finest diplomats? Those are my barons, and I need them here, commanding my warriors."

"Then allow me to go in your stead."

He began pacing back and forth. "You brought us a great victory, though it irks me to be forced to withdraw." He looked around at his nobles, who'd gathered to celebrate their victory. In the face of the harsh reality of their current situation, they grew sombre. "What think you, Lord Hagan?"

The Baron of Mulsingen cleared his throat. "By giving us victory this day, Your Grace, Lady Beverly demonstrated her superior skills in warfare. Her strategy of withdrawing to Zurkirk seems the best course of action given our current circumstances."

"And what of sending her north to seek aid?"

"I believe it's worth the effort."

"But would it bear fruit? I'd hate to send her north when we might need her here to help defend our lands."

"It's worth the gamble, Your Grace. More men are needed to continue the fight. If we sit here and wait, the enemy will only bring additional legions to overwhelm us."

"Agreed, but that gives them the opportunity to replace their losses." The duke turned to Beverly. "What say you to that?"

"That's precisely what we want them to do, Your Grace. It also gives us time to rebuild our own numbers, providing the Northern Alliance can be persuaded to intervene on our behalf."

Lord Alain let out a sigh. "We shall gather our wounded, bury our dead, and then withdraw across the border to Zurkirk. I shall draft a letter immediately asking Andover and Reinwick to come to our aid."

Brother Cyric pushed through the crowd. "If I may, Your Grace, might I accompany them?"

"I was not aware this was Church business."

"Strictly speaking, it's not, but my contacts in Andover and Reinwick might prove advantageous to this pursuit."

"Would that be acceptable to you, Lady Beverly?"
"Most certainly, Your Grace."
"Then it's settled. You'll leave first thing in the morning."

THIRTY-SEVEN

Under the Mountain

SPRING 968 MC

The mountain shook, releasing a cascade of dust from the great pillars of Ironcliff's Royal chambers.

"It's getting worse," grumbled Thalgrun.

"It is," replied Agramath. "With the fall of the outer city, they've resorted to hurling great rocks at us with their trebuchet. It appears they mean to tear the mountain apart one stone at a time."

"They'll have a hard time breaking into the under-mountain."

"So it would seem."

"You don't agree?" asked the vard.

"The Halvarians don't appear the type who take on a task-halfheartedly. This bombardment must be part of their plan. The key is determining what their next move will be."

"Have the guild masters gathered?"

"They await you in the great hall."

"Then let's go and have a chat, shall we?" Thalgrun brushed the loose stone from his sleeves and then entered the corridor. Outside stood two guards, their golden armour marking them as members of the elite Hearth Guard. They quickly fell into step behind their vard as he made his way towards the great hall.

"I have to hand it to them," said Thalgrun. "That trebuchet is a fine piece of engineering. You don't suppose it's Dwarven, do you?"

"I doubt it. From what the rangers saw, it had no gears, merely a giant sling."

"Still, it's a remarkable piece of weaponry. I never imagined Humans capable of such work."

They paused as a guard ran forward to open a door. Beyond lay the great hall of Ironcliff, wherein the guild masters waited.

Thalgrun took a deep breath, and then entered, Agramath following two steps behind. The vard nodded at those present, taking his place on the throne. Ironcliff boasted over thirty guilds, although only a few held any real power. His gaze settled on the Guild Master of the Warriors Guild.

"Garnik," he began, "of all those here today, you are the most knowledgeable concerning siege operations. What do you make of this recent development?"

"It is no threat to us, my vard. The Humans could throw rocks at the mountain for all eternity, and it would make no difference."

"I beg to differ," said Agramath.

"I am the expert in such matters. Are you suggesting I don't know my business?"

"No one else in Ironcliff would know more, but you do not take into consideration our enemy's motives."

"Meaning?"

"They are no fools. If they throw rocks at the mountain, it's for a reason."

"And what reason would that be? Surely you're not suggesting they can collapse the entire mountain?"

"Let us keep a civil tongue," warned Thalgrun. "We are here to discuss our current situation, not get into arguments."

Strodar Goldeye, the master of the bankers guild, took a step forward. "You speak with great wisdom, my vard. If I might make a suggestion, let us follow Lord Agramath's line of reasoning." He held up his hand as Garnik opened his mouth. "I know you disagree with his assessment, but humour us if you would." Strodar paused, looking around the room. "We know the enemy seeks to defeat us, but then what? Are they intent on sealing us up in our mountain, or are they bloodthirsty enough to wipe us out entirely?"

"How would we know?" called out Selia Ironfist, master of the mining guild. "We've had little interaction with Humans, aside from Merceria."

"That's true," said Agramath, "but we cannot dismiss the fact they might be employing magic to guide them, possibly even those skilled in the application of working rock and stone."

"True," added Thalgrun. "Let's not forget the lesson of Dun-Galdrim."

"Dun-Galdrim?" said Garnik. "No evidence suggests the Halvarians had anything to do with its loss. All we know is it went silent some fifty years ago."

Agramath shook his head. "Given its likely proximity to the areas claimed by the empire, can there be any other possible explanation? We mountain folk don't abandon our cities, particularly one as well fortified as Dun-Galdrim."

"Even if that's true, and I'm not ready to concede that point, it has little bearing on our present circumstances. The Halvarians captured the outer city and are now hurling boulders at the mountain. I could understand were they intent on destroying our great doors, but that doesn't appear to be their objective."

"I wonder," said Selia. "Could they be attempting to bury the front door behind a rockfall?"

"You tell me," said Garnik. "You're the expert on such things."

"Agreed," said Agramath. "What are your thoughts on the matter, Selia? Is our enemy following bad advice, or is there an inherent threat to this bombardment?"

She stepped forward, then turned to face them. "We have known for a while there are fractures in the mountain. It's possible they might be trying to exploit them."

"Fractures?" said Thalgrun. "Are you suggesting the entire mountain is in danger of collapse?"

"No. At least not without centuries of such abuse. Picture the mountain as a large piece of flint. When striking such a stone, a small piece might slew off, while other times a much larger piece does."

"We're not children," insisted Strodar.

"True, but the full explanation is complicated. To the senior members of the mining guild, the mountain is like a living, breathing creature. It has its strengths, as most people know, but it also has its weaknesses. I can only assume the enemy learned of a way to take advantage of them."

"How do they know where to strike?"

"I haven't the faintest idea."

"No," said Agramath, "but I have. We know the empire employed Earth Mages near Stonecastle. I put forward the idea that they brought some to Ironcliff to exploit those weaknesses."

"But how in the name of Gundar's Forge would they be able to read the mountain without entering it?"

"As you all know, I am an accomplished master of rock and stone, yet even I don't know everything."

"How much time do we have?" asked Thalgrun.

"That's difficult to say," replied Selia. "I would need to make a more detailed examination of the areas they've been targeting."

"Can you give us a rough estimate?"

"Three weeks, perhaps four?"

Thalgrun sat back on his throne, his mind whirling from this revelation.

Would he be the last Vard of Ironcliff, his people doomed to be forgotten to history? How did one counter such a threat? His thoughts turned to his subjects. There was no escape from beneath the mountain; the enemy army had seen to that. How could he best serve his people? Should he surrender? The thought was quickly dismissed. No Dwarf worth their beard would consider such a thing, yet he saw no other way out of this predicament.

"We should begin evacuation," suggested Agramath. "We could use the casting circle to send our people to Wincaster."

Thalgrun sat up, his mind falling into sharp focus. "Begin at once."

"Is that wise?" asked Strodar. "We can't possibly hope to save everyone. How do we decide who goes?"

"We will start with the wounded. Guards, fetch Hayley Chambers and Revi Bloom. I would seek their opinions on the matter."

"Bring them here, my vard?"

"No. Such matters are best discussed in private." He turned to the guild masters. "Much as I appreciate everyone's ideas, we haven't the time for debate. You must excuse me. I have a lot to see to." With that, he rose, waving for Agramath to follow as he left.

"So? What do you think?" Thalgrun took a gulp of his ale.

"We can begin evacuation whenever you like," replied Revi, "but I'm not certain that's your best course of action. We're currently short on mages, and each recall spell uses a considerable amount of our strength. We can only manage three castings a day, and that's not accounting for the return trips."

"I was afraid you'd say that. Just as well, I suppose. We'd have nothing but arguments over who to save. What do you think, Commander?"

"It's a grave situation, indeed," replied Hayley, "but not as bad as it sounds. It might be just the break we've been waiting for."

"I'm not sure I understand?"

"You say they're hammering the mountainside, but trebuchets aren't the most accurate weapons."

"What are you suggesting?"

"What if we gave them something to take advantage of?"

"And how would we do that?"

"I assume you have tunnels near the weakened areas?"

"We do," replied the vard.

"Then I propose we weaken the area even more."

"How do we do that?" asked Revi. "It wouldn't be safe to dig while they're hurling giant stones at us."

"Ah, but they stop at night, don't they?"

"They do," said Thalgrun. "If I understand what you're proposing, we dig out the walls, leaving only a thin face of rock on the outside of the mountain. Then, when the next attack hits, it'll break through, presenting the enemy with an opportunity to get inside."

"Precisely. You'd have your best warriors standing by to fight them in the tunnels, where Halvaria's superior numbers can't be used to any advantage."

"I'll go you one better," said Thalgrun. "We lure them deeper into the mountain, then collapse the walls and ceilings, burying them alive."

"That's an extremely dangerous game," said Revi, "especially if any Earth Mages are amongst their army."

"Very few things in war are not dangerous, and as for the Earth Mages, I don't think even they could stop a cave-in that large." Thalgrun looked at Hayley. "I doubt your rangers would be of much use. It's not as if they could loose their arrows in the restricted space of the halls. I don't suppose I could convince your queen to send more footmen?"

"I'm afraid we have none to spare, not while Stonecastle and Trollden are under attack."

"Any news from those areas?" asked the vard.

"The last I heard, the Dwarves of Stonecastle were preparing for a siege. As for Trollden, I've heard nothing. Then, again, it's a pretty remote region of the country."

"Do you think the south is safe?"

"As safe as it can be, given our present circumstances," replied Hayley. "However, I'm more concerned with Ironcliff. Is what I proposed even feasible?"

"I will need to consult with the mining guild, but I don't imagine it would be too difficult, especially considering it gives us a way to strike back."

"It's only a temporary measure," said Revi, "not a solution. It will undoubtedly buy us some time, perhaps even inflict casualties, but it won't win the war."

"Tell me," said Hayley, "is it true the entire mountain is riddled with pits and traps in case of attack?"

"Aye, it is," replied Agramath. "I oversaw much of the work myself. Why?"

"I was thinking it might be helpful to capture some Halvarians."

"I doubt they'd cooperate, if that's what you're thinking."

"It wasn't. I'm looking for more Halvarian armour and weaponry to supplement what we took in the raid."

"To what end?"

"Spreading confusion."

"Interesting," said Thalgrun. "Are you suggesting your rangers impersonate Halvarian warriors again?"

"While in the tunnels, yes. How better to get in behind their lines?"

The vard laughed. "You have steel flowing through your veins."

"That's one way of putting it," added Agramath, "but it still doesn't solve the bigger problem, which is how we get these invaders off our doorstep."

"Wait," said Revi. "What about Heward? Couldn't we coordinate our efforts here with his command attacking the enemy's lines?"

"We could," replied Hayley, "but timing it would be difficult since we don't know exactly when that trebuchet might break through."

"Or if the Halvarians will seek to take advantage of it," added Agramath. "They might continue bombarding us with stones rather than trying to gain entry."

"That's a risk we'll have to take," said Thalgrun. "Even if they don't do what we want, it gives my people something to focus on. A kingdom without hope is a dangerous thing."

"Well said, my vard. When would you like us to begin making preparations?"

"As soon as that trebuchet of theirs packs it in for the night."

"How long before the walls can be prepared?" asked Revi.

They all looked at Agramath.

"That's difficult to say," replied the master of rock and stone. "I shall arrange a meeting with Selia Ironfist as soon as we're done here."

"Oh yes?" said Thalgrun with a twinkle in his eye. "Eager for some one-on-one time with her, are you?"

The mage cleared his throat. "I assure you we will conduct the affair with the greatest professionalism."

"An interesting turn of phrase. Very well, my friend. Seek her out, and see what she thinks of this proposal."

Agramath left in a hurry, an action that amused the vard.

"Am I missing something?" asked Revi.

"Let's just say my master of rock and stone and the master of the mining guild share a history."

"A history of what?"

"Does he have to spell it out for you?" said Hayley.

Revi stared back, confused, so she leaned forward and whispered in his ear.

Thalgrun had no idea what she said, but the Life Mage must've received the message, for he blushed profusely.

"Now," said Hayley. "Let's see about contacting Heward, shall we?"

Lord Arandil Greycloak watched the Elven warriors of the Darkwood march past, a familiar face amongst them. "I must admit to some surprise at seeing Delsaran with our troops."

"I do not see why," replied Shalariel, Lady of the Darkwood. "Ever since he returned from Stonecastle last year, he has talked of little else. Small wonder, then, that he should wish it liberated."

"War is no joke, and a bard is ill-equipped to fight against an enemy such as the one that awaits us."

"He will adapt," she replied, "as we all have in recent years." She paused to return a salute as a group of riders rode past, their armour a deep grey, as were their cloaks.

"The Grey Wardens," said Arandil. "They have not ridden to war in more than two thousand years."

"A new age is dawning in which Elvenkind returns, taking their rightful place amongst the people of Eiddenwerthe, not as conquerors, but as allies."

"You forget. We fought alongside our Mercerian friends before."

"I have forgotten nothing. We fought by their side, but that was only a portion of our army. Now, we march in numbers not seen since the Great War."

"There it is," announced the bard three days later. "The Forlorn Tower."

Lord Arandil halted to view the soaring stone structure built up against the side of an immense cliff. A large, double door stood at its base, though no windows were visible. "How does it work?"

"The floor inside is wide enough to carry a wagon," replied Delsaran. "Dwarven engineering lifts it to the top of the cliff using a series of strange mechanisms. I do not claim to be an expert with such things, but I must admit it is most impressive." The bard's gaze returned to the tower, where he noted an individual exiting its base. "Ah. That must be one of the guards."

"Greetings," called out the Dwarf. "I'm Taldur, the gatekeeper to the Forlorn Tower. Who might you be?"

"I am Lord Arandil Greycloak, Lord of the Darkwood. My army has come to aid Vard Khazad, the Lord of Stone."

The Dwarf raised his eyebrows. "Is that so? I hate to disappoint you, but I'm afraid you're a little late."

"Late?"

"Yes. Haven't you heard? The siege has been broken."

Lord Arandil dismounted, then moved closer, along with Shalariel. "Would you be so kind as to tell us what you know, Master Taldur?"

"It would be my honour, but I shall give you the quick version; I shouldn't like to delay you unnecessarily. The Halvarians reduced the outer city to ruin, then moved its warriors in to begin work on breaching the doors to the under-mountain."

"From your apparent delight, I assume they were unsuccessful?"

"That's putting it mildly. Master Herdwin and his companions hid amongst the rubble for days on end. Then, when an opportunity presented itself, they took out the empire's general."

"Took out?" said Shalariel. "I am not familiar with that term."

"He means killed," replied Arandil. "Master Herdwin has once more demonstrated his finest qualities, no doubt with the assistance of Kasri Ironheart. Were there any survivors amongst the besiegers?"

"Aye. They say quite a few fled east, back towards Kharzun's Folly, but last I heard, the vard has yet to pursue."

"Then allow us to help by doing so on his behalf. We will scour the mountain passes of these vermin and then carry the war into the very heart of Halvaria."

"I'm sure the vard would be most pleased with the offer," said Taldur. He leaned to one side, looking at the Elven host. "Out of curiosity, how many of your warriors did you bring?"

Arandil smiled. "Why, all of them."

THIRTY-EIGHT

Contemplation

SPRING 968 MC

Gerald stared into the fireplace, his mind elsewhere. As if sensing his unease, Storm padded over, placing his massive head in the marshal's lap.

"He senses you're troubled," said Jane. "If you share your burden, you might see your way clear of it."

He absently stroked the dog's head. "We defeated the attempted invasion in the south, and word has reached us that Stonecastle is free of the enemy."

"But surely that's good news?"

He forced a smile. "It is, but now I must contemplate our next move."

"Which is?"

"How to take the war to the enemy."

"Wouldn't it be better to sue for peace?"

"No. According to Aubrey's reports from the Continent, the empire believes it's their destiny to rule over all of Eiddenwerthe. If we make peace now, we only delay the inevitable."

"It is quite the dilemma," replied Jane, "but how do you wage war against an empire about which you know so little?"

"That's the very matter I was just considering."

"What conclusions have you come to?"

"We have prisoners from Trollden, and although I've yet to see a full report from the Siege of Stonecastle, I imagine there'll be more from there."

"I'm not sure I understand what you're suggesting?"

"Collectively, those prisoners will know a lot about the Empire of Halvaria. If we convince even a few to talk to us, it'll help us map out their lands."

"But isn't the empire huge? Who can collate all that information and make sense of it?"

Instead of answering, he smiled.

"Surely you're not suggesting Her Majesty would do all that work?"

"It's exactly what Anna delights in, and, if you recall, she has a perfect memory—an ideal match for just this sort of thing."

"Once you have this map, how will you proceed? We barely had enough people to hold off their attack. It's not as if we have men to spare to invade the empire?"

"It all hinges on Beverly. If she leads the Petty Kingdoms to victory in the east, we can add additional pressure here. Think of this as a coordinated attack."

"But the distances involved are incredible. Has this ever been tried before?"

"Not that I know of," said Gerald, "but I doubt anyone other than us has used Orc shamans to coordinate their armies."

"Well, if anyone could take on the empire and win, it would be you."

A knock at the door interrupted their discussion. Evard Brenton poked his head into the room. "My pardon, sir, but Master Kraloch is here."

"Send him in," said Gerald, rising from his chair. He moved to the door, shaking the hand of the Orc shaman. "Good to see you," he said. "You have news from the east?"

"I do," said Kraloch. "Lady Beverly led the Army of Erlingen to a great victory, destroying an entire Halvarian legion."

"That's wonderful news, but surely you should tell the queen this?"

"And I will, but Lady Aubrey wished me to pass on a piece of news she thought you would find particularly interesting."

"That being?"

"Beverly found a Halvarian weakness she feels you may be able to exploit."

"You have my full attention."

"It appears that, while the empire's legions are highly disciplined, they rely on a strict command structure. She won the battle by isolating enemy forces on a forest road. Without their higher-tier leaders, they were disorganized and lacked initiative."

"How interesting," said Gerald. "That's precisely why we ensure that even the lowest-ranking sergeant knows the objectives."

"This was Beverly's thought as well."

"Does their campaign continue?"

Kraloch shook his head. "Unfortunately, they were forced to withdraw back across the border due to the presence of a second legion."

"Does Beverly still command?"

"Aubrey informed me they've chosen to head north, hoping to persuade others to join their cause. In her absence, the Duke of Erlingen will command his army in person."

"I'm not sure if that's good news or bad."

"Good, surely?" said Jane. "If there's another legion in the area, they'll need all the help they can get."

"Under ordinary circumstances, I'd agree," said Gerald, "but from what I've been told, the duke lacks military experience."

"This is true," added Kraloch, "though he did take part in the Battle of the Pines. A fitting name for the engagement, considering the terrain."

"I trust all our people are uninjured?"

"They are. Lord Aldwin assisted Lady Aubrey in tending to the wounded during the battle. Krazuhk also played an important part in the victory."

"Krazuhk?" said Jane.

"She is a master of air," replied Kraloch, "and intends to return to Merceria with the rest of our people."

"A welcome addition. I don't believe Merceria has any Air Mages, do we?"

"No," said Gerald, "and that's been troublesome to us, especially considering Edwina has a gift for it."

"Then it's fortuitous they found Krazuhk. When can we expect to see them back in Wincaster?"

"It'll be some time, particularly as I need to coordinate our efforts with them. Of course, none of that matters if they can't defeat their own invasion."

"But you know their weakness now," said Jane. "Surely that accounts for something?"

"It certainly helps," replied Gerald, "but we still have so much to do. Trollden must be retaken, and that fleet still sits off our southern coast."

"What of Stonecastle?" asked Kraloch.

"Lord Arandil leads the Army of the Darkwood through the mountain passes even as we speak. I'm certain Vard Khazad will send warriors to assist in clearing out the remainders of the enemy legion."

"And what of Master Herdwin?"

"He and Lady Kasri will return here, to Wincaster, before heading north. I imagine they'll want to take part in the liberation of Ironcliff, and I can't say I blame them."

"When can we expect that?" asked Jane.

"We'll need to deal with the situation down south first. Once the coast is clear of that fleet, it'll free up men to bolster Heward's command."

"There's the Gerald I fell in love with, the energetic leader."

"Energetic?" he replied. "Hardly that. Some days, I find it difficult just to get out of bed."

Kraloch bowed. "Please excuse me, Your Grace. I must make my report to the queen."

"If you don't mind, I'll join you."

Braedon kicked the ball, then ran across the room, almost colliding with the Marshal of Merceria.

"Careful, now," chided Anna. "You don't want to hurt Grandpa."

"He's full of energy," said Gerald.

"I wish our mages could tap into it; they'd be able to cast spells for the rest of their lives." She collapsed into a chair, exhausted.

"You know, you have servants to look after him."

"I spend so little time with him, thanks to this war. I want to cherish what I can, even if it is exhausting. Tell me, was I this much trouble when I was younger?"

"Oh, you were much worse but were a little older when we first met. Braedon has some catching up to do if he wants to match your childhood."

"Well," replied Anna, "at least he has a mother who loves him."

"You turned out well despite your own mother's absence."

"I have you to thank for that." She kicked off her shoes and put her feet on a footstool. "There, that's better. Now, tell me this plan of yours."

"It's very rudimentary, but I'll refine it as we learn more about Halvaria."

"I'm concerned about events in the east," said Anna. "Erlingen defeated an Imperial legion, but there's no guarantee they can do that a second time. If they lose, it frees the empire to send more men against us."

"I'll admit it's a gamble, but if we wait too long, we risk losing what little advantage we have. The empire won't sit idly by, allowing us to build our strength in peace. They'll come back, determined to defeat us with even larger numbers."

"Explain how this strategy of yours would work."

"We liberate Ironcliff, then send a large expedition through the Gap. We've learned the northern provinces are former Petty Kingdoms the Halvarians have absorbed over the last few centuries. I hope marching through them will stir up the locals to fight back against the empire."

"A clever tactic," said Anna, "but dangerous should they prove loyal to the emperor."

"To my mind, the key to this campaign is portraying ourselves as liberators. I would also divide our army into smaller brigades to cover a larger area."

"And if the enemy threatens?"

"Then we gather to fight them. Smaller commands give us greater flexibility, and we now have an abundance of seasoned commanders at hand."

"I have no objection to this plan," replied Anna, "but we must first deal with southern shores. I won't send our army into enemy territory only to have the empire return."

"We are in agreement on that."

"Excellent. Now, as to their fleet, I have some words of encouragement."

"Those being?"

"Alric managed to assemble a fleet. Before you get too excited, there are some issues, chief amongst them being that, based on Tog's observations, the empire's ships still vastly outnumber ours."

"Does Alric have a plan to deal with that?"

"Not entirely," said Anna, "but I do. Do you remember the Siege of Riversend?"

"I could hardly forget it. Why? What have you got in mind?"

"If you recall, the Kurathians used those massive creatures to pull their barges."

"Yes, I remember now. According to Beverly's report, they were chained to the ships and controlled by mages. Surely you're not suggesting we do the same?"

"Lily told me creatures such as those live in the southern parts of the Great Swamp. I thought we could try using magic to convince them to aid us."

"Who will go down there and speak to them? We have no ships to speak of. Or are you suggesting a few ships from Weldwyn could slip past the invasion fleet?"

"No. I hoped Albreda would use her magic to summon them. It works for horses."

"Yes," said Gerald, "but horses are land-based animals; those other creatures are likely aquatic. Would her magic even work with them?"

"I have no idea, but I believe it's worth investigating. Don't you?"

"Definitely, but I'm concerned about time. The southern coastline is hundreds of miles long, and we have no idea where these creatures may be found. It'll take weeks to get someone down there, let alone search the entire coast."

"We could use the Saurian gates to go to Erssa Saka'am."

"The gates are dangerous," said Gerald. "You saw the effect they had on Revi."

"That was a prolonged exposure, and I'm confident he's learned his lesson."

"You're suggesting we send Revi Bloom?"

"He has the advantage of having been there before. Besides, you know he'd relish the opportunity to return there and look for his next great discovery."

"I can't argue with that, and he knows the recall spell, so he'd be able to return at a moment's notice."

"You have reservations?"

"We don't have many Life Mages available right now. I can't say I like the idea of sending our most experienced one into the swamp."

"Even if it means defeating the Halvarian fleet anchored off our shores?"

"You've convinced me," said Gerald, "but we can't send him alone."

"I hadn't intended to."

"Who do you propose we send with him?"

"Hayley and some of her rangers."

"But she's needed up in Ironcliff."

"There's not much they can do while holed up inside a mountain."

"But she's my regional commander."

"We both know you will go up there and assume command. It's part of your master plan; you said so yourself."

Gerald grinned. "I see you've outmanoeuvred me yet again. When would you like to begin this search of yours?"

"I should think sooner rather than later. As you said earlier, we haven't a lot of time."

"I'll send word to Revi and Hayley before the day is out."

"Good, but let's make it a request rather than a command."

"Might I ask why?"

"He still believes I haven't forgiven him for stranding Aubrey, Beverly, and Aldwin out east. He'll view this as an opportunity to get back in my good graces."

"Does that suggest you're still upset with him?"

"No. I now appreciate the complexities of what he was trying to achieve. It also proved advantageous in the long run, although that ultimately depends on what happens when Beverly goes north to Reinwick."

"Learning more about the Petty Kingdoms' politics would be helpful," said Gerald. "Right now, we only know there's some sort of Northern Alliance."

"Oh, we know a great deal more than that. If you recall, Kraloch is in contact with a shaman of the Red Hand, a female Orc named Shaluhk. She's given us a much more detailed account of the Duchy of Reinwick."

"She has? Why wasn't I told any of this?"

"It didn't seem important at the time," replied Anna.

"Well? What do you know about the place?"

"A tribe of Orcs is there: the Ashwalkers, known for using Fire Magic."

"Will they be able to help Beverly?"

"Kraloch has already taken steps to contact them."

"What other secrets are you keeping from me?" asked Gerald.

"I don't consider them secrets; they're more like a collection of information. I've spent years accumulating what others might consider trivial details. They seem to rise to the surface when I least expect them."

Gerald smiled. "That's your gift, Anna. It always has been. Would any of Shaluhk's people be of use?"

"I couldn't say; their home is much farther to the east, although I believe they have powerful magic at their disposal."

"Really? I can't imagine anyone stronger than Albreda, although it's difficult to compare mages of different disciplines. Just out of interest, what kind of magic do they employ?"

"Water and Fire, primarily, though Shaluhk herself is a gifted shaman in her own right. You know, theoretically, they're our allies."

"They are?"

"Yes," said Anna. "If you recall, Urgon told us we were allied to all the Orcs, not only his tribe."

"That's right. Still, that was years ago."

"Six and a half, to be precise."

"Was it really?" said Gerald. "It seems like longer. Do you think they would honour that commitment?"

"Given their present circumstances, they might consider it."

"Meaning?"

"They live in Therengia, a realm scorned by most of the Petty Kingdoms."

"Wouldn't that make them less likely to help rather than more?"

"Perhaps," said Anna, "but this gives them an opportunity to prove their value to the rest of the Continent."

"How far east did you say they were?"

Anna laughed. "I didn't, but it's an extremely long trip for them. Still, there's a possibility they could travel to Reinwick by ship, assuming they agree to help."

"Interesting," said Gerald, "but perhaps the question remains: would they make a meaningful contribution? You can only fit so many on a boat."

"The Halvarians managed to embark an entire legion."

"True, but they used their own ships and had a lot of time to prepare. The same cannot be said for the Orcs of the Red Hand."

"Ah, but I think you're missing an important element. The Red Hand and Therengia are one realm."

"Are you suggesting the entire kingdom would march west to aid the Petty Kingdoms? That's a lot to ask."

"We know the empire threatens the existence of everyone, not just us, but we don't know if they see things that way. If not, we must hope Beverly and Aubrey convince the Northern Alliance to march to Erlingen's aid and pray that will be enough."

"You've given me much to think on," said Gerald, "but it won't affect my plans in the short term. We still need to clear the empire from the swamp, and not even the Petty Kingdoms can help with that." He paused, then walked over to Braedon, asleep on the floor. He lifted up the young prince, then set him onto his mother's lap. "There," he said. "Right where he belongs."

"As are you, Gerald. Without your presence, we never would have survived this invasion."

SPRING 968 MC

Exalor, the High Strategos of the Halvarian Empire, watched as the shattered remains of the Third Legion made their way back across Kharzun's Folly. They had suffered a defeat of monumental proportions, all because their commander-general was more concerned with personal glory than following the plan.

He thought back over his strategy. It called for a three-pronged attack on Merceria, but two prongs had been repulsed. How had his plan failed? Not the type to admit personal culpability, he blamed it on the men under his command. It now fell to him to salvage the situation, but how?

The eastern side of Kharzun's Folly was defensible, and he could use mages to destroy the temporary bridge that spanned the ravine, making it even more so. As for the southern coast, the failure of that landing stung, but the empire maintained control over the Sea of Storms. Their presence alone forced Merceria to garrison men there to repel any possible future attack, so they were, in a sense, still carrying out their duty.

He held out hope Ironcliff would fall. Once that happened, the Seventh Legion would be freed up to deal with the troublesome army holding the western end of the Gap, but to ensure success there, he needed to oversee the assault in person. He would have to entrust his current location to the Marshal of the Empire, someone with whom he seldom saw eye to eye.

He was pondering this very thought when he noted the arrival of his aide, Wingate, whom he'd left back in the capital to look after things. The fellow wound his way through the retreating legionnaires, halting before his master.

"Your Grace," he said, out of breath. "I bring news."

"If it's about the failed seaborne invasion of Merceria, I'm fully aware."

"That's not it at all, Your Grace. It concerns the campaign in the east."

"There is no campaign in the east. What in the name of the emperor are you babbling on about?"

"Four legions crossed into the border kingdoms some time ago, intending to complete the Great Dream."

"That's impossible! Only I, the High Strategos, can authorize such a thing!"

"That is not entirely true, Your Grace. The invasion carried the emperor's blessing."

"Have I missed something? Was I relieved of my position?"

"No, Your Grace."

"Who led this invasion?"

"Edora Sartellian."

"She's not even a marshal!"

"True," said Wingate, "yet somehow she was given command of the frontier. I fear you have been left in the dark by design. I only learned about it myself when I was mistakenly delivered a message meant for someone else."

"And you came straight here?"

"I did, Your Grace, but I fear, without magic, it took me far too long."

"You did well," said Exalor, "though this news could not have come at a worse time. My offensive is in tatters, and now elements within the Royal Council plot to usurp my authority."

"What do we do?"

"What I should have done months ago: return to the capital and seize the Crown for myself!"

<<<<>>>>

Cast of Characters

MAIN CHARACTERS

Merceria & Allies
Aldwin Fitzwilliam - Master smith, married to Beverly
Alric - King of Weldwyn, married to Anna, father of Braedon
Anna - Queen of Merceria, married to Alric, mother of Braedon
Arnim Caster - Viscount of Haverston, married to Nikki
Aubrey Brandon - Baroness of Hawksburg, Life Mage
Beverly Fitzwilliam - Baroness of Bodden, General, married to Alric
Gerald Matheson - Duke of Wincaster, Marshal of the Army
Hayley Chambers - Baroness of Queenston, High Ranger
Herdwin Steelarm – Dwarf smith, friend of Queen Anna
Kasri Ironheart - Dwarf warrior, daughter of the Vard of Ironcliff
Krazuhk - Orc, Master of Air, Sky Singers
Nicole (Nikki) Caster - Viscountess of Haverston, married to Arnim
Owen - Knight of Erlingen

The Empire of Halvaria
Exalor Shozarin - High Strategos
Nevarus - God Emperor
Wingate - Aide to Exalor

SECONDARY CHARACTERS

Dwarves

Agramath - Master of Rock and Stone, Ironcliff
Brogar - Bodyguard to Princess Althea, Mirstone
Caldrim - Captain, arbalest company, Weldwyn
Galman Boldhammer - Captain, Stonecastle
Garnik Hardhand - Guildmaster, Warriors Guild, Ironcliff
Gelion - Captain, cousin to Herdwin, Stonecastle
Grolik - Warrior, Forlorn Tower, Stonecastle
Khazad - Vard, Stonecastle
Margel – Stonesmiths guild, Forge mate to Gelion, Stonecastle
Murdan - Arbalester, Gelion's company, Stonecastle
Rotmir - Warrior, Forlorn Tower, Stonecastle
Selia Ironfist - Guildmaster, Mining Guild, Ironcliff
Skodan - Arbalester, Gelion's company, Stonecastle
Strodar Goldeye - Guildmaster, Bankers Guild, Ironcliff
Taldur - Warrior, Forlorn Tower, Stonecastle
Thalgrun Stormhammer - Vard, Ironcliff
Tindal - Warrior, cousin to Margel, Stonecastle
Tulfar Axehand - Dwarf, Baron of Mirstone, Weldwyn

ERLINGEN

Alain Heinrich - Duke of Erlingen
Deiter Heinrich (Deceased) - Previous Duke of Erlingen
Eadric - Therengian traveller
Emerson - Captain, Army of Erlingen
Galrath of Paledon (Deceased) - Knight of the Sceptre
Hagan Stein - Baron of Mulsingen
Kinmar - Therengian traveller
Milgyrd - Therengian traveller
Myles - Knight of the Sceptre
Rosalyn Stein - Baroness of Mulsingen
Rudolf Sturgess - Mercenary Captain, Torburg Wolves
Wulfrum Haas - Baron of Regnitz

HALVARIA

Agalix Sartellian - Inner Council, Fire Mage
Agostino Feranti - Captain-General, 1st Imperial Cohort, 4th Legion
Alitor Verathras - Earth Mage, Halvaria
Bastien Lambert - Commander-General, 7th Legion
Beaufort - Aide to Marshal of the South
Castimar Stormwind - Marshal of the South, Water Mage
Claudio Zalango - Captain, 4th Legion

Desjardin - Captain, 5th Legion
Edora Sartellian - Inner Council, Fire Mage
Enelle Sartellian - High Purifier, Fire Mage
Erkinwald (Deceased) - First emperor of Halvaria
Esteve Solinak - Commander-General, 3rd Legion
Fadra Stormwind - Inner Council, Water Mage
Freya Stormwind - Inner Council, Water Mage
Grafford Sartellian - Fire Mage, Halvaria
Grim - Aide to Commander-General Vorinus Moreau
Hamath Nordin - Commander-General, 5th Legion
Idraxa Shozarin - Acting Marshal of the North
Janek - Servant at the Imperial Court
Jansen Borke - Captain, 5th Legion
Kaladesh (Deceased) - Ruler of ancient Halvaria, pre-empire
Kelson Shozarin - High Sentinel, Enchanter
Korvin Bandros - Commander-General, 11th Legion
Kozarsky Stormwind - Admiral, Storm Fleet, Water Mage
Nedermeyer - Captain of Horse, 5th Legion
Praxar Shozarin - Marshal of the Empire, Enchanter
Rhedra - Earth Mage
Ryfar Shozarin - Halvarian Agent, Clanholdings
Stivern Lindman (Deceased) - Captain-General, 2nd Imperial Cohort, 7th
Legion
Umberto Rakert - Commander-General, 8th Legion
Vadym Stormwind - Halvarian Agent, Clanholdings, Water Mage
Vorinus Moreau - Commander-General, 9th Legion
Zoran - Captain of foot, 9th Legion

MERCERIA
Albreda - Mistress of the Whitewood, Earth Mage
Aldus Hearn - Earth Mage
Andred (Deceased) - Former King of Merceria
Ansel (Deceased) - King of Merceria, Husband of Queen Evermore
Arandil Greycloak - Elven ruler of the Darkwood, Fire Mage/Enchanter
Bertram Ayles - Ranger
Braedon Gerald - Prince of Merceria, Son of Anna and Alric
Brenton - Royal guard, Wincaster
Edgar Greenfield - Retired Bodden warrior, queen's courier
Edwina - Former princess of Weldwyn, Air Mage in training
Evard Brenton - Royal Guardsman

Evermore (Deceased) - Queen during Merceria's first Golden Age
Galloway - Captain, Colbridge
Gral - Troll, Trollden
Harold Wainwright - Captain, Wincaster Bowmen
Harper - Royal guard, Wincaster
Heward 'The Axe' Manton - Baron of Redridge, Knight of the Hound
Hugh Gardner - Captain, Wincaster Light Horse
Jane Goodwin - Lady of the Weldwyn court
Kiren-Jool - Kurathian Enchanter
Lanaka - Kurathian cavalry commander
Lightning - Beverly's Mercerian Charger
Lily - Saurian
Montrose (Deceased) - Executed traitor
Preston Wright - Baron of Wickfield, Knight, married to Sophie Wright
Randolf - Former Knight of the Sword
Revi Bloom - Royal Life Mage, Enchanter
Richard 'Fitz' Fitzwilliam (Deceased) -Baron of Bodden, Beverly's father
Robbins - Archer Captain, Colbridge
Shalariel - Elf, Mistress of Thorolandrin, The Darkwood
Sophie Wright - Baroness of Wickfield, married to Sir Preston
Storm - Kurathian Mastiff, Queen Anna's pet
Swiftfeather – Hawk, Merceria
Tog - Troll, Earl of Trollden, Leader of the Trolls
Valmar (Deceased) - Former Marshal General of Merceria

NORLAND

Asher - Earl of Beaconsgate, nephew of Lord Hollis
Bronwyn - Queen of Norland
Calder - Earl of Greendale
Creighton - Earl of Riverhurst
Hollis (Deceased) - Former Earl of Beaconsgate
Jendrick - Advisor to Lord Hollis, Necromancer, Elf in disguise
Marik - Former champion of Lord Hollis
Marley - Earl of Walthorne
Rutherford - Earl of Hammersfield
Waverly - Earl of Marston

ORCS

Bloodrig - Shaman, Sky Singers, Deisenbach
Ghodrug - Chieftain, Black Ravens, Norland
Gorath - Deputy High Ranger, Black Arrows, Merceria

Kraloch - Shaman, Black Arrows, Merceria
Kurghal - Shaman, Black Arrows, Urgon's sister, Merceria
Meghara - Mythical mages of ancient Orc origin
Rulahk - Shaman, Black Ravens, Norland
Shaluhk - Shaman, Red Hand, Therengia
Urgon - Chieftain, Black Arrows, Merceria

The Twelve Clans (Clanholdings)

Althea - Princess, Dungannon
Flint - Goblin, Tinker, Stonewall
Glisnak - Goblin, Stonewall
Grazuk - Goblin, wolf rider, Stonewall
Haldrim - Dwarf, Captain, Dragon Company
Lochlan - Clan chief, Dungannon
Tarzil - Goblin, wolf rider, Stonewall
Virdu - Goblin, bender, Stonewall

The Fighting Orders

Alonso - Temple Captain, Saint Mathew
Bernelle - Temple Captain, Saint Agnes
Charlaine - Temple Commander, Saint Agnes
Cyric - Temple Knight, Saint Mathew
Enna - Temple Captain, Saint Agnes
Giselle - Temple Captain, Saint Agnes, Deisenbach
Isabeau - Temple Commander, Saint Agnes
Johanna - Temple Knight, Saint Agnes
Marlena - Temple Captain/Commander, Saint Agnes
Petra - Temple Captain, Saint Agnes, Erlingen
Roland - Temple Commander, Saint Mathew
Vitaly - Temple Captain, Saint Mathew, Erlingen

Weldwyn

Aegryth Malthunen - Earth Mage
Beric - Earl of Southport
Dryden - Earl of Loranguard
Gretchen Harwell - Enchanter
Jack Marlowe - Cavalier, Viscount of Aynsbury
Julian Lanford - Earl of Falford
Leofric (Deceased) - King, Weldwyn, Father of Alric
Oliver Weldridge - Earl of Faltingham, Weldwyn
Osbourne Megantis - Fire Mage, Weldwyn

Parvan Luminor - Elf, Baron of Tivilton, Weldwyn

OTHERS
Argalin Krantz - King, Gotfeld
Athgar - Fire Mage, Therengia
Axalon (Deceased) - Ancient army leader, Thalemia
Burghild Raina - Duchess, Angvil
Corella - Maid, Neiburg, Angvil
Delsaran - Elf bard, the Darkwood
Engle Bertran - General, Angvil
Ernst Falkenberg - Older brother of Temple Commander Marlena
Gwayne - King, Rudor
Kip - Youth, Angvil
Ludmilla Stormwind - Water Mage, Advisor to Queen of Deisenbach
Ludwig Altenburg - King, Hadenfeld
Natalia Stormwind - Water Mage, Therengia
Rilan Paldrin - Manservant, Neiburg, Angvil
Wilmot - Baron, Rudor

PLACES

HALVARIA
Aloria - Ancient kingdom bordering Halvaria
Auverney - Conquered kingdom, now province, Halvaria
Calabria - Kingdom, coast of the Shimmering Sea, absorbed by Halvaria
Dun-Galdrim - Dwarven stronghold, fell to Halvarian fifty years ago
Guilford - Keep, Auverney, Halvaria
Varena - Capital of Halvaria
Wyburn - City, Northwest Halvaria
Zefara - Port city on the west coast of Halvaria

MERCERIA
Bodden - Town, Barony
Colbridge – City
Erssa Saka'am - Saurian city/temple
Great Swamp - Massive swamp
Haverston - Village, viscountcy
Hawksburg - Town, Barony
Queenston - Town, Barony
Redridge - Village, Barony
The Whitewood - Great forest

The Queens Arms - Inn/Tavern, Wincaster, Merceria
Trollden - Town
Wickfield - Village
Wincaster - Capital City

The Petty Kingdoms

Abelard – Kingdom, northeast coast
Andover - Kingdom, north of Erlingen
Angvil - Duchy
Arnsfeld - Kingdom, adjacent to Halvaria
Burgemont – Kingdom, north of Angvil
Deisenbach - Kingdom
Erlingen - Duchy
Gotfeld - Kingdom
Hadenfeld – Kingdom, bordering Deisenbach
Ilea - Kingdom, South Coast
Oberfeld - Kingdom, south of Gotfeld
Reinwick - Duchy, Northern Coast
Rudor - Kingdom, adjacent to Halvaria
Talstadt - Duchy
Thalemia - Ancient Empire on the Shimmering Sea
Zowenbruch – Kingdom, bordering Deisenbach

Weldwyn

Aldgrave – Barony
Grand Edifice of the Arcane Wizards Council-The Dome, Summersgate
Loranguard – Earldom
Mirstone - Dwarf Mine, Barony
Stone Tankard - Tavern, Mirstone, Weldwyn
Summersgate – Capital
Tivilton - Elf Barony

Cities, Towns and Villages of the Petty Kingdoms

Adelwel - Village, Duchy of Erlingen
Chermingen - City, Duchy of Erlingen
Herani - The Holy City, birthplace of humanity
Kurslingen - Capital, Zowenbruch
Lidenbach, - Capital, Arnsfeld
Neiburg - Capital, Duchy of Angvil
Rasgalen - Village, Gotfeld
Saints Crossing - Village, Gotfeld

Salzing - City, Duchy of Erlingen
Santrem - village, Deisenbach
Torburg - Capital, Duchy of Erlingen
Volkenstag - Village, Kingdom of Gotfeld
Zurkirk - Village, Duchy of Erlingen

TWELVE CLANS

Banburn - Clanholding
Drakewell - Clanholding
Dungannon - Clanholding
Galchrest - Clanholding
Halsworth - Clanholding
Klinridge - Clanholding

OTHER LOCATIONS

Antonine - City State governing the Church of the Saints
Darkwood - Elven Realm, between Merceria and Stonecastle
Forlorn Tower - Great lift/elevator, Stonecastle
Great Northern Sea - Sea north of the Petty Kingdoms
Grey Peaks - Mountain range forming eastern border of Merceria
Halvaria - Large Empire to the east of Merceria
Ironcliff - Dwarven Stronghold, Kingdom
Kharzun's Folly - Great bridge across a ravine, Stonecastle
Korascajan - Magical academy, Sartellians
Nockwood - Forest, North Gotfeld
Norland - Kingdom north of Merceria
Ogre's Hill - Hill in eastern Angvil
Rasfeld - River separating Erlingen and Angvil
Sea of Storms - Sea west of Halvaria and South of Merceria
Shimmering Sea - Sea south of the Petty Kingdoms
Stonecastle - Dwarven Stronghold, Kingdom
Stonewall - Goblin Enclave, formerly Dwarf mine of Tor-Maldrin
Stormtop Mountains - Separates Halvaria from Petty Kingdoms
Sullen Peaks – Halvaria's name for the Stormtop Mountains
Sunset Peaks - Mountain range, western border of the Clanholdings
Terengaria-Old name of region: Merceria, Weldwyn, Norland, the Clans
The Fox and Hound - Tavern, Torburg, Erlingen
The Gap - Flat land between Thunder Mountains and Grey Peaks
The Grey Goose - Roadside inn, Zowenbruch
The Silver Chalice - Gentleman's club, Salzing, Erlingen
Therengia - Realm east of the Petty Kingdoms

Thunder Mountains - Mountain range north of Norland
Traverne River - North Gotfeld
Volstrum - Magical academy that trains Stormwinds, Ruzhina

BATTLES
Battle of Beggar's Reach (968 MC/1110 SR) - Halvaria defeats Angvil
Battle of Chermingen (953 MC/1095 SR) - Erlingen defeats Andover
Battle of Lidenbach (961MC/1103 SR) - Temple Fleet defeats Halvarians
Battle of Rasgalen (967MC/1109 SR) - Halvaria defeats Gotfield
Battle of Saints Crossing (967 MC/1109 SR) - Halvaria defeats Rudor
Battle of Temple Bay (956 MC/1098 SR) - Church defeats Halvarian in Reinwick
Battle of the Brinwald (961 MC/1103 SR) - Arnsfeld defeats Halvarian invasion
Battle of the Pines (968 MC/1110 SR) - Erlingen defeats Halvarian legion.
Battle of the Standing Stones (962 MC/1104 SR) - Therengia defeats Holy Army
Battle of the Wilderness - Alternate name for Battle of the Standing Stones
Siege of Riversend (961 MC/1103 SR) - Weldwyn defeats Kurathian seaborne invasion
Siege of Wincaster (962 MC/1104 SR) -Queen Anna captures capital of Merceria

THE LEGIONS OF HALVARIA ASSIGNMENTS
1st - Southern Frontier
2nd - Southern Frontier
3rd - Attacking Stonecastle
4th - Attacking Trollden
5th - Attacking the Petty Kingdoms
6th - Facing Ilea
7th - Attacking Ironcliff
8th - Attacking the Petty Kingdoms
9th - Attacking the Petty Kingdoms
10th - Southern Frontier
11th - Attacking the Petty Kingdoms
12th - Facing Ilea

GODS

Gundar - God of the Earth, Creator of Dwarves
Malin - Goddess of Wisdom, Patron goddess of Weldwyn
Saxnor - God of Strength, Patron god of Merceria
Maleus - Ancient god of Halvaria

Saints

Anges - Protector of Women
Cunar - The Warrior
Mathew - Protector of the Sick and Poor

Orc Tribes

Ashwalkers - Reinwick
Black Arrow - Merceria
Black Ravens - Norland
Red Hand - Therengia
Sky Singers - Deisenbach

Other Things

Afterlife - Where good people go when they die
Bender - Goblin healer
Captain-General - Leader of a Halvarian Cohort
Cohort - Subdivision of Halvarian Legion, 600 men.
Commander-General - Leader of a Halvarian Legion
Great Dream - Halvarian goal to conquer the entire Continent
Grey Wardens - Elite mounted Elven troops from the Darkwood
Grunt - Goblin hunter armed with spear
Hearth Guard - Elite Dwarven warriors, Ironcliff
High Lord of Herani - Ancient ruler of Herani
High Strategos - The highest military rank in Halvaria
Knights of the Sceptre - Order of Knighthood, Erlingen
Lobber - Goblin hunter armed with ranged weapons
Marshal - Highest military rank in most kingdoms
Mountain Wolf - Large wolf native to the Sunset Peaks
Nature's Fury - Beverly's hammer, imbued with the power of the earth
Northern Alliance - Military alliance: Reinwick and Andover
Old Kingdom - Name given to ancient kingdom of Therengia
Outer City – Dwarven city that lies outside the mountain
Primus - Leader of the Church of the Saints
Runt - Young Goblin
Saurians - Lizard like race
Sky Singers - Tribe located in Deisenbach

Teeth of the Serpent - A Dwarf tactic to allow retreat from battle.
Thalamites - Race of people from Thalemia
The Gilded Throne - The Throne of Halvaria
The Greens - Bowmen of Wincaster
Tinker - Goblin smith
Torburg Wolves - Mercenary company
Under-mountain - Dwarven city that lies beneath a mountain
Underworld - Where not-good people go when they die
Vard - Dwarven Ruler
Wolf Rider - Goblin, mounted hunter

A Few Words from Paul

While Enemy of the Crown dove into the background of those behind the invasion of Merceria, Peril tells of a broader conflict, a war spreading across the Continent. The Halvarian Empire is at its height, its legions unmatched throughout the entire world of Eiddenwerthe, when they come up against Merceria, a kingdom that has been at war for most of its existence.

On the surface, it would seem the two are well matched, for both have disciplined, experienced warriors, but whereas the empire has its marshals and commander-generals, Merceria has its secret weapon: Gerald Matheson and the veteran army he's developed since becoming marshal.

Not to be forgotten are the accomplishments of Beverly, Aubrey, and Aldwin, for without their presence, the enemy would have conquered the Petty Kingdoms and then turned its full attention on Merceria.

Though the first victories have been achieved, there's still much work to do and a war to see through to its final conclusion.

The story will continue in Heir to the Crown, Book 14, Saviour of the Crown.

A book is the result of hard work and dedicated efforts of several people aside from myself. I must thank my wife, Carol Bennett, for her tireless work in editing, cover design, and promoting this book, along with being my inspiration for these tales.

I would also like to thank Christie Bennett, Amanda Bennett, and Stephanie Sandrock for their encouragement over the years, as well as their moral support. In addition, I must thank Brad Aitken, Stephen Brown, and the late Jeffrey Parker for their part in building the foundation for these characters.

My BETA team, as always, deserves thanks for their feedback, which has proved crucial to these books, so thank you Rachel Deibler, Michael Rhew, Phyllis Simpson, Don Hinckley, Charles Mohapel, Debbie Reeves, Susan Young, Anna Ostberg, Joanna Smith, Lisa Hanika, Keven Hutchison, Brad Williams, and Lisa Hunt for your assistance.

Perhaps most importantly, I must thank you, my readers, for enjoying these tales as much as I enjoy creating them. I look forward to continuing this journey into the history of Eiddenwerthe with you.

About the Author

Paul J Bennett (b. 1961) emigrated from England to Canada in 1967. His father served in the British Royal Navy, and his mother worked for the BBC in London. As a young man, Paul followed in his father's footsteps, joining the Canadian Armed Forces in 1983. He is married to Carol Bennett and has three daughters who are all creative in their own right.

Paul's interest in writing started in his teen years when he discovered the roleplaying game, Dungeons & Dragons (D & D). What attracted him to this new hobby was the creativity it required; the need to create realms, worlds and adventures that pulled the gamers into his stories.

In his 30's, Paul started to dabble in designing his own roleplaying system, using the Peninsular War in Portugal as his backdrop. His regular gaming group were willing victims, er, participants in helping to playtest this new system. A few years later, he added additional settings to his game, including Science Fiction, Post-Apocalyptic, World War II, and the all-important Fantasy Realm where his stories take place.

The beginnings of his first book 'Servant to the Crown' originated over five years ago when he began running a new fantasy campaign. For the world that the Kingdom of Merceria is in, he ran his adventures like a TV show, with seasons that each had twelve episodes, and an overarching plot. When the campaign ended, he knew all the characters, what they had to accomplish, what needed to happen to move the plot along, and it was this that inspired to sit down to write his first novel.

Paul now has four series based in his fantasy world of Eiddenwerthe, and is looking forward to sharing many more books with his readers over the coming years.